Black Gold

Also by Charles O'Brien

Mute Witness

Black Gold

Charles O'Brien

Poisoned Pen Press

First Edition 2002

10 9 8 7 6 5 4 3 2 1

Library of Congress Catalog Card Number: 2001098493

ISBN: 1-59058-010-9 Hardcover
ISBN: 1-59058-021-4 Trade Paperback

Poisoned Pen Press
6962 E. First Ave. Ste 103
Scottsdale, AZ 85251
www.poisonedpenpress.com
info@poisonedpenpress.com

Printed in the United States of America

For Elvy

Acknowledgments

I would like to thank Giles Mercer, Headmaster, Lesley Richards, and the dedicated staff of Prior Park College for showing me about the house and discussing its history; the Bath City Archives, the Bath Central Library, and the Bath University Library, for their willing and gracious assistance; Del Davies and the University Housing Office, for making research in Bath both pleasant and convenient.

Marilyn Wright has read *Black Gold* critically at various stages and offered generous insightful comment. Jennifer Nelson of Gallaudet University and David Manning of The Clarke School for the Deaf have given many practical suggestions concerning issues of lip reading and deafness. I am also grateful to Eileen Spring for expert advice on English eighteenth-century custom and law on marriage and divorce; to Ray Gaudette for lending his computer skills; to Gudveig Baarli, for help with the maps; and to Barbara Peters, Rob Rosenwald, and the talented professionals at Poisoned Pen Press.

To my wife Elvy I owe special mention for her expert editorial reading of the book and her many supportive suggestions for its improvement.

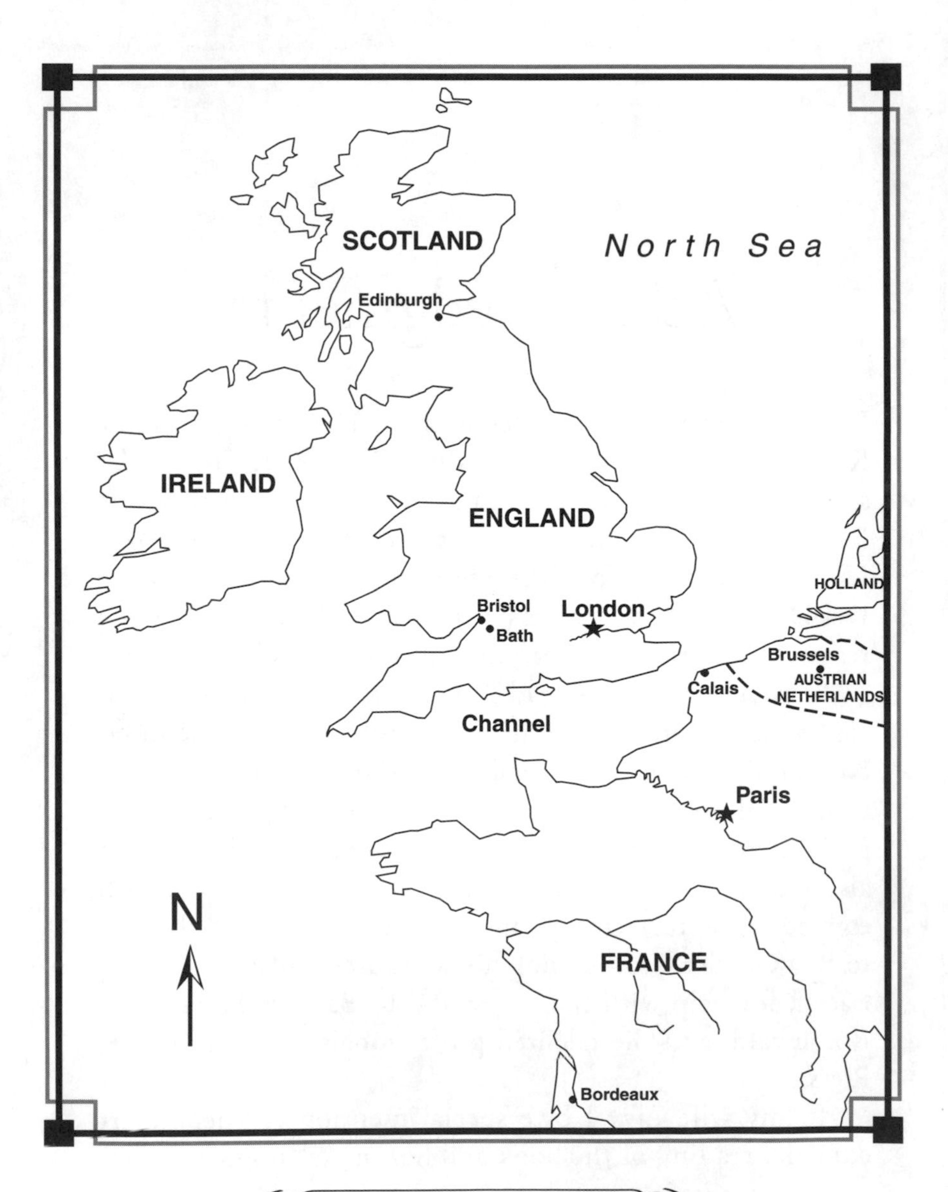
SCOTLAND
North Sea
Edinburgh
IRELAND
ENGLAND
HOLLAND
Bristol
London
Bath
Brussels
Calais
AUSTRIAN
NETHERLANDS
Channel
Paris
N
FRANCE
Bordeaux

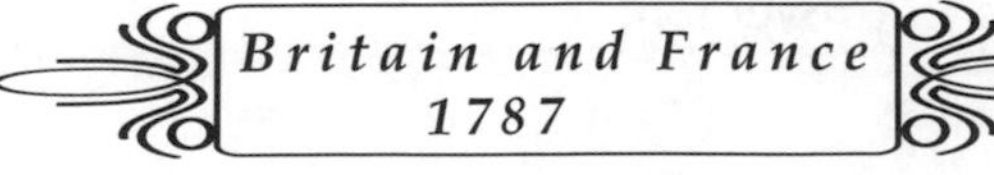
Britain and France
1787

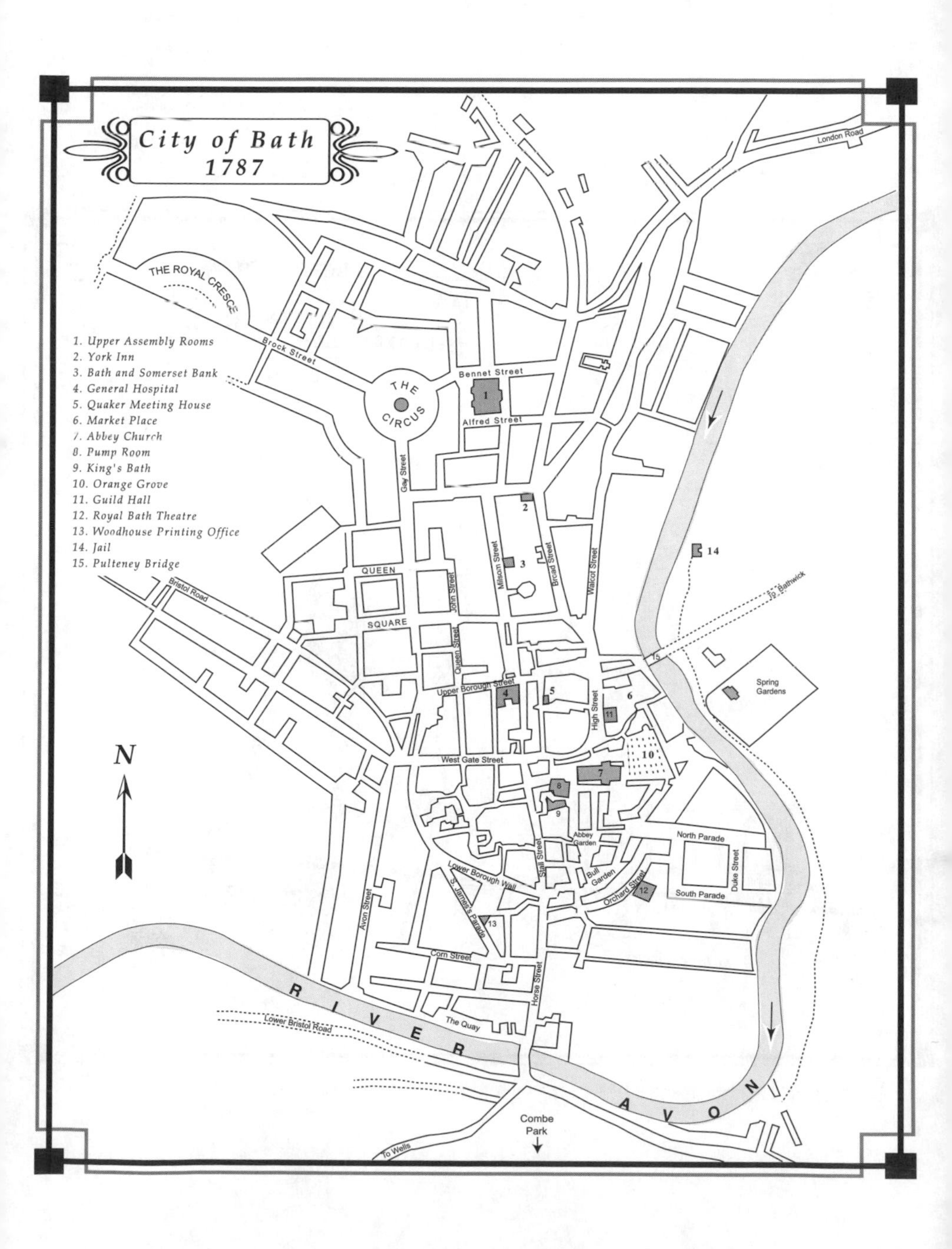
City of Bath
1787
1. Upper Assembly Rooms
2. York Inn
3. Bath and Somerset Bank
4. General Hospital
5. Quaker Meeting House
6. Market Place
7. Abbey Church
8. Pump Room
9. King's Bath
10. Orange Grove
11. Guild Hall
12. Royal Bath Theatre
13. Woodhouse Printing Office
14. Jail
15. Pulteney Bridge
THE ROYAL CRESCE
Brock Street
THE CIRCUS
Bennet Street
Alfred Street
Gay Street
London Road
Milsom Street
Broad Street
Walcot Street
QUEEN
SQUARE
John Street
Queen Street
Bristol Road
To Bathwick
Spring Gardens
Upper Borough Street
High Street
West Gate Street
Abbey Garden
Bull Garden
North Parade
South Parade
Duke Street
Orchard Street
Stall Street
Lower Borough Wall
St. James's Parade
Avon Street
Corn Street
Horse Street
The Quay
Lower Bristol Road
RIVER AVON
Combe Park
To Wells
N

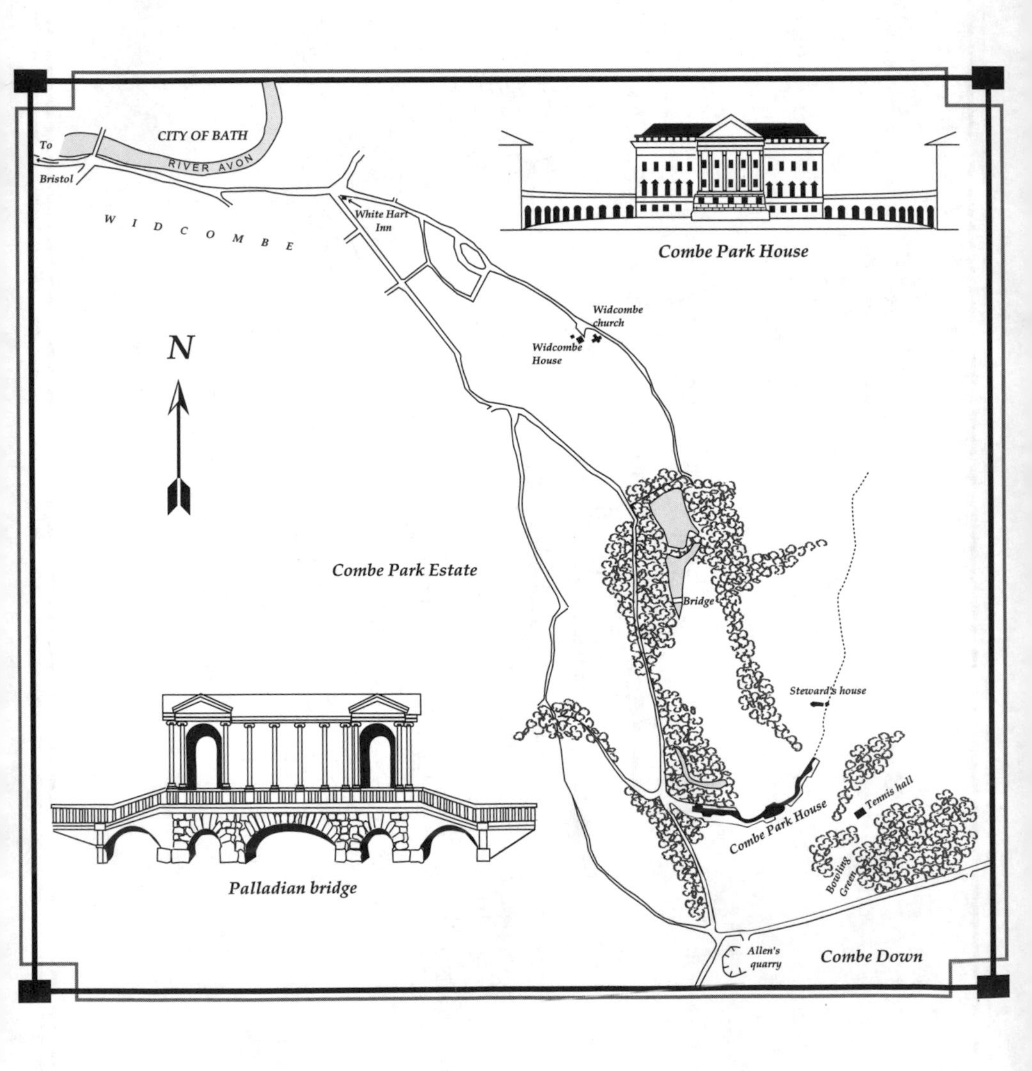

CITY OF BATH
RIVER AVON
To
Bristol
WIDCOMBE
White Hart
Inn
Combe Park House
Widcombe
church
Widcombe
House
N
Combe Park Estate
Bridge
Steward's house
Palladian bridge
Combe Park House
Tennis hall
Bowling
Green
Allen's
quarry
Combe Down

Cast of Main Characters in Order of First Mention

Contents

Chapter 1

A Family Matter, Winter 1787

Saturday, January 6

The sky was overcast, the thin light of day rapidly fading. Gusts of freezing wind whipped up dust in the courtyard. Colonel Paul de Saint-Martin left his cabriolet in the care of a groom and stepped into the entrance hall. He shivered. The room was unheated and the chill of the ride from Paris was in his bones. His Aunt Marie had suddenly called him to Chateau Beaumont, her country residence a few miles south of the city.

"May I take your cloak, sir? The Comtesse is with Baron Breteuil in the library." The doorman gathered the garment on his arm. "She is expecting you."

A liveried footman led the colonel through the building to a closed door and knocked. At a soft command from within he opened the door.

Saint-Martin entered the library, raised his arm in greeting. A strange, heavy atmosphere pervaded the room. Darkness seeped through the windows; dozens of candles struggled to dispel the gloom. Their light flickered on the gilded spines of books. Eerie shadows danced on the high stuccoed ceiling.

"I understand we're gathered here to deal with a family matter," said Saint-Martin with a frisson of apprehension. He glanced at his mentor and distant relative, Baron Breteuil, who rose from his chair. The man was grim-faced. And so was Comtesse Marie, who came forward to greet him, her brow knitted with concern. What could be so serious? True, the baron often looked grim these days when dealing with affairs of state as the king's minister for Paris. The government was virtually bankrupt. Its critics demanded deep cuts in expenditures and the right to approve new taxes. The baron mumbled a greeting through tight lips, then fell silent.

But Aunt Marie? What troubled her? Saint-Martin could not recall ever seeing her in such distress. She was usually lighthearted and gay, a welcome tonic when his own spirits were depressed. This evening she gave him a weak, distracted smile and inquired about his health.

Servants arranged three chairs at a small table. Tea was poured, sweetcakes served, and the servants withdrew.

When the door closed, the baron put his cup down with a clatter. His hands gripped the arms of his chair. He threw a glance toward the comtesse, then addressed Saint-Martin. "I'll come right to the point, Paul. I'm asking you to pursue a certain Irishman, Captain Maurice Fitzroy, at one time in our king's service in the Dillon Regiment."

"We've never met, though I've heard his name mentioned—a gambler and a rake."

"An expert gambler, indeed! He has won large sums of money from Comtesse Clare, my cousin." The baron paused for a deep breath. "I could forget about the money. She was foolish to risk it. But I cannot overlook what he did to my godchild, Sylvie."

The baron yielded to Comtesse Marie, who reminded her nephew, "She's my godchild as well, and your distant cousin."

Saint-Martin felt a tightening in his chest. He knew Sylvie de Chanteclerc from summers he had spent at Chateau Beaumont a decade ago. She'd have been eight or nine years old at the time. A sunny child, always eager for a new game.

A few months ago over coffee in the Palais-Royal, they had renewed their acquaintance and promised to meet again soon. He had been struck by her uncanny resemblance to his friend, Anne Cartier—lively blue eyes, blond hair, fair complexion.

"She's a spirited, sensible girl of nineteen," the baron continued. "For some time, the Irishman attempted to court her. At first, she found him handsome and charming. They met on a few occasions, but she came to distrust him. Polished on the surface. Mean and deceitful underneath. When she tried to discourage him, he pressed his suit even more ardently. Two days ago, she finally rebuffed him." The baron paused, swallowed, then went on, his voice just above a whisper. "The monster found her alone, beat and raped her. He spread the rumor that she had complied gladly, that I had punished her." The baron looked down, stroking his forehead.

Saint-Martin gasped, turned to his aunt. "When did this happen? I hadn't heard. I just got back from Rouen."

"Late Thursday evening," she replied. "At the baron's chateau while he was in Paris. Sylvie had sent Fitzroy away. But he only pretended to leave the estate and hid somewhere on the grounds. When everyone had gone to bed and the house was quiet, he sneaked through a window he had earlier unlatched. In a footman's disguise, he made his way to her room, bound and gagged her, violated her. A pair of trusted servants found her unconscious yesterday morning."

The comtesse excused herself and pulled on a bellrope. A maid appeared. The comtesse spoke into her ear and sent her off, then resumed her account. "When Sylvie recovered consciousness, she was in shock and wouldn't talk to anyone. She was brought here last night, started to feel better, and told me what had happened. I wrote to the baron at once."

"Aunt Marie..." Saint-Martin struggled for words. "I can hardly believe it! Poor Sylvie!"

"But it's true." The comtesse fell silent and took a deep breath. "She allowed me to verify the evidence on her body."

"And you can see for yourself," came a strained voice from behind Saint-Martin. He heard the rustle of a garment and looked over his shoulder. A young woman wrapped in a plain brown dressing gown stepped out of the shadows. Her hair was covered by a gray bonnet that shadowed her face. Obviously in pain, she managed to hold herself erect.

She bowed to the baron and the comtesse, then approached Saint-Martin, who rose from his chair. "Colonel," she said, curtseying stiffly before him.

"Sylvie." His voice faltered. Shocked by her altered appearance, he glanced toward his companions. Their eyes had fastened on him.

Untying the bonnet, she moved a step closer, then bent forward into a candle's light. "He did this, Colonel." She removed the bonnet and tentatively touched her face with her fingers, as if to confirm the damage. The left side was deeply discolored, the eye half-closed. Her lips were swollen.

Saint-Martin felt his gorge rising. "My God!" he breathed.

Stepping back, she pulled open her gown and let it fall over the cord at her waist.

Out of respect, Saint-Martin instinctively tried to avert his eyes. But Sylvie held his gaze. She pointed to dark bruises on her side. She coughed slightly, grimacing with pain.

"He kicked her and broke two ribs," said Comtesse Marie. She hurried to the young woman, wrapped her again in the gown and gently embraced her.

Sylvie cast her a thin smile, then turned back to Saint-Martin. Wrath worked the lines of her mouth. "Fitzroy claims I invited him to my room and the baron beat me for having dishonored the family name. But I swear before Almighty God, the Irishman lies." Her voice dropped to a hoarse whisper. "I want you to kill him."

The baron rose to his feet and shook his fist. "Death would be much too quick, too gentle!"

Sylvie sagged into the comtesse's arms, then forced herself upright. "Kill him!" she cried, her voice low and hoarse. The two men looked on while Comtesse Marie helped her from the room.

When the door closed behind the women, the baron began to pace the floor furiously, staring ahead, pounding his fist into the palm of his hand. After a few minutes, he sat at a desk and waved Saint-Martin to a chair facing him. He held up a document. "This is the king's *lettre de cachet*, a secret order for Captain Fitzroy to be held in solitary confinement for the rest of his life in a royal prison." He handed it to Saint-Martin, adding, "I'm ordering you to execute the royal command."

Shocked by Sylvie's tragedy, Saint-Martin could only nod his assent. For a few seconds he struggled to control his feelings, then found his voice. "The captain's behavior revolts me, sir. Where shall I catch him?"

"The scoundrel disappeared from Paris yesterday, after claiming he was about to be accused of a crime he hadn't committed. I assume he'll flee to England, but he may go there by way of the Low Countries. He knows we will watch the French channel ports closely. I want you to organize a search. Alert the posts of the Royal Highway Patrol at the frontiers. As far as the public is concerned, he is wanted for questioning concerning allegations of fraud."

"May I inquire, sir, why you secured the *lettre de cachet* instead of a warrant for his arrest?" Saint-Martin took a dubious view of this arbitrary procedure that lent itself so easily to abuses of the worst kind. An innocent man could be plucked from his home in the middle of the night and imprisoned without trial, without knowing his accuser or the crime of which he was accused.

The baron leaned forward, arms on the desk, hands clasped tightly. "I want to spare Sylvie the horror and shame of a public trial. She would have to reveal what happened. Judges would question her testimony, probing into the most intimate details. Every hack scribbler in Paris would spread lurid tales about her."

Saint-Martin agreed. "She should not have to endure the tearing open of such a wound." And, to make matters worse, he thought to himself, she could lose the case. Fitzroy might go free. The crime of rape was difficult to prove. And the baron had powerful enemies in high places who resented his great influence at court or had been stung by his sharp tongue. They would be eager to credit Captain Fitzroy's tale.

"Well, there you have it," said the baron, rising from the desk, the discussion at an end. "Fitzroy is guilty beyond a doubt and must be secretly imprisoned. Once in chains, I can assure you, he will suffer the torments of the damned."

Tuesday, March 20

Colonel Paul de Saint-Martin removed his gloves and flicked specks of dust off his red lapels. Baron Breteuil had summoned him to his office in the royal palace at Versailles. The colonel sighed softly. Ten weeks had passed since Captain Fitzroy had assaulted Sylvie and the rogue was still at large.

Saint-Martin surveyed the antechamber. At this late morning hour the room was crowded with petitioners waiting for an audience, most of them supercilious aristocrats, fashionably dressed. They passed the time exchanging bits of court gossip. To judge from the impatient glances they threw at the baron's door, each of them felt entitled to enter immediately.

The colonel smiled to himself. He would be shown into the office before any of them. The baron's message was cryptic and urgent. Something must have happened concerning Captain Fitzroy.

Punishing the knave lay very close to the baron's heart. He had been sorely troubled that the search had thus far been fruitless. Fitzroy had indeed fled to the Low Countries, keeping a step ahead of the French agents pursuing him. Saint-

Martin himself had travelled to Brussels and received full cooperation from the Habsburg authorities. In vain. Fitzroy had disappeared, most likely into Germany or England.

A liveried servant opened the office door and with a bow invited Saint-Martin in. The waiting crowd stirred. A titter of chagrin trailed after him.

Baron Breteuil rose from behind his desk and greeted the colonel with a smile. "Paul, I believe we've found the Irish scoundrel." He sat down again, beckoning Saint-Martin to a chair opposite him. "I can't tell you how pleased I am."

"Where is he?"

"In England." The baron was silent for a moment, allowing the new diplomatic complications of the case to sink into Saint-Martin's mind. "One of my agents, Madame Gagnon, a milliner, has spotted him in Bath under his own name. Maurice Fitzroy! Would you believe it! The bold villain!"

The colonel weighed the baron's words carefully before replying. "That's bad news for us. He's a devil, not a fool. He must have found powerful men to protect him, so he now feels secure."

Breteuil shrugged his shoulders, then pushed a sheet of paper across the desk. "A description of the milliner and the address of her shop. I want you to call on her."

So that's what this conversation was all about, Saint-Martin thought. He must pursue Fitzroy in England. He folded his arms across his chest and leaned back listening, while the baron went on about the milliner's report. Saint-Martin's mind soon began to wander, distracted by a large map of western Europe on the office wall. His eyes fixed on England. Suddenly, London leaped out at him.

Unbidden, an image crept into his mind. A tall, lithe young woman with golden blond hair and blue eyes. Anne Cartier. He had longed for months for her to return to Paris. Fond memories surfaced: beads of dew dripping from a rose onto her sleeve, a ride together in the woods near Wimbledon. Was

Providence now sending him to her? From her last letter, he knew she would be in London yet a little while longer. They could surely meet again as he passed through en route to Bath.

The baron tapped his fingers on the desk. "A certain aspect of this mission seems to appeal to you, Colonel. Bath may be the loveliest city in Britain and offers pleasures to suit every taste. But you will be there on serious, dangerous business."

Caught day-dreaming, the colonel quickly collected himself. "I'm fully aware of that, sir. Fitzroy's wily as well as ruthless." From the report of others, Saint-Martin had formed a mental picture of this foe he had yet to meet. Medium height, slender build, wavy black hair, soft blue eyes, high forehead and refined, delicate features. This almost feminine appearance masked the strength and agility of an athlete. An accomplished fencer, he was also expert with dueling pistols.

"May I ask, Baron, why you have chosen me for this mission rather than, say, an experienced agent like Inspector Quidor?"

"We're dealing with a family matter, Colonel, as well as a crime. You have a personal interest in the mission and the discretion to carry it out properly. I can trust you to avoid diplomatic complications. You know the English and their ways and speak their language. Our relations with them are tense at present. They fear we shall intervene in the quarrel among the Dutch, clash with the Prussians, upset the balance of power in the region. In a few words, you will abduct Fitzroy for me without making a mess. Quidor is clumsy, as we learned in the necklace affair."

Saint-Martin smiled inwardly. A little more than a year earlier, Quidor and his ruffians had tried to kidnap Comte de la Motte, who was in England selling off diamonds from the notorious stolen necklace intended for the French queen. Debarking near Newcastle like a small invading army, they witlessly stirred up the authorities and had to flee in confusion.

"I suggest you travel as a private person on vacation. I'll supply the money and documents you'll need."

"And what of my duties as a provost of the Royal Highway Patrol?"

"I'll find someone to act in your place." The baron paused, his voice took on a conspiratorial tone. "I do not intend to inform our foreign minister. He might become unduly alarmed. Our embassy in London, therefore, will not be aware of your mission. As I've said, this is a family affair. Thc less that's known of it, the better."

The baron reached into a pile of papers on his desk, then looked up as if to say, if there's nothing else…?

"I understand what you expect of me," said Saint-Martin, rising from his chair. "By the way, I'd like to takc my adjutant, Georges Charpentier, with me as a valet."

"By all means. Good man. Knows England. How soon can you leave?"

"By Friday, the 23rd, arriving in Bath a week later, with a couple of days in London en route."

The baron wrinkled his brow in an afterthought, then drew a small silver case from his pocket. "Take this with you, Paul. And study it from time to time."

Saint-Martin opened it to a recent miniature portrait of Sylvie in a gauzy white summer dress. She gazed at him with a happy, innocent expression. He felt profoundly saddened, then angered. A precious part of the young woman's spirit had been brutally destroyed. He snapped the case shut and muttered through tightly pressed lips, "This should help me remember why I'm going." He bowed stiffly to the minister and stalked out.

Outside the baron's office, Saint-Martin's mind was churning. How could he apprehend a wily, ruthless, well-connected villain in England, a foreign country, France's enemy for centuries? He walked rapidly through the state apartments of the royal palace, oblivious to the bustle of courtiers and clerks around him. By an instinct he had learned to trust, he sought out the great palace garden that André Le Nôtre had built for Louis XIV over a century ago.

From the terrace outside the palace, Saint-Martin gazed out over this vast symbol of the Sun King's glory. Broad flights of stone steps led from one level down to another. Wide graveled avenues cut through a regimented forest of trees. Water jetted from fantastic fountains or mirrored the sky in still, pellucid pools. Colossal statues struck every conceivable attitude. A marvelous symmetry and balance ruled over all.

Saint-Martin drew a deep breath. The garden's formal grandeur, so striking in early spring with trees and bushes just beginning to bud, reassured him that the human mind could master even the most wayward impulses of nature. The human variety, included.

This place had once been little more than shifting sand and marsh. Louis XIV had decided it would become a great garden, cost what it might. His architect Le Nôtre designed an ambitious plan, brought in earth, water, and stone, set thousands of men to work to create a masterpiece of cultivated taste and intelligence, a symbol of the absolute authority of the French state and its monarch.

Saint-Martin felt certain that a similar intelligence and energy could be brought to bear on Fitzroy. Beneath his polished, elegant surface, the captain was a primitive man, a wily brute, all sand and marsh. Baron Breteuil was as determined as the great king and willing to spend whatever it would take to outwit and capture the miscreant. Like the king's architect, Saint-Martin would have to devise a credible plan and execute it. A daunting task, but in an odd way he felt lifted up by the majesty of the state. Its ideal of justice would inspire him, and its power would enable him to prevail.

He left the terrace and walked down the steps into the garden. The parterres to left and right still slept, awaiting their floral robes. In the Apollo basin, a gusty spring breeze rippled water around the sun god in his chariot rising from the depths.

In the distance, the Grand Canal stretched out nearly to the horizon. A few pleasure boats drifted lazily on its shimmering surface.

He imagined himself out there with Anne, her hands dangling in the water while he rowed. "That's for a warmer season," he murmured to himself, for the sun had slipped behind a cloud and the breeze had turned chilly. He found a sheltered bench with a view of Apollo's fountain, pulled a small case from his pocket, and opened it to a miniature portrait of Anne. Their deaf friend Michou had painted it last summer. Saint-Martin had carried it with him ever since.

As he gazed at Anne's image, his mind drifted back to that time. He and Anne had stood side by side at this very fountain after a private royal audience. She had handed over to the king the priceless stolen jewels she had recovered, having been wounded in a struggle with its thief. As a reward, the king had given her a fine cabochon emerald set in gold and hung on a gold chain.

In the fountain's reflected light, she had asked Saint-Martin to help her put it on. He had slipped behind her and fastened it around her neck. She had turned her head and ravished him with a tender smile. His heart leapt. It was a moment he would never forget.

Later in September, as Anne was leaving Paris for London, they had agreed to be friends. He had wanted a more committed relationship, perhaps marriage, but had cautiously yielded to her yearning for independence. She had said she'd only be gone for a few weeks, visiting grandparents and friends.

Saint-Martin looked up to the sky, searching for the sun, then sighed. The "few weeks" had stretched out into seven months. Anne had nursed her grandmother through a lingering fatal illness. Her letters had expressed an ardent wish to see him soon. But delay followed delay until he wondered if she were losing interest in returning to Paris, to Abbé de l'Épée's school, where she had been learning to teach deaf children. Had she been trapped into caring for other aged relatives? She might stay in England forever.

He stared again at Anne's portrait as if his gaze could somehow bring her back to his side. How he longed for her! He returned the case to his pocket, leaned back on the bench, and thought ahead to his forthcoming visit to England. He would seek her out in the village of Hampstead near London where she was staying with her grandfather. Would her face light up, her arms reach out, when he appeared on her doorstep?

Buoyed by a fragile hope, he imagined the two of them riding in the lovely green English countryside, her blue eyes teasing him, her cheeks flushed with pleasure. The prospect lifted his spirits. But a quiet voice within warned him not to let his hopes rise too high. Or distract him from his task. He rose from the bench and walked purposefully back to the palace.

Chapter 2

A Change of Plan

Tuesday, March 20

The scent of hay and freshly oiled leather filled the tackle room. A young woman stepped back to inspect her work and gave it a nod of approval. She believed in caring for her own saddle and her boots, never mind what the men thought. Out in the stable a mare whinnied softly, then snorted. The horse had been fed, now she wanted more personal attention.

"I'm coming, Mignon." The young woman walked into the stable and stroked the fine-boned black thoroughbred's gleaming neck. It whinnied with pleasure, bent its head toward the young woman, and nuzzled her.

An old man's voice, still robust, came from the house close by. "I'm home, Annie. You've another letter from Paris. Can't *imagine* who sent it." The language was French with a Norman accent, though the old man had lived his entire adult life in England. He had just returned from Hampstead with the mail. A daily morning ritual.

Anne Cartier smiled ruefully. She had detected an undertone of concern in her grandfather's teasing voice. He knew very well who had sent the letter. The French colonel. She closed the stable door behind her and hurried up the garden path to the house, a modest two-story brick building set on a gentle rise of land and surrounded by great oak trees and lush, grassy meadows.

Monsieur André Cartier sat quietly at the table on the garden terrace cleaning the barrel of a pistol. A square, ruddy-faced man with dark bushy eyebrows, he had about him even in repose an air of authority. Thick wiry steel gray hair attested to his seventy years. The recent loss of his wife had dulled the brilliance of his blue eyes. But he still managed a large gun shop in Hampstead a mile away, crafting duelling pistols, fowling pieces, and the like for wealthy customers. As Anne approached, he smiled at her with obvious affection.

Sheltered by the house from a cool spring breeze, the terrace gathered the full warmth of the March sun. The letter from Paris waited for her on the table. She took a seat facing her grandfather, drew a small case from her bag, and opened it to the miniature portrait of Paul that her deaf friend Michou had painted in Paris. For a few moments she gazed at the portrait, drawing in Paul's presence, then picked up the letter.

After reading a few lines, Anne wondered if she shouldn't have retired to the privacy of her room. Her face surely betrayed her yearning for this man. On the other hand, she had always felt comfortable confiding in her grandfather. Months ago, she had spoken about Paul de Saint-Martin. A provost of the Royal Highway Patrol, he had helped her clear the name of her stepfather, Antoine Dubois, falsely accused of murdering a woman in Paris, then killing himself.

During that investigation, she and Paul had grown fond of one another, despite the great social distance between them. It had been hard for her to leave him last September and return to England for a visit.

Her grandfather had listened to her patiently but with a skeptical ear. He had heard of the man before. Years ago, Anne and her parents had sung his praises. They had met him, then a young officer, during summers spent in France before the

American War. Unfortunately, as a child, the old Huguenot had learned to hate the French monarchy and its church. His parents had suffered imprisonment and the loss of their property at the hands of the king's agents. Relatives in France were still subject to force and guile designed to bring about their conversion. As he grew older, he judged individual Catholics on their personal merits. But the ancient antipathy welled up whenever he pictured Colonel Paul de Saint-Martin in the king's uniform.

Sometimes Anne wondered if her grandfather also feared that another man might take away his beloved granddaughter. When she first mentioned Saint-Martin, Cartier had suggested the colonel might have ulterior motives in befriending her. Was he a typical nobleman looking for a mistress? Or, did he have marriage in mind? If so, was that in her best interest? Would his family accept her? Would he expect her to adopt his religion?

She had wrestled with these questions for the past several months. Her grandfather had suggested she stand back and take a sober look at Saint-Martin. Allow time and distance to test her feelings for him.

That she had done, aided by delays she could not avoid. In the end, as her reaction to today's letter confirmed, she wanted to be with Paul more than ever. But, marriage was a different matter. As she had said to her grandfather, she didn't want to *belong* to anyone. She wanted to manage her own life.

Her grandfather now seemed to read her mind. "Our law and customs are creating this quandary." He reached across the table and held her hand. "You and the colonel could marry according to society's conventions but agree to treat each other as free and equal. That agreement would depend solely on the sincerity of your promises. Whether within or outside of marriage, your best guarantee of remaining your own person is the integrity of his love for you. Thus far, it has survived the test of separation."

He gazed at her thoughtfully. A tinge of sadness came over his face. "Annie, consider the situation of your Protestant relatives in France. In public, they have to conform to the law requiring them to marry, baptize, and worship according to the rites of the Roman Catholic Church. In private, they act according to their consciences. It's galling to have to compromise in such matters but unavoidable." He sighed deeply.

Squeezing his hand, she thanked him. The future remained unclear, but glancing again at the miniature portrait of Paul lying next to the letter, she felt hopeful. Michou had caught the frank cast of his brow, the quiet humor in the lines of his mouth, the glint of desire in his eyes. Anne caressed the portrait with her fingers.

She read Paul's letter again. He was still working on the special assignment Baron Breteuil had given him in January. A difficult, very troubling case. One day he would tell her about it. In the meantime, he missed her and was looking forward to a ride together at Chateau Beaumont.

He was referring to an early morning during the past summer. A tender moment. They were about to mount their horses when news came of a murder on a nearby estate. Reluctantly, they had to abandon the ride. The ensuing investigation absorbed their attention and the moment was lost.

Anne's desire to return to Paris strengthened with every line of the letter. She would resume her studies with Abbé de l'Épée and master his system for educating deaf children. And she would renew her friendship with Paul. At the end of the second reading, she laid the letter on the table and looked up at her grandfather. His smile was sad but accepting. She felt a tug at her heart.

"I'll be leaving for Paris by the Dover coach on Monday the 26th."

"Yes, we've talked about it before. There's risk, but you've given it enough thought. Go to him. He seems to be an honorable man."

"But I hate to leave you, especially since Grandmother is gone." Anne imagined her grandfather alone in the house, its rooms filled with the mementos of a long married life. They would constantly remind him of the loss of his wife.

"Don't worry. I'll be fine. With spring coming, my mind will be busy with work on the estate as well as the gun business. I'll have my sister Adelaide. She'll soon come to live with me."

Anne felt relieved. Her recently widowed aunt was an amiable, sensible person. They would comfort one another. Blowing him a kiss, Anne rose from the table. "I'm going to ride over to Hackney to say good-bye to Mr. Braidwood."

Since returning to England in September, she had often visited his institute for the deaf, where she had worked prior to becoming involved in the Dubois case. Braidwood had entrusted a few of his students to her for tutoring and shown keen interest in her report on the work of Abbé de l'Épée in Paris, whom he viewed with suspicion as a rival.

"Julien will ride with you to Hackney," said Monsieur Cartier in a voice that admitted no contradiction. "There's safety in numbers, especially on English highways."

A few hours later, Anne Cartier rode sidesaddle on her thoroughbred down the gravel path that led to the highway. Julien, Monsieur Cartier's trusted groom, followed a few paces behind. Like his master, the groom had fled from Normandy to England as an infant together with his French Huguenot parents. He too had kept his mother tongue. Neither man felt entirely at home in England.

Anne cast a sidelong glance at him and smiled. He merely nodded back, but she could see a hint of pleasure in his eyes. A taciturn man, he spoke only when he thought he had good reason to do so. Yet she felt comfortable with him. And grateful. He had shared with Anne his knowledge of horses—he had served several youthful years in a British mounted regiment. Thanks to him, she could ride and shoot like a cavalryman.

On this day, Anne was especially happy that Julien allowed her to pursue her own thoughts. Halfway to Hackney, they passed by Islington, where she had fond memories of rope dancing and tumbling at Sadler's Wells, first with her stepfather, Antoine Dubois, and then, later, by herself.

There were darker, painful memories also, from a year and a half ago, when Jack Roach and his cronies attacked her at night outside her Islington cottage and trumped up charges of lewd solicitation and assault against her. She had spent the night in a wretched jail. The next day, Roach's ally, the magistrate, Tom Hammer, had condemned her in a farce of a trial. The crowd in the village marketplace had shouted, "French whore." On the scaffold Hammer had cropped her thick golden hair. Even now, she shuddered at the thought of that bitter, humiliating experience.

With relief she spurred her horse toward Hackney. When she had felt depressed, Mr. Braidwood had given her comfort and rewarding work to do. She owed him a great deal.

At the institute an ancient servant showed her in, then gestured in the direction of Braidwood's reception room. "You know the way, Miss Cartier, you're at home here." He bowed slightly and returned to his post.

She felt pleased to be thought of as one of the family. Wending her way through the building, she renewed her acquaintance with students and teachers. They greeted her warmly, if briefly, for the students—some twenty of them—were in the midst of their daily vocal exercises, tediously learning the position of lips and tongue for every sound their teachers wanted them to make.

Anne stopped at an open door to watch Mr. Braidwood's son John work with three young children. One student at a time, he shaped their mouths with his own fingers. Then he pronounced the vowels, and they followed his lead. To correct their mistakes, he chose a rounded silver instrument the length of a tobacco pipe, flattened at one end, with a small ball at the other. Placing it in the students' mouths, he moved their tongues to the exact position for each vowel.

Frustration flashed across the students' faces as their teacher calmly repeated the exercise again and again. But they endured it more or less patiently for they realized its purpose. They must learn to articulate clearly, or no one would ever understand what they said. Finally, he put the device in its case and smiled. They would move on to something more enjoyable.

The door to Braidwood's office stood ajar. Anne knocked, then cautiously stepped inside. Bent and gray, Braidwood was standing by the window, looking out at the garden. Hearing her enter, he turned and immediately straightened up. "What a pleasant and, I must say, fortunate surprise. For I've just now been thinking of you. In this morning's mail I've received a most troubling message. Let me tell you about it."

The day was still warm and sunny, uncommon for March. He ordered tea, then led Anne to a sheltered table at the far end of the garden. When tea had been poured and they were alone, he met Anne's eye. "I'm concerned about little Charlie Rogers. You recall him, I'm sure. The eleven-year-old boy from Bristol. You tutored him frequently and got on well with him."

"Of course. A sweet, bright child, rather small and frail, suffers from asthma. He's away on holiday with his parents at a spa, isn't he?"

Braidwood sighed. "Yes, he's in Bath. I learned this morning that he needs a new tutor for the next four or five weeks." The old man shifted in his chair and took a sip of tea, as if gathering courage. "And you came to mind."

Alarm bells rang in Anne's head. Several weeks tutoring in Bath? She wanted to leave Hampstead for Paris in six days!

Braidwood apparently failed to notice her consternation, for he went on explaining the "troubling message." It came from Lady Margaret Rogers, the boy's mother. "His tutor Mary

Campbell has suddenly died," he said, his voice breaking. "Lady Margaret asks me to send a replacement."

Anne drew back in horror. "That's incredible! How did it happen?"

"Accidentally. She fell. Lady Margaret didn't say how."

Anne knew Mary Campbell, a likeable, conscientious seventeen-year-old whose parents were deaf. A hearing person herself, she was familiar with oral training of the deaf.

"Her parents studied with me in Scotland many years ago," Braidwood continued. "We've kept in touch. Mary visited us here in Hackney in January when she moved to London. A kind, friendly girl. I thought she'd be a good companion for little Charlie, if not exactly a tutor. I recommended her to Lady Margaret." Braidwood stared at the ground, shaking his head. "I feel devastated by her death and partly responsible for it. After all, I sent her to Bath."

"Don't punish yourself." Anne struggled for words that would console the stricken man. "You couldn't foresee an accident like this."

"Thank you, Miss Cartier, for your kindness." He looked up at her, knitting his brow. "But I should have done something. She had complained to her parents that the family was a hornet's nest. When I heard that, I should have called her back and sent an older person. She was perhaps too young and inexperienced. I also worry about the boy's well-being in such a family. His parents have little understanding of his disability and treat him as a nuisance or an embarrassment."

Though realizing he desperately wanted her to take Mary's place, Anne remained silent. Her heart was set on her reunion with Paul. Moving into a strange household wasn't at all what she wanted to do. Yet she owed Braidwood a favor, and a small inner voice urged her to repay him.

"Couldn't someone from the staff here in Hackney be sent to replace her?" It shamed Anne that she was trying to evade his clear desire.

"My son's health is too delicate for the journey and for what are surely stressful circumstances. My assistants are needed here and are also too young and inexperienced." He paused for a moment, then raised his hands palms up and smiled tentatively. "I thought of you from the start. You have worked with the boy over the past several months, and he likes you." He paused, then continued with a more confident voice. "You are a mature, resourceful, and courageous woman, as you recently proved in Antoine Dubois' case. I would be most grateful if you could relieve my mind of this concern."

"This comes as a complete surprise to me," Anne responded as calmly as she could. "I have made plans to return to France this coming Monday. But, I see the urgency of Charlie's situation. Give me an hour's time and a quiet place to think it over."

"I appreciate your willingness to consider my request. The garden is yours for as long as you need it." Braidwood rose from the table, visibly hopeful, and returned to the house.

Anne paced up and down the garden paths, recalling Charlie's slender, delicate features, black wavy hair, high forehead, soft blue eyes. He was small and immature for his age, but an unusually intelligent and sensitive boy. Three years ago, a high fever had taken away his hearing. His parents placed him with Braidwood, who had just opened his institute in Hackney. Sharp-eyed and alert, the boy developed a remarkable talent for reading lips. Since he had acquired the habit of speech before his illness, he articulated well enough to be understood. But his voice had become monotone and unnaturally loud and high pitched. He stumbled on new words and certain sounds, like "ch."

At home, Anne understood, the boy spoke reluctantly, fearing criticism or ridicule. She knew little about the boy's family, other than it was rich. Braidwood had mentioned that the father had made a fortune in West Indian trade, and his wife was an Irish baron's daughter. Under the circumstances, Anne reasoned, she could set her own terms: decent accommodations, good pay, and a suitable measure of freedom and respect. It was only for a month or so. The boy was isolated and lonely. Or, worse.

She glanced across the garden at the institute. Teaching here had helped her recover from her humiliation at the hands of Roach and Hammer. She owed Braidwood for that. He could have taken advantage of her but he didn't. And he wouldn't have asked her today if he had any other choice. Rising from the bench with a heavy heart, she knew she must postpone her return to Paris and travel immediately to Bath.

On her way to Braidwood's office, she began considering the preparations she must now make. Harriet Ware, her best friend from Sadler's Wells, was working as a singer and dancer at a theater in Bath. Anne would write to her this evening, announcing her imminent arrival. Then she would write to Paul. A tear escaped from her eye. She hoped he would understand.

Chapter 3

Despair

Thursday, March 22

Shortly after dawn, Colonel Paul de Saint-Martin strolled through the enclosed garden of his residence on Rue Saint-Honoré. The marks of winter were still visible everywhere: fallen twigs, moldering leaves, dry stalks of plants. But spring had arrived. In a few hours, the full heat of the sun would beat down on the flower beds. Daffodils were about to bloom.

He had risen early to ready the garden for its new season. It was his last opportunity. Tomorrow, he would leave Paris for England and didn't know how long he would be gone. He regretted that he might miss the spring flowers already making their way out of the ground. They cheered his spirit after the dreariness of winter. For over an hour he cleared away the debris and left it in a pile for servants to dispose of.

At seven o'clock, he broke off work. Time to talk to Georges about the trip. Up to this point, he had not involved his adjutant in the pursuit of Fitzroy. Georges Charpentier was an older man in his late forties, with a broad knowledge of policing. While Saint-Martin was away from Paris, Georges had capably managed the provost's office and investigated several crimes. Saint-Martin's substitute, a retired colonel, was happy that someone else looked after affairs. Had Georges been of noble birth, he could have expected to rise to a position of authority in the Royal Highway Patrol.

Saint-Martin had ordered breakfast to be served in his office. Georges appeared promptly, just as a servant was setting the table with plates and cups, baskets of bread, butter, preserves, and cheese. He poured coffee, set the pot on the table, and left the room. The adjutant rubbed his hands with relish, took a seat, and broke off a piece of bread.

Before he could bring it to his mouth, the colonel cleared his throat. "Georges, can you be ready to leave for England tomorrow?"

The adjutant blinked. "You're joking, aren't you?" He grinned and wagged his head.

"No. The baron gave me orders two days ago. Couldn't reach you yesterday. Fitzroy's been spotted in Bath. I need you to help me catch him and bring him back."

Georges put down the bread, his brow furrowed. "I thought Fitzroy was a family matter. Should I be involved?"

His tone of voice was neutral, his expression detached. Still, the question had an edge that caught Saint-Martin by surprise and disquieted him.

"The baron wants to keep the affair out of the public eye. But, family honor isn't the only issue. Fitzroy raped and beat a young woman, who happens to be my cousin. He shouldn't be allowed to do that to anyone. I'm treating this as a serious criminal offense. Normally, we'd ask the English to give up a suspected felon. But, in this case, the procedure would expose Sylvie to public shame. And, the English might refuse to cooperate, preferring to accept Fitzroy's version of the incident." He paused to gauge his adjutant's mind and noted his growing interest. "Now, to answer your question: Yes, I think you should be involved in catching Fitzroy; he's a fugitive. Furthermore, you're familiar with the English and speak their language. I couldn't find a better man in all of Paris."

"That's true," Georges remarked candidly. "Sartines was my master!"

The colonel had often heard Georges' homage to Lieutenant-General Sartines, the man in charge of French police more than a decade ago. Georges had in fact served Sartines as a spy in England.

Georges palmed the imaginary hair on his bald pate, grinning lecherously. "Well, it looks like the women of Paris will have to find another lover for a while. I'll warn them I'm being called away suddenly on business." He lifted his cup and took a sip of coffee. "What role am I to play?"

"My valet. I'll be travelling as a tourist." The colonel explained they would cross the Channel at Calais, spend a few days in London, then go on to Bath. "Baron Breteuil has arranged for Lieutenant Faure from Villejuif to move into this office while I'm gone."

"Will we see Miss Cartier?" Georges asked, a sly look in his eye.

"I hope so," Saint-Martin replied with feeling.

The two men had nearly finished breakfast when a message arrived. "From Comtesse Beaumont," said Saint-Martin, scanning the page. "She wants me to visit her on Rue Traversine. Sylvie's with her. Something's wrong." He stared at the note, then turned to his adjutant. "You had best come along, Georges."

The two men hurried on foot through busy crowded streets to the comtesse's town house. She and Sylvie had come to Paris a few days ago. The young woman had been convalescing at Chateau Beaumont and had recovered to the point where she might benefit from meeting people, shopping, enjoying something light at the theater, attending a concert.

A maid met the two men at the entrance and showed them into Aunt Marie's parlor on the first floor. She and Sylvie were lingering over breakfast. Saint-Martin introduced Georges to Sylvie, who studied him with curious interest. The comtesse smiled a greeting; she already knew him. The men declined an offer of coffee but agreed to join the women at the table. When Georges hesitated to take a chair, the comtesse insisted.

While chatting about the unusually fine March weather, Saint-Martin observed Sylvie with growing concern. True, her facial bruises were gone. Her ribs appeared to have mended for she moved her body easily. But, her long blond hair was combed back severely and tied in a tight knot. She had lost weight, giving her an emaciated, haunted appearance. Her blue eyes were downcast, deep-set and dark. She spoke seldom, and then in flat, halting words.

In the course of conversation, Saint-Martin mentioned that he and Georges would leave Paris for England tomorrow.

Sylvie looked up with a start. "Have you found him?"

"Yes, we know he's in Bath."

"Why do you bother going there? He said he had friends in England." She spoke emphatically, her voice laced with scorn. "They'll believe his story and protect him."

"He may be overconfident," Saint-Martin replied. "With Georges' help, I intend to catch him."

She glanced at Georges, then at Saint-Martin. "Good luck." All feeling drained from her voice, her shoulders sagged. "Please excuse me." She turned to the comtesse. "I'll retire to my room."

When the young woman had left, Comtesse Marie sighed deeply, then explained that, yesterday, she and Sylvie had gone shopping in Palais-Royal close by. They had enjoyed themselves, trying on the enormous hats that had become fashionable. When they were tired, they stopped for tea in Café du Foy. Hardly had they sat down when Comtesse Louise de Joinville entered the restaurant together with several elegantly dressed men and women.

Saint-Martin grimaced; this tale could not come to a good end. Louise, his cousin, thirsted for malicious gossip. "What happened?" he asked apprehensively.

"She noticed us. Rushed over to express her sympathy. It was obvious to me, and certainly to Sylvie, that Louise was merely curious to see how much damage Fitzroy or—as she might have thought—Baron Breteuil had done. 'Oh, Sylvie, you poor thing' she said again and again. Finally, she left us and joined her companions at another table. From their sidelong glances and their tittering, one could tell they were tattling about Sylvie." The comtesse fell silent, glanced at Georges then at Saint-Martin. Finally, she shook her head, unable to continue.

Her nephew offered her water from a pitcher on the table. She sipped at her glass, took a deep breath, and went on. "That was one of the worst moments of my life. I had been nursing Sylvie for over two months. I knew exactly how she felt. She looked up at me and asked to go home, as if all hope had died within her."

While his aunt recounted the incident, Saint-Martin thought of Sylvie. A good, sensible person, yet she had aspired to the conventional life of her class: parties, seeing and being seen, a successful marriage. Since Fitzroy's assault, she had come to realize she could no longer thrive in society. The rape had cast a deep shadow of shame over her and lessened her attractiveness to suitable men. Life seemed nothing but a dark abyss.

A sudden fear gripped Saint-Martin, his aunt, and Georges at the same instant. They stared at one another for a moment, then Comtesse Marie pulled a bell rope and called a maid. "Go to Sylvie's room and see if she's comfortable."

In a minute, the maid came back. "She's not there, my lady. Shall I continue looking?" Comtesse Marie leaped from her chair, anticipating Saint-Martin and Georges by only a fraction of a second. "Paul! Check outside. The maids and I will search the house."

Saint-Martin beckoned Georges. "To the stables! Follow me!" They ran downstairs, crossed the courtyard, and tried the stable door. Locked. "The bar drops down into a slot.

Maybe I can force it out." He slipped his sword through a narrow space between door and frame and lifted up. The door swung open and he saw her. "Go around the back way," he whispered to Georges.

Sylvie stood in her shift on a stool, her clothes piled in front of her. She had thrown a rope over a low transverse beam and was tightening it around her neck. Saint-Martin took a step into the room, then stopped for fear of provoking her to jump. She stared at him blankly. "Go away, Paul. This is the end."

"Stay alive, Sylvie, for the sake of those who love you. Louise and her kind are false friends. Vipers. There's much more to life than pleasing them."

Her eyes widened but her mind appeared not to grasp what he was saying. She looked up to see whether the rope was secure on the beam. Georges crept into the room behind her. Saint-Martin, his throat parched, kept on talking. Suddenly, she gave him a faint, despairing smile, then jumped, kicking the stool aside.

At that instant, Georges leaped forward and slashed the rope with his sword. She fell to the floor, the rope coiling loosely over her. Saint-Martin felt weak in the knees, but he stumbled up to her. Georges was already easing the rope from her neck.

She clawed at his face, thrashed about, moaning, "No! No! Let me die." They quickly restrained her and carried her into the house.

Aunt Marie met them on the way. "She's alive," said Saint-Martin, "but desperate. Watch her constantly."

"I'll see she gets the care she needs. There's surely a way out. She's a sound young woman."

"Yes, dear aunt, there's hope for her." But only a slim hope, he thought sadly. It would be difficult to save a woman who was determined to kill herself. "I want to know her progress. Write to Madame Francine Gagnon, Milsom Street, Bath. She can be trusted to pass your messages on to me."

On the walk back to the provost's house on Rue Saint-Honoré, Georges was unusually quiet, head bent down studying the pavement. At the entrance, he leaned toward Saint-Martin and hissed through lips drawn tight with anger, "Colonel, I'm with you all the way. By God, we'll bring the bastard back to France!"

Chapter 4

Family Problems

Monday, March 26

"Bath ahead," the coachman shouted. Anne felt a tingle of apprehension. Her meeting with the wealthy Rogers family drew near. She stirred nervously, wondering how she would be received. Differences of social rank mattered less in Bath than in London, she had heard. That was encouraging. She glanced out the carriage window at newly green fields, hedge rows blossoming, swallows swooping among the cottages along the road. The weather had been overcast and warm all day but now a cool westerly wind cleared the sky. As the carriage entered the city on London Road, it passed by serried ranks of gracious honey-colored terrace houses. Anne gasped with pleasure. Her anxiety ebbed away.

Her travelling companion, Mrs. Mowbray, a wealthy widow from Hampstead and frequent visitor to Bath, had also been gazing out the window. Now she turned toward Anne and exclaimed, "The city is at its best this evening. The wind's blown away the haze and smoke that gathers in the river valley." As an afterthought, she added, "Shall we make a slight detour? I could show you some of Bath's marvels."

Anne gladly agreed. Once she had assumed her duties at Combe Park, she might not be as free as she'd like for sightseeing.

At her companion's instruction, the driver turned off London Road and drove to a large two-story stone building between Bennett and Alfred Streets. "The Upper Assembly Rooms," she pointed out. "Grand place, isn't it!" Low, slanting rays of the sun bathed the building's surface, turning its honey color into gold. Monumental, nobly proportioned, it occupied an entire city block. Did even London have such a fine building? Anne wondered.

"In an hour," her companion continued, "the cream of society will come here to gossip, drink tea, dance, gamble. For myself, I prefer private parties where I can find smaller, more agreeable company, chat freely, and win a penny or two at whist."

They drove on through a large circle of handsome identical attached houses crowned with balustrades of giant stone acorns. "The Circus," Mrs. Mowbray remarked. "Only the very rich can afford to live here."

"Have you heard of Combe Park?" asked Anne, recalling the wealth attributed to Sir Harry Rogers. She was eager to learn how her future employer was regarded.

"Yes, indeed," the widow replied. "Bath's pride. I've been there on a few occasions. Sir Harry's a splendid host—select company, good food and music." Her voice dropped conspiratorially. "And gambling for high stakes. Too high for me."

How high will the stakes be for me? wondered Anne to herself, aware that her sojourn at Combe Park would truly be a gamble. "A hornet's nest," Mary Campbell had said.

By the time they left the Circus, the sun had set; street lamps were lighted. Elegant men and women appeared on the wide sidewalks. Finally, Anne alighted at the York, Bath's most comfortable inn, and bid good-bye to her companion.

As the carriage drove off, Anne felt charmed by the appearance of the city in which she would spend the next several weeks. But, what manner of mischief, she wondered, went on behind its beautiful facades?

The morning after Anne arrived, she was awakened by a maid entering her room with a large tray. Behind her came Anne's friend, Harriet Ware, her large brown eyes sparkling with delight. "Sorry, Annie. I couldn't meet you here last night. On Monday evenings I dance at the Bath Theatre. But I've ordered breakfast for the two of us. Hope you don't mind. Your room's really the best place to talk. Afterwards, I'll take you to Combe Park."

Anne roused herself, threw on a robe, and embraced her friend. Then, holding her at arm's length, Anne glanced at her fine yellow woolen gown and its intricate brown embroidery. A costume rather beyond a dancer's means. "Bath's been remarkably good to you, Harriet!" They had last seen one another a year and a half ago. Anne took stock of her friend. She had grown into a self-assured young woman at ease in the world.

"Thank you," she replied, flushing slightly. "Now, tell me exactly why you're here. You wrote earlier about working at Combe Park."

Anne sat facing Harriet at the breakfast table over coffee, warm rolls, sweet butter, and ginger marmalade. "I've agreed to tutor the Rogers' eleven-year-old deaf boy." She went on to speak about the death of Charlie Roger's young tutor, Mary Campbell, and the boy's painful inability to communicate with his family, and they with him. "This turn of events distressed Mr. Braidwood, and he asked me to step in. I really wanted to return to Paris, but I couldn't turn him down." Anne hesitated, then added, "You know why, Harriet."

"I was there. The market place in Islington. Last year. It's etched in my memory. Mr. Braidwood helped save you from Tom Hammer, Jack Roach, and his cronies."

"So, here I am," Anne said. "What can you tell me about Mary Campbell and her accident?"

Harriet finished a bite of her roll and sipped her coffee. Her face took on a somber cast. "I knew her well. She was a lively, pretty girl with a willowy figure. I gave her dancing lessons, showed her the Pump Room and Spring Gardens. At first, she seemed happy at Combe Park, caring for Charlie, going to parties. Lately, she appeared troubled but she didn't want to complain. Said she'd work things out."

"Did she have any friends?"

"Captain Fitzroy took a liking to her. I saw them together in the ballroom and in the garden."

"Captain who?"

"Fitzroy. Irish. Handsome gentleman. Lives at Combe Park. You'll meet him today."

"Do you have any idea what Mary's troubles were?"

Harriet shrugged. "Perhaps Fitzroy became too ardent. Once she told me, he's best kept at arm's length. After she died, a rumor in the town claimed she had stolen silver spoons from the Rogers' cabinets. I'd say someone was maligning her."

Anne started at Harriet's reference to the spoons, the first she'd heard of them. A dubious rumor. Stealing seemed out of character, to judge by what Braidwood had said about the girl.

Harriet detected Anne's surprise and wagged a finger. "Bath loves gossip; rumors are its common currency. We hardly believe a particle of what we hear, but we repeat it anyway."

"How did the accident happen? Braidwood would like to know for her parents' sake."

"She fell down the servants' stairway in the middle of the night and broke her neck. A footman found her dead. I'll show you the spot."

"Yes, I'd like to see it." Anne reflected for a moment. "Poor Mary! What a pity! And what a loss for little Charlie." She leaned back in her chair, steepled her fingers at her lips. "Tell me what you know about his family."

"I often meet his parents—Sir Harry more than Lady Margaret."

A certain overtone in her voice aroused Anne's curiosity. "What sort of man is he?"

A blush spread over Harriet's smooth creamy skin. "About fifty. Tall and strong. Barrel-chested. Square ruddy face. Women find him handsome, charming in a rough way." She paused, gazing inward at her image of the man. An uneasy, enigmatic smile played on her lips. She took off her bonnet and released a cascade of dark brown wavy hair on to her shoulders. "He's full of energy and ideas. Things happen when he's around."

An uneasy look in her friend's eye alerted Anne. "Do you know him well?" She felt the need for caution. Her friend was a dancer and singer, very beautiful, still young and a little foolish.

Harriet appeared only slightly embarrassed. "He comes to the dressing room after performances and speaks to me as well as to the other girls. I'm one of his favorites, I suppose. He invites me to sing and dance at Combe Park. Pays well. Most evenings, it's the liveliest place in Bath. The best food, drink, and music. Guests can flirt on the dance floor, or in the garden if the weather's fair. There's gambling, for those who want it. Much more fun than the stuffy Assembly Rooms where dull, respectable people gather to gawk at one another."

Anne smiled in tentative agreement. She too might prefer the parties at Combe Park. "Sir Harry seems to enjoy playing the generous host," she remarked. "I've heard his fortune comes from West Indian trade. How did he manage? Slaves and sugar are risky business."

Harriet spread marmalade on a bun, bit into it, then laid it down. "Harry's the son of a shipwright," she explained. "Went to sea as a boy, worked up to captain of a Bristol slave ship, then charmed and married the owner, a wealthy widow. With her money he expanded his trade in slaves and West Indian goods, especially sugar. His wife died after six years, and he inherited her wealth."

Harriet's familiarity with the life of Harry Rogers intrigued Anne. "Did Harry and the widow have any children?"

"No," Harriet replied. "But he took in his nephew, William Rogers. Sent him off to school. His manners need polish, so he's spending the spring season in Bath." Harriet grimaced. "You'll meet him today. A big fifteen-year lad. Resembles his uncle but lacks his charm and energy." She hesitated, searching for the right words. "I'd better warn you, don't trust him. A cheat and a bully. I've heard he annoys the servant girls and teases poor little Charlie."

"Who is in charge of William while he's here?" Anne asked.

"Harry's hired a tutor, Mr. Edward Critchley, who arrived a couple of months ago. Watch out for him too. They say he's learned, reads Greek and Latin, French, and Italian, and studies the stars with a telescope. But I think he's odd. Makes my skin creep. He looks down his long skinny nose and sniffs at me as if I smell bad."

"Thanks for the warning," said Anne. "But I'm more concerned about Sir Harry at the moment."

"He's rich!" said Harriet with a touch of awe. "During the American war he made a small fortune financing privateers. His shipping business still turns handsome profits, and so do his investments. He invites wealthy people to his parties and makes deals with them. They think he has a nose for money."

Anne's curiosity grew livelier. "The son of a shipwright! How did he get the 'sir' in front of his name?"

"He bought it! I don't know how. Then he married Lady Margaret, an Irish baron's young widowed daughter. In a way, Harry bought her too, paid off her father's debts." Harriet's eyes sparkled with irritation. "Lady Margaret indeed! Holds her nose up in the air. Doesn't see me or the other girls when we come to the house." Harriet mimicked the woman, pursing her lips in distaste.

"You are to the manner born," Anne chuckled.

Harriet rose from her chair, glided back and forth across the floor, primping, issuing orders to imaginary servants. Arms akimbo, she turned to her friend. "No need to be born to the manner, Annie. With enough money and the right connections, any actress could play the baroness."

"True." Anne smiled patiently.

Harriet returned to her chair. "Lady Margaret soon gave birth to Charlie, heir to Sir Harry's fortune. At first, he doted on the boy and set great hopes on his future." She frowned. Her voice darkened. "When Charlie became deaf, Harry began to dislike him. That's what I'm told. The situation has grown much worse since Captain Fitzroy arrived here late last month with Lady Margaret. He's her cousin, they say."

Anne sat up, puzzled. "What does the captain have to do with Charlie?"

"I'd rather you see for yourself," replied Harriet, shaking her head and sighing. "Harry turns away from Charlie as if he can't stand the sight of him. It's sad."

"Combe Park," shouted the coachman from the driver's seat as he brought the carriage through the entrance. They passed between a large outbuilding on the left and the retaining wall of a grassy upward slope on the right. Ahead stood the rectangular block of a great house, built of the same honey-colored stone found in Bath's finest buildings. As the carriage neared the house, the road offered Anne and Harriet a brief northward view over Bath and the River Avon under a thin veil of midafternoon mist. The carriage continued on to the house's south side and its main entrance.

A tall footman approached, lowered the carriage step, opened the door, and extended his arm to help her descend. Anne gasped, then immediately recovered her composure. He was a black man in crimson livery trimmed with silver. A silver band circled his neck.

"Lord Jeff," whispered Harriet in Anne's ear.

While the women walked to the door, the black servant lifted Anne's trunk from the rack on the back of the carriage and pointed the coachman toward the stables where he could water his horses.

Harriet leaned toward Anne. "Sir Harry's probably in his study, watching us." With a tilt of her head she led Anne's gaze to a window to the right of the entrance where a figure dimly appeared. "He really enjoys showing off his slave."

Anne stopped in her tracks, as if shot. She glanced over her shoulder at the footman a few paces away, her trunk resting lightly on his hip. She stared incredulously at Harriet. "A slave? Here in England?"

"Where've you been, Annie!" whispered Harriet in mock amazement. "There are thousands in London, Bristol, and Liverpool. And many in Bath too. Mostly domestic servants. They come with the West Indian trade."

The black man showed the two women into the study, a large well-lighted room facing south. A beautiful Turkish carpet covered the floor. Sir Harry rose from behind a mahogany desk and strode toward Anne, took her hand, and kissed it. "Welcome, Miss Cartier!" He stepped back, head canted, inspecting her. "I'm happy to see that Mr. Braidwood has sent us a woman this time rather than a girl. He has assured me of your competence as a tutor. And Harriet has mentioned some of your other talents." He threw a mischievous glance at Anne's friend, who had begun to blush. His gaze shifted back to Anne. "Singing, dancing, and tumbling. We shall put you to good use at Combe Park."

Anne thought it wise to let Sir Harry know from the beginning what could be expected of her. Later on, she would offer to entertain occasionally. "I have come mainly to be helpful to your son, Charlie. When might I meet him?"

"At dinner. Mr. Critchley's looking after the boy temporarily. They're taking a walk in the garden." Rogers put his hand at her elbow and guided her to the door. "Dinner will be in two hours. Lord Jeff's in the hall and will show you to your room."

At the door, Anne turned to Sir Harry. "If I may be allowed to ask, sir, why do you call him Lord Jeff? It would seem an odd name for a slave."

Rogers smiled, his eyes hooded, then beckoned the footman. "What is your Christian name?"

"Jeffery, sir." The man spoke out clearly in a deep soft lilting voice.

"And who was your father?" Rogers affected a serious mien.

"A great warrior in Africa, a noble in the service of his king." The footman appeared to raise his chin a little higher.

"So, Miss Cartier, there you have it: Lord Jeff!" Rogers burst out laughing.

Anne stared at the black man. His face was impossible to read. Was this some kind of cruel joke?

Rogers' mood turned serious. Pride flashed in his eyes. He stepped out into the hall and gestured to Anne's large trunk. Jeffery hoisted it effortlessly to his shoulder. Rogers patted the black man's upper arm, bulging in the sleeves of his coat. "Like his father, Jeff's also a great warrior, the best boxer in Britain. He'll soon prove it, too."

"Yes, sir," said Jeffery, his lips frozen in the hint of a smile.

Anne's room was located in the southwest corner of the chamber story. Jeffery went in first with the trunk, laid it down, and pulled the drapes aside. As Anne and Harriet entered, the sun broke through the clouds and flooded the room with light. The footman bowed and left, closing the door quietly behind him.

From the center of the room, arms crossed on her chest, Anne examined the furnishings with a critical eye. A few nondescript engravings hung on the cream-colored walls. A large sofa stood against a wall. There were a table and some upholstered chairs by the window. The furniture and rugs were worn and mismatched, though of decent quality. An ornate mirror stretched nearly from floor to ceiling.

Harriet, who had been observing Anne, remarked, "A curious mixture, isn't it. After the original owner died, the heirs took out whatever could be moved and sold." She pointed to the mirror. "That's built right into the wall, or they would have taken it too. When Harry leased Combe Park a few years ago, he furnished the house with items from an estate sale. These chamber story rooms mean little to him. It's different downstairs where he meets the public."

"The wealthy people he wants to impress," Anne remarked, surprised again by her friend's knowledge of Sir Harry's affairs and her familiar use of his name.

Harriet shrugged. "I suppose that's true." This line of thought seemed to carry Harriet into deeper, troubled waters. Creases of concern appeared on her brow. "Sometimes I think he puts a price on everything, even people. But that's how men are."

While Harriet rested on the sofa, Anne lay restless on the bed, her mind preoccupied by Mary Campbell's fate. She roused her friend. "We have a little time before dinner, Harriet. I want to see where Mary fell to her death."

"Then come with me." Harriet led her down the hall into a narrow unlighted side corridor. A plain door opened to a small landing from which steep stairs ascended to the floor above and descended to the floor below. "She was found down there." Harriet pointed to the landing below. "The doctor who examined Mary said the fall bruised her head and body, but she died of a broken neck."

Anne stood silently staring at the stairway. "It's easy to see how she could have tripped on her skirts or caught her heel on a step." She imagined servants hurrying up and down, often careless or distracted. "I'm amazed that the builder of this house thought so little of his servants' safety." She shook her head. "What puzzles me most is why Mary was here in the middle of the night."

Harriet appeared reluctant to reply. "Malicious gossips say she was hastening to a tryst with a lover. Captain Fitzroy is one of those mentioned."

"That's hard to believe," said Anne. "But I haven't seen the captain. Come, Harriet, this place depresses me. Let's go back to my room."

A short while later, Jeffery announced dinner and led the way downstairs. The two women were waiting in the hall outside the dining room, when a tall thin man approached with little Charlie. Anne greeted the boy with a kiss. His eyes brightened but he remained silent and stiff, working the corners of his mouth as if about to cry. He seemed thinner and more withdrawn than when she had last seen him.

Mr. Critchley bowed slightly to Anne. "We've been out for a walk in the garden to work up Charlie's appetite for dinner. Sir Harry thinks the boy needs more meat on his bones." Critchley was a middle-aged man, wizened-faced, as if life had drained out of him. Everything about him seemed long and thin: legs, arms, fingers, hair, head. He spoke with a cultivated tongue in nasal tones and in precise clipped phrases. His eyes were set deep and narrow. He looked down at Charlie and patted his head. Anne thought the boy shuddered.

"I'll leave him with you," remarked the tutor, offering the semblance of a smile. Harriet also excused herself and followed him into the dining room. Anne was alone with the boy.

Tears filled Charlie's eyes. Trembling, he attempted to speak but could not form the words. "I'm so glad to see you," he finally said. "I want to go back to Hackney. All my friends are there. I hate Bath, and especially this place."

Anne hugged him, calmed him with the promise of a long talk after dinner.

The family had gathered near the table to meet Anne. The first person to approach her was Lady Margaret, a stunning beauty in a silk gown worked with gold on a green ground, a wheatsheaf of emeralds in her lustrous auburn hair. She inspected Anne with a cursory glance. "You have trained with the deaf in Paris, Miss Cartier. How interesting." Her voice lacked even a trace of enthusiasm. "I'm sure Charlie will appreciate your instruction." She glided toward her chair at the lower end of the table. Sir Harry gave Anne a broad smile and patted her on the arm. He sat himself at the opposite end of the table. Critchley mumbled something through tight lips and sat to the right of Sir Harry. Finally, William Rogers sauntered up to her and smirked. "We're an odd bunch, aren't we!"

"William!" exclaimed Lady Margaret.

The young man ignored her and took a chair to his uncle's left. Sir Harry seemed unperturbed by his ward's display of insolence. Anne and Harriet sat opposite one another in the middle of the table, and Charlie next to Anne and to his mother's right. The chair to her left remained empty.

"I thought your cousin said he was coming to dinner," said Sir Harry, addressing his wife, a clear note of irritation in his voice.

"Business in the city has delayed him slightly. He is in his room, dressing, and will join us after the soup." She gave an order to Jeffery at the sideboard. He began to ladle clear broth from a porcelain tureen, then helped a maid serve the table. Leaning around Anne, he placed a steaming bowl on her plate. For a moment, his musty scent enveloped her. His hand was huge, his fingers thick. She noticed scars on his knuckles. From the boxing, she supposed, though she knew little about the sport. She watched him serving the soup to the others, then later clearing away the bowls. He moved gracefully, light of foot and supple of body. Amazing for such a large man.

In the interval following the soup course, Captain Fitzroy entered the dining room. Lady Margaret gave him a sidelong glance, then touched the empty chair to her left. He stood, his hands gripping the back of the chair, while she introduced him to Anne. He stared at her quizzically for a moment, as if she were somehow familiar to him. "Mademoiselle Cartier from Paris," he remarked in French. "Perhaps we've met in the Palais-Royal. Or, at the variety theater."

"Perhaps." Anne smiled with a shrug of her shoulders. She could not recall ever having seen him, but he might well have watched her performing on stage. She sat back and observed him speaking to his cousin. His hair was black and wavy, hers was rich auburn; his eyes soft blue, hers green. But there was also a likeness. Similar fine facial features: high forehead, aquiline nose, full sensuous mouth. His skin had browned and coarsened from years in the military. Hers was still clear, and as smooth as Dorset cream.

Anne glanced to her left at Charlie, who stared at Fitzroy across the table. She studied the boy's beautiful profile, his black wavy hair, then nudged him. He turned to her, his soft blue eyes expectant, a sweet smile on his fine featured face. Good God! It dawned on her, what Harriet had earlier insinuated. The captain was Charlie's father.

Surely not, Anne thought. Nature had merely played a trick among relatives. Persons hungry for scandal had leaped to an absurd conclusion.

At that moment, she sensed a hush had come over the room. All eyes had fixed on her, watching her reaction. Her throat tightened, rendering her speechless. She felt her face flush with embarrassment. Sir Harry sat back, his usually animated face now a rigid, unsmiling mask. His wife reclined in her chair, her chin thrust out as if defiant. Captain Fitzroy settled into his place, spread a napkin on his lap, seemingly oblivious to the conspiracy of silence around him. From across the table, Harriet winked, "I told you so."

It was Harriet who broke the spell. "Sir Harry. Tell us about the boxing match you're arranging for next week." She glanced at the black footman standing impassively at the sideboard. "Is Lord Jeff getting ready?"

Rogers forced a smile; he appeared to appreciate Harriet's intervention. "Yes, indeed. He trained all morning in the tennis hall, sparred with Sam the Bath butcher." Conventional table conversation then took over. The tension in the air dropped to a bearable level. Anne carried on as if nothing untoward had happened. But she couldn't help thinking: something dreadful is going to happen here.

After dinner, Harriet left for the city and Anne returned to her room in the chamber story. She paced back and forth, reflecting on her meeting with the family. Their indifference to Charlie distressed her greatly. They had ignored him at the table. Even more troubling was the intimation of scandal concerning his parentage.

She approached the large wall mirror, removed the pins from her hair, and shook it loose. Her brow creased with concern. Behind the family's facade of polite manners, a crisis was building, though she couldn't see the shape of it clearly.

In front of the mirror she managed to unhook and untie herself from her clothing. She had just changed into a dressing gown when someone knocked on the door. She opened to Charlie Rogers, who stood uncertain in the antechamber between their rooms. At her beckoning he entered hesitantly. She guessed he had come to unburden himself.

He attempted to speak but was so upset that he slurred and garbled the words. His lips quivered and he cried. Anne put her arm over his shoulder and held him until he grew calm. Then, she faced him and encouraged him to tell her what was the matter.

"When I try to speak, people ignore me or make a face. At Braidwood's school I can talk to people and they listen."

As he grew more composed, his eyes began to dart around the room, as if he were afraid someone would spy on him.

His gaze seemed to catch on the wall mirror. Anne became suspicious. If he whispered in her ear, she assured him, he could safely tell her what was wrong.

He nodded, then warned her in his flat monotone, "Don't look. There are peep holes in the frame of that mirror."

"Do you know if anyone is spying on us now?"

"I don't think so. Master Critchley and William have gone to Spring Gardens this evening."

She studied the mirror closely and discovered holes in the deeply recessed eye sockets of a faun sculpted on the left side of the mirror's frame. She checked the matching faun on the right side and found two similar peep holes.

"How did you find out about these?" she asked.

"One day, when I was on the servants' stairway, I saw Master Critchley and William in front of the storeroom next to your room, trying to see if anyone was coming. They didn't see me, so they sneaked in. A few days later, I was in the storeroom getting a blanket when I saw the door handle move. I guessed it was them. I ducked under a table. They came in. I watched them open up the wall. When they left, I did what they had done and found the peep holes."

"Show me." Anne went into the hallway and looked up and down. No one in sight. She gestured to the boy. He took her by the hand and led her into the storeroom, a place for drapes and bedding. Charlie pulled a hidden lever in a tall case. It turned on a pivot, opening up a shallow windowless closet. Two stools stood against the opposite wall below two sets of peep holes, each concealed by thin sliding panels. Anne opened one of the panels and peered into her own room. With mounting anger, she imagined Miss Mary Campbell standing in front of that mirror, brushing her hair, disrobing.

She closed the panel and returned with the boy to her room. Were the men content merely to watch the young tutor? A suspicion began to dawn on Anne. Could this violation of the girl's privacy have had anything to do with her death?

"Did you ever see Master Critchley or William bother Miss Mary?"

"Yes, Mr. Critchley. One day I saw him sneak into her room. I told her, and she went in and caught him. He shut the door behind them. So I went into the storeroom to watch through the peep holes."

"What did you see?"

"Miss Campbell had her back to me. I don't know what she said. She was shaking her finger at Mr. Critchley. Six silver spoons were on the table. Mr. Critchley was facing me up close, so I could read his lips. He said, don't tell anyone or he'd say she stole the spoons. Then she'd be hung. She threw the spoons at him and pointed to the door. His face looked angry. He picked up the spoons and left."

Anne stopped the boy. He was trembling. His speech was becoming fast and impossible to understand. She sat down with him on a bench and held him again until he quieted down. Then she asked what he knew about the theft of the spoons.

"I think Mr. Critchley took them. He pinches things when no one is looking. But I've seen him do it. The next day, when I was in the kitchen, he brought the spoons to Cook. He said he found them somewhere."

The boy glanced at Anne, his face blank, as if overwhelmed by what he had seen. Anne struggled to suppress the horror she felt. Finally, she asked, "What happened to Miss Campbell after the man left her room?"

"She told me she would talk to my mother in the morning. That same night she fell down the stairs."

Could there be a connection? Anne wondered. Critchley might have feared being exposed. Had he killed her that night? Unsupported conjecture, Anne realized, but worth keeping in mind.

In any case, something had to be done to shelter the boy from the tutor's evil influence, though she didn't know what.

She didn't trust his parents enough to bring the matter to either of them.

She consoled the boy. "We'll be best friends. Pretend you didn't tell me anything."

The boy smiled and touched his heart.

"I have an idea, Charlie. Bring me your modeling clay and your paint and brushes."

Half an hour later, Anne and Charlie stepped back, inspecting their work. They nodded to one another and laughed. The two fauns framing the mirror stared at them through new, brightly painted, bulbous eyeballs.

Chapter 5

Tracking the Prey

Tuesday, March 27

Colonel Saint-Martin and his adjutant, Charpentier, arrived in London tired and hungry after four-and-a-half days of traveling from Paris. It was a cool, foggy morning. The city bustled, wide awake, its narrow streets thick with traffic. Georges paid off the coachman who had brought them from Dover to the George & Blue Boar Inn in Holborn, a point of departure for post coaches to Bath. They had planned for only two days in London, so they went directly to work.

Georges arranged for breakfast and unpacked. Saint-Martin sent messages by courier to Monsieur André Cartier and Anne, announcing his arrival and asking to meet them. He also wrote to two friends, Captains James Gordon and William Porter, whom he had met while serving with French forces in the American War. "Do you know a certain Captain Fitzroy?" he inquired. He gave that message to another courier and sent him off posthaste.

The two officers replied shortly by the same courier, and suggested Saint-Martin join them at noon in London Tavern on Ludgate Hill. "Best selection of wines in London," Gordon had written. "Near St. Paul's Cathedral. You can't miss it."

They did know Fitzroy, a dashing fellow about town. He spoke proudly of his escape from France.

After a short rest in their rooms, Saint-Martin and Georges walked to the restaurant and were shown through the noisy, crowded public hall to a private room. As they entered, the British officers rose to greet them. "We reserved this room," said Porter. "Too many curious ears out there." Porter shook the colonel's hand, then glanced skeptically at his adjutant.

Saint-Martin drew Porter aside out of ear-shot of Georges. "He's my chief investigator. Part ferret, part bulldog! First-rate soldier. Served with valor at Minden. I want him to hear what we say about Fitzroy."

Porter nodded to the colonel, smiled amiably to Georges, then showed the two Frenchmen to their seats. In a few minutes, a waiter came to take their orders. "The turtle soup is famous," suggested Porter. They chose the soup, hot beef, and a fine red Bordeaux. When the waiter left, they sat back recalling old times and exchanging recent news of one another. There was much to talk about.

The British officers had been prisoners of war in the colonel's custody for several months following the fall of Yorktown. The three men had become friends and had met again during Saint-Martin's visit to London last year. Gordon was a tall, red-haired canny Scot with broad shoulders and narrow waist. His family were wealthy landed gentry who traditionally gave a son to the British army. Porter was also tall, but corpulent, fair-skinned, and black-haired. His father was a wealthy merchant in Essex, north-east of London. An educated man and amateur playwright, Porter had helped Saint-Martin perfect his English.

They had avoided military duties since returning disillusioned from captivity in America four years ago. Business and politics bored them. Their chief interest was the pursuit of pleasure. They shared comfortable quarters in London, and frequented its coffee houses, theaters, and gambling dens.

Saint-Martin thought he knew the officers well enough to trust them with his plans. There was still some risk. Gordon and Porter were, after all, British officers and might regard what he intended to do as an affront to British honor. On the other hand, they had probably heard rumors concerning Fitzroy and Sylvie and could easily suspect he was pursuing the Irishman.

When conversation began to lag, Porter cocked his head and asked, "Paul, what brings you and your aide to England? And how has Captain Fitzroy captured your interest? I can guess but I'd rather that you told us."

"This is for your ears alone," the colonel replied. "Baron Breteuil has sent us to apprehend Fitzroy and return him to France. Privately. Discreetly." Saint-Martin went on to describe his mission from its beginning in January up to his forthcoming trip to Bath. His friends soon dropped their nonchalance and leaned forward, fully engaged. When he described Fitzroy's assault on Sylvie and her attempted suicide, both men flinched.

At the conclusion of the story, they remained deathly silent for a moment, shaking their heads. They glanced at one another. "Fitzroy! What a blackguard!" exclaimed Gordon. "He's been telling a different story. The young woman was willing enough, he claims. For her sins the baron beat her."

Porter seconded his companion with a vigorous thump on the table. "The captain's a liar, a villain, and deserves to be horsewhipped and shot!" Then he turned to Saint-Martin. "We'll tell you what we know about him."

The colonel settled back in his chair and listened. His friends had met the Irishman many times during the months he spent in London. "He's a handsome one!" said Gordon, the livelier of the pair. "And has charmed many a bird out of the trees. At the beginning of the year, he lived in the town house of a woman he called his cousin. A tall, auburn, green-eyed beauty. We saw her usually from a distance, walking in Green Park or dancing with him at a ball. He never brought her into our circles or talked about her."

The turtle soup arrived at this point. While a waiter was ladling it into their bowls, Saint-Martin leaned over to Georges and whispered in French, "Find out that cousin's address and what the servants have to say about her and Fitzroy." Saint-Martin switched back to his friends. "What's the local opinion of Sylvie de Chanteclerc?"

Porter tasted the soup, smacking his lips with satisfaction, while he considered the question. "Most people are inclined to believe Fitzroy. The woman is just another French tart. Disappointed in love, she cried rape. They say a man like Fitzroy doesn't have to beat a woman to get what he wants."

"Sylvie's different," insisted Saint-Martin with some heat. "She kept him at a distance. He had to force himself upon her."

"I'm not surprised to hear this," Porter conceded. "I've seen his violent side. Often gambled with him. Once, he accused a man at our table of cheating at cards. Picked him up and threw him right out the window into the street."

"And he wasn't charged either," added Gordon.

"Who protects him?" asked Saint-Martin, amazed. "He left England a decade ago to escape arrest. Why has he been allowed to return?"

Porter, the more knowledgeable of the two, replied. "According to credible rumors among his fellow officers, Fitzroy has brought information from France that seems useful to the British government."

Saint-Martin raised an eyebrow. "He hasn't been privy to any secrets about our armament or tactics. The only strategy he knows is what he's learned in a boudoir or gambling den."

Porter smiled. "Quite right. And that's where he has gathered his tales of sexual and financial corruption at high levels of the French king's army and navy—who can be bought and for how much. Fascinating tidbits to feed to our spies in your country."

"In return for those tidbits, our government has cleared away old charges against him and obstructs new ones," added

Gordon. "For good measure, he now has the rank of captain in the Royal Horse Guards and carries a sword. Two armed officers, a major and a captain, look after him. It's not clear exactly what they're supposed to do. Keep him out of trouble? Protect him from French agents?" Gordon's voice took on a warning tone. "Fitzroy's an expert fencer and marksman; he can actually protect himself."

This discussion broke off while waiters cleared away the soup dishes and served hot beefsteaks. The red Bordeaux arrived and was poured. The waiters withdrew again. Saint-Martin brought the conversation back to Fitzroy.

"He has the devil's own luck," observed Gordon, who went on to tell tales of the Irishman's prowess at the faro table. "He will wager on almost anything and usually wins."

At the end of the meal, Porter ordered drinks and pipes, then turned to Saint-Martin. "Now you see more clearly the lay of the land. If we learn anything else about Fitzroy, we'll let you know."

Gordon picked up the thread. "Paul, if you need help, call on us. Catching that rogue will be a daunting task."

The next day, under heavy clouds, and a brisk wind blowing against them, the colonel and his adjutant set out in a hired cabriolet for Hampstead. Monsieur Cartier's message had urged them to come to his gunshop, but regretted Miss Cartier had departed for Bath two days earlier. Momentarily, Saint-Martin felt disappointed, but his spirits revived quickly. He would meet Anne in Bath. How extraordinary!

On their way, Georges reported that Fitzroy's alleged cousin, the "striking beauty," was Lady Margaret Rogers, daughter of an Irish baron and married to Sir Harry Rogers, a rich Bristol slave trader. At Lady Margaret's London town house, the servants had been shy talking to a stranger. "But there's always one I can buy with a pint of ale or a guinea," George observed wryly.

He had insinuated himself into the company of Rogers' coachman, Peter Hyde, who was staying briefly in the town house. His master had sent him to London to run errands in preparation for a boxing match near Bath in the first week of April. Georges found the man in a nearby inn, bought drinks for him, and soon had him talking.

"Fitzroy and Lady Margaret are an odd brace of cousins. Hyde says you can feel the tension between them, like love and hate mixed together."

"Did he go to Bath with her?"

"Yes, sir, several weeks ago."

"Sounds like a *ménage à trois.* How does her husband feel about that?"

Georges shrugged. "I couldn't draw the coachman out. He's loyal to Rogers, enjoys his confidence. They talk mostly about horses and sports, especially boxing."

After an hour's drive, the cabriolet reached Cartier's gunshop, a large two story building on the edge of the village of Hampstead. At the front door the two Frenchmen entered the business office and asked for the proprietor. The hum and clank of machinery could be heard behind the office wall. The clerk went into the workshop, releasing a burst of noise as he opened the door. In a few minutes he returned with a stocky, gray-headed man.

The colonel extended his hand. Monsieur Cartier hesitated a fraction of a second, then gripped it. That cost him an effort, thought Saint-Martin. He had heard from Anne of the family's flight from religious persecution more than fifty years ago. An officer of the French king could expect his visit to awake bad memories.

Cartier addressed the visitors in French with a Norman accent. His greeting was courteous but cool, his eyes wary, searching their faces. He asked if they would like a quick tour of the shop. With a slight bow, the colonel replied that he and his adjutant would be delighted.

A dozen men were busy at work in a large, well-lighted room, speaking French for the most part. Some operated lathes and drills, producing gun barrels. Others carved and polished wooden stocks, while a few cut and engraved brass fittings. "Let me show you samples of our firearms." Cartier opened a wall cabinet to rows of short fowling pieces. In another cabinet stood long sharpshooting rifles. In a third lay racks of pistols. "Business is good. My men can hardly keep up with the demand."

"Last year at Wimbledon, I fired one of the pistols you gave to your granddaughter. A beautiful weapon," Saint-Martin remarked. "How do you achieve such perfection?"

"I still have friends in Normandy who help me select the very best apprentices. I train them myself and when they become expert, I pay them well. That's my secret!" His manner had relaxed as he walked through the shop, exchanging words with his men. He clearly enjoyed their respect.

As they were passing by a stack of canes, Georges asked if he could study them while Monsieur André and the colonel visited privately. "I suspect they contain hidden weapons."

"Indeed! Devilishly clever ones—stilettos, swords, pistols, even a mace. They are much in demand among gentlemen who walk in the city at night." Cartier signaled a young man nearby polishing a cane. "He'll show you how they work."

As Cartier led the colonel out of the shop, he smiled for the first time. "We can talk better upstairs where many of the workers live. I keep a couple of rooms for myself. Sometimes I work late at night or the weather is bad."

One of his rooms served as a simply furnished parlor. Cartier sat his guest at a table and offered him cider. "You must excuse my manners, Colonel. You noticed a lack of warmth in my welcome. I never thought I'd shake the hand of a French policeman. As we fled from Normandy, your troopers were biting at our heels." He paused, stared into his glass, as if recalling a faded memory. He sighed. "That was many years ago, and times have changed. There's more tolerance. Still, old wounds lie hidden deep in our souls and bleed when we least expect them to."

"I understand," said Saint-Martin gently. "No offense taken."

"Annie's told me how you cleared the name of Antoine Dubois last year. She's grateful. Counts you as her friend." He gazed intently at Saint-Martin, as if struggling toward a decision. "An unusual young woman, don't you agree? I've encouraged her to be her own person. But that sets her apart from most other people, exposes her to loneliness. She needs a true friend and, may I presume to say, not just a husband."

"I share your opinion," Saint-Martin remarked. "I've tried to be that friend and consider myself privileged."

Cartier's features softened, his eyes moistened. "She's more precious to me than all of this." He waved a hand over his business in the rooms below. "Be good to her."

That was a grandfather's benediction, Saint-Martin realized. From the heart. Difficult to make. He felt humbled. "I'll do my best."

The two men finished their cider and rose from the table. "Too bad you've missed her," Cartier remarked. "She'll be in Bath for a month tutoring a deaf boy." The old man seemed genuinely sorry.

"Our good fortune," said Saint-Martin at the door. "Bath is our destination. We shall leave tomorrow and meet her there. Do you have any messages for her?"

Cartier seemed delighted. He said he would write one and have it delivered to their inn before nightfall, together with messages from Mr. Braidwood and her solicitor, Mr. Barnstaple.

"Where is she living?" asked Saint-Martin, almost as an afterthought.

"With the family whose son she's tutoring. The Rogers. Sir Harry and Lady Margaret. They've leased Combe Park, a large fine estate complete with servants. Near the city." Cartier smiled with satisfaction as he spoke.

Saint-Martin felt the blood drain from his face. His heart missed a beat. My God! he thought, Fitzroy might live there with his cousin Lady Margaret.

Cartier glanced sharply at Saint-Martin. "What's the matter, Colonel?"

"At supper last night, I heard a disturbing report about a certain army officer who has accompanied his cousin Lady Margaret to Bath. I'm sure Anne is resourceful enough to deal with him. But, Georges and I shall make certain she's safe."

Cartier breathed a sigh of relief. "Trouble appears when you least expect it. I'm happy you will join her. God has sent her a friend she can count on."

Chapter 6

An Accident?

Wednesday, March 28

Anne glanced at the faun's bright eyes staring at her from the mirror and grinned. Charlie had been so pleased with their work. She felt relieved. The boy had rebounded from his depression. Her pleasure, however, was tempered. William and Critchley would eventually discover that their peepholes were blocked. What new mischief would they attempt?

A young maid arrived to help her dress for the day. Anne chatted with her for a while, putting her at ease. Then, while the maid was hooking up the bodice, Anne seized the opportunity to inquire about Mary Campbell.

"She was no better than she should be," remarked the maid dismissively. "She never took notice of me." Then, sensing her opinion had discomfited Anne, she added, "Mind you, she took good care of Charlie."

Other servants reacted to Anne's questions in a similar way. They told her mostly what she had already heard from Harriet, except that they were annoyed by Mary's superior attitude as tutor. She had been in the household only a month and had not become one of them. As a tutor, she held a position apart and slightly above the other female servants. That she was young and bold further irritated them.

The servants lived mostly in the garret rooms far from the site of the accident. None of them observed anything unusual about Mary before going to bed. Nor did they hear any screams or other sounds of violence in the house during the night.

It was almost ten in the morning when Anne went to Lady Margaret's apartment in accord with the lady's wish to discuss Charlie's tutoring. She sat at a breakfast table in a buff dressing gown with a pot of tea and a half-eaten biscuit before her. She gazed idly out the window. Jeffery stood off to one side attending her.

Her maid announced Anne's presence.

"Miss Cartier, do come closer." She beckoned to a chair.

Anne sat down facing her, observing evidence of an ill-spent night. Heavy eyelids, lines of irritability at the mouth. After a polite exchange about Bath and its weather, Lady Margaret inquired if Anne's accommodations were satisfactory. Anne replied she was pleased, avoiding mention of the peepholes. She sensed Lady Margaret did not wish to hear of trouble.

When the conversation turned to Charlie, Anne explained how she intended to work with the boy. They would practice lipreading and oral articulation. She went on to briefly describe her devices and techniques to make the instruction more palatable.

Lady Margaret groaned occasionally, due perhaps to a headache, but she listened as well as could be expected, occasionally asking a pertinent question.

When the lady professed to be satisfied, Anne begged to raise another matter. "Mr. Braidwood would like to know the circumstances of Mary Campbell's death in order to assuage the grief of her deaf parents." Out of the corner of her eye, she noticed a flicker of interest flit across Jeffery's face.

"I wrote them a message of condolence," Lady Margaret said wearily. "If you need more, you must speak to the steward. I have placed this regrettable affair in his hands." She nodded a dismissal to Anne and gestured to Jeffery to remove the breakfast tray. The visit was over.

Anne found Mr. Cope, the steward, in his office in Combe Park's east wing, a large two-story structure joined to the main house by a low open arcade. The office walls were lined with shelves of files and account books. The steward sat behind his desk, quill in hand, busy with a sheet of paper.

Anne stood at the open door and cleared her throat. Mr. Cope looked up. A frown creased his brow.

"Yes? Do I know you, Miss?"

"Anne Cartier. Charlie Rogers' new tutor. Please excuse the interruption. If it's convenient, I'd like to ask you a few questions."

He studied her for a brief moment, then smiled hurriedly. "Allow me a minute to bring this letter to a close." With his quill he pointed to a chair.

She sat opposite him and took in his appearance. A once-handsome, elderly man, he had a tired look about him, a heaviness of spirit. His hair was thin and gray, his cheeks were pallid, his lips had a tint of blue. After a long minute, he laid down his pen, blotted the paper, and looked up at Anne. "What can I do for you, Miss Cartier?"

By his speech, she judged him to be intelligent and well-educated. Encouraged, she began to lay Mr. Braidwood's desire before him.

The steward repeated the common understanding of how the body had been found. As far as he was concerned, her death was clearly accidental. The doctor had found no evidence of violence, and a magistrate had concurred.

"And her body? What was done with it?" Anne asked.

"Placed on board a ship bound for Scotland the next day," he replied.

This seemed remarkably abrupt, Anne thought with dismay.

Her face must have betrayed her feeling. The steward leaned forward, hand clasped before him, and met Anne's eye. "Lady

Margaret wanted the incident closed as neatly and quickly as possible."

"Miss Campbell was a decent, upright woman," Anne persisted. "Were not prayers said for her? A parson called?" She wondered, was any mark of respect shown to her?

"This is not a religious house, Miss Cartier. Sir Harry has converted the chapel into a ball room. No one living or dead should expect prayers here." He paused. His face darkened. A tinge of asperity crept into his voice. "I might add, Miss Campbell was a brash young woman who often forgot her place. I gather that many here had felt the lash of her tongue. Though no one wished her ill, or was glad of her accident, they are pleased she is gone."

Anne sensed that the steward might have been one of the targets of Miss Campbell's blunt speech. There was something furtive and insincere about him. Anne concluded nothing more could be gained from further questioning. She thanked him and left. On the way back to the house, she regretted that a sharp-eyed investigator like her friend Georges Charpentier had not examined Mary's body.

As Anne approached the servant's entrance to the house, she suddenly became aware of Jeffery at her side.

"Have you learned what you set out for, Miss Cartier?" There was a note of doubt in his voice.

"Only enough to make me want more." She stopped at the door and turned to him. "Did you know Mary Campbell?"

"Only a little. She was kind and helpful to little Charlie. Spoke her mind. Fought for her rights. But, at Combe Park, one should be cautious." A warning look in his eye seemed intended for her.

"Oh! What do you mean?"

He shook his head, unwilling to be drawn out. "I think you should speak to Mrs. Powell, our cook. She knew Miss Campbell better than anyone. I'll bring you to her."

He opened the door to the basement and let her into the hallway. They were immediately embraced by scents and sounds from the kitchen and bake house, mixed with those from the laundry, the beer cellar and the wine vault. Jeffery peered into the kitchen, exchanged a few words with someone inside, smiled, and beckoned Anne.

"Miss Cartier, this is Combe Park's cook, Mrs. Martha Powell." Jeffery stepped aside while the two women shook hands. "You've been here hardly a day, Miss Cartier, but I've already noticed a change in Charlie. He's a much happier boy since you arrived."

The cook was as tall as Anne but heavy-boned. Her face was round and red, her hair dark brown streaked with gray. She spoke with a heavy west country accent that Anne found difficult at first. At a glance Anne could tell that the woman was lord in her own kitchen but appeared friendly as well.

She wiped her hands with her apron and greeted Anne. "You may call me Martha. Join me for tea." She sat her visitors at a small wooden table by a window and directed a kitchen maid to make the tea.

"Could we speak about Mary Campbell?" asked Anne cautiously, when tea had been served and the maid had joined others in the scullery next door.

Martha glanced at Jeffery, who nodded ever so slightly. She cocked her head. "What would you want to know?"

Anne explained Mr. Braidwood's interest in the matter, then asked, "Why was Mary in the stairway so early in the morning?"

"She was taking care of Charlie. His asthma flared up." The cook spoke emphatically, as if to counter the rumor of a tryst. "For several days, he had been waking up early in the morning, gasping for breath. It helped when he sat up in bed, drank hot herbal tea, inhaled its vapors. I always prepared a pot for him and set it in the hearth. I'm sure she was coming to fetch it when she fell."

The cook's voice hesitated on the word "fell," prompting Anne to wonder if she suspected foul play. "So, someone else could have known she might be using the stairway at that time of night," Anne remarked.

"The kitchen maids knew, so did Jeffery. Perhaps others." She glanced at the footman. "But it wasn't broadcast upstairs."

"Was there someone 'upstairs' who shouldn't know?"

Martha hesitated to reply.

Anne pressed on. "Did anyone in the house wish to harm her?"

The cook sighed. "Captain Fitzroy had been courting her ever since he arrived from London. She was a very pretty girl and wonderfully light on her feet. Loved to dance. For a time, she was flattered by his attention and pleased to be his partner in the ballroom upstairs. Later, she grew to dislike him. A vain, brutal man. He took offense at her attempts to avoid him."

She glanced over her shoulder before continuing. "The day before she died, he found her alone in the kitchen gathering dried crumbs for the geese in the pond. I was in the scullery. Suddenly, I heard raised voices and a loud slap. I stepped into the kitchen to see what had happened. He had tried to kiss her and she had hit him smartly. He stalked out without a word."

She paused for a sip of her tea. "I could tell by the set of his jaw he was angry. So I called Jeffery and asked him to look after Mary on her way to and from the pond. The captain might try to hurt her."

"I went after her right away." A hard expression had settled on the footman's face.

"It's a good thing he did," continued Martha. "On Mary's way back, about half-way up the path to the house, Fitzroy suddenly came out of the woods. In an instant, Jeffery was there. The captain took one look at him, mumbled an excuse and left. Jeffery walked Mary back to the house."

Martha shook her head. Her voice wavered. "We thought Fitzroy had learned a lesson—he had better leave Mary alone.

She seemed no longer in danger. Anyway, Jeffery couldn't stay up all night to guard her after he'd worked all day."

A heavy silence descended over the table. The cook appeared overcome by Mary's fate and by the feeling she might have failed to prevent it. Jeffery seemed saddened as well.

Anne stirred, then took the lead. "You've probably heard the rumor that followed the captain from London..." She could see from expressions of distaste on their faces that they had.

Jeffery answered, "Yes, the captain himself spreads it about. It's a lie. He was the one who hurt that French girl, and he would have hurt Mary, if I hadn't stopped him."

"Could he have killed her in the stairway?" Anne asked.

Martha shrugged. "He claims he was gambling with friends in the city at the time."

"Did she have any other enemies?" asked Anne.

"None that disliked her enough to kill her," said the cook. Jeffery agreed.

In the discussion that followed, Anne realized they were unaware of Mary's conflict with Mr. Critchley over the stolen spoons. She briefly reported what Charlie had told her.

"I'd swear he snitches things from the pantry, but I can never catch him at it. I suspected him from the start when the spoons went missing last Wednesday after a fancy dinner upstairs. I was in the scullery. He came in, stood near to the silver, and chatted while I was washing it. Later, when I counted the lot, I was short six pieces. I went to Mr. Cope who looks after the silver, keeps it under lock and key. He might search for the spoons in Mr. Critchley's room, I said. Late in the morning after Mary died, Mr. Cope came to me. He had found the spoons, he said. Where? I asked. None of your business, he replied."

The cook glanced from Jeffery to Anne. "What do you make of that?"

"It appears that Mr. Cope and Mr. Critchley are friends of a sort and have reached an understanding," Anne replied. "Have you heard the rumor that the spoons were found in Mary's room after her death?"

Both Jeffery and Martha nodded.

"Mary's threat to report Critchley may have sealed her fate," offered Anne.

Jeffery had listened attentively without saying much. He rose now from the table, thanked the cook, and excused himself. He had to return to work. "Mr. Critchley might have wished to kill Mary that night," the footman remarked. "But he was seen at The Little Drummer on Avon Street until dawn." Jeffery left without another word, the two women staring at each other bewildered. How did Jeffery know? Had he been there?

As Anne left the kitchen, she had to admit to herself that it was possible Mary simply tripped and fell to her death. Still, she wouldn't report as much to Braidwood yet. Her mind was too uneasy. The captain's alibi needed to be checked. Despite what Jeffery had said, Critchley was still suspect.

And, there could have been someone else.

Chapter 7

French Agents

Friday, March 30

Colonel Paul de Saint-Martin stood outside at the main entrance to the York Inn, cast his eyes upward to the sky, and frowned. Dark clouds hung heavy with moisture over Bath. A steady drizzle muted somewhat the city's raucous voice. An inauspicious beginning, he thought, as he raised his umbrella and stepped out into the street. His adjutant, Georges Charpentier, was about to follow when two rough-looking men carrying a sedan chair jogged by, nearly knocking him down.

"Mind your manners!" shouted a hotel footman at the backs of the retreating pair. He turned to Georges apologetically. "Could've saved my breath. The chairbearers of Bath regard neither man nor beast."

Georges sputtered some unprintable French in agreement, then hastened to catch up to his superior. They had arrived at the inn very late the night before in a hired carriage, driven at top speed, heedless of highwaymen and deep holes in the road. When they had awakened early this morning, they ached in every joint. But, they had dressed and breakfasted quickly. A full day's work lay before them.

At eight o'clock, Milsom Street was already crowded with traffic, though the shops had only just opened. The drizzle made the pavement slippery and walking treacherous. Carefully placing his feet, Colonel Saint-Martin threaded his way among carts, carriages, sedan chairs, and other morning traffic. Georges followed close behind, chilled, muttering to himself. The colonel peered through the crowd and saw the imposing bowed colonnaded facade of the Bath and Somerset Bank. "That's our landmark. Madame Gagnon's shop should be directly across the street." Anticipation crept into his voice. This woman would know whether his prey, Captain Fitzroy, had in fact settled down in Combe Park.

In the millinery shop, a few dowdy ladies examined hats, feathers, bolts of fabric, ribbons, laces, buttons, hooks, and the like, anxiously preparing to display themselves to the gimlet eyes of their neighbors. Saint-Martin had learned earlier that a fancy ball would take place on Monday evening at the Upper Assembly Rooms. Many distinguished visitors and the cream of Bath's society would attend, he'd been told. He gazed critically at the plain women in front of him. Were they a representative sample?

A short, stout middle-aged woman held up a yard of linen for a gaunt, nearsighted lady who examined it with the aid of spectacles. "A cloth of the highest quality, Madame. It is French manufacture. From Lyons."

Saint-Martin concluded from the short woman's accent what he had already deduced from her proprietary manner: she was his Madame Gagnon. At virtually the same moment, she met his glance and nodded. She would be with him in a minute. Her dark brown eyes darted back to her customer, then to the other ladies and the shopgirls. She seemed alert to everything going on in the store. A spirited woman, Saint-Martin observed, and, years ago, a pretty one.

After a few minutes, she freed herself from the nearsighted lady and approached him cautiously, a cool smile fixed on her face, her head tilted slightly. Something in his manner, he realized, betrayed him. He was not merely a stranger. Bath was full of strangers whom nobody noticed. He was French and a policeman. Her scrutiny was almost palpable. That pleased him. She would be a deep well of information.

"Sir?" She addressed him in English. Seeing he understood, she continued. "You have recently come to Bath? May I show you something? Perhaps fine ribbons for your lady?" She motioned him toward a counter at the rear of the room where there were no customers. Georges drifted away to one of the shopgirls.

"Yes, Madame," Saint-Martin replied in English. "My footman and I arrived late yesterday and are staying at the York Inn. I wish to purchase a gift for a young noble lady in Paris." He added softly, "Baron Breteuil's goddaughter."

She smiled politely as she would for any fine gentleman. But her eyes took on a harsh, knowing glint. She had a personal interest in Sylvie de Chanteclerc's misfortune. "For that kind of gift, sir, we need to agree on a time when we can discuss her wishes privately. In an hour, shall we say? An extra shopgirl will arrive then who can take my place."

"Of course, Madame. I'm pleased to deal with a person who promises to be so helpful." The colonel bowed, collected Georges, and left the shop.

The Upper Assembly Rooms were only a few minutes' walk to the north. Saint-Martin had decided while waiting in the shop that Monday's fancy ball might offer something useful to his purpose. Fitzroy and his noble cousin would likely be there. Within the hour he had bought a ticket for himself. Georges offered to spend that evening mingling with the motley mob of chairbearers, pickpockets, and beggars who usually gathered around the building as the fine folk entered and departed. He was sure to pick up helpful gossip.

Georges then left to build a network of informants and to acquaint himself with the city's constabulary and watchmen.

Some cooperation might be required of them in order to spirit Fitzroy out of Bath. Baron Breteuil had provided generously for such expenses.

The colonel returned to Madame Gagnon, who greeted him again as a rich prospective customer. "Let us discuss the young woman's desires in my parlor in the English manner over a cup of tea."

The milliner led him to her living quarters above the shop. Her parlor was a small room overlooking Milsom Street, from which rose a constant low rumble of traffic. Saint-Martin soon ceased to notice it as they introduced themselves and began to converse in French. "Baron Breteuil has indicated I should expect you," she said, seating him at a small table. She took a chair across from him. A servant came with tea and biscuits, then left. Madame Gagnon poured while he told her what he had already learned about Fitzroy.

She seemed to anticipate a question forming in Saint-Martin's mind. "Yes, I know the baron. And Sylvie. Years ago, I worked as a dressmaker for her parents." That harsh glint came back to her eyes. "Let me tell you what I've learned about that Irish rogue."

She explained that the captain and his cousin, Lady Margaret, had come to Bath six weeks ago in the company of a Major Tarleton and a Captain Corbett. "Odd chaperons," she added. "Faces scarred in battle or brawls, they seem better suited to transport hardened criminals from Newgate to the hangman's scaffold. They are Fitzroy's constant companions in public. He appears to feel perfectly safe and takes no other precautions."

"I've been warned he's always armed," remarked Saint-Martin. "He's also ruthless and cunning. It will be difficult to apprehend him."

"Difficult, to be sure," the milliner agreed. "But he's over-confident. That's to our advantage." She went on to described his skill at the gaming tables and his charm at the cotillions and balls. The news of his affair with Sylvie had followed him from London. Most people in Bath seemed willing to accept his version. "The English are inclined to think the worst of us French," she observed tartly.

Saint-Martin smiled, bit into a biscuit. "I understand he lives with Lady Margaret and her husband, Sir Harry."

"Yes, at Combe Park, a mile and a half southeast of the city."

"Fate plays odd games with us," exclaimed the colonel. "A friend of mine has recently entered Sir Harry's service as tutor to his deaf son. I plan to visit her."

Madame Gagnon appeared to hesitate. "I would be anxious for any friend of mine in the Rogers household." She explained that Sir Harry's chief passions, next to making a great deal of money in the slave trade, consisted of playing court tennis and training a black man to be a bare knuckle fighter. Lady Margaret, on the other hand, neglected to supervise her household, leaving the task to a steward. Her only concern was to preserve her beauty. "She makes it clear to everyone that she prefers the company of her cousin to that of her husband."

Saint-Martin leaned forward with increasing interest. "And how does Sir Harry deal with that?"

"Like a cat watching a pair of birds on a branch overhead. Only his eyes betray him. He holds the urge to kill just below the surface. The cousins have not openly challenged him. He has not openly reproached them. He seems to be waiting for them to take a false step."

"Why does he tolerate the captain's presence at Combe Park?"

She shrugged her shoulders. "Perhaps to lull him into a false sense of security, then suddenly strike out at him. Perhaps to better observe the affair and gather incriminating evidence in case he wishes to secure a divorce."

"A guileful man, this Harry Rogers."

"And a hypocrite, as well. They say he has a mistress hidden somewhere in Bath."

The colonel's concern shifted to the young deaf boy whom Anne was tutoring. "Charlie Rogers, how is he affected by the conflict between his parents?"

Madame Gagnon pursed her lips, then studied the contents of her cup. "There's a rumor—I can't vouch for it—that Sir Harry isn't the boy's father." With a nod she acknowledged the consternation that seized Saint-Martin. She continued soberly. "Charlie bears a remarkable family resemblance to Fitzroy. That shouldn't surprise anyone, if indeed they are kin. It's Fitzroy's attitude that's most telling. I sense—and so do others—that he regards Charlie as his son. And I fear Sir Harry senses that as well. Since he first saw the captain several weeks ago, he has grown cold toward the boy."

Saint-Martin thanked the milliner and said they should keep in touch. "It sounds like Combe Park is a tinder box about to ignite," he said as he rose to leave the parlor. He added silently to himself, "And Anne is in the midst of it." He hastened back to the inn.

"Finished." Saint-Martin laid down his pen and picked up the draft of the letter he had just written. His adjutant across the table sat up expectantly. The colonel continued, "I must make the acquaintance of Sir Harry Rogers. Tell me what you think of this, Georges." He began to read.

> *Sir Harry Rogers, Combe Park.*
>
> *My dear Sir: I would like to call on Miss Anne Cartier, tutor to your son, Charles, this afternoon at a time convenient to her and to you. The messenger, Monsieur Georges Charpentier, will await her reply and yours. I have messages for her from her grandfather in Hampstead, her solicitor Mr. Barnstaple, her employer Mr. Braidwood, and her patron in Paris,*

my aunt Comtesse Marie de Beaumont, who supports Miss Cartier's work with deaf children at Abbé de l'Épée's institute in that city. I particularly desire to make your acquaintance, either this afternoon or on another occasion. I have heard of your prowess at court tennis. Perhaps you would be so kind as to include me in one of the games at your hall in Combe Park. I am considered to be rather good at the sport. I also understand you have trained a black man to be an outstanding bare knuckle fighter. As a colonel in the French Royal Army on holiday, I would like to know more about this manly English art and perhaps invest some money in it.
Yours respectfully,
Colonel Paul de Saint-Martin, York Inn.

Georges approved with a nod. "It's got the right bait for Rogers and I see why you are casting it. The man has ships lying in Bristol's harbor. He hates his wife's cousin, Fitzroy. Perhaps he could be persuaded to put the rogue on one of his ships and drop him off in France."

"You've grasped the nub of my strategy." The colonel struck the letter with the back of his hand, smiling wryly. "The devil will come in the details."

Georges rubbed his bald head, reflecting for a moment. "It might work, sir. Let's see what kind of fish we have in Sir Harry."

"Good. Make a clean copy of this draft for my signature and bring it to Combe Park. Meanwhile I'll write a note to Miss Cartier to take with you."

While Georges copied, Saint-Martin leaned forward staring at a blank sheet of paper. Faint echoes of Mozart's sweet melodies drew his mind back several months. A string quartet was playing in his sitting room as Anne was about to leave Paris. Moved by the music, they wondered what direction their friendship should take. Marriage perhaps? No, it would cost Anne her freedom. He had thought they might later leap that hurdle. In the end, they agreed they should part. Separation would test their love.

The scratching of Georges' pen brought Saint-Martin back to the present. He breathed deeply, drew Anne's miniature portrait from his pocket, gazed at it, laid it next to his paper, and picked up a pen. His hand trembled, then found assurance and began writing. *My dearest Anne…*

In the middle of the morning, on her way to Sir Harry's study, Anne saw a stocky, bald-headed man standing hat in hand in the entrance foyer. She gasped in disbelief and rushed up to him. "Georges!" she cried out. "What are you doing here?"

Before she could embrace him, he winked and brought a finger to his lips. "Secret police business," he whispered. "The colonel and I, we're incognito, at least for the moment. I've brought messages to Sir Harry from Colonel Saint-Martin. One of them is for you. He's requesting an invitation to Combe Park."

For a moment, she stared at Georges, stunned speechless. Paul hadn't even hinted he might come to England. She said softly, "It's wonderful to see you, Georges. I hope to meet you and your colonel very soon and find out what you're doing. Now I must run. Sir Harry has called me."

As she entered, Sir Harry rose from his desk, the messages in his hand. Hers was unopened. He gave it to her and gestured to a chair. "I'll read aloud the message the colonel sent to me. It concerns you. You may prefer to read your letter privately."

"Yes, Sir Harry, that would please me."

He raised the sheet of paper and began to read. In a polite and formal way, Paul asked Sir Harry for permission to visit her and, on the same occasion, to make his acquaintance. Having met Georges, Anne was prepared for the invitation, so she paid more attention than she might have otherwise to *how* Sir Harry read the message. His eyes engaged the words, as if drawing hidden meaning from them. The prospect of the visit had clearly intrigued him.

"Tea at about two o'clock should suit us," Sir Harry said, glancing up at Anne. "This evening we shall also entertain here at Combe Park. Perhaps we could continue our visit with the Frenchman then. He might add some spice to the occasion. I'll dash off a reply."

As the hour of Paul's visit drew near, Anne watched the driveway from the window of her room on tiptoes of anticipation, still feeling the effects of this morning's surprise. She held his message open in her hand. "My dearest Anne," he had begun. "How marvelous that Providence should bring us together in Bath. I have much to tell you."

A hackney cab rattled up to the great house's main entrance. Anne opened the window and leaned out. Paul stepped down, aided by a footman, and entered the house. Georges paid the driver and turned to follow the colonel. Anne waved a handkerchief. Georges glanced up, saw her, and broke out in a big smile. She drew back from the window, thinking she would visit with him later. For the present, typically, he would join the servants for tea and draw gossip from them.

On the way downstairs, Anne suddenly realized she had waved to Georges but not to Paul. What had held her back? A hidden doubt about him? Stung by this unexpected and unwanted scruple, she grew increasingly impatient with herself. She had looked forward so eagerly to seeing him. As she came to the entrance hall and heard his slightly accented voice, she began to grow light-headed. Any lingering doubt slipped away. Her eyes met Paul's. She felt a surge of joy. It was as if they had been apart, not several months but a few days.

He bowed, took her hands, kissed her on the cheek. When they had exchanged greetings, Sir Harry directed them into his study and sat with them at a tea table. "Lady Margaret regrets not welcoming you and excuses herself," he said. "We shall have a party here this evening. Cards, games of chance, dancing. The preparation for such an occasion takes her the better part of the day. Would you like to meet her this evening?"

"Yes, of course, I'd be delighted," Paul replied, lifting an eyebrow slightly as if surprised by this sudden, unexpected invitation.

"Then consider yourself invited. Lady Margaret will be easy to recognize. Look for the most beautiful woman in the room." He paused, then winked at Saint-Martin. "Feel free to bring a companion."

"Perhaps Miss Cartier would be willing to accompany me." He looked at Anne hopefully.

Her eyes gently teased him. "With pleasure, Colonel. I've also promised Sir Harry to sing a few songs."

The black footman entered the study with the tea service. Paul scanned the man's muscular body, his eyes widening in wonder. Sir Harry watched, barely containing his amusement. Paul engaged Jeffery's eye and smiled a compliment, then turned to Sir Harry. "Your fighter as well as your footman, I assume."

"Yes, strong as an ox. Clever and quick, too. Spars every day. Return here tomorrow and watch him. His real test will come in five days. His opponent stands a half-head taller and weighs one stone more. Fights like a bull. Hasn't lost a match—yet."

During this talk about sports, Anne took the opportunity to observe the two men in friendly conversation. Paul did not presume upon his higher noble rank, nor did Sir Harry defer to him. They went on to spar over the merits of French and English manners. Paul argued for the subtle Frenchman, Sir Harry for the blunt Englishman. At the same time, they appeared to be studying one another.

Sir Harry rose to end the visit. "Colonel, this has been brief but most pleasant. Please stay overnight as my guest. Then tomorrow, after you've seen Lord Jeff in his morning exercises, you might like to join me in a match of court tennis."

"I'm pleased to accept your challenge."

"You and Miss Cartier may use the parlor for your visit if you wish." He gestured to the door across the hall from the study. With a wave of his hand he walked off toward Jeffery in the entrance hall.

The parlor was a northerly room, cool and dark in the late afternoon. Glowing embers of a dying fire drew Anne and Paul to the fireplace. They stood for a moment, side by side, in the fleeting warmth. As if triggered by a spark from the fire, they turned toward one another and began in unison, "I've missed you so...." They broke off in a burst of laughter and embraced, then kissed ardently.

"I *have* missed you, Anne." He pressed her tightly to himself.

"We have much to share with each other. Let's begin now." She caressed his cheek. "What are you telling people in Bath about us?"

"We're acquainted through your work with deaf children in Paris. But someone as perceptive as Sir Harry has already concluded we're friends."

Anne noticed an inflection in his voice that asked, "And more than friends?" She was silent for a few moments, wondering how to reply. Not yet, she thought.

Paul pulled up chairs and stirred the embers to life. Anne lit several sconces. When they were seated, Paul reached into his valise and drew out letters. "From Mr. Braidwood, Mr. Barnstaple, and your grandfather, André." He handed them to Anne.

"I'll read them later," she remarked. "Thank you."

He brought out another letter from the valise. "And this is from Comtesse Marie. I'd like you to read it now. It deals with a mutual friend of ours."

Anne eagerly opened the envelope. Besides brief news from the comtesse, it contained a separate sheet of bravely written lines from Michou, a young woman, deaf from birth and uneducated, but gifted with a remarkable painter's eye. Anne had befriended her, and introduced her into Abbé de l'Épée's institute for the deaf. Anne read aloud:

> *I learn read write a little. I live by students at school. They are kind helpful. I miss you. I send gift. I love you. Michou.*

Anne was too moved to speak. She looked up at Paul. He was also touched, his eyes moist.

He reached again into his valise. "Since you left, Michou's been painting diligently and did this for you. I had it encased." He handed Anne an oval silver case.

It opened to a miniature self-portrait of Michou as Anne remembered her from their last meal together. In a soft yellow silk dress, she sat erect, her green eyes alert, gazing at her friend. Anne shared the portrait with Paul.

"A remarkable likeness," he said. "She speaks eloquently with her eyes."

"She's teaching sign language to Aunt Marie." Anne handed him the comtesse's letter, adding, "She admits it's about time she learned."

He scanned the single sheet, then gazed fondly at Anne. "Perhaps you will teach me."

Anne nodded. "I'd like that." She imagined him in voiceless conversation with her. It seemed more intimate than spoken words. After all, the language of love was gesture. Signing might help overcome his reticence in matters of the heart.

"Then we shall begin my instruction when our business in Bath is finished." He carefully folded the letter and returned it to her.

"And what is that business, if I may ask?"

"The capture of Captain Fitzroy, who lives here. Georges and I must bring him back to France for a crime he has committed. You have met him by now and might be familiar with his character."

"I do know him. In fact, he is among those whom I suspect caused the death of my predecessor, Mary Campbell." Anne then told him what she had learned about that incident and the captain's possible part in it.

"That sounds like something Georges and I must look into. The captain's abuse of women would seem to follow a pattern."

"Sir Harry surely suspects you are a French police officer in pursuit of the captain."

Paul's eyebrows shot up. "How would he have discovered that?"

"When Sir Harry learned I was coming to tutor Charlie, he asked Harriet about me. She's a dear friend but easily led. I fear he has charmed her. She told him I had worked with you last year in Paris to clear Antoine's name. At the time no one knew you were coming to Bath, but Sir Harry had heard about Captain Fitzroy and the baron's goddaughter. When you arrived, he was sure to suspect who you are and why you've come."

"Hm, I see." Paul leaned forward and stared into the fireplace, hands clasped. "Fitzroy must also know. So much for the element of surprise."

"I've heard his version of the story. Tell me what really happened," she asked. "I sense in him a deceitful character."

Paul stirred the fire, then turned toward her. "Back in January, Fitzroy brutally beat and raped Sylvie de Chanteclerc, my cousin and Aunt Marie's goddaughter as well. Since then I have been pursuing him. This is the mysterious case I mentioned in my letters to you. Sylvie is depressed and has recently attempted suicide."

"How horrible! Poor woman! The captain deserves to be punished. But how will you bring him back to France?"

"I don't know yet. I've come to Combe Park to find a way." Paul paused for a moment. A puzzled expression crept over his face. "Why has Sir Harry been so welcoming? Surely he wants more from me than a partner in court tennis."

"He apparently believes you might be useful to him. That's how he thinks about everything. What's most on his mind right now is how to deal with Lady Margaret and Fitzroy."

Paul's jaw tightened. He spoke with steel in his voice. "Perhaps I can help him solve that problem."

Chapter 8

Mortal Enemy

Friday, March 30

Anne went to her room with the unopened letters Paul had delivered to her and sat by the window to gain its late afternoon light. Her grandfather André's message was brief but poignant. A deep man of few words, he missed her sorely but hoped she was enjoying Bath. He reported on his visit with Colonel Paul de Saint-Martin. Friendly, a genuine man of honor, he could be trusted. Anne should invite him to stop over in Hampstead on his return journey to France.

She gazed at her grandfather's bold signature, her eyes tearing. His reaction to Paul pleased her, all the more because she understood his strong resentment toward officers of the French king.

The letter from Barnstaple, her solicitor, provoked a frisson of apprehension. He rarely wrote. She quickly broke the seal and read:

> *My dear Miss Cartier,*
> *I should alert you to the fact that Mr. Jack Roach is living in Bath. He may pose a threat to you. Although I've known his whereabouts for a year, I've had no reason*

to mention it until today when I heard you were travelling to that city.

Anne shuddered at the reference to Roach and laid down the letter. Last year she had told her solicitor she didn't want to hear about the man unless absolutely necessary. Even the thought of him had distressed her. She should have spoken to Barnstaple before leaving Hampstead. With a sigh, she resumed reading.

I've learned of a new development in your case against Roach. The magistrates of Bath had previously chosen to ignore my requests that he be held for the assault he committed upon you in Islington. This morning, I heard from Mr. Dick Burton, a Bow Street officer. Bath's magistrates have called upon him to look into fraud and extortion Roach is alleged to have committed in their city. The officer believes he may also give you justice. He has your address, so I presume he will call upon you.

Respectfully yours, Edward Barnstaple, Esq.

Anne reread the letter, then rose from her seat, troubled by this rash of disconnected, unexpected events—her call to tutor Charlie, Paul's arrival in pursuit of Fitzroy, and now the news of Roach's presence in the city.

A knock on her door startled her. A maid walked in with hot water and towels. Time to wash and dress for this evening's party. Anne folded the letters and slipped them into a drawer. She would deal with their implications later.

When the maid had gone and Anne was alone in her room, she heard faint sounds of music. Without warning, an attack of nerves struck her. She breathed deeply to calm herself.

Tonight would be a special evening. She and Paul would dance together for the first time. She nervously smoothed the folds of her light blue muslin gown and studied its delicate pattern, then tightened the dark blue sash at her waist.

Glancing at herself in the mirror, she pouted half-seriously. Other women would be much more splendidly dressed and adorned with expensive jewelry. They would notice the paste diamonds on her necklace and bracelets. Hopefully her appearance would please Paul. Nothing else mattered. She stepped a country dance around the room, flaring her skirt, and pronounced herself ready.

She left her room, crossed the antechamber to Charlie's door and knocked, forgetting for a moment the boy was deaf. Then she remembered the cord hanging to the left of the door that worked a mechanical signal in the boy's room. Still no response. Tentatively she opened the door and saw Charlie absorbed in a book. He seemed to sense her presence and glanced over his shoulder. Startled at first, he smiled wanly, then gazed at her. "You're beautiful, just like a princess," he said, his eyes wide with a child's wonder.

"Thank you, Charlie." She was deeply touched by his remark. "I'm going to the party downstairs. I'll look in on you later." How lonely he must feel, she thought, no companionship with children his own age, no affection from his family. Delicate, as well. Little wonder that he should look and act like a boy of nine rather than eleven. She waved to him from the door.

At the stairway she met Paul, dressed for the evening in a well-tailored buff suit with a fawn vest. His eyes shone when he saw her.

"You look lovely, Anne." He bowed and kissed her hand. "This is for you, from Paris." He handed her a small spyglass encased in mother-of-pearl. "A clever little invention. The lens points forward or diagonally. I bought a little telescope for myself."

"Thank you, Paul. I'll try it now." She stood at a right angle to the bust of a Roman emperor in a nearby niche and looked straight ahead. Then she turned the lens to the diagonal position, lifted the spyglass to her eye and focused on the sculpture. "What an evil-looking man!"

"That's Nero," Paul remarked. "Mean crafty eyes, fleshy features, malign twist of the lips."

"Reminds me of Jack Roach." She slipped the glass into her purse. "Barnstaple says the rogue's in Bath. A Bow Street officer is coming to investigate him."

Paul looked at Anne with concern. "Georges and I shall be on guard."

"Roach be damned!" She took his arm. "Let's join the party."

They descended the stairs together to find the first floor rooms already filled with a lively, fashionable crowd. Lady Margaret was standing in the entrance hall, as her husband had said, easily the most beautiful woman in the room and well aware of it. She had chosen a high-waisted, low-cut dark green silk gown to accent her creamy white skin. A golden silk ribbon embroidered with pearls crowned her lustrous auburn hair.

Sir Harry was at her side smiling easily, belying the rumors of a rift between them. Anne marveled that his lightly patterned cream colored suit subtly matched her complexion. He greeted newcomers with characteristic affable charm, passing them along to his wife. Nearby in crimson livery stood Jeffery, the tall black footman, at their beck and call. Anne found herself momentarily gaping at the three of them, an extraordinarily attractive group on display.

Sir Harry presented Paul to Lady Margaret. "I've heard from my husband about you, Colonel," she said, her green eyes gaining brilliance as they studied him. "He told me you speak English and have a taste for sport. But I sense you are also gallant. You must grant me the pleasure of a dance later in the evening."

"Your wish is my command, Lady Margaret." Paul bowed, then stepped back to allow an arriving guest to approach her.

Anne and Paul left the hall. "What was that light I saw in her eyes?" she whispered in his ear.

"Ardent desire," he whispered back with a teasing smile. "If she has an ulterior motive, I don't know what it is. Like Sir Harry, she probably knows who I am and why I'm here. Would she also want Fitzroy packed off to France?"

Anne shrugged. "She may be more cunning than we give her credit for."

They reached the drawing room which had been converted into a gambling den and was doing a brisk business. "Isn't faro illegal in England?" Paul asked Anne, tilting his head toward a table at the far side of the room. A banker sat there selling chips and dealing cards.

"Indeed, it is," replied Anne. "But the magistrates prefer not to enforce the law in great private houses like Combe Park." She pointed to a tall, fashionably dressed young man approaching the faro table. "That's William Rogers, Sir Harry's nephew. He's usually away at school but is here for the season. His friends are fops his own age whom Sir Harry detests and won't allow in Combe Park. He wants William to learn the social graces of a gentleman. By the look of it, he's fonder of the vices."

They drew close to the table and stood next to Rogers. He acknowledged Anne with a scant sidelong glance as if to say he would do as he pleased and didn't care who observed him. But his hands trembled, beads of perspiration gathered on his forehead. He bought fifty pounds worth of chips and bet them on the sequence of the last three cards. Five other gamblers also placed bets on the remaining combinations. The banker dealt out the first, then the second, finally the third card. The young man groaned.

"Better luck next time," Anne said politely, though she felt little sympathy for him. She had long known that a fool and his money were soon parted. Rogers had lost in a minute what a hard-working artisan might earn in a year.

William glanced from Anne to Paul, apparently calculating whether he might borrow from them.

"Mr. Rogers," Anne began, "you've not met Sir Harry's guest for this evening, Colonel Paul de Saint-Martin from Paris."

The young man mumbled a hasty, distracted greeting, concluded these people weren't likely to lend him money, then looked around the room for more compliant faces.

Several persons avoided his gaze; others shook their heads. He was well known to visitors at Combe Park. With a pull on his coat lapels and a careless air, he left the room.

"What should I know about that young man?" asked Paul, drawing Anne off to a quiet corner.

"His late father left him a modest legacy that Sir Harry administers. He grants William a small allowance, not nearly enough to support his gambling. He must be in debt to someone. His character is nasty. I've heard he torments the young house maids. He's also a sneak."

She described the peepholes in her room. "He had an unhealthy interest in Mary Campbell. I'm wondering if he might have had something to do with her accident. He would be the third man who might have wished to harm her, together with his tutor, Critchley, and Captain Fitzroy."

"I'll tell Georges what you've told me. He may have opportunities here and in the city to learn more about Miss Campbell. I'm particularly intrigued that Fitzroy might be involved. If British justice were to overtake him, we would have come here in vain."

Paul then glanced toward the faro table which had attracted three eager young men. "The banker looks confident."

"He works for Sir Harry, turns a profit for him. It's like stealing candy from children." The frenzied atmosphere of the room began to irritate Anne. "Have you seen enough, or do you want to lay a bet?"

"I'd rather dance with you before Lady Margaret catches me."

Anne took his hand. "Follow me." She led him back through the entrance hall, evading Lady Margaret's eye, and on to the far end of the building into a large ballroom that had once been a chapel. To the left on the rear wall was a gallery supported by slender pillars. To the right on a stage in the former chancel, a band of musicians were playing the last notes of an air.

"After a short intermission," Anne said, "we'll have a country dance."

Paul appeared hesitant. He explained that his London friends, Captains Gordon and Porter, had introduced him to the dance while in America, but he needed coaching.

Anne took him aside and walked him through the steps, humming a tune all the while. By the time the musicians reassembled, Paul professed he wouldn't seriously embarrass himself or Anne.

After a hesitant start, he proved himself competent. The dance was simple, and it was easy to imitate the other couples. Anne felt exhilarated. They spun around the hall, exchanged partners, came together again. When the music ended, they were breathless.

As they left the dance floor, Lady Margaret entered the room and looked about. Anne tapped Paul on the shoulder. "Her Ladyship has arrived." He turned as if about to go to her, but Anne seized his arm and drew his attention to another man moving toward Lady Margaret. "There's your villain, Captain Fitzroy, the man you've been pursuing since January. He's going to ask her for the next dance. Let's watch."

They were a striking, well-matched pair. He was a dashing figure in a blue military coat with red lapels and gold epaulets, buff waist coat and breeches. His hair was powdered and brushed high. When she took his hand and bowed, her face seemed to gain color and her body tensed in anticipation. He called to the musicians for a minuet. The other dancers yielded the floor. Alone, the center of the crowd's attention, the cousins executed the elaborate movements of the dance with perfect grace. As they drew near, Anne observed that Paul's face had grown taut. A frown worked on his lips. She shuddered. His contempt for Fitzroy was almost palpable.

The next time the cousins danced past him, he seemed to have mastered his feelings. He took out his little telescope and studied the pair. "They appear to enjoy what they're doing, but do they really care for one another?"

Anne looked through her spyglass. "The smiles aren't genuine. And the eyes are hard to read. It's as if they're wearing masks."

Midway through the dance, the cousins again drew near. "They are speaking to one another," said Paul. "But I can't hear them over the music and the chatter of the onlookers. You read lips. Can you make out what they're saying?"

"Not enough to make sense. They move too fast. I can't get a clear view of their lips. Wait. He's looking this way. I think he's talking about you: 'French colonel…' And she's answering…" In a few moments the couple danced out of range.

"What did she say, Anne?" Paul insisted, brow furrowed.

Anne had grasped the lady's facial expression much better than her words. "I'm not sure, but I think she told the captain to mind his own business."

Paul reflected for a moment. "I guess he tried to warn her away from me."

The dance finished to a round of applause. Still smiling but avoiding one another's gaze, the cousins bowed, left the floor, and disappeared into the crowd.

Anne and Paul remained in the ballroom to hear Harriet sing an air. Anne then joined her on the stage in a duet. Sir Harry was in the crowd, his eyes fastened on Harriet, his lips slightly parted as if he were panting. The man's infatuated, Anne thought with horror, her voice threatening to break. She struggled to gain control of her feelings. As the women finished their song, Sir Harry slipped away.

After a few more dances, Anne and Paul had had enough and left the ballroom. They were walking in the hallway when Jeffery came toward them with a tray of drinks. He knocked on the door to Sir Harry's study. A voice sounded. The slave opened the door and entered just as Anne and Paul were passing by. She glanced into the room, gasped, then gripped Paul's arm. "Keep walking," she flustered. "Look straight ahead."

All the rooms on the first floor bustled with guests eating, gambling, singing, and dancing. There wasn't a quiet spot to be found. "Let's go to your room," said Paul, a note of alarm in his voice. Still gripping his arm, her heart pounding, Anne nodded.

He closed the door behind them and drew chairs up to the fireplace. After stirring the embers, he sat opposite her and took her hand. "What has shocked you, Anne?"

"When Jeffery opened the door to the study, I could see Sir Harry standing by his desk."

"Yes?"

"He was talking to Jack Roach."

"Do you think Roach recognized you?" He slowly released her hand and sat back in his chair.

"No. But he might have seen me earlier." She stared into the fire. "What could Sir Harry and Roach have been talking about? About me? Or, someone else?"

"We must find out quickly. But what concerns me now is whether Roach might attack you tonight."

The fire slowly died down. Paul drew a deep breath, then rose to his feet. "I'll ask Jeffery if Roach is still with Sir Harry in the study. And, whether he's a guest in this house. Georges will have Roach followed until we're sure he's no danger to you." He knelt by her side and put an arm around her shoulder. "I'll get back to you as soon as I can."

"I'll check on little Charlie," she said, regaining a measure of calm, "and lock myself in."

Downstairs, Saint-Martin found the black slave in the entrance hall awaiting calls for his service. As the colonel approached to ask him about Roach, he saw a man step out of the study, turn around, and bow to someone within, presumably Sir Harry. The door closed behind the departing visitor, a large fleshy man with sandy hair, slack-jawed, wearing a red coat and tight buff breeches.

"Jack Roach?" murmured Saint-Martin. "The Red Devil?"

"The same," responded Jeffery, barely moving his lips.

Roach crossed the hall, peered into the parlor, then walked toward the ballroom. He's looking for someone, Saint-Martin thought. For Anne? He asked Jeffery to call Georges Charpentier to the entrance hall.

Georges arrived just as Roach left the ballroom followed by a tall thin man with lank hair and ill-fitting dark clothes. "I know the thin one," Georges whispered. "Mr. Critchley. Recently hired to tutor William Rogers. Serves also as Sir Harry's personal clerk—and spy. The cook says he's a petty thief."

Roach turned, said something out of the side of his mouth to Critchley. The thin man nodded and stepped back into the ballroom. "Watch the man in red," Saint-Martin whispered to Georges. "That's Jack Roach."

Roach walked through the entrance hall and out onto the dark portico, passing by them with a preoccupied air.

"It's cold, damp, and windy out there," said Georges. "He'll have the place to himself."

"Wait," the colonel cautioned. "He'll soon have company."

In a few minutes, the thin man left the ballroom, passed through the entrance hall as preoccupied as Roach had been, and joined him on the portico. "You can be sure Roach is dealing in mischief," said Saint-Martin. "We'll wait for them." Ten minutes later, the thin man left the portico and returned to the party, a smile on his face. Shortly afterward, Roach also left, but he went directly to the main entrance and out the door. "See that he leaves Combe Park, Georges. I'll wait for you here."

Georges returned to the entrance hall in twenty minutes. "A servant and I followed him to the river and watched him cross the bridge into the city. The servant will keep watch on him. But I doubt he'll come back tonight."

"What can he be doing with Sir Harry's clerk?" Saint-Martin asked.

"Critchley's nose is in everything," Georges replied. "He must spy for Roach as well as for Sir Harry."

"That means Roach is aware of Miss Cartier and planning to harm her. Find out where he lives. Have someone follow him for a few days. We may discover what's going on in this house."

Chapter 9

A Curious Invitation

Saturday, March 31

The night fell eerily quiet. No sound came from her footsteps. She approached the dirt lane to her cottage and grew anxious. A light shafted fitfully through her hedge. Darkness pooled between its thin rays. Suddenly, a huge figure leaped out into the light in front of her. A ray lighted his face. Jack Roach! He leered at her, bared his teeth. Slowly he drew near. His mouth opened wide, his teeth were long, sharp, like fangs. She was stricken, couldn't move.

Then a voice came from a great distance. Roach's face froze in grotesque surprise. The voice again. Her name. Roach vanished. A rap sounded on her bedroom door. The maid was trying to come in with breakfast. Anne now dimly recalled having latched it before going to bed.

Dazed, half-awake, Anne stumbled barefoot in her scant nightdress to the door and unlatched it. Georges strode in with a tray. "I told the maid I'd bring your breakfast. Thought I'd make sure you're all right. Why didn't you answer?"

Anne let out a sigh of exasperation. "I'm fine," she muttered crossly. "The maid could have told you that." She glared at him and pointed toward the table. He hastened to set down the tray, muttered an apology, and backed quickly out the door.

Anne shuddered for a moment, reliving her nightmare, then shook it out of her head. She stared in the mirror, her face wild and angry. She burst out in a fit of laughter. "Poor Georges," she exclaimed. He guarded her like a nervous sheep dog.

After breakfast, she dressed in a pale green morning gown. She had just finished combing her hair when she heard a knock at her door. Paul was there, affection brimming his eyes. He'd also come to check on her, Anne thought. She led him into the room.

"Are you well?" he asked, searching her face.

"Yes," she replied. "After the initial shock, I'm back to feeling I can cope with Jack Roach." She took his hand and drew him close. "I regret we've been too long apart."

He brushed his cheek against hers. "But a kind Providence has brought us together again." He cupped her head in his hands. She clasped him tightly and they kissed.

She gently eased back from him. "Late last night, Sir Harry sent me a message." She picked up a folded paper on the dressing table and handed it to Paul. "I'm to bring Charlie to Lord Jeff's training session this morning. Sir Harry insists the boy must learn what it means to be a man."

She mimicked the father, growling, swaggering around the room, pounding her fist into her hand. "Charlie needs toughening up, he says. Hasn't been to a session since Miss Campbell died." She paused while Paul read the message. "What do you think of it?" she asked dubiously.

"It might not be as bad as you imagine, Anne. I understand these training sessions are much less brutal than bare knuckle battles. The fighters wear padded mittens so they won't hurt one another. In London even gentlemen take part. Builds courage, they say. That may be what Sir Harry has in mind."

A maid arrived with towels and warm water. From behind a screen Anne finished her toilette and chatted with Paul as she dressed. Her reservations about taking Charlie to the training session decreased if they did not entirely disappear.

Shortly before ten, they found the boy at his desk. He turned from a book he had been reading and glanced uncertainly at Paul. Anne introduced him to Charlie, who smiled shyly. Paul signed a greeting he had learned from Anne. The boy beamed with pleasure. Then she said his father wished him to watch the training session. His lips quivered. Anne grew alarmed. She was of a mind to plead with Sir Harry to excuse the boy, but Charlie put on a brave front and insisted on going.

It was a cool, damp morning. In the distance, a gray haze shrouded Bath. Anne and Paul, with Charlie between them, hurried over a gravel path toward the tennis hall in the park. A grove of pine trees hid it from view until they reached a clearing. Before them stood the large honey-colored stone building, simple in its lines and well-maintained.

The main entrance opened into a hallway with pegs on the walls for coats and hats. As they entered, Charlie looked up anxiously and reached for Paul's hand. Sporadic volleys of loud shouts and thuds drew them through an antechamber into a training room off to the left.

Jeffery stood in the middle, stripped to the waist. Fine beads of perspiration glistened on his body. At his feet lay two large iron cannon balls. Behind him stood Sir Harry, who ignored the newcomers and barked out a command. Jeff lifted and lowered the weights again and again, the muscles of his chest, shoulders and arms rippling gracefully. His skin shone like polished ebony. Anne's flesh tingled at the sight of it. She recalled Louis Fortier from Sadler's Wells, the "French Hercules," as large and perhaps as powerful as Jeffery but with nothing like his inner grace.

Sir Harry shunted the visitors off to one side while he exercised the slave with increasingly heavier iron weights until Jeff's muscles seemed strained to their utmost. The training continued with a series of progressively lighter weights and then a brief rest.

Meanwhile, Sam the Bath butcher arrived, stripped to the waist, stretched, and also exercised with the iron. He was Jeff's height but thicker in the body and much heavier. Sir Harry came to Anne's side and pointed to the butcher. "He lifts the carcasses of oxen as if they were chickens and does it all day long. Lord Jeff needs to train hard to gain that much strength. Before you came, he had run down to the river and back twice."

For the sparring match, the two men donned padded mittens and moved from the training room to the tennis court. Servants had laid out a large thick pad in the center of the court to lessen the danger of injuries from slipping or falling on the hard wooden surface. The spectators gathered at a safe distance.

At a signal from Sir Harry, the butcher went on the attack, charging Jeff like a bull. The black man dodged nimbly, peppering the butcher with jabs. The butcher then advanced more cautiously, throwing powerful punches from the shoulder at Jeff's head, which he parried with ease. For an hour the two men worked their way through a repertoire of punching, grappling, and feinting.

Anne watched with more interest than she had expected. She had acquired a visceral dislike of the sport from seeing large, rough men bloody one another in Islington's market place. But she had to acknowledge Lord Jeff's remarkable stamina and skill. Paul stood fascinated, face taut, arms akimbo. Little Charlie averted his gaze and pressed up against her side.

Exasperated, Sir Harry shouted at the boy to be a man. To no avail. Charlie began to tremble. His father left the pugilists to fend for themselves. He seized his son by the arm, dragged him away from Anne, and struck a fighter's pose—left foot forward, fists clenched and raised, eyes cold and hostile. "Do as I do," he shouted to the boy.

Charlie stood stock still, staring blindly, hands at his side, paralyzed with fear.

The father glared at Anne. "Tell him to fight, damn it!"

Anne tried to sign but couldn't get Charlie's attention.

"Bloody coward!" shouted Sir Harry, and threw a left jab that grazed the boy's cheek. He cowered in front of his father, tears streaming from his eyes.

With a hand raised in protest, Anne walked quickly up to Charlie and wiped his face, then turned to his father. "He's too young and too frightened, Sir Harry. Let him be." Without waiting for a response, she drew the boy away. "I'd better take him back to his room." She gave Paul a warning glance over her shoulder and left the hall.

On the path back to the house, her arm around the boy's shoulder, Anne reflected on the scene she had just witnessed. Sir Harry's irritation with Charlie, in the beginning perhaps that of a stern father with a recalcitrant son, had escalated into something sinister, a passion akin to hatred. She detected it in the man's face, though Sir Harry himself was probably unaware of it. For a moment, when he threw that punch at the boy, it looked to Anne as if he were striking out at Fitzroy, like a man seeking revenge.

When Sir Harry began to bully his son, Paul was standing at the edge of the pad, close to the fighters. He observed the incident out of the corner of his eye and was preparing to intervene when Anne took the initiative. He remained by the fighters but alert to Sir Harry's moves. As Anne and Charlie were leaving, Sir Harry took a step as if to pursue them, then stopped, apparently sensing Paul's presence. Fists still clenched, Sir Harry glared at the departing figures until the door shut behind them.

With a mumbled curse, he turned to Jeff and the butcher. During this incident, they had merely gone through the motions of attack and defense, glancing sideways at the father and his boy. "That'll be enough for today," barked Sir Harry and waved them out of the room. Still fuming, he walked over to Paul, paused for a moment, drew a deep breath. "I need a game of tennis. Singles. Will you join me?"

Paul nodded. "Gladly."

Near the end of the tennis match, Paul sensed that Sir Harry had finally spent his wrath, or at least gained control of his feelings. Up to then, he had wielded the racket like a club and struck the ball as if he meant to kill it. As a result, he played badly and lost. Paul had to perform well below his usual game to keep the score close.

"That wasn't my best effort, Colonel. I apologize. Training Lord Jeff is too much on my mind. We'll have to play again soon."

"I'd be delighted, Sir Harry. I understand the challenge of making a champion of him."

The two men left the court and walked to the dressing room across the antechamber from the training room. While they sponged the sweat off their bodies, Paul sensed that Sir Harry, eyes cast down, had something to say to him and was pondering how to say it.

Finally, he looked up. "Colonel, I think I'm a good judge of men. I've hired many a ship's captain. Though I've known you for little more than a day, I see that you and I have much in common."

An overriding interest in Captain Fitzroy? Saint-Martin asked himself. How does he imagine I can be of use to him?

Sir Harry paused for a moment, meeting Saint-Martin's eye. "I wish you to be my guest at Combe Park during your stay in Bath. Be as free as you like. Make use of my stable and the servants." He extended his hand. His voice took on an enigmatic tone. "You'll find Combe Park most convenient for your purpose."

"I'm pleased we share so much, Sir Harry. Your kind invitation is most gratefully accepted." The men shook hands and finished dressing. On leaving, Saint-Martin opened the door for Sir Harry. "Shall we play tomorrow? I must offer you an opportunity for revenge."

Rogers stopped instantly in his tracks, probed Saint-Martin with narrowed eyes. Then, smiling wryly, he replied, "Yes, Colonel, an opportunity for revenge. I look forward to it eagerly."

Chapter 10

A Poor Rich Boy

Saturday, March 31

Georges walked briskly to the city, urged on by a wet, mild, southwesterly wind. His spirit was troubled and gray, like the clouds scudding overhead. He had just served breakfast to Anne and assured himself she had passed the night safely. But she had been testy with him. And rightly so. He had rudely entered her room, embarrassed her. And for no good reason. The maid could have told him all he needed to know.

"Georges, you bungling idiot!" he exclaimed aloud. He took aim at a stone in his path and gave it a mighty kick. He wanted Anne to think fondly of him, and he had made her angry. Well, the experience would teach him a lesson. Even a police officer must show consideration to others. He would try to improve his manners, especially toward women.

A light rain pattered on his oilskin coat. He could have taken one of Combe Park's carriages, but he preferred walking to driving in the city's crowded streets, and walking helped clear his mind. He needed to find a way to deal with Jack Roach. A dangerous fellow, slippery as an eel. At Milsom Street he discovered with dismay that the shop was closed. Odd, he thought. Then he noticed a sign in the window: the shop would open at ten. He glanced at his watch. Barely eight o'clock. A bit early to call on a lady without warning. He shrugged, drew a deep breath, and knocked boldly on the milliner's door.

Pleading urgency, he persuaded a reluctant maid to lead him upstairs to the parlor and call her mistress. A few minutes later he faced an irate Madame Gagnon at table in a pink silk dressing gown, hair in disarray. He recalled with shame his recent commitment to good manners. To salvage some self-respect, he spoke his best French, wrinkling his brow with regret. "I'm sorry, Madame, but there's no time to lose."

She glared relentlessly at him over coffee and rolls and said nothing.

He increased the sympathy in his voice and began to plead. "Baron Breteuil will be most grateful for your help."

"What's so urgent that brings you here unannounced?" she huffed. "You routed me out of bed. Didn't even allow me time to put on a decent face."

Georges knew how to appear contrite, and it was necessary in this instance. For Madame Gagnon's features, suffering from the ravages of time, required significant cosmetic remedies. He excused himself with as much solicitude as he could muster. "I would not dream of intruding like this, Madame, were it not that a life is in danger." He explained how Jack Roach had attacked Anne Cartier in Islington a year and a half ago and once more threatened her. "We will take every precaution to protect her, but we must also anticipate his moves. Roach may have stumbled upon Miss Cartier at Combe Park by accident. In any case, he'll try to harm her. He may also be mixing his hand in the question of little Charlie Rogers' paternity, which could complicate our pursuit of Captain Fitzroy."

Madame Gagnon sighed, sipped her coffee, gathered her thoughts. "The Red Devil's well-known to me. He lives in the North Parade, a row of fine town houses. It's a short walk to the Pump Room where he spends much of his time digging up scandal. He can be seen there shortly."

Georges made a mental note to visit the place.

The milliner warmed to her story. "I know for a fact he extorts money from several of my customers or their husbands. His spies discover that these people—they're usually wealthy merchants—deal in smuggled goods. Tea, brandy, lace. He threatens to expose them to the excisemen. His victims agree to pay him part of their profit from the illegal trade. If they don't, he informs the excisemen, who confiscate the smuggled goods, fine the culprits, and give Roach a reward for the information. He seems to enjoy what he's doing, and it earns him a good living."

"And the hatred of his victims," Georges remarked. "It's a wonder he's still alive."

"He's shrewder than he looks." Madame Gagnon bit into a roll, chewed thoughtfully for a moment. "You say he's meeting with Sir Harry. That tells me Roach is branching out into an even more rewarding line of work." She gestured to the pot of coffee.

Georges leaned forward, filled her cup, and poured one for himself. "Nothing we know about Sir Harry suggests he's a likely victim of extortion. Where's he vulnerable? Selling slaves is perfectly legal, a respectable trade in this country. Adultery? That's hardly ground for extortion. Wealthy, powerful men like Rogers cheat their wives without shame."

The milliner broke in. "But if *she* were unfaithful, Roach would be very interested. Sir Harry might have asked Roach to help him make a case for divorcing her. He'd have to convince Parliament. A long, hard task."

"Assuming you're right," Georges conceded, "when could she have done anything to justify a divorce? The servants say Mr. Critchley, Sir Harry's personal spy, keeps her under close scrutiny."

Madame Gagnon stared into her cup for a moment, then looked up. "Roach would need to go back eleven years. Harry Rogers, a wealthy widower, went out in search of a bride. He found Margaret Pakenham of Westmeath in Ireland, a striking beauty and recent widow, the youngest daughter of an Irish baron in need of cash. Rogers paid off the father's debts and received Margaret in return. Shortly after their engagement, Rogers sailed to Jamaica for several months on business. Upon his return to England, they married and he bought his title."

"Aha!" Georges sat up straight. "Was she faithful while he was away? Is Charlie Sir Harry's boy? That's the question."

"But no one asked it then." The milliner shrugged. "Charlie was born eight and a half months after Rogers' return. Neither he nor any one else suspected her, not for many years afterwards. Then Captain Fitzroy appeared at their town house in London in January. Gossips recalled he had visited Margaret at Pakenham Hall while Rogers was in Jamaica. They concluded she had had an affair then with Fitzroy."

"Gossip isn't enough," Georges interjected. "Rogers would have to prove to Parliament that Margaret had deceived him on an essential point of the marriage contract, like Charlie's paternity. Even then, Parliament might not be persuaded to grant a divorce with the right to marry again."

"The House of Lords approves only three or four private bills of divorce per year," Madame Gagnon admitted. "But, difficult as they may be, Sir Harry seems bent on getting one. I'm sure he's willing to pay Roach a handsome sum to find the necessary witnesses, documents, or other evidence."

"How did you come by this information?"

"Mostly from Lady Rogers' maid. She often shops here. If she comes later this morning, I'll have her to tea. She might know someone familiar with the time Sir Harry was away."

Georges rose to leave, then had an afterthought. "Could you tell me the inns that Roach frequents?"

She shook her head. "I'll contact a few people who would know." She winked at Georges. "If you could give me an hour, I'll take you to the Pump Room and show you Jack Roach at work."

At nine, Georges returned to the millinery shop and found Madame Gagnon groomed for public viewing in a fine gray woolen dress, her hair brushed and lightly powdered. She had engaged chairbearers who carried them to the Abbey Yard, the busy open area in front of the great church. They made their way on foot across the yard to the Pump Room, a simple, elegant structure whose most prominent feature was the north facade of five large rounded bay windows.

Inside, a mixed crowd of men and women gossiped or gawked at one another, glasses in hand. Among them were a lord or two, a few bishops, country parsons, wealthy merchants and country gentry, as well as several preening dandies and courtesans. Many of the visitors, afflicted by gout and other diseases, limped about, leaned on canes, or sported bandaged limbs. To them, the water promised relief or a cure. Georges gave a snort of disbelief.

"Would you care to try the water?" the milliner asked in a teasing tone. The pumper and his maids were selling the warm sparkling fluid at a nearby counter, while musicians played lively tunes in the gallery. Georges purchased two full glasses and gave one to his companion. Guarding their drinks, they wove through the crowd to an open bay on the south side of the room. "Down there is the King's Bath," said Madame Gagnon, pointing to a small shallow pool crowded with pink-faced bathers up to their necks in hot sulphurous water, men and women alike wearing shapeless canvas garments for modesty's sake.

Georges had raised his glass and was about to sip when a wayward thought entered his mind. He stared at his glass. "Where does this water really come from?" He glanced down at the pool.

Madame Gagnon caught his meaning, wrinkled her nose. "Not from there, silly man!"

Georges twirled his drink, then sniffed. Rotten eggs, he thought. His thirst vanished. He lowered the glass and began scanning the crowd for signs of Jack Roach.

"There he is," said Madame Gagnon, pointing to a man in a red coat pressing his thick body up to the counter. "Watch him carefully."

Roach bought a glass of the mineral water and looked around the room. A flash of recognition lighted up his face. He walked over to a fashionably dressed lady conversing with several other women. She froze momentarily as he approached, regained composure, spoke a few words. He smiled thinly and stepped back to the water counter. A few minutes later, the woman beckoned her servant standing by and ordered him to fill her glass. Unnoticed by her companions, she slipped a small package into the servant's hand and whispered in his ear. He went to the counter, gave Roach the package, and ordered water for his mistress.

"That's typical of him," said Madame Gagnon in a pained voice. "I'll leave you now. I must return to the shop. Call on me early in the afternoon. I hope to have something for you." She slipped away into the crowd. Georges moved closer to Roach, who sipped from his glass, glancing over the rim at the people milling about him. At one point, he lifted the glass to a nondescript man who sidled up to him and spoke in a whisper out of the side of his mouth. Roach replied in like fashion. The man drifted away. Part of Roach's gang, Georges thought.

From the Pump Room, Roach moved to a public breakfast in Spring Garden across the Avon, Georges following at a safe distance. Musicians entertained while a crowd chatted noisily over their food. Georges recognized many of them from the Pump Room. Roach took payments from another well-dressed woman and a man and met with a pair of dandified cronies.

At one o'clock in the afternoon, eager to match wits with Roach, Georges returned to Milsom Street. Madame Gagnon led him into a private room in the rear of her shop. Cabinets lined the side walls. Rolls of ribbons, a measuring stick, and cutting shears lay on a long table in the middle. Sunlight sifted evenly through a large high window in the back wall.

"I have something for you," she said. "The maid from Combe Park knows of an elderly Irish woman from Pakenham Hall, Betty Murphy, who nursed and raised Lady Margaret, then looked after Charlie until he went to Braidwood's institute. She's retired on a pension from Sir Harry. Lives with a younger invalid sister in Bristol. The maid didn't know the address."

"That's a good start," Georges said. "We must find Betty before Roach does."

Madame Gagnon furrowed her brow. "What does this have to do with capturing Captain Fitzroy?"

Georges leaned against a cabinet and took a moment to gather his thoughts. "Roach would try to bribe the old nurse to testify against Lady Margaret. If Parliament were to grant the divorce, Sir Harry would cut Lady Margaret and Charlie off without a shilling, and Charlie could no longer inherit Sir Harry's fortune. That money is what Fitzroy is really after. Without at least the likelihood of it, he would leave Combe Park and his capture would become problematic. Therefore, we must make sure nurse Betty does not give out any damaging information about Lady Margaret. I'll try to persuade Colonel Saint-Martin to get that address in Bristol and go there tomorrow. In the meantime I must keep track of Roach. Where can I find him in the evening?"

"At The Little Drummer on Avon Street." Tapping her chin, the milliner stepped back and inspected Georges. "If you go there, you'll want a disguise." She opened a closet. "Old, worn costumes from the theater. Take your pick." She pressed a key into his hand. "Use the back door. It opens on to John Street. Come and go as you like. No one will notice you."

After the stress of the training session, which had left Charlie overwrought, Anne felt she must divert the boy's attention to something positive. She coaxed him to the classroom with the promise of a treat later on. From eleven o'clock until noon, they worked hard at reading lips, a difficult but essential art he happened to be good at.

Today's lesson followed their usual routine. They began with letters, words, and short phrases the boy encountered almost every day, as simple as "come" and "go." He read them off cards and observed while Anne spoke them. She also taught him to distinguish words that looked the same to the eye by discerning their context. In the classroom, for example, Mr. Critchley would tell him to "mark" not "park" or "bark" his lesson.

He needed to anticipate words and phrases that people around him were likely to use and especially to grasp the meaning of their gestures and facial expressions. Anne had earlier devised a pantomime of typical activities at school. This time, just for the fun of it, they would switch roles: Charlie the teacher, she the pupil. She guessed the boy had a talent for mimicry. Fear of offending others kept him from using it at Combe Park. She assured him he could express himself freely with her.

He hesitated, glanced up at her shyly. "Really?" he asked.

"Yes, really."

He drew himself up straight, mouthed a phrase rather carelessly and questioned her with a look of authority. She hesitated, unable to discern his meaning. He cupped a hand to his ear for an answer, then shook his head. She made a guess. He shook his head and asked again with a frown. She tried once more. Shifting his weight from one leg to the other, he listened impatiently, raised his arms in despair, and began pacing the room. He suddenly stopped, jabbed a warning finger at her, mouthed the phrase again, cocked his head attentively for a moment. She guessed correctly this time. With a condescending smile, he patted her on the shoulder.

"Is *that* how I look?" she asked with mock indignation.

"Well, not exactly," he confessed. "I exaggerated a little."

Anne was pleasantly astonished. The boy spoke fluently, once free of the fear of ridicule.

At lunch with Charlie in the servants' hall, Anne glanced out the window. A steady drizzle fell from a leaden sky. For the boy's treat she'd have to think of something to do indoors.

"When we've finished eating, let's go to the tennis hall. It should be empty then. I'll teach you a new trick."

Intrigued, the boy clapped his hands and swiftly cleared his plate.

As they entered the building, they were met by loud grunts. Jeffery was in the training room, stripped to the waist, stretching his muscles. "I felt stiff from sparring this morning," he explained with a fleeting glance toward Anne and Charlie. While the boy gaped at him, Jeffery began rhythmically lifting a pair of large iron balls. His skin soon shone with sweat.

"We shall leave Jeffery to his exercise," Anne said to the boy, leading him to the tennis court. She found a trove of tennis balls in a corner of the room. For several minutes she and Charlie tossed the balls back and forth. "Watch me," she said and began to juggle three of them. Charlie stared eagerly, his mouth gaping in amazement. She kept the balls flying for several seconds, then caught them.

"Now, you try it, Charlie." She smiled encouragement and tossed two balls to him.

After several attempts, Charlie managed to keep both balls in the air at the same time. "You'll soon juggle three," Anne told him. His coordination was excellent.

He juggled the balls ever higher until he lost control and they fell to the floor. Turning to Anne, he smiled broadly, then glanced over her shoulder. His smile faded. Anne swung around apprehensive. Roach?

In the shadows of the antechamber, Jeffery was watching them. Aware he had been noticed, he came forward. "I'm sorry to have disturbed your game." He bowed and started to leave.

On impulse Anne called to him, "Would you like to try it?"

He hesitated for a moment, then returned to the training room. He came out with three sixteen pound balls cradled in his arm. He said to Charlie, "I learned this as a boy and still enjoy doing it." He tossed the three balls in the air, one after the other, until all three were rising to incredible heights.

He kept the balls going for a minute or so, with little apparent effort and much grace. In her many years at Sadler's Wells, Anne had never seen such strength and skill. She glanced at Charlie: in his mind the black man had reached heroic stature.

Sensing the boy's admiration, Jeffery winked at him and caught the balls. He beckoned Charlie to follow him, paused, and turned a questioning eye to Anne. She picked up her skirts and joined them outside. The mouldy scent of decayed wet leaves filled her nostrils, but the drizzle had stopped. Thin shafts of sunlight broke through the clouds. Jeffery led them to a level clearing in the pine grove that served as a bowling green. It stretched to an embankment at the far end, where a large square block of wood rested on top of a thick pole.

Jeffery had brought one of the iron balls along. He took a balanced stance, swung the shot a couple of times, stretched out his left arm toward the target, drew back his right arm with the shot clasped in his huge hand, and threw it. The shot knocked the wood off the pole. He must often practice here, Anne realized.

The boy gestured, he'd like to try it. Jeffery found a small bowling ball and gave it to the boy, who imitated Jeffery's pitch. It missed the block but not by much. Pleased, he turned to Anne. "May I play with Jeffery?" he asked, articulating each word clearly and glancing toward the black man.

Anne gave Jeffery an inquiring look.

He shrugged. "I'm free for a few more minutes."

"Free?" Anne asked herself. Yes, even a slave could elude his master's grip for a short while and do what he wished. She watched the boy and the slave in conversation, Jeffery squatting to Charlie's level explaining the rules of bowling. What an incongruous pair! She couldn't keep from smiling. Charlie might have found a friend.

"Visit Bristol tomorrow?" Saint-Martin glanced at his adjutant over lunch in the colonel's room. Georges had just returned from a morning spent following Roach and had reported what he had learned from Madame Gagnon.

"I think we must," Georges replied, then explained the visit's connection to capturing Fitzroy. "Let's hope we reach Charlie's old nurse Betty before Roach does."

"We'll leave early tomorrow morning." Saint-Martin laid down knife and fork and leaned back reflecting. Betty would be frightened off by two strange men at her door, asking questions about Lady Margaret. They had to find a way to gain her trust. In an instant he had a solution. Charlie, the boy she loved. She'd open her door for him. "What do you think, Georges? Shall I ask Miss Cartier to join us and bring little Charlie along?"

"Shrewd idea, sir. Wish I'd thought of it."

Saint-Martin resumed his meal, then paused again. "And another thing, Georges, after our talk with nurse Betty, we should visit the harbor. That's where we'll embark for France, if we ever lay hold of Fitzroy."

In the late afternoon, Anne and Paul found Sir Harry, Lady Margaret, and Captain Fitzroy together in the parlor. Unsmiling, stiffly facing one another, they were drinking tea and straining at conversation. Jeffery stood by, waiting to serve them. Anne had welcomed Paul's suggestion. Now she addressed the proposal to Lady Margaret with side glances to Sir Harry: a Sunday in Bristol with Charlie, leaving by Combe Park coach at about eight in the morning and returning in the late afternoon before sunset. Charlie would pay a visit to his old nurse and see the ships in the harbor. Colonel Saint-Martin, who also wished to inspect Bristol's celebrated harbor, would accompany them for safety's sake.

Lady Margaret appeared surprised by the request. "Charlie's nurse?" She stared blankly for a moment. "Yes, of course, old Betty! It's been three years since Charlie's seen her. She was so good to him." She smiled radiantly at Anne, then at Paul. "That would be lovely. I have the address somewhere. I'll write a note for you to take along."

While Anne spoke to Lady Margaret, Paul observed Captain Fitzroy, who was questioning Sir Harry about the forthcoming fight and the terms of a bet. They reminded Paul of a pair of his fellow officers arranging a duel. At Anne's mention of a visit to the old nurse, the Irishman glanced at her, then at Paul, and an odd, calculating expression flitted across his face.

As Paul and Anne left the parlor, Sir Harry walked them to the door. He touched Paul's elbow. "When you visit Bristol harbor, call on my ship, *The African Rose.* Critchley will write a note to introduce you to the captain. The ship's being refitted for a voyage to Africa." It was a brig with a copper-sheathed hull, he explained, one of the fastest ships in his fleet. During the American War, it carried twenty guns and captured many prizes. "By the way, *The Rose* will make a call at Bordeaux and take on a shipment of wine. There's nothing like fine French wine to help us build good will with the governors of our forts on the slave coast."

"I agree," remarked Saint-Martin politely, then stepped into the hall. When the door closed behind him, he thought how convenient for the ship to stop at Bordeaux.

~~~

Colonel Saint-Martin went to the stables to arrange for a coach. Peter Hyde, Sir Harry's coachman, had just returned
~~~

from London. He was a heavy middle-aged man of medium height with thinning gray hair and the broad, battered face of a fighter. Sunday should be his day off, he said gruffly, but he would consider making a trip to Bristol. The colonel promised to pay him well.

"I'll prepare a coach for you and drive it myself. I like your man, Georges. Stout fellow. Met him Wednesday in London. Owe him a pint of ale. He can ride guard with me up front."

Saint-Martin felt reassured and returned to his room where he laid out his traveling clothes. At eight o'clock in the evening, as he was writing in his diary, Jeffery came with an invitation from Lady Margaret to join her, Captain Fitzroy, and other guests for billiards in the parlor. According to Jeffery, Miss Cartier had excused herself and had retired to her room to write letters and to rest.

The colonel accepted the invitation reluctantly, knowing he would have to meet Fitzroy sooner or later. They were living across the hall from each other. But he would need to steady himself mentally. Their meeting could explode the revulsion and anger he felt toward the man. This antipathy had been refreshed by learning that Fitzroy had accosted Mary Campbell in the kitchen and that his alibi for the night of her death came from his two dubious companions, Tarleton and Corbett. The captain had apparently pursued her with the same brutal instinct as he had Sylvie.

As Saint-Martin entered the parlor, Lady Margaret approached him. "So glad you could come. I've been abandoned. Harry's gone to the theater to watch his protégé, the sweet young Harriet Ware." She made a pouting grimace, then smiled mischievously. "So, on the spur of the moment, I decided to have a little party." She gazed boldly at Saint-Martin, assessing him with a flirtatious eye. "You will fit very nicely into Sir Harry's place." She took his arm and ushered him around the room, introducing him to her guests.

At the billiard table she drew Captain Fitzroy away from the game, the cue still in his left hand. "I believe you two have not yet met," she said, placing her hand on the captain's shoulder. "This morning, my husband invited Colonel Saint-Martin to be our guest and gave him the room across from yours. I'm so pleased we shall enjoy his company."

Fitzroy bowed slightly to her and smiled. "Is that so, Margaret?" He turned to Saint-Martin, extending his right hand. "Welcome to Combe Park, Colonel."

For an instant, Saint-Martin experienced a powerful wrenching sensation. Fitzroy appeared transformed into a beast of a man, punching and kicking Sylvie. Tearing off her clothes. Throwing himself upon her. Lust and anger distorted his face into a savage, grotesque mask.

Gripped by wrath, Saint-Martin felt an urge to seize Fitzroy's throat and strangle him. Fortunately, the horrific vision left as suddenly as it had come. It must have registered on his face, he thought. But Fitzroy did not appear to have noticed anything unusual. He stood at ease in his fine blue uniform, his mouth curled into a cool smile, his right hand waiting. Saint-Martin numbly shook it while uttering a polite greeting.

When Fitzroy turned his attention back to the billiard table, the colonel felt relieved and seized the opportunity to observe him again. Last night, he had seen him at a distance, youthful and handsome, dancing gracefully with Lady Margaret. This evening, standing close to him, Saint-Martin detected the incipient marks of a dissipated life—sagging jowls, cold lusterless eyes, a nervous tick of the mouth.

Lady Margaret beckoned Fitzroy's companions, the two British officers, from the far side of the table. Both wore red military coats with blue lapels; swords hung at their waists. "Major Tarleton, Captain Corbett," she remarked to Saint-Martin, "your old enemies from the American War. Perhaps you could make peace with them in a friendly game of billiards."

"If they agree, Lady Margaret," he replied cautiously. They did not appear friendly. Tarleton was a stocky, red-faced man, whose beady black eyes belied the hearty manner he affected. Corbett was small, dark, and wiry. His protuberant eyes gave the impression he was perpetually astonished. Gripping their cues like spears, the two officers measured Saint-Martin for a moment, then shook his hand.

"Good!" declared Lady Margaret. She called out to the black footman standing near a sideboard of food and drink. "Jeffery! Bring us two more billiard cues. The colonel and I shall join these men."

The colonel was momentarily surprised. He was accustomed to French noblewomen playing billiards for high stakes. But Lady Margaret's clear creamy skin, her hauteur had led him to believe billiards would bore her. Caring for her beauty had seemed to be her only concern and had left her little time or energy for anything else.

Sensing his attitude, she threw him a teasing glance, took a cue from the footman, and laid a wager on her first shot. With a practiced hand, she knocked the ball smartly into the pocket. In the match that followed she proved herself equal to the men.

Saint-Martin felt himself at a disadvantage. In the English version of billiards, he needed to drive the balls into the table's six side pockets. In the French version to which he was accustomed the table had no pockets. The balls caromed off the cushioned wooden sides, striking one another. He was also used to playing with a French cue, called a mace. Its tip was large, square, and curved slightly upward for resting on the table while in play. The English cue tapered to a small round tip, requiring special skill from the player.

That the other players earned higher scores mattered not in the least to Saint-Martin. He had come to observe, not to win. What intrigued him was the competition between Lady Margaret and Fitzroy. Contrary to the convention of women deferring to men, she played with keen determination and threatened to beat him. The final score was close, Fitzroy winning by a point or two.

They all moved to a table where Jeffery served a fine port wine. Under its influence, Lady Margaret grew talkative, teased the men, laughed loudly. Fitzroy became sullen and glared at her. With a toss of her head, she rose, stood behind his chair, and petted him playfully. He yielded a grudging smile and agreed to a game of whist.

For yet a short while, the colonel played billiards with Tarleton and Corbett, then excused himself. On the way back to his room, he walked out on the large empty portico off the entrance hall for a breath of fresh air. The night was cool and damp. The moon breaking through the clouds cast a fitful light between the tall columns.

He pulled his coat tightly around him, looked out over the city in the distance, and set to thinking. Sir Harry had intimated his willingness, nay eagerness, to provide the ship to take Fitzroy to France. The problem was how to get the Irishman securely on that ship without, as Baron Breteuil had said, making a mess. That did not look easy, now that he had met the man and his two guardians.

A click clack of heels on the stone floor alerted Saint-Martin. He swung around and recognized the shadowy figure of Captain Fitzroy advancing toward him. Instinctively, the Frenchman tensed. His right hand rose, clenched, then dropped to his side. The Irishman's posture didn't seem menacing.

"Enjoying the view, Colonel Saint-Martin? I'll join you. It's time we get better acquainted."

"We appear to know a good deal already about each other, Captain."

Fitzroy shrugged. "I'm intrigued to know why Sir Harry invited you so quickly to be his guest at Combe Park."

"He enjoys my company at court tennis."

"And it's remarkable that Miss Cartier, Charlie's tutor, is also your *particular* friend."

"You and I understand one another better than I could have anticipated."

Fitzroy leaned silently on the balustrade, then straightened up and turned to the colonel. "Are you confident you'll achieve what you set out to do in England? I should imagine Baron Breteuil has paid a pretty price for your trip."

"I believe I shall, God willing."

The mask of frivolity dropped from Fitzroy's face. "You'll need more than God's help, Colonel. The baron has sent you on a fool's errand. Gallant knight indeed! Will you avenge the stain on Sylvie's honor? Preposterous! No one in England believes she's been wronged or trusts the word of her godfather, a minister of the French king. The baron beat her, not I."

"The English may believe what they wish," Saint-Martin retorted. "I know what happened to Sylvie—and also perhaps to Miss Campbell." He looked askance at the captain. "Why are *you* staying here?"

"Looking after the interests of Lady Margaret. As even a half-wit can see, Sir Harry is infatuated with another woman and searching for a way to divorce my cousin, leaving her and her son penniless. She's easily bullied. If I weren't here to advise and defend her, he could coerce her into confessing an infidelity she never committed."

"What's in it for you, Captain?"

"Honor. Beyond that, who knows?

Saint-Martin arched an eyebrow, kept an ironic silence.

"Look here, Colonel, I should warn you off any foolish move. I'm protected by two British officers who know my situation, and I'm armed at all times." He drew a small pistol from inside his coat and aimed it at Saint-Martin's head. "Do you understand?"

"Perfectly," he replied, gazing calmly at Fitzroy. "You've wasted your advice on me. I plan no foolish move." He held the captain's eye and with a finger gently moved the barrel of the pistol to one side. "Don't point it at me," he said softly. "If it went off, you'd be hung. A pity. I have in mind a more appropriate fate for you."

Disguised in the simple, decent gray suit of a traveler, Georges sipped a glass of brandy in The Little Drummer. He had time on his hands. Jack Roach wasn't expected for at least an hour. The Frenchman had chosen a small table with a clear view of the room and sat on a bench with his back to the wall. He had peeked into several inns on Avon Street, most of them small, dark, seedy venues for prostitutes and thieves. The Little Drummer, in contrast, comprised a large wood-panelled public room with a low ceiling. Oil lamps on the walls cast a friendly glow. The wooden furniture was worn but decent.

Clerks and artisans were drinking amiably and playing cards. At a table near the bar sat three women in cheap finery, still young and attractive. Local people called them "Nymphs of Avon Street." A stairway at the end of the bar led up to their first floor rooms. Georges recognized in these women a way to pursue Mary Campbell's case.

At Anne's urging, Georges had made the acquaintance of Jeffery, the black footman. Their conversation had come around to Critchley's claim to have spent the night of Mary's death at The Little Drummer. His partner, according to Jeffery, had been a nymph named Fanny. That's all the footman would say though it was clear he knew more.

Georges approached the women's table with the ease of a man who had had some experience with their kind. He gave them his most engaging smile and asked if he could buy them drinks. Won by his friendly manner, they invited him to sit at their table. He explained he was French, a footman on an errand in Bath for his employer, a Scottish family. On closer inspection, he noticed that their gowns, though of inexpensive material, were well-made and fitted perfectly. He complimented the women. They thanked him and gave the credit to Sarah, a dressmaker next door. By this time, he had identified Fanny, a short, buxom country girl. He asked her, "Could we get to know each other better in your room?"

She rose smiling and led him up the stairs.

As he closed the door behind them, she began to unhook her bodice. He asked her to stop, then gestured to a pair of wooden chairs. "We'll talk instead. I'm willing to pay you well for certain information." He reached over and pressed a shilling into her hand. "That's for a start. The Scottish family I serve are the parents of Mary Campbell. They want to know what happened to their daughter."

Fanny stared at him, nonplused and wary.

"Have you heard of her?"

"She's the one that fell and broke her neck...a fortnight ago."

Georges nodded. "On that night, you were in this room with Mr. Critchley, were you not?"

"What if I was," she snapped. "What's that to you?"

"It's all the same to me. Were you together until dawn?"

She frowned perplexed. "So we were."

"Isn't that unusual in your line of work?"

"He paid for the whole night." She grew exasperated. "What does that have to do with Mary Campbell?"

Georges pressed another shilling into her hand. "What did you do all night?"

"Frolicked in bed. Drank an ale. Slept."

"Did he get up in the night?"

"I wouldn't know," she growled. "I slept like a dead woman. Didn't wake up till he shook me at dawn and said he was leaving."

"You've been very helpful, Fanny. I had to learn exactly what Mr. Critchley did that night. I suspect he put a potion in your drink, went about other business, and returned at dawn to rouse you."

A troubled expression came over her face. "That *was* odd. I usually wake up in the middle of the night. Use the chamber pot. So, he drugged me, the old sneak. Why would he do that?"

Georges waved a warning. "You're a clever woman, Fanny." He pressed three more shillings into her hand. "If you value your neck, speak to no one about this, not even to your friends downstairs. Just tell them what a great lover I am." He rose to leave, put both hands on her shoulders, and looked her in the eye. "Mr. Critchley may be dangerous," he said in a low voice. "Do you grasp my meaning?"

"Yes, sir," she said in a small voice. "I do indeed."

Back in the public room Georges fretted over another brandy as the minutes passed. His disguise couldn't hide the fact that he was a stranger. The regular patrons might resent him and wonder what he was doing there. In case he was asked, he was prepared to admit he was French. Patrons of The Little Drummer were likely to think he was in the smuggling trade, which he knew well enough to carry on a conversation.

At nine o'clock, Roach appeared at the entrance in his characteristic red coat and squinted into the room until he recognized someone near Georges. He made his way to the table of a scar-faced beetle-browed man with wiry gray hair and sloping forehead. Roach ordered drinks and the two men began to exchange loud, foul remarks belittling the nymphs, who pretended not to notice. After Roach and his companion were served, they leaned toward one another in more serious conversation. Roach passed a folded piece of paper to the man, who tucked it into his pocket.

A few minutes later, two men looking like strangers walked into the inn and spoke to the barkeeper. He nodded toward Roach's table. The newcomers approached him and a brief conversation ensued. Then the four men moved to a private room at the end of the bar.

Georges watched all this, increasingly perplexed. The newcomers were wearing plain brown suits, but Georges could recognize military officers even if they were naked. Tarleton and Corbett. Madame Gagnon had described them. Georges rubbed his neck. What kind of business did they have to discuss with Jack Roach?

A short while later, Roach and his three companions left the inn—without paying for their drinks. The barmaid grimaced sourly to their backs. Georges beckoned her to his table. "Has the Red Devil been here earlier today?" He pressed a penny into her hand.

She pierced him with a wary look. "You an exciseman?"

"Do I talk like one?" he asked, as if insulted. "I'm a French traveler, just getting acquainted in Bath."

His accent disarmed her suspicions. She drew close to him, so as not to be overheard. "Nothin' wrong saying he was here a couple hours ago. Met a pale thin man what looked like a clerk. Does regular business here with the Red Devil. Don't make me rich."

"Critchley doesn't pay for drinks either," said Georges softly to himself, as the barmaid moved on to another patron. Georges stared into his glass at the last few drops of his brandy. Smuggled, he was sure.

Paul lay in his bed, eyes open, restless. He had slept fitfully for an hour. Now he was wide awake. A distant clock struck midnight. When he had first considered the idea of a trip to Bristol, he and Georges had thought it would be safe to travel during the day on a well-used road. Even after his encounter with Fitzroy on the portico, he had gone to bed, his mind still at ease. But a seed of doubt had been planted, and it grew while he slept.

He got up from the bed, opened the window, and stared out into the early morning darkness. Might Fitzroy dare to attack him so soon after threatening him? Would he also risk injuring little Charlie? Or Anne? Would Roach learn of their trip and try to cause her harm?

He ran his fingers through his hair. His questions seemed pointless. These scoundrels would choose an unlikely time and place to strike where their blame could be concealed. Surely not in broad daylight on the Bristol road.

Unlikely? But wasn't that precisely the point? Finding it impossible to release this nagging concern, Paul got up, retrieved his military pistols from a drawer and loaded them, then went back to bed and fell into a fitful sleep.

Chapter 11

A Day in Bristol

Sunday, April 1

Anne rose early, dressed and breakfasted, and crossed the antechamber to rouse Charlie. To her surprise, he was ready and eager to go. He was usually a slug-a-bed. They had just stepped out into the hallway together when Paul approached them. Anne started. He was wearing two holsters beneath his traveling coat.

He followed her gaze. "Anne," he said in French as they embraced, "send the boy downstairs to the entrance hall. Georges is waiting there. I need to speak to you."

Hiding her concern as best she could, she did as she was told. Charlie dashed off, skipped down the stairs, and was soon out of sight. "What's happened, Paul?"

He took her under the arm, walked her back into the antechamber, and closed the door. "I've grown concerned for our safety," he began evenly, then went on to tell of his encounter with Fitzroy on the portico, his sleepless speculation about Jack Roach. "My fears may be groundless, the stuff of an excited imagination. But, I've taken this precaution." He patted the pistols. "Georges has also armed himself."

For a moment, Anne remained silent, biting on her lip. Should they cancel the trip? After all, she was responsible for Charlie. But was the danger real or imaginary? They would travel on the main road in broad daylight. It would be folly to allow vague, ungrounded fears to govern one's life. One might as well be in prison. Finally, she said with more determination than she felt, "We'll go. But I'll bring along my duelling pistols."

The morning sun struggled through a crevice in a bank of clouds; a thin mist hovered over the Avon. Hitched to four fresh horses, the coach rolled out of Combe Park down the road to the river valley. Mindful of the real or imaginary dangers ahead, Peter Hyde drove with a blunderbuss at his side. Next to him, Georges held a short-barrelled musket in his lap. Two pistols were hidden beneath his seat.

At the Bristol road the coach met an early morning rush of wagons and carts. Families from nearby villages were arriving, smiles on their faces in anticipation of the city's Sunday pleasures. A few travelers were leaving for Bristol. In the coach, the sense of danger vanished. Paul laid his pistols on the floor. Across from him, Anne left her pistols in their case at her feet.

Charlie sat next to her, lips parted, delighted to be going on an outing. At first, scenes along the road caught his eye. Sheep grazing on a lush green hillside. Men playing at skittles outside a country inn. Children chasing one another up and down country lanes. After a little while his excitement slackened, and Anne involved him and Paul in word games with signs and gestures.

The coach reached Bristol in an hour and a half without incident. Hyde, who knew the city, drove into fashionable Queen Square. "Sir Harry owns that one," he shouted, pointing out a house in a long row of elegant residences. "He rents it to one of his partners in the shipping business." Rogers had lived there for several years until he tired of Bristol's inbred cliques.

He now divided his time between a London town house and Combe Park.

The coach halted in front of a small cottage a mile from the city center. Daffodils were blooming in plots to the left and right of a graveled walkway. Georges remained with the coachman, while Anne led the others to the door. She put Charlie in front and rapped.

At the sight of the boy, Betty cried out his name, hugged him, and welcomed his companions. She was a stout, vigorous, nimble-witted woman with a thick Irish accent. Except for a few gray hairs and wrinkles, Betty wore her seventy years lightly.

"Charlie, my boy!" she exclaimed, "I thought I'd never see you again."

Her accent baffled him, but he easily guessed her meaning, smiled, and spoke a few clear words of greeting.

"The school's done you a world of good." She held him at arm's length and looked him in the eye. "How do you like Bath?"

He shrugged his shoulders. The corners of his mouth turned down.

For a moment she was silent, then said quietly, "I understand." She turned to the other visitors.

Anne and Paul introduced themselves and delivered Lady Margaret's note. As Betty read it, a cloud seemed to cross her face but didn't lessen the warmth of her welcome. She seated Charlie and his two companions in her tiny parlor and treated them to tea and biscuits.

After pouring the tea, she read the note again and sighed. "Lady Margaret doesn't know my sister's recently passed away. It's hard to write about it. I'll have to send a note back with you to Combe Park." Betty's voice was cheerful, but it couldn't mask the grief and loneliness of a person whose life had just lost much of its purpose.

Her attention turned to Charlie. Their conversation was difficult because of her accent. Nonetheless, with Anne's help, he spoke of his teachers and friends at the institute in Hackney.

Betty understood most of what he said, and clearly enjoyed his wide-eyed exuberance. Paul remained in the background, a kindly expression on his face. Betty gradually warmed to him and congratulated Anne on having such a fine, handsome friend.

Anne cast a grateful sidelong glance at Paul, then ventured cautiously into Betty's years of service with Lady Margaret.

"Yes," she said, smiling wistfully, as if conjuring up the past in her mind. "I nursed her as a child and later was her lady's maid. She's the most beautiful woman I've ever known. Always a pleasure to dress her."

"And her son?" Anne asked.

"I raised Charlie as well and cared for him during the illness that cost him his hearing. Such a fever he had! A lucky boy to have come out of it alive. I felt sad when he went away to Hackney, but it was for the best."

Betty was intensely loyal to Lady Margaret, Anne realized. How would she react to the gossip swirling around her mistress? Withdraw behind a wall of silence? Anne sent Charlie out to pet the horses, then turned to the nurse. "I've no interest in Bath gossip, but I'm troubled for Charlie's sake by what I hear and see." She explained the tension in the Rogers' family and its effect on the boy.

Betty listened with increasing distress. "I didn't know Fitzroy had returned to England. Poor lovely Margaret. She's doomed." Betty pressed a hand to her mouth. Tears trickled down her cheek. She patted them away with a fine linen handkerchief. "It's a gift from her," she said, folding it neatly.

"I wouldn't ask you to betray a confidence," Anne began. "But something is terribly wrong in the Rogers' family. Could you tell us what's at the root of it? I fear it threatens Charlie."

"I'm sorry, I promised Lady Margaret years ago I would carry her secrets to my grave. I know I must also watch out for Charlie's best interest. But at this time, I can do nothing."

With a trusting look, she glanced at Paul, then at Anne. "I do care. Please let me know what happens."

"Were we the first to speak to you about Lady Margaret?" Anne asked. Too many people knew about this visit for it to remain a secret.

"No, you weren't! A big man in a red coat came here an hour ago. I didn't let him in. Didn't like the looks of him. He offered me money if I'd talk about her affairs with men years ago. I slammed the door in his face." She paused, shuddered a little. "He said he'd be back."

After lunch at an inn, they drove to the harbor and found Sir Harry's ship, *The African Rose*, rocking gently alongside the quay at high tide, its sails furled. It appeared to be over a hundred feet long and about thirty feet wide. The hull's copper sheathing glistened above the water linc.

"Paul, you must know something about ships," Anne remarked, aware he had sailed to America and back during the war with Britain. "What kind is it?"

"A brig," he replied, pointing to the two square-rigged masts. "Look at its sleek lines. It can serve as a privateer. I see ports for twenty guns. With a well-disciplined crew, it should sail faster than most brigs—a great advantage when carrying slaves on the Middle Passage. They're more likely to arrive healthy."

"Middle Passage?" she asked, unfamiliar with the phrase.

"The voyage from Africa to the West Indies. A slave ship runs great risk of foul weather, disease, slave mutinies. With bad luck, even a fine ship like this could lose half its crew and cargo."

Paul went on board with Sir Harry's message. In a few minutes he returned with the captain, who had just finished a meal in his cabin at the ship's stern. He was a weather-beaten man about forty years of age, hale and hearty, with a sailor's rocking gait. His blunt speech inspired confidence. Anne had no doubt of his ability to manage a difficult voyage. Without hesitation, he offered to lead the visitors on a tour of the ship.

They started on the main deck. "This being the Sabbath, half my crew is ashore today." He added with a wink, "at their prayers." The refitting of the ship continued, nonetheless, if at a slower pace. Sailors were hauling kegs of ship's supplies up gangways and lowering them below deck through open hatches.

For the occasion, Anne had deliberately chosen a dark brown frock of light-weight wool and a sensible pair of shoes. She intended to be as free to walk and climb as possible. The captain raised a warning hand to her. "You'd better stay on deck with a ship's officer, young lady, while I take the gentlemen below."

She stared at him with cool determination. "I came prepared to hitch up my skirts. I'd like to see everything." Then, nodding toward Charlie, she added, "Sir Harry's son is deaf. I must explain things to him."

The captain's expression softened. He gazed at Charlie for a moment. "I had a boy his age. Lost him at sea in a storm." He opened his hands in a gesture of welcome to Charlie and smiled.

The boy's eyes brightened. "Thank you," he said carefully.

Anne took note of the captain's gesture. "How do you speak to black people?"

"Natural signs aren't enough. If I can't recruit a crewman who knows their languages, I make a point of buying a black man who speaks English."

Anne thought she must have looked doubtful, for the captain went on to say, "On the African coast, many speak our tongue. Sir Harry's footman, Lord Jeff, he was one. I bought him and his mother ten years ago. Prime domestic servants. Sold them in Jamaica to a planter for twice the average price." He appeared to reminisce. "Yes, I recall Jeff. Had an

African name back then. Big strapping fellow. Spoke like an English school boy."

"Jeffery was on this ship?" asked Anne, incredulous.

"That's right," the captain replied. "Smart. Knew what was good for him. His mother fell sick. We took care of her; he helped us."

The captain led them down a hatchway to the lower deck. They shuffled between bunk beds, trunks, racks of muskets and cutlasses, a cook's galley. Anne thought it incredible so much could be packed into so little space. Between decks she could barely stand upright.

The captain signaled for them to climb back up to the main deck. Anne protested, "I'd like to see the hold for the slaves."

The captain frowned, waved away the idea, as if she had asked to taste the bilge water.

"This is a 'respectable trade,' is it not?" she asked. "Where do you put the human cargo?"

Nettled by her irony, the captain turned to Paul, who seconded her request. The captain pointed to a heavy door with a small barred window. "There's another entrance at the far end of the hold." He pulled the door open, remarking wryly, "We keep it locked and barred when the blacks are in there, three hundred and fifty of them and just thirty-five of us." He explained that the slaves could also be reached from hatches on the main deck that were normally covered with heavy iron grates. These were now open to receive goods to be sold in Africa in exchange for the slaves who would be brought to Jamaica.

Anne peered through the door. The slave hold occupied the central portion of the ship. With Charlie in hand, she entered the low, dark, cavernous space, already half-full of cargo. Small, high portholes allowed for some circulation of air. She forced herself to imagine hundreds of men, women, and children lying manacled side by side for weeks on end.

Charlie tapped her arm and asked, "What did the captain say about Jeff?"

"He was taken with his mother from his home and put on this ship. Might have lain here."

The boy looked around the hold, his face screwed up with distaste. Shuddering, he drew close to Anne. She put her arm on his shoulder.

The captain stared at her. "I know what you're thinking, Miss. The Abolitionists say we're brutes who maim and kill the blacks for the pleasure of it. Well, I find my pleasure in bringing as many of them to market as I can." The captain swung his arm out in a sweeping gesture. "We put them in this cramped place for six to eight weeks or more. Without proper care, they'd nearly all die. We can't afford to let that happen, so we keep the place clean. Weather permitting, the blacks come up on deck during the day. We make them move about, dance, even if they don't want to."

Turning to Paul, he remarked, "During the war, Colonel, I transported our soldiers to America in conditions worse than this."

The slave trade was taking on a lurid aspect in Anne's mind. She had seen black men and women in London but had thought of them only as exotic servants. They bore no visible marks of servitude or mistreatment. She had paid little attention to controversy over the slave trade. But this visit to *The African Rose* roiled her mind. She saw herself lying in the hold among the slaves, chained, naked, filthy, overpowered by stifling heat and the stench of excrement and urine. Horrid images of the Islington jail seeped into her imagination. She began to feel nauseated and trapped. Her companions swayed, the wooden floor rose up toward her.

Paul moved quickly to her side, held her under the arm. "Fresh air, Anne?"

For a moment, she leaned against him, her hand on his shoulder. "I'll be all right." Drawing a deep breath, she steadied herself and thanked him. Turning to the captain, she asked as evenly as she could, "How many slaves die before you reach Jamaica?"

"About one in twenty during a fifty-day voyage," he replied, then added apologetically, "Some slave ships lose half. That's a waste. We buy strong healthy blacks and don't pack in as many per square foot as other traders. Our ship's doctor tends to the sick." The captain warmed up to his topic. "We're able to sell more slaves in good condition at the other end and at a higher price than anybody else. That's sound business, says Sir Harry."

Anne whispered to Paul, "Sounds like Satan's business, I'd say."

"Yes," he replied softly. "Unfortunately, it's thriving."

Their tour ended in the captain's quarters where he served Charlie a hot chocolate and the adults a fine brandy. In the course of conversation, Paul inquired about the ship's call in Bordeaux.

"Thanks to the new commercial treaty between our countries," the captain replied, "we shall exchange English woolens for French wine."

"Do you take passengers?"

"Occasionally officers bound for duty on the slave coast travel with us. When we've had space, and for a good price, we've also carried a few convicts in irons, condemned to servitude at British posts in Africa."

Paul's face brightened. He and Georges exchanged glances. Anne read their minds. With Sir Harry's connivance, they could conceivably put Fitzroy in irons on the ship and drop him off in Bordeaux. She wondered, it was almost too good to be true.

From his seat next to the coachman, Georges peered into a darkening, late afternoon mist. He and his companions had driven without incident halfway back to Bath. Traffic was light, but the friendly greetings they received from a few fellow travelers warded off their fears. At a bend in the road a coach from Bath slowed down as it passed, and a hand drew back a curtain but did not wave. Soon afterwards, a large hooded horseman from Bristol overtook them at a gallop and was soon lost in the mist.

Then they came upon a wagon that had lost a wheel and was blocking the road. Georges became immediately suspicious. Why hadn't the Bath coach or the horseman stopped to help? Could the accident have happened in the last minute or two? An unlikely coincidence, he thought.

An elderly man and woman left the wagon and started walking toward the Combe Park coach. No one else was in sight. Thick hedges lined the road. Peter Hyde reined in his horses and turned to Georges. "A trap?"

He nodded. "An old trick." Leaning over, he called out a warning in French to Colonel Saint-Martin in the coach. Hyde picked up the blunderbuss and Georges the short-barrelled musket.

The coachman ordered the couple to go back and push their wagon out of the way. Instead, they drew pistols and dashed forward, firing. One of the shots took Georges' hat off. At the same moment, four bandits charged out of the hedges, pointing their pistols toward the coach.

Georges shot the old man just as he reached the horses. Hyde's blunderbuss blasted away at the woman, who fled limping into the hedge on the left. Anne fired from her window. Two of the bandits dropped to the ground. Saint-Martin felled the leader of the band and one of his companions, then leaped from the coach and picked up their loaded pistols. Anne reloaded her weapons and trained them on the wounded men. From behind the hedge came the sounds of horses galloping away. The combat was over as suddenly as it had begun. Only the smell of gun powder lingered in Georges' nostrils and the echo of the shots rang in his ears.

He pulled out his pistols and jumped down to the colonel's side. Searching the hedges, they determined that the bandits must have numbered at least eight. Besides the six who had attacked the coach, two more must have guarded the horses hidden behind the hedges.

"It was a large, well-organized ambush," Georges said. "The coach with the drawn curtains stopped traffic behind us to gain time for the attack. And the rider galloping past us must have alerted the bandits ahead."

"A clever, daring plan," the colonel agreed. "But they didn't expect us to come heavily armed and alert."

Three of the bandits lay unconscious where they had fallen. The fourth man, who had posed as elderly, sat up moaning in pain from a shoulder wound. The bandit leader was dead. Georges looked closely at his scarred face. "I saw him with Roach at The Little Drummer last night." In the man's pocket, Georges found a description of the coach and its passengers with Anne and Charlie's names underlined, the two Frenchmen crossed off.

With Anne and Paul standing by, Georges leaned over the wounded man and demanded to know what he and his companions had intended to do. At first, he refused to speak. But, when Georges placed a pistol at his temple, then cocked it, he admitted they had orders to tie up the coachman, kill the two Frenchmen, and bring the young woman and the boy to an abandoned cottage a mile from the road. Then their leader "Scarface"—that was his name—would pay them off with watches, jewelry, and gold coins. The injured man claimed to have no idea what Scarface had planned for the captives.

"That's probably true," said Georges to Anne and Paul, "And with Scarface dead, we'll never know what he intended." Georges and Peter Hyde tied up the wounded men and laid them on top of the Combe Park coach together with the body of their leader. The disabled wagon was pushed off the road, and the coach set out again for Bath, forty minutes away.

Not until they settled back in their seats did shock set in. Anne felt limp and numb. Paul seemed tense and anxious, the color drained from his face. At the same moment, both of them glanced at Charlie, but he appeared untouched. When the shooting began, Anne had pushed him to the floor of the coach. While the others were engaged with the bandits, Charlie had gotten up and hung out the window, intent on the scene. His eyes were now bright and lively, his lips parted in amazement. The spectacle had exhilarated him.

When their spirits returned to normal, Anne remarked to Paul, "This is frightening. The bandits knew who we were and where to find us."

"Thank Critchley," Paul exclaimed in a voice heavy with irony. "As soon as he had prepared Sir Harry's message to the ship's captain, he must have gone to Roach. Then, last night at The Little Drummer, Roach instructed the bandit leader to attack us."

She studied the paper from the dead man's pocket. "Why was he told to kill you and Georges? Roach doesn't know either of you."

"But Captain Fitzroy does. And his guards, Tarleton and Corbett, met with Roach last night to negotiate an alliance. Apparently the captain didn't yet know that Roach was helping Sir Harry build a case against Lady Margaret."

"Curious allies." Anne traced the underlining with her finger. "I also seem to have been one of their targets, Charlie the other." She spoke in French as calmly as she could, aware that Charlie was watching her lips.

With a glance at the boy, Paul also spoke French. "Underlining your name and Charlie's doesn't tell us what they meant to do. We can only guess. Perhaps Scarface was supposed to carry you away to Roach, while holding little Charlie for ransom."

"Assuming Roach is the mastermind," Anne suggested, "let's suppose someone wanted Roach to kill Charlie too."

"And who might that be?"

Anne replied with a low, strained voice, "A passionate man, duped by his wife and her lover. Such a man would see in Charlie the living symbol of that betrayal."

∞∞∞

It was twilight when they drove into Bath, the bandits trussed and unconscious on top of the coach. At the market place, Paul hired a carriage to bring Anne, Charlie, and himself up to Combe Park. The Rogers' coach with Georges and the wounded bandits drove on to the prison.

On the way through the city, Paul and Anne agreed to tell Sir Harry and Lady Margaret about the incident, but without suggesting that Roach was behind the attack or that Critchley had informed him. To accuse them without proof would risk alienating Sir Harry, who was depending on those men for evidence against his wife. Only Scarface could have implicated Roach.

The sun had set and guests were entering the house as Paul, Anne, and Charlie arrived. Jeffery lowered the step on the carriage for Anne to descend. She thanked him with new feeling born of her experience on the slave ship. He might have noticed the change in her voice. His brow lifted slightly.

Lady Margaret, regal in a purple silk gown trimmed with gold thread, stood in the entrance hall and greeted the guests as they arrived. Nearby, relaxed and jovial in an embroidered white suit, Sir Harry spoke to a fashionable gentleman about the forthcoming boxing match. When the host and hostess were free, Paul and Anne approached with Charlie between them.

Lady Margaret first smiled, then looked uncertain and touched her husband's arm. Paul drew them together and asked softly, "Could we meet privately in the study? The hall is unsuitable for what we have to tell you."

Startled, the Rogers glanced at one another, sensing that something untoward had happened. Lady Margaret beckoned the steward who was passing through the entrance hall. "Mr. Cope, please show the guests in. Sir Harry and I have been called away for a minute."

Sir Harry closed the study door behind them and distractedly gestured for everyone to find chairs for themselves. "Now, tell us, Colonel, what can be the matter?" His voice betrayed some irritation.

"On our return journey, Sir Harry, forty minutes from Bath, a large band of armed men attacked us." Paul paused, allowing the shocking news to sink in. Lady Margaret raised a hand to her heart. The creamy whiteness of her face turned to gray. Sir Harry's irritation gave way to an expression of dismay.

Anne picked up the story. "Fortunately, none of us were injured. Charlie, in particular, is well." She put a hand on the boy's shoulder and faced him so that he could read her lips. "He was a brave fellow."

Charlie drew up his courage and said, "One of the bandits is dead."

"And his four companions are now in prison," Paul added. He went on to describe what had happened. Sir Harry interrupted frequently with questions. Lady Margaret appeared confused and said nothing. She glanced repeatedly with concern at Charlie.

Leaning back in her chair, Anne studied Sir Harry's reaction for signs of complicity or guilt. The news of the attack appeared to surprise him. But what troubled him, Anne thought, was not the danger to his son but the size and boldness of the band. "Very puzzling," he said again and again. It seemed unlikely to Anne that he was behind the attack.

By the end of Paul's report, Sir Harry's brow had deeply furrowed. "Robbers are common on the roads out of Bath, but they usually work in the dark singly, or in two's or three's at the most. And they use clubs, or swords, rarely pistols.

Your attackers carried on like a band of desperate smugglers." He clasped his thighs in a gesture of determination. "I'll speak to the mayor. We must root them out!"

He rose from his chair and gathered his wife. "It's time to return to our guests. We're glad you're all safe and sound. Join the party." As they walked out the door, Sir Harry hailed a guest in the hallway. Music drifted toward them from the ballroom. Voices melted into a general din.

The three travelers started to follow the Rogers. Suddenly, Anne stopped, closed the door, and looked at Charlie. He was fighting back tears. She hugged him, stroking his head. In French she said to Paul, "While you were speaking of violent men charging our coach, our pistols firing—his son in the gravest danger—Sir Harry never once looked at him."

Chapter 12

Laying Blame

Paul led Anne and Charlie from the study, through the milling crowd in the hallway, and up the stairs. At the door to her antechamber, she turned to Paul. "I can't go down to the party tonight. Charlie needs care, and his parents won't give it to him. He and I will play with hand puppets and cards until he's ready to sleep." Pale and drawn, she glanced anxiously at Charlie and put an arm over his shoulder. "I feel guilty for taking him to Bristol." She looked tenderly into Paul's eyes. "Will you visit me after you leave the party?"

"If it's not too late." He caressed her hand. "I'll report to you whatever I discover." When she had gone inside with the boy, he listened to their fading steps, to doors closing. For a moment, he stood quietly holding her worried face in his mind's eye. His heart went out to her.

If there was any guilt from the trip, it was his. He had taken advantage of Charlie, put him in harm's way. Should he have been more cautious? More concerned that his pursuit of Fitzroy did not harm innocent bystanders? Fortunately, the boy wasn't injured. Indeed, the adventure seemed to have done him good. And, the trip had been worthwhile. Roach would not get evidence against Lady Margaret from Betty. Her neighbors were alerted and would protect her. Fitzroy would remain within reach. The prospects for shipping him to France seemed better than ever.

Distant sounds of music jarred the colonel back into the present moment. He hurried to his room, changed to fresh linen and a brown dress suit, and went downstairs to the party.

Moving among the guests, he snatched bits of conversation, much of it about wagering on Jeffery's boxing match at noon on Wednesday. Large sums, eager faces. He also eavesdropped on guests discussing the afternoon's attack. How quickly the news had spread. He learned nothing useful, except how anxious the English were about violent crime on their highways. And yet they wouldn't dream of allowing their king to establish a royal highway patrol as in France.

The sound of music drew him to the ballroom. As he entered, Miss Ware was singing an air to a rapt audience. Her voice, a strong well-trained soprano, filled the room with a lilting melody. A fetching young woman, dark-eyed and comely. Sensuous, yet touchingly innocent. Sir Harry was standing nearby, off to one side, his eyes locked on her. Whenever she looked in his direction, his face beamed with joy. At the end of her song, he led the applause.

The trumpets gave out a resounding flourish. The music director announced a country dance. As Miss Ware stepped down from the stage to the ballroom floor, several men approached her, faces bright and hopeful. Sir Harry brusquely elbowed them out of his way and seized her for himself. She seemed a little startled but pleased by the competition.

The band struck up the music, and the dancers began stepping about the room. For a large, rugged man, Sir Harry was remarkably light on his feet. And skillful. He executed the quick steps with ease and grace. His broad ruddy face exuded the delight he drew from his lovely young partner.

A tap on the shoulder interrupted Saint-Martin's observations. "Shall we dance?" asked Lady Margaret, her emerald eyes inviting him with a warm inner glow. She extended her arms toward him. "The hostess' privilege, Colonel."

Momentarily at a loss for words, Saint-Martin bowed gallantly and murmured his pleasure. He quickly summoned his courage, uttered a silent prayer to the muse of the dance, and stepped out on the floor. Navigating the rapidly changing figures of the dance left him little opportunity for small talk. He did notice his partner casting swift barbed glances at her husband and Miss Ware and sensed each time a tensing of her hands. At the end of the dance, he felt fortunate to have maintained a semblance of dignity. He could easily have tripped them both.

While the musicians rested, Saint-Martin and Lady Margaret strolled from the floor. He looked at her sideways. A woman of uncommon beauty and aristocratic hauteur, but cunning and self-serving. A mercurial woman of Irish temperament, her moods shifting swiftly from frigid to torrid behind a mask of sangfroid. Law and convention had trapped her in an unhappy marriage. She could be a desperate, dangerous woman.

"Isn't it odd, Colonel, that the bandits appear to have known precisely where and when they could find you?" She tilted her head, a knowing expression in her eyes. "Who do you suppose betrayed you?" Before he could respond, she added, "And my son?"

"I do suspect someone, Lady Margaret, but I really shouldn't name him until I have more evidence."

"Mr. Critchley is your man, Colonel. My husband's personal spy."

Saint-Martin inadvertently shuddered. Her implication was obvious and shocking.

Lady Margaret turned away to speak to other guests and left Saint-Martin with his dark thoughts. He didn't believe Sir Harry had organized the attack or attempted to kill his son. But to his wife, at least, he seemed capable of such a crime.

Saint-Martin set out to find Georges, who should have returned from his business at the city's jail. The search ended in the basement gun room. Georges was seated at a work table. The weapons they had discharged that afternoon lay before him.

He looked up and smiled. "Take care, Colonel. Don't soil your ruffles." He waved his hand with a flourish over a litter of cleaning rods and oily rags. "The pistols are ready to go back into their cases."

"Let's talk here," said the colonel, sitting across from his adjutant. "No privacy upstairs." He reached gingerly for Anne's duelling pistols and held one in each hand, balancing them, taking aim with one and then the other. "If I ever had to duel Fitzroy, I'd borrow one of these. I couldn't miss." He shook his head. "Too bad, we must bring the man back alive." He placed the pistols in their case. "I'll take them to Miss Cartier when we've finished."

At a word from his superior, Georges reported that the two most seriously wounded bandits were in the city's hospital. The third man had died shortly after arriving there. Under interrogation, the lightly wounded man, whom Georges had already questioned, admitted Scarface had recruited him and four other men late Saturday night on Avon Street with the promise of a heavy purse of gold coins. Tomorrow, bailiffs would move the man to the prison in Taunton to await trial.

"At the jail, I mingled with constables and watchmen I've gotten to know." Georges rammed a cleaning rod down the short barrel of his musket. "One of them said Roach left the city on horseback at mid-morning and didn't return until after sunset."

"He could have been at the cottage, even near the scene of the attack," said Saint-Martin.

"Or the big man who galloped by us." Georges cocked his head quizzically. "You don't think Sir Harry hired Roach to kill Charlie, do you?"

"Seems unlikely to me, though I can't say why." Saint-Martin found himself reluctant to accept such an idea, perhaps because he had come to depend on Sir Harry for the capture of Fitzroy.

"You have to admit Sir Harry *could* have done it," Georges insisted. "He looks like a bluff, hearty, smiling man. But that's just on the surface. There's dark evil in his heart. After all, he once captained a slave ship and continues to trade in slaves. A brutal business!"

"I grant you that. Still, I'll give Sir Harry the benefit of the doubt. I'm inclined to think Roach alone directed the attack and did so mainly for revenge against Anne—and, for whatever reason, Fitzroy paid him. Most likely, to eliminate me. I can't fathom Roach's intentions toward the boy. Perhaps later on he'd 'rescue' him to win favor and a reward from his parents."

Shrugging his doubts, Georges pulled the cleaning rod out of the musket and inspected the weapon carefully. "Finished finally. I'll wash up, change clothes, and question the servants." He put the musket in a rack, then glanced at the colonel. "In all the excitement, I almost forgot to tell you. I've demolished Critchley's alibi in the Campbell case." Georges went on to relate his conversation with Fanny. "Either he or Fitzroy could have pushed her down the stairs."

"But how can we prove it?" asked Saint-Martin. For a moment he was lost in puzzled thought. "No one admits to seeing either of them at the scene of her fall." He rose from his chair, waved to his adjutant, and left with Anne's pistols. As he went lightly up the stairs, he pictured Anne waiting for him. As she heard his steps nearing the door, her blue eyes would brighten, her soft lips would part. The thought pleased him immensely.

Resplendent in Combe Park livery of crimson and silver, Georges adjusted his powdered wig and joined the party. At nine in the evening, he was standing in the hall near the main entrance when Jack Roach arrived in a cab and attempted to enter. On duty at the door, Jeffery blocked his way, saying only invited guests were allowed inside.

"I want to speak to Sir Harry," Roach growled. "He left a message at my apartment."

"Sir Harry is in his study with several gentlemen discussing business," said the footman with perfect courtesy. "May I tell him you are here?"

Roach cursed Jeffery for an ignorant savage but handed him a personal card to announce his arrival.

Leaving Roach standing outside, the footman walked to the study with the card. Georges followed him discreetly, his curiosity aroused. After a minute in the study, the footman emerged holding Roach's card in his hand.

As Jeffery approached the entrance hall, Georges beckoned him off to one side behind tall potted plants where they wouldn't be noticed.

"I saw Roach send you to Sir Harry with his card. Could you tell me what Sir Harry replied?" Georges fully realized Jeffery needed a very good reason for doing anything that would put him in jeopardy with his master. Therefore, he added in a low voice, "I'm investigating the Red Devil's part in this afternoon's attack. It's possible Sir Harry was involved with him. Maybe not. I've got to find out."

For a moment, Jeffery stared at Georges, searching his face. Then, he smiled regretfully and held up the card so that it showed his master's handwriting on the back. "Don't know," he murmured, "Can't read. Sir Harry didn't tell me."

Georges took a step closer and quickly scanned the message:

I'm busy now. Meet me in the training room in ten minutes

"Thanks anyway, Jeffery. I understand." Georges winked and took a step back. He suspected the footman *could* read but didn't want his master to know.

"Sir, you are a friend of Miss Anne. I trust you."

Georges pointed to the card. "Can you make Roach wait five minutes for it?"

"Gladly." Jeffery pocketed the card and sauntered away, losing himself in the crowd.

The footman's delay gave Georges enough time to dash to the tennis hall ahead of Roach and slip into the training room. It was pitch dark, but he found his way to the closet in the back wall and hid inside. The louvers in the door gave only a partial view of the room, but he should at least be able to hear what was said. He felt around the closet for brooms, mops and pails and put them out of his way. He could not afford to make a noise and be discovered.

After a few minutes, he heard footsteps in the antechamber. The door opened and a large figure entered carrying a lantern. As he set it down on a small table, his face was illumined. Jack Roach! He glanced nervously around the room. With an audible sigh he drew a pair of stools up to the table and sat down, wringing his hands.

Suddenly, he looked up. At the same moment, Georges heard footsteps. A frisson of excitement raced through his body.

"Roach, is it you in there?"

"Yes, Sir Harry."

Rogers walked in, wearing a cape and carrying a lantern. His eyes darted about, searching the room. Satisfied they were alone, he sat at the table facing Roach. "Have you seen Critchley? Has he reported to you on Lady Margaret's billiard party Saturday night?"

"No," Roach replied, "I've been out of the city most of the day and haven't spoken to him yet. Should I?" His voice had an impertinent edge.

"Well, I have, so save yourself the trouble." Sir Harry unclasped his cape and laid it on a nearby bench. "Critchley spent the evening hiding on the portico, peeking into the parlor. He claimed my wife played an excellent game of billiards. The French colonel had better stick to tennis. But that's not why I've called you here. Have you heard that bandits attacked my coach on the Bristol Road this afternoon?"

Roach nodded tentatively.

"Would you happen to know the man they called Scarface? Or any of his men?" Rogers' voice had taken on an undertone of contempt.

"In my business," Roach replied defensively, "I meet many criminals. Scarface was one of them. A bold villain. I might recognize some of his band."

"I value your familiarity with Bath's criminal element. That's why I ask you, how could so many seasoned villains expect to profit from robbing travelers on an outing to Bristol? A few watches, a handful of guineas, divided among so many is next to nothing for each of them. Did they think the coach was transporting bars of gold to the Bank of England? They were well-armed and equipped with horses. Surely, they should have sought out a better investment for their efforts."

Roach shrugged his shoulders. "Their leader may have deceived them."

"And have risked the wrath of several armed villains by paying them a pittance or anything less than he had promised?" Sir Harry rose from the table and began to pace the floor, stabbing the air with his finger. "No, someone had contracted with Scarface for the attack, not merely to steal a few watches and gold coins, but to assassinate one or all of the passengers. I think the principal target was Colonel Saint-Martin. The man who hired the band, I suspect, was Captain Fitzroy. He has good reason to fear the colonel and want him out of the way."

"I see," murmured Roach thoughtfully. He stirred as if about to add his opinion.

Sir Harry cut him off. "From his hiding place last night, Critchley saw the captain threaten the colonel with a pistol."

Roach gasped loudly.

Rogers leaned over the table and shook a menacing finger in Roach's face. "I want you to find out if indeed Fitzroy was behind the attack on the coach. Report to me any future conspiracy he might aim at the colonel."

~~~

Hidden in the closet, Georges mulled over what he was hearing. He had thought Rogers had called Roach to the training room to account for a failed attempt to kill little Charlie. Now it appeared that Rogers didn't suspect that the attack might have been aimed at his son and was unaware of Scarface's note, which Colonel Saint-Martin had kept secret. Nor did Rogers indicate in any other way that he was behind the attack. He blamed it on Fitzroy, who had been out riding in the country at the time and had not yet returned.

Sir Harry's version seemed plausible to Georges. By abducting Anne and Charlie, the bandits intended to spare them from the slaughter—Anne, in order that Roach might have revenge on her; Charlie, in order to allow him later to escape or to set him free for a ransom. Fitzroy wanted the boy to live. He would eventually inherit Sir Harry's wealth for Lady Margaret to hold in trust and the captain to exploit.

Georges listened carefully. The men were leaving. He waited a few minutes, then cautiously stepped out of the closet. His mind was spinning, but slowly a sequence of events fell into place. Saturday afternoon, Fitzroy had been in the parlor and heard about Sunday's trip to Bristol. He must have then contracted with Roach. Overnight, Roach and Scarface assembled a band of six. On Sunday afternoon, Tarleton and Corbett in disguise led the band to the site of the ambush, hid behind the hedge, and directed the attack. It was most likely Fitzroy himself who rode in the Bath coach, identified
~~~

the target, and sent a messenger, a big man, perhaps Roach, galloping off to the band.

The more Georges considered this view of Fitzroy's role, the more convinced he felt it might be true. He'd think about it again after a good night's sleep and tell the colonel.

Sir Harry and Roach had long gone when Georges shook the cold out of his bones, felt his way through the dark building, and hastened back to the house.

Chapter 13

Fancy Ball

Monday, April 2

Early in the morning, half-awake, Anne left her bed and padded over to the window. The sun had just begun to climb above the brow of Combe Down. The sky had cleared to the south. She opened the window and breathed in fragrant spring air. In the eaves above her, doves cooed softly. A perfect hour for a ride.

She washed with cold water and brushed her hair, then reached into her wardrobe for the riding outfit she often wore in Hampstead. Black cap, light brown wool coat, tan breeches, black boots. Paul wouldn't be shocked; he had seen her astride a horse before in Wimbledon, shortly after they had first met. He had seemed surprised but pleased.

A few minutes later, she met Paul in the servants' hall. "This is the ride we promised each other many months ago," he said as he embraced her. Mrs. Powell had laid out a breakfast of coffee, bread, and butter at a table where they could be alone. While they ate, Paul shared with her what Georges had overheard last night in the training room.

"I now believe Fitzroy and Roach arranged the ambush on Bristol Road," Paul remarked. "Of course, Roach could have acted on his own."

Anne felt relieved to hear that Charlie had not been a target, but she was reminded of the threat to Paul. For a moment she stared at him, suddenly aware that she could have lost him yesterday. Her throat tightened. When she tried to speak, she thought she would choke. Finally, she stammered, "Fitzroy will try again. He'll find some other way. What shall we do?"

"We'll be ready," he answered calmly. "But, since we have no proof of his complicity, we must behave as though we don't even suspect him."

The stable was bustling when they walked in. Stableboys stopped to stare at Anne, then returned to cleaning the floor. At the far end of the building, Peter Hyde was instructing a young groom to prepare coaches for the day. He turned and waved. Georges came out of the stalls, leading two thoroughbreds, saddled and eager to go, a black mare for Anne and a chestnut hunter for Paul.

They mounted their horses and trotted on paths through the estate to a country road south of Combe Park. Its packed dirt surface was in good condition, and they had it to themselves. When they came to a long straight stretch, they urged their horses to a gallop. The mare was eager to run. The wind soon whistled in Anne's ears. Paul's hunter took up the challenge and the horses raced neck and neck.

At Ralph Allen's stone quarry they reined in their mounts, tethered them to a tree at the edge of a grassy clearing, and walked toward the works. Decades of cutting had gouged a large amphitheater out of a steep hillside, exposing thick layers of limestone. Great blocks of cut stone littered the quarry's floor as if giants at play had tossed them helterskelter.

Anne took off her cap, shook her hair. The sun had risen high enough to throw its rays against the western wall of the quarry, drawing out the honey color so characteristic of Bath's buildings. Black martins darted in and out of crevices in the stone, swooping swiftly from wall to wall. Their twittering echoed like a fairy band of tiny flutes. She and Paul gazed quietly at the scene until workmen began arriving—insects measured against the walls of stone towering above them.

"Anne, with you at my side I could stay here forever."

She stared fondly into his eyes. The magic of this place had joined her spirit to Paul's in a kind of sacred communion. His voice resonated with yearning to seize, to celebrate this tender miracle, lest it vanish without a trace, like the echo of birdsong against the rock. A keen desire stirred deeply within her. She wanted to hold on to this moment and share it with him. They turned to each other. His lips met hers in a long, fervent kiss.

Even gripped by passion they were still aware they were out in the open, exposed to public view. They drew apart.

"Another time, Anne."

"Another place, Paul."

At Combe Park's gate, they encountered Jeffery in old clothes, trotting toward them, breathing easily. He had run down to the river and back, Anne thought. When he saw them, he waved and joined them on the road into the estate, keeping pace with the horses. He glanced with interest at Anne, then stared. She didn't take offence. The footman might never have seen a woman astride a horse. But she noticed Paul seemed startled and annoyed. Jeffery averted his eyes and veered off toward the house.

Late that morning, Anne wanted some aids for her lessons with Charlie. A few puppets or picture books would do. Critchley was the person most likely to know where to look. She didn't like to deal with him, especially since he had betrayed her to Roach, but she decided to approach him anyway. He was at his desk in the classroom, dictating Latin passages to William. As she entered, he looked up at her with cold, hostile eyes. William snickered. But Anne managed to maintain her civility. She asked if the tutor knew where she could find toys.

"Try the attic above the ballroom," he said curtly and resumed dictation.

Anne found the door to the attic unlocked and stepped into a large chamber above the ballroom. To the left stood a harpsichord. She carefully lifted the cover but raised little dust. Someone must have recently uncovered the instrument. Its veneer was badly cracked and stained. Water damage, she guessed. She began to play a tune her mother had taught her, but several keys didn't work. She replaced the cover and looked around.

Shelves lined the walls; trunks and storage boxes littered the floor. At the far end of the room, yet another door opened to a space over the former chancel. Inside she heard a low intermittent sound. She stopped, listened. The sound came again, very low.

To her left she noticed a small puppet theater. On a shelf straight ahead were hand puppets, dolls, painted lead soldiers, and other toys. To her right stood a wall of freestanding bookcases that enclosed the southwest corner of the room. The sound came from behind the books.

She edged through an opening between the cases. Suddenly, to her left, she saw a very large man in crimson livery sitting in a dormer window space. Light poured on him. It was Jeffery, bent over a small table, his head resting on an opened book. He was snoring. She gasped and stepped back, bumping into a case and rattling its contents. The footman raised his head and looked around, his eyes half-closed, as if he didn't know where he was.

"I'm sorry for disturbing you," Anne stammered.

He glanced down at the book, then leaped to his feet, sending the chair tumbling behind him.

Mouth agape, Anne backed into the case again. She gulped, "I'm so sorry...I'll go away." She turned to leave.

"Please, Miss. Don't go...Let me explain." He raised his hands, palms out. "I didn't steal it...."

His entreaty was so earnest that she stopped, her heart thudding with visceral fear. She was alone with this huge, strange, powerful black man! Yet he didn't threaten her, he was pleading. She froze, speechless, staring at him.

He lifted the book from the table and handed it to her. It was a collection of stories from the Bible in very simple English. He must have found it in one of the cases behind her.

"I never thought you stole it," she said quietly, returning the book to him. "But why do you come up here to read?"

He held the book in his hands like a treasure. "The law doesn't allow slaves to read or write. That's what the master says. If I disobey, he says, I'll go back to Jamaica on the next boat and cut sugar cane the rest of my life."

"I surely will not tell anyone you are reading unless you want me to." She was about to excuse herself again and leave, when she noticed a profound sadness in his face, an unfulfilled yearning. She asked him, "What's the matter?"

"I read poorly. No matter how hard I try. I come here after training, like now. I come often at night. I learn the words but not what they mean. There's no one here to teach me." He caressed the book with his fingers, then put it on a shelf and picked up the chair.

A surge of pity flooded Anne's heart. No one in the household would defy the master's orders. They might report an infraction by the slave. Outside the house this huge black man attracted instant attention. Even if he were free, he wouldn't have the time or money to go to a school or hire a tutor.

Could she teach him, she wondered. She'd have only a month to do it. How much could she accomplish in a few furtive hours? And if they were discovered? She'd be ridiculed. And, she shuddered, glancing up at the man, she'd be suspected of something far more scandalous than teaching him to read! Paul would not doubt her virtue, but he would think she was thoughtless and reckless. Teaching Jeffery had nothing to do with apprehending Fitzroy, he would say. And, it might seriously complicate relations with Sir Harry.

"Miss Cartier!" Critchley's high, reedy voice called out. Anne heard foot steps from the servants' stairwell. They stopped. He had reached the attic landing. She grabbed Jeffery by the arm, pulled him between the cases and out into the room, then pointed to the puppet stage. "Quick, pick it up and follow me." She dashed to the shelf, seized an armful of hand puppets, and raced into the large storage room, the footman after her. They were half-way through the room when Critchley entered, wheezing heavily.

"Thank you so much for coming to help me," Anne exclaimed, her voice carrying far more concern than she felt. "You really shouldn't have climbed the stairs." The man stood bent and breathless but staring with gimlet eye at Anne and the black man. As she passed by, she smiled to Critchley and glanced back at Jeffery. "I asked the footman to help me with the puppet stage. It would have been too much for a woman to carry down the stairs." Once out of earshot of the clerk, she thought she heard a sigh of relief from Jeffery.

After introducing Charlie to the little puppet theater, Anne returned to her room. She felt sad and helpless. There was little she could do for Jeffery. She gave a shrug and decided to deal with another problem that had been festering in the back of her mind. Harriet! Sweet, foolish girl! Had she encouraged Sir Harry's infatuation? Was she even aware of it?

Anne leaned back against the door and let her mind range freely. The pieces of a puzzle were falling into place: Harriet's fine clothes; her familiarity with Combe Park and its master; the remarkable progress of her career, from dancing in the chorus at Sadler's Wells to singing solo at the Royal Bath Theatre. A powerful, hidden hand must be working for Harriet.

Anne found it hard to imagine Harriet as Sir Harry's mistress. She had too much self-respect and integrity to exploit a man or to allow herself to be exploited by him. She also came from a devoutly religious family. But she had left home for the theater. She was also only human. Perhaps she had been charmed by Sir Harry. At the very least, she might well be Sir Harry's protégé, and unaware of the risks involved. For all his charm, he was a brutal and self-serving man, not likely to respect any woman for long, whether as beautiful as Lady Margaret or as personable and talented as Harriet.

She had invited Anne to tea at her apartment at two o'clock, following a rehearsal. Since Anne's arrival in Bath, she and Harriet had little time for a serious talk. Now Anne saw an opportunity. She paced back and forth. Should she ignore Harriet's predicament or warn her? With a deep breath, Anne chose the latter, fully aware that even the best of friends might not appreciate uninvited counsel.

A little before two, Anne reached Queen Square, a grassy park enclosed by a wrought iron railing. A tall, slim pyramid stood in the middle. Rows of stately buildings with uniform facades gave the square a dignified, well-mannered aspect. She had just begun searching for Harriet's residence, when she recognized a crimson carriage parked on Gay Street at her friend's address. Alarmed, Anne stopped to consider what to do. Had Harriet invited Sir Harry to join them at tea? There would be no chance then for sisterly advice!

She happened to notice a couple walking on a graveled path near the sharply tapered pyramid. Their conversation seemed strained. The man was leaning toward the woman, chopping the air with his hand. She was looking ahead, keeping a polite distance between them. She recognized Anne and waved. It was Harriet, together with Sir Harry. Anne walked into the park to meet them.

He bowed stiffly to Anne, as if she were intruding. Harriet seemed relieved to see her. They had come from the Upper

Assembly Rooms, where Harriet had rehearsed for the evening's musical entertainment. He had watched, since he would otherwise miss her performance. He was supposed to meet his sporting friends to discuss Wednesday's boxing match.

"Sir Harry, would you please excuse us," Harriet said as they reached the entrance to her building. "Anne and I have much to talk about. We've been out of touch for over a year." Her tone was soft and gentle, her manner mollifying. He seemed assuaged. She extended her hand and he kissed it, looking up boldly into her eyes. He bowed politely to Anne, then strode to his carriage and drove off.

While Harriet hunted for her key, Anne studied the building's simple, elegant facade of Bath stone. This was a much too fashionable address for a young singer and dancer. Who paid the rent? A plausible answer immediately came to her mind, but she withheld judgment. There had to be a better explanation.

The two women walked up to Harriet's apartment on the first floor. A young maid let them into the parlor and took their coats. Anne surveyed the room, increasingly disconcerted by the level of refinement and comfort she was discovering. A tea table was set for two near windows offering a lovely view of Queen Square. In one corner stood a harpsichord. On the walls were many scenes of Bath—including the same view of Queen Square she had just enjoyed. Over the fireplace hung a masterful painting of a beggar girl and a boy, depicted in half-figure. They stood in a clear golden light against a dark woodland background.

Anne was instantly charmed. The girl was perhaps fourteen, her slim body wrapped in a gauzy shawl. Her oval face had the color of pure rich cream. Her eyes were dark brown, her gaze wistful and inward. A light wind blew through her thick wavy dark brown hair. Her companion was a few years younger and more childlike. His light brown hair was tousled and his complexion enlivened by a touch of pink. He bent forward and looked up at the viewer with guarded hope.

"Elizabeth Linley and her brother Tom," said Harriet over Anne's shoulder. "My aunt's favorite painting by Gainsborough. The children are probably posing for a play or piece of music. Aunt Caroline likes it because it reminds her of me."

Anne glanced at her friend. There was indeed a resemblance, even more remarkable today, when Harriet's expression also seemed wistful—and a little troubled.

"Aunt Caroline?" asked Anne, suddenly aware she wasn't acquainted with Harriet's family. She and Harriet had become friends during a summer season at Sadler's Wells, where performances and camaraderie had preoccupied them.

"Yes, that's her painting." Harriet extended her arms in a broad, sweeping gesture. "And this is her apartment." A hint of reproach crept into her voice. "Annie, you know I can't afford all this! Who do *you* think is paying for it?" She stared severely at Anne, then a teasing smile appeared on her lips.

"I'm sorry…." stammered Anne.

At that moment, the maid came with a tea tray and served them. The tea service had Derby's deep blue underglazing, further evidence of Aunt Caroline's wealth and good taste.

When the maid had left, Harriet remarked, "I know you are wondering…." She hesitated briefly as if unsure she should continue. "You are wondering about Harry and me. And so are others. You may have heard rumors about a mistress." Harriet's back grew rigid. She struggled for words. "Well, if he has one, it's not me."

Anne didn't comment. She frankly felt relieved, but she tried not to show it. With a smile she urged Harriet on.

"Aunt Caroline bought this apartment years ago and came to it every season. She loved Bath, especially its music, and was fond of the Linley family while they performed here. Elizabeth was the finest soprano in England, and her sisters sang almost as well. Tom wrote music, played the violin like a master, but he drowned a few years ago. Their home was 'a nest of nightingales,' Aunt Caroline used to say. She's now widowed, invalid, and housebound in London. She could have leased to someone. Instead, she insisted I live here with a maid and proper clothes. Didn't want her niece starving penniless in a garret!"

"How fortunate you are, Harriet, to have such a generous, cultivated aunt."

"Yes, she has given me so much. And she knew Maestro Rauzzini. For years she had encouraged my singing in church choirs. So, when I came to Bath, she arranged for him to give me voice lessons."

"I'm pleased to hear this. But, if I may ask, what is Sir Harry's interest in you?"

A confused expression came over Harriet's face. "Let's see if I can explain." She described first meeting Harry, a year ago. She had sung several airs during intermission at the theater and was returning to the dressing room. "He came up to me, this finely dressed, big burly man. There were tears in his eyes. He managed to say, 'Your songs touched my heart. May I see you later?'"

Stunned by his ardor, she had agreed. They met after her last performance that evening. He promised to do something for her. Bring her forward. Since then, he had been true to his word. Thanks to him, she had sung in the best houses in Bath and Bristol. But, at a cost she was only now beginning to reckon.

"Until a few months ago, it seemed he wanted only my friendship and my voice." They had gotten on well together, singing, dancing, even teasing one another. Harry acted like an overgrown boy—spontaneous, natural, lively. With Lady Margaret, he was a different person—tense and withdrawn. His wife's icy, aloof manner seemed to cast a pall over his spirit. "I felt sorry for him. So, he often confided in me."

Harriet looked up wistfully, like the beggar girl in the painting. "Since Captain Fitzroy has come to England, there's been a big change. Harry wants to put Lady Margaret and Charlie aside and start a new family. As soon as I understood this, I told him I would have no part in adultery—I'm a religious person. But I saw he was suffering and it didn't seem his fault. So, I've tried to stay friendly, but without encouraging him to think I would ever become his wife. I know him well enough to realize that would be foolish."

Anne recalled the scene in Queen Square when she arrived. "Sir Harry seemed to be pressing himself upon you."

"He's been doing that recently," Harriet conceded. "And he has grown more and more protective. Takes me home in his carriage from the theater or the Assembly Rooms. Doesn't want me to walk alone. Wants to be close to me, touch me. I'm beginning to think he's jealous. Fears someone will take me away from him. I'm not sure how to deal with this."

Anne felt unprepared to offer a solution to Harriet, but she thought she saw a glimmer of hope. "Let's keep in touch. Something may happen to bring Sir Harry to his senses."

As Anne returned to Combe Park in a cab, she wondered, if Fitzroy were removed from the Rogers' household and imprisoned in France, would Sir Harry's anger toward Lady Margaret diminish? If so, he might then reconcile himself to continuing their marriage and end his infatuation with Harriet. If Fitzroy remained at Combe Park much longer, Anne feared, Sir Harry might resort to desperate measures and Harriet would be hurt.

In the feeble light of a few sconces, Paul and Anne spun across the floor in a country dance. Combe Park's empty ballroom echoed with the sound of their feet. "You dance well, Paul," she said encouragingly. He had asked her for a lesson before the Fancy Ball that evening. Hundreds of the city's most distinguished residents and visitors would gather in the Upper Assembly Rooms and many of them would watch him, a French nobleman. He wanted to dance with more assurance than he had last night with Lady Margaret.

"Would you care to rest for a moment?" she asked. "You're puffing."

"Thank you. That might be wise." He explained he had spent the morning at the training session, where he lifted irons and sparred with Lord Jeff. The footman had been mercifully gentle, like a cat with her kitten. Nonetheless, Paul had finished the session bruised and tired. Afterwards, Sir Harry had insisted on a match of tennis.

"You must be starved, Paul. Let's have a bite to eat. Jeffery will fetch something for us." She stopped a servant in the hall and asked for the footman. Gone to the city on an errand, she was told, but the servant offered to bring food to the dining room.

As they lunched, Anne reported on her encounter with Jeffery in the attic. "I fear what might happen if Sir Harry finds out his slave is attempting to learn to read." She broke a piece of bread, took a bite, then laid it aside, a question growing in her mind. "What do you suppose Jeffery does when he runs errands in the city? Could Georges look into that?" She knew he had created a wide network of spies with Baron Breteuil's money.

Paul gazed at her doubtfully. "I don't see how Jeffery's errands concern our pursuit of Fitzroy. Still, I'll ask Georges. Very little escapes his notice."

That evening, a coach left Combe Park for the Fancy Ball at the Upper Assembly Rooms. Sir Harry had excused himself for an important sporting conference in his study. He might come to the ball later. Georges sat alongside Peter Hyde, the coachman, with Mr. Critchley and William behind them. Lady Margaret had invited Anne and Paul to ride inside. They sat opposite her and Fitzroy. The captain attempted to appear unperturbed by his cousin's arrangements, but he nervously fingered the hilt of his sword and cast furtive, baleful glances at Paul. After a few moments of strained silence, the men paid compliments to the ladies: Lady Margaret in a mauve silk gown, Anne in delicately patterned soft red muslin, a gown that Madame Gagnon had altered and lent to her.

Having exhausted that topic, they chose the weather. An unusually mild spring, they agreed. Blossoms had appeared on walnut trees. At the carriage entrance, they left the coach and went their separate ways. Georges mixed among the footmen and chairbearers.

Anne and Paul began to explore the building. It was their first visit. In the ballroom, they found five hundred men and women jamming themselves into a space that would comfortably accommodate half that number. Anne glanced up to the musicians' gallery where Harriet stood hesitant for a moment before she began to sing. The din of the crowd, together with the instruments of the band, overwhelmed even her strong voice. Anne couldn't hear a word.

The Master of Ceremonies stepped on to a platform and invited persons to dance in order of rank, beginning with an earl and working downward.

"It will be a long while before we might be called," Paul said, taking Anne under the arm. "Let's move on. We may learn something useful." In the Tea Room they saw Madame Gagnon at a table with three other ladies dressed in fine muslin. Their fans fluttered, their heads nodded or shook in response to whatever the French woman was telling them.

"Persons of quality," whispered Anne.

"It's remarkable that such well-born, fashionable women would sit in public with a milliner," Paul remarked. "That would never happen in Paris."

"Nor in London. But Bath is different. A city of strangers seeking pleasure and diversion. Manners and dress are what count here. The three ladies have probably come from London for the season and do not know each other well. They may have visited Madame Gagnon's shop, where she teased them with bits of gossip. Now she's feeding them the latest rumors."

Madame Gagnon's gaze swept the room. She excused herself from her companions and strolled toward Anne and Paul, stopping on the way to greet friends and customers.

"You've led me to believe she deals in more than ribbons," Anne whispered to Paul.

He threw her a teasing smile. "That's a state secret." He rose to greet the French woman, then introduced her to Anne.

"Miss Cartier, I've heard about your adventure yesterday afternoon on the way back from Bristol. Very instructive. When women learn to shoot, men will pay them more respect. By now, the story's all over town." She leaned forward and whispered in French, "Whom do you suspect was behind it?"

"Jack Roach," Anne whispered back.

The milliner glanced over Anne's shoulder toward the door. "Don't look. The Red Devil has just appeared. He'll probably torment some of his victims this evening and keep his eyes open for new ones."

Roach stepped into the Tea Room, looked around, apparently didn't see anyone he wanted to meet, and left.

"Let's see where he goes," Paul said to Anne. He rose from the table and bowed to Madame Gagnon. "Excuse us, Madame, we'll talk more later." Anne took her spyglass from her purse and held it ready.

They followed Roach into a noisy octagonal antechamber, where he spoke familiarly to an elderly man accompanied by a much younger attractive woman. Anne raised her glass and studied them, using Paul as a shield. The elderly man was visibly distressed, his eyes avoiding the confused gaze of his companion. No money was passed, but Anne managed to read from Roach's lips his parting words. "Pay or else."

Anne repeated this to Paul.

"I smell scandal and extortion," he said softly. Suddenly, he touched her arm. "Wait a moment." He led her eyes to a man in a plain gray suit, walking with a limp. "I know him. Watch. I think he's following the Red Devil into the Card Room."

Roach wandered through the room, greeting many of the players by name, saying a few words at a table, then moving on to the next one. The man in gray sat alone against the wall appearing to listen to the musicians in the gallery. Anne and Paul also found a small table. Hiding her spyglass with a fan, she studied the stranger. Perhaps fifty years old, he was of medium height, thick-set body, square face, and a full head of pepper-gray hair.

"Now I recall his name." Paul leaned toward Anne. "Dick Burton, a Bow Street officer! "

Anne nodded. "Barnstable's letter mentioned him coming to Bath. Do you think he can deal with Roach?

"Burton's shrewd, well-informed, experienced. We had lunch together in London last year. I hired him to help me locate you. The limp is new."

The room grew crowded and very warm. Roach approached the table where Lady Margaret and Captain Fitzroy were playing whist with another couple. She ignored Roach's greeting. Unabashed, he bent over Captain Fitzroy's shoulder as if inspecting his hand of cards and spoke a few words into his ear. The Irishman clenched his teeth and muttered out of the side of his mouth what looked like a curse. Roach merely smiled and moved on. The four people at the table glanced at one another, startled and confused.

"I thought the captain and Roach were in league against us," whispered Anne.

"Yes, they were," replied Paul, "but they now appear to be enemies. The attack failed. Perhaps they blame each other or quarrel over the expense."

Eventually, Roach left the Card Room. Burton rose and followed him into the Ball Room. The crowd there was so dense, the atmosphere so stifling, that Anne and Paul gave up any hope of dancing. And there didn't seem to be any profit in following Roach and Burton any further.

"William Rogers has found companions," remarked Paul, glancing off to his left. In a corner of the room the young man and a pair of fops had gathered around three young women in fashionable low-cut gowns. Mr. Critchley was out of sight.

"No chaperons," observed Anne, studying the group with her spyglass. "William has dipped deeply into the punch bowl. His cheeks are as red as ripe apples. He and the other men are bargaining with the women. He knows them, takes the lead. This is not the first time."

"Is there a gentleman nearby overseeing the transaction?"

"Yes, a tall hard-faced man," Anne replied, intrigued by Paul's question, "but very well-dressed and polished in his manners. Is he really what I think he is?"

Paul nodded. "In Paris it's the same. This 'gentleman' must work for a luxurious brothel, probably located nearby, and is in charge of the three women. To deceive the Master of Ceremonies, he pretends to be their escort. The English would call him a pimp."

"William is too young for that sort of thing," said Anne, but she immediately imagined him at the peepholes leering at Mary Campbell.

"He's big and *looks* older than his years," Paul observed. "Critchley should take better care of his student. This evening's pleasure will cost the boy a small fortune, not to speak of what it will do to his character—and perhaps to his health. The brothel of course will extend credit to him—nephew of the richest man in Bath—but there will be a harsh reckoning. I doubt Sir Harry will pay for this."

Eventually, an agreement was reached. The young men sauntered toward the exit, the young women on their arms.

Anne stared after them. "Incredible! Pandering at a fancy ball!"

"Yes, but it won't come to the Master of Ceremonies' attention so long as it's elegant and discreet."

Back in the Tea Room Anne and Paul hoped to join Madame Gagnon for a light supper. She wasn't in sight. They had just sat down at a table partially sheltered from public view when Paul saw Burton walk in. "I think he's going to eat. Shall I ask him to sit with us?"

"Of course. We share a common interest in Jack Roach."

As Paul approached, Burton's eyes narrowed for a brief moment, then brightened with recognition. He followed Paul to the table. "Delighted to join you," he said to Anne. "I had intended to find you, but I've only just arrived. Staying at the York."

As he took his seat opposite her, Anne noticed a long thin scar on his left cheek from ear to mouth. Suddenly, she realized he had caught her staring.

"A French sabre, Miss Cartier. Battle of Minden. Many years ago." The officer cast a quick wry glance at Paul. "No hard feelings, Colonel." With a smile, he turned their attention to the fashionable dress of the crowd around them, the indifferent quality of the musicians, and the heat and noise of the place.

Anne sensed Burton was assessing Paul. Apparently reassured of his character, the officer leaned forward and addressed Anne. "As solicitor Barnstaple has explained in his letter to you, I've come to investigate extortion and fraud by Jack Roach. A group of wealthy Bathonians stand ready to pay a generous commission if I rid the city of this pest."

He paused, gave Anne a hopeful smile. "God willing, I shall also bring him to justice for his assault on you."

"And you, Colonel Saint-Martin...." He tilted his head quizzically. "I'm wondering what has brought you here. Official business? I understand a certain Captain Fitzroy is also in Bath, wanted by French authorities for fraud. According to rumor, he had an affair with Baron Breteuil's goddaughter."

"In truth, sir, he beat and raped her. But, to satisfy your curiosity, I'm here privately. By coincidence—believe it or not—I met Miss Cartier, who has added greatly to the pleasure of visiting this beautiful city. I'm staying at Combe Park as the guest of Sir Harry Rogers."

"Rogers?" Burton glanced at Anne, then at Paul. "I've overheard talk concerning an attack on a coach belonging to the family."

While Paul briefly described the incident, Burton stroked his chin thoughtfully. "Roach's behind it, you believe? How did he know about your trip to Bristol?"

"I suspect Rogers' personal clerk—Critchley's his name—betrayed our plans to Roach," Paul replied.

"Mr. Critchley's one of his spies? Fancy that! Personal clerk to Sir Harry? Very interesting." Burton gave Paul a crooked smile. "Bath, city of intrigue, wouldn't you say, Colonel."

Paul agreed, hoping Burton would continue. He obviously had more to say about Critchley. But Anne, pointing toward the door, broke in with an excited whisper. "Lady Margaret and her cousin have arrived."

They sat themselves at a table occupied by the two British officers Tarleton and Corbett.

Burton followed Anne's gaze to the newcomers and raised an eyebrow. "Yes?"

Paul had barely begun to explain, when Jack Roach also entered the room, walked directly up to Fitzroy and Lady Margaret, and bent down to speak to them. After a heated exchange, the Irishman leaped to his feet, shoved Roach back, and slapped him hard across the face. In an instant, Tarleton and Corbett were at Fitzroy's side, ready for battle. Roach stood stunned for a moment, then turned abruptly and left the room.

"That's cause for a duel," exclaimed the Bow Street officer. He rested his arms on the table, clasped his hands, and stared at Anne and Paul. "What do you make of it?"

Chapter 14

Fateful Theft

Tuesday, April 3

Anne rose early after a restless sleep. In her dreams she had seen Roach, like a leering red monster, strut through the Card Room, lean over Lady Margaret's shoulder, and bare fang-like teeth as if to bite her. With a shudder, Anne sat herself in front of the mirror and began brushing her hair. There was a soft knocking on her door. She drew a light blue robe over her shift and opened to Paul.

"Sorry, I'm early," he said, taking her hands. "I wanted a minute alone with you."

She stepped back, gazing at him. Although it was only seven o'clock, he was dressed for a day in the city: light brown coat, dark brown breeches, and pale yellow waistcoat.

"I'm going to meet Burton after breakfast," he said, after they embraced, "and visit the Pump Room together...." Before he could say more, there were footsteps outside.

"Breakfast!" Georges' voice echoed in the antechamber. Anne smoothed her robe, opened the door again, and stepped back. He swaggered in, a large round breakfast tray balanced on one raised hand. As he passed her, he twirled the tray, grinning like a clown.

Her hand flew to her mouth. "Georges! Be careful."

Paul had moved to the table and was checking his watch. At Anne's exclamation, he looked up, alarm clouding his face.

Georges stopped, blinked, apparently having expected his superior to arrive a little later. "Sorry, sir," the adjutant mumbled, lowering the tray.

With a flourish he laid out the cups, saucers, plates, quince marmalade, butter, and the basket of rolls. Anne and Paul seated themselves at the table. Georges poured coffee for them.

"Lady Margaret and Captain Fitzroy have only just arrived home," said Georges, dropping a lump of sugar into the colonel's cup. Anne declined with a shake of her hand. Georges continued, while serving butter and rolls. "Shortly after you returned to Combe Park, they left the Assembly Rooms in a rush. Lady Margaret had torn her gown and insisted on going home to have it repaired. The captain was angry. Had a party in mind with friends in the Crescent. 'Faster,' they shouted, though Peter the coachman was driving at breakneck speed."

At a gesture from his superior, Georges pulled a chair up to the table. He had brought an extra cup and poured for himself. Between buttered rolls and sips of coffee, he explained that Lady Margaret had been in the house no more than ten minutes when out she came, calm and smiling. Then off to the party. The coachman had to wait outside for them all night long. Georges chuckled. "He gave us an earful of it in the servants' hall."

Paul asked, "Have you heard *why* they left the Assembly Rooms so abruptly?"

"Not yet." Georges looked up from his cup, puzzled by the question.

"I'm surprised." Paul went on to inform his adjutant about the incident in the Tea Room.

Georges frowned. "While I was talking to the servants, I did hear that Fitzroy struck Roach, and Roach walked away. But that doesn't account for Lady Margaret's panicked return home." A puzzled frown creased Georges' forehead. He put his cup on the table and sat still for a moment, eyes cast down, fingers tapping together.

Suddenly, he looked up. "Aha! the torn gown! You couldn't know that Lady Margaret tore the gown herself. Deliberately. In the Ladies' Parlor off the Tea Room. Must have been just after the incident you witnessed. Madame Gagnon was watching her for me and saw her sneak into a corner and rip the hem. At the time we couldn't understand why she did it. But, now I see. She wanted an excuse to go home first rather than drive directly to the private party."

That puzzled Anne. What did Lady Margaret want to do at Combe Park that she couldn't reveal to her escort? Something prompted by Roach's remarks in the Tea Room. Something important that required only a few minutes. She turned to Paul.

He anticipated her question. "Roach probably hinted he had discovered evidence of scandal concerning Lady Margaret and Fitzroy and would conceal it for a certain sum. Otherwise, he would pass it on to Sir Harry."

Georges scratched his head. "At Combe Park, Lady Margaret must have looked for that evidence, then left the house believing Roach didn't have what he claimed. But, I don't think he was trifling with her. He's a serious gambler playing for high stakes. And very clever."

"His cleverness is about to meet its match," observed Paul. The conversation turned to Dick Burton, whom Georges had not met. "Burton was the London officer who helped me find Anne. Our contact was brief."

Georges' eyebrows arched. "Shall we tell him about our pursuit of Fitzroy?" He glanced doubtfully at Anne, then at Paul.

The colonel shrugged. "He already knows why we're here. That could be a problem. He's loyal to the Crown and might obstruct our plans to abduct a man who enjoys its protection. We must find ways to convert him into an ally."

"We can help him arrest Jack Roach," Anne interjected. "For that I personally would be most grateful."

Georges drained his cup and stood up to leave. "By the way," he said to Anne, "your friend Harriet left the ball shortly before you and Colonel Saint-Martin."

"Yes?" Anne stared apprehensively at Georges.

"She climbed into an unmarked coach, shades drawn. I recognized it. From Combe Park. When she opened the door, I could see a man inside. Too dark to tell who he was. The chairbearers say they've often seen the coach at the theater."

Anne sighed. "Sir Harry. He's her patron, not her lover. He hopes for a more intimate relationship. I fear he'll hurt her."

When Paul and Georges left, Anne paced the floor, mulling over the aftermath of the Tea Room incident. Why had Roach deliberately precipitated Lady Margaret's panicked rush home? When he had first conceived the idea of prying into scandal at Combe Park, he must have felt confident he would somehow find evidence to justify Sir Harry's divorce. Thus far, he had gotten nothing. The old nursemaid Betty had refused to speak to him. Nor had he uncovered much of use at the Assembly Rooms or other cesspools of malicious gossip. Lady Margaret and Fitzroy had appeared circumspect: playing whist, dancing and dining always in company. So, Roach would have to conclude the most likely place for any damaging evidence was at Combe Park. But where?

Anne stared out the window. The wind drove a cold, steady drizzle against the glass. Spring in Bath was not a season for the cousins to have romantic trysts out of doors. That ruled out the park. In the public rooms of the house there were too many servants, guests, and, of course, the gimlet-eyed Critchley, William Rogers, and Sir Harry himself. By a process of elimination, Anne was left with few choices: Roach must focus on Fitzroy's room or Lady Margaret's or both.

She turned and leaned back against the window sill. Raking her fingers through her hair, she glanced at the large ornate mirror on the wall. One of the fauns seemed to ogle her with its bright protuberant eyes.

Peepholes! Lady Margaret's suite was directly below Anne's own room. Could the closet that was used to spy on her also have served for spying on Lady Margaret?

Anne immediately hurried next door to the storeroom. No one there. She pulled the hidden lever, entered the shallow closet, and studied the panels hiding the peepholes to her room. She had left them slightly ajar. They appeared to have been moved. Closely examining the floor, she found a section that could be raised and, beneath it, an ingenious optical instrument that could be pointed through small openings into Lady Margaret's dressing room and her bed chamber. Without knowing much about lenses and the like, Anne was sure this was an elaborate, expensive device. Who could afford it and would want to spy on Lady Margaret? Only Sir Harry himself. And, Jack Roach.

Alarmed by her discovery, Anne carefully plotted her next move. It was time she and Charlie went to his mother's rooms. She liked to visit briefly with her son during her breakfast, though she couldn't communicate with him very well. He was shy and she was impatient. She had asked Anne on the six previous days to come along and help the conversation. Each of those visits had been a little more cordial and natural than the previous one: the boy, more at ease with his mother; she, more patient and appreciative of him.

This morning, however, she seemed nearly exhausted. Her hands trembled; her eyelids were half-closed. A night of gambling and brandy had taken its toll. Nonetheless, she struggled through questions about the boy's progress in writing, reading lips, and pronouncing words. Charlie performed well enough to bring a tired smile to her lips.

While the boy showed his mother some sketches he had made, Anne examined the walls for the openings she had discovered upstairs. Since she knew approximately where they had to be, she quickly found them in the corner molding, masked by sculpted garlands. With the optical device, the peeper could watch Lady Margaret if she brought Fitzroy to her room or tried to hide anything.

After breakfast and the conversation with Charlie, Anne followed the boy to the door, wondering how to reveal the spying to his mother. Anne told Charlie to go on to his lessons, she would soon follow. She stepped back into Lady Margaret's room. The woman started, then frowned at this intrusion.

Before she could object, Anne raised her hand in a warning. "Someone is spying on you in this room." She beckoned her to the corner and pointed up toward the garlands. "If you look carefully, you will see the openings. A clever instrument is pointing through the molding. And I'm sure there are similar openings in your dressing room. A spy can watch almost every movement you make." Anne paused for a moment, then added, "And I'm almost certain someone spied on you last night."

Lady Margaret stepped back as if struck, stared up at the garlands, then looked at Anne with shock and disbelief. "Roach tricked me." She rushed to a small writing table, fumbled frantically with it and opened an ingeniously hidden drawer. "It's gone," she cried, staring down into a shallow empty space. With an anguished, childlike moan, she clutched at her throat and swayed. Anne caught her and eased her into a chair. For several minutes she sat there, leaning forward, hands clasped tightly in her lap, whimpering softly.

What could have been hidden in the drawer? Anne asked herself. Jewels? Incriminating love letters?

The whimpering slowly subsided. She sat up. A flash of anger crossed her face. "Where's Sir Harry?" she demanded.

The question took Anne aback. Shouldn't the woman keep track of her own husband? Anne happened to know the answer and replied calmly. "He told Colonel Saint-Martin he was going to a place near Calne with several other men to inspect the arrangements for tomorrow's match."

Lady Margaret fell silent, her shoulders slumped, her face lined and pale. She glanced up at the hidden instrument in the corner, then turned to Anne. "Go to Charlie. There's nothing you can do for me."

Colonel Saint-Martin put on his coat, inspected himself in the mirror, and walked toward the door of his room. He was on his way to the city. Georges was behind him, about to go downstairs to the servants' hall. There was a knock on the door. The colonel opened it and Anne rushed in, breathless, face flushed. "I've run up the stairs." She paused for a moment, breathing deeply. "Lady Margaret has just learned she's been spied upon in her rooms. She's taken it badly."

Anne described the optical device, the lady's discovery of the empty drawer, and her despair. "I'm sure she'll be here in a minute looking for Fitzroy." She waved a hand toward the room across the hall.

"Do you want to wait here and see what happens?" Paul asked.

"Sorry. I can't stay. Charlie's expecting me." She smiled apologetically and slipped down the hall toward the boy's room.

Paul watched until she disappeared, then closed the door. "We'll wait here," he told Georges. A few minutes later, they heard steps in the hall, then sharp knocking.

"What in God's name do you think you are doing?" the Irishman barked. "I'm trying to get some sleep."

"Something awful has happened," stammered Lady Margaret. "May I come in?"

A moment later, the door shut. Saint-Martin and Georges could no longer hear what was said, only murmuring. It seemed unwise to eavesdrop from the hallway. Saint-Martin opened his door an inch. The sound from Fitzroy's room increased. Suddenly, the Irishman shouted loudly. The words were indistinct but the tone was angry. Saint-Martin stepped into the hall. The crack of a hard slap came from the room, followed by a woman's shriek. More slaps and louder shrieks.

Leaving Georges behind, Saint-Martin crossed the hall and knocked on Fitzroy's door. "What's going on in there?" he shouted. The room instantly fell silent. After a few moments, Lady Margaret came out and edged past him, the clear creamy color of her face now a blotched pink. Blood trickled from her nose and the corner of her mouth. "It's nothing, Colonel. Please excuse me." She gathered her skirts and hurried away to the stairs.

For an instant, the image of a battered Sylvie de Chanteclerc surged into Saint-Martin's mind, almost blinding him. Then, the crumpled form of Mary Campbell at the foot of the stairs. Through the open door he noticed Fitzroy staring out the window. "Captain! What evil spirit compels you to beat women?"

Fitzroy spun around and advanced toward Saint-Martin. "Colonel, this is my affair." His face was gray, his eyes narrow slits. Without another word, he slammed the door.

Concealed by a screen of large green plants, Georges waited in the entrance hall. Captain Fitzroy wasn't the kind of man to sulk in his room when he came under pressure. His violent reaction to Lady Margaret indicated he had been unaware of what she had hidden and was furious when he found out. Love letters? Private journal?

While waiting, Georges wondered who had actually spied on her and discovered her hiding place. Not Sir Harry. He had come to the Fancy Ball by that time. Nor nephew William, who was mired in sin at a brothel. Roach also had remained in the city. That left only Roach's confederate, Critchley. He had quit the Fancy Ball early in the evening. After observing Lady Margaret open the drawer, he must have found a way to steal its hidden contents. Had he stolen her key? Bribed a maid?

"Hmm," Georges murmured. Critchley now held a valuable secret. Had he shared it with Roach?

Georges heard the sound of approaching steps. The Irishman entered the hall with his valet, whom he left at the door with instructions to watch his room. Georges remained behind the screen until the valet withdrew, then followed Fitzroy down the road to the River Avon and into the city. In the market place, the captain bought an inside seat on the post coach to Bristol that was about to depart. Georges hastened to a nearby stable and rented a decent horse for the day.

The weather was misty, but Georges managed to keep the coach in view. Shortly before noon, Fitzroy alighted at the Bush Tavern and went inside, presumably to reserve a seat for the return trip to Bath in the afternoon. Georges left his horse in the care of a groom and followed the Irishman on foot through narrow, crowded city streets to the harbor.

Fitzroy walked up and down the quay, speaking to ships' officers standing by their vessels until he found one who nodded and smiled. After an amiable exchange of words, the officer beckoned him on board.

Georges retired to a tavern on the quay, ordered an ale, and sat by a window with a clear view of the ship. It was the *Hampton*, a large brig, sails furled, with ports for eight guns. An American flag hung limp and sodden on its pole. Dockers were carrying casks up the gangplank and piling them on deck. Fitzroy and the officer had disappeared into a cabin in the ship's stern.

An hour later, Fitzroy reappeared, weaving his way among the casks to the gangplank. With a smile on his face, he waved to the officer and descended to the quay.

Rather than follow him again, Georges decided to find out what had happened on board. He approached the officer, who had resumed his post on the quay, and asked to which port the ship was destined. To New York was the reply. "Then I may be in luck," Georges remarked. "Are you taking on passengers?"

The officer gaped at him. "Why yes, another gentleman reserved passage just a few minutes ago, but there's room for a few more."

"Any ladies among the passengers?" Georges asked, thinking of Lady Margaret. Would she bolt from Combe Park and abandon her son? Before the officer could respond, Georges quickly added, lest he be misunderstood, "Ladies add a touch of refinement to a long voyage."

"None so far, unfortunately," replied the officer, smiling. With a gesture toward the casks, he explained that the ship should be ready to sail in a week or two.

Georges thanked him and said he'd think it over. He walked back toward the Bush Tavern, taking care to avoid Fitzroy. Hedging his bets, the captain was prepared to abandon Combe Park and Lady Margaret, if need be. And soon!

Chapter 15

Secrets

Tuesday, April 3

Charlie bent over the page of Latin grammar Mr. Critchley had assigned and began conjugating the verb "to love," *amare*. He wrote down the inflected forms, carefully shaping each of them with his lips: *amo, amas, amat, amamus....* The memory of his visit to his old nurse Betty slowly crept into the forefront of his mind. Her hand on his shoulder, her caring smile. It made him feel warm to think of her.

It was midmorning. Charlie was at his writing table in the schoolroom. He looked up from his book, peered at the map of Italy on the wall in front of him. Rome, Venice, Florence, Naples. Places Mr. Critchley loved to talk about. The boy squinted to see more details, but the room's two large windows cast a thin northerly light on the wall, dulling the colors of the map and blurring its features. Charlie glanced to his left. William Rogers, his cousin, stared vacantly into space, elbows on the table, hands cradling his jaw. His book lay closed before him. Charlie turned back to his Latin grammar.

Absorbed in his work, he didn't notice Mr. Critchley enter until he stood right in front of him. Charlie flashed a smile. He was enjoying school today. Mr. Critchley cast a sour glance in the boy's direction and walked over to William, who only now noticed his teacher.

Something about Mr. Critchley was different, Charlie thought. A heightened color on his pale face, a bounce in his step. The deaf boy watched guardedly, as Critchley beckoned William with a jerk of the head to follow him to the window.

Intrigued, Charlie spied on the two men as much as he dared. Miss Cartier would want to know what he saw. Unfortunately, William's back was to him. But Mr. Critchley stood almost opposite. Charlie could see his lips and his gestures and grasp the gist of what he was saying. He seemed to be commanding William to do something. William shook his head, then shrugged his shoulders. Charlie wrote down all the words he could grasp. Miss Cartier could put them together.

Anne sat at the table in her room, Charlie by her side. She laid down her pen and patted the boy's notes together. He had caught much of what Critchley had said and had sketched with a child's simplicity the man's facial expressions and gestures. She faced the boy, then spoke clearly. "Well done, Charlie. I've puzzled out what you saw in the classroom." It seemed the cook was sending the black footman on an errand to the city markets that afternoon. Critchley had ordered William to follow him, apparently suspecting Jeffery would use this opportunity to do something contrary to his master's wishes.

Stroking the boy's head, Anne told him not to let on to Mr. Critchley that he had been watching him.

"I shall not tell him," he said, carefully enunciating each word, obviously pleased at what he had accomplished. Anne gave him a writing exercise, and he returned to his own room.

Leaning against the door, Anne asked herself if she should tell Jeffery he was being followed. He surely knew that already and might resent her prying into his affairs. From servants the night before, Georges had learned that the black man was often seen on Avon Street. Too big to miss, they had agreed. Critchley might have found out what he wanted to know concerning Jeffery and had given William the task merely to keep him busy.

That line of thinking didn't satisfy Anne. Since her visit to *The African Rose*, and the episode in the attic, she had grown concerned for the slave, a huge, powerful man, yet so vulnerable to abuse. Perhaps Critchley wanted to confirm his suspicions before denouncing Jeffery to his master.

She reached into the cabinet for her street clothes. He might not realize the danger to him was serious. Brushing aside her own arguments to the contrary, she decided to follow him and discover what was going on. If he were in trouble, he should be warned before it was too late.

Anne fingered a large worn shawl she had found in a storeroom and pulled it snug over her shoulders. Underneath she was wearing a plain brown woolen dress and on her head a matching bonnet. With a small basket in her hand, she hoped to be taken for a domestic servant. As she crossed the bridge over the River Avon, she saw Jeffery turning left onto the quay. For the direct route to the markets, he should have chosen Horse Street. William Rogers furtively followed him.

The footman carried a large empty basket. A long coat covered his livery. He didn't take any other precautions. He turned right onto Avon Street and made his way through a dense crowd of peddlers, urchins, fish mongers, and other dregs of Bath. He stopped at a seamstress shop next door to The Little Drummer. A half-hour later, still in livery, the basket under his arm, he emerged and continued on Avon Street toward the markets.

Anne debated, should she follow him? She noticed William had ignored the footman's departure and continued to loiter in a doorway opposite the shop. He knows something I don't, Anne thought. She waited, her curiosity aroused.

A few minutes later, a tall, handsome light-skinned black woman about Jeffery's own age left the shop. William fell in behind her. Anne followed them up Avon Street, into Cock Lane, and on to the Quaker Meeting House, where the young woman knocked on a side door. William slipped into an alleyway and watched. The woman knocked again and a small wiry middle-aged man with thick gray hair and high cheek bones greeted her and showed her in. At that point, William shuffled off in the direction of Combe Park. Anne sensed that William had done this before. He seemed bored.

While the woman was inside, Anne made inquiries in the neighborhood and learned that the Quaker, Mr. David Woodhouse, was a leader of the society's anti-slavery movement. He owned a printing shop on St. James's Parade. Several men called him a troublemaker who encouraged slaves to run away from their masters. Local sentiment was generally unfavorable to blacks, accusing them of begging and pilfering. Anne lacked experience with black people, but she doubted the accusations she heard. Though Jeffery was poor, he didn't beg or pilfer. And it seemed shameful for the people of Bath who benefitted in so many ways from slavery to despise its victims.

An hour passed before the woman emerged and returned to her shop. Anne followed. Shortly thereafter, Jeffery reappeared, his basket filled with bread, cheese, and sausages. He entered the seamstress shop and remained for perhaps a half hour, then left with his basket still full. Anne followed him back as far as the bridge, when it became clear he would return to Combe Park.

A plan formed in her mind. She turned around and walked to Milsom Street and Madame Gagnon's shop. As she entered, a frisson of anxiety gripped her stomach. She had met the Frenchwoman only yesterday to borrow a gown, and hesitated to impose on her so soon for a second favor. Paul and Georges had warned she was touchy, but would be helpful if approached with tact.

The milliner greeted Anne politely, eyes wondering. "How may I serve you, Mademoiselle Cartier?"

"I wish to speak to you privately."

The Frenchwoman hesitated a fraction of a second, gave Anne a searching glance, then led her into the back room. When they were alone, Anne explained how the Rogers' black slave's effort to free himself might distract Sir Harry and complicate the pursuit of Fitzroy.

"I need to investigate what he does on Avon Street. The Little Drummer is a good place to start."

Madame Gagnon stepped back, quickly studied Anne's domestic servant's gown. "You can't go like that. The only women there are barmaids and prostitutes. Let's see what I have here." She opened the thespian closet.

A few minutes later, Anne was dressed as a valet in a worn gray suit with black embroidered designs, her facial color dulled with powder. Madame Gagnon gave her an approving pat on the shoulder and opened the rear door. Anne hurried back to Avon Street.

It was nearly three o'clock when she entered The Little Drummer. A half-dozen patrons occupied the public room. She sat alone at a table to the right of the door, her back to the wall. In front of her was the stairway to the first floor rooms. Nearby, three young women were chatting over large mugs of ale while they waited for customers. At a table in the middle of the room a pair of rough seamen slouched in their chairs, talking loudly, their voices slurred with drink. Anne guessed they had come from Bristol for some evil purpose. No one seemed inclined to talk to her.

A barmaid approached. Anne thought she might glean information from her, but, as it turned out, she was new to The Little Drummer and couldn't help. A few minutes later, the seamstress' daughter entered the inn and, to Anne's surprise, took the fourth chair at the nymphs' table. For the young woman didn't carry herself like a prostitute. The young women smiled and called her Sarah. She signaled the publican behind the bar. Nodding, he reached for a mug.

At that moment, the two surly seamen noticed Sarah and exchanged lewd comments loud enough for all to hear. One of them hitched up his breeches and swaggered over to the nymphs' table. "How much?" he asked the young black woman.

"I'm not for sale," she replied curtly and turned her back to him.

The man pulled out a long thin knife, grabbed the woman from behind by the jaw, and set the blade at her throat. "I want some dark meat, understand?" He lifted her to her feet and pushed her toward the stairs.

Anne signaled the publican, a small, older man, who lowered his eyes. The other patrons turned away. The young women sat wide-eyed, paralyzed with fear. Anne waited quietly until the bully passed, then slipped behind him. To negotiate the first step of the stairs, he put the knife between his teeth and reached for the rail. Anne seized his arm and twisted it brutally behind his back. Screaming with pain, he dropped the knife from his mouth and released the woman.

The other seaman leaped from his table, knife drawn, and rushed toward his struggling companion. Half-way across the floor, a pewter mug hit him full in the face. Gathering courage, the young women pelted him with bottles and more mugs. The publican, wielding a thick iron rod, led a few brawny patrons into the fray. Anne pushed her man into their hands and turned to Sarah, who sat dazed on the steps.

"Are you all right?" Anne asked, kneeling in front of her. Blood trickled from a slight cut on her neck. Anne stanched the flow with a clean cloth.

The young woman's eyes blinked, trying to focus. She nodded and breathed, "Thank you."

Anne helped Sarah to her feet. "May I escort you home?" Anne glanced over her shoulder at a commotion behind her. The seamen were being thrown out of the inn, badly beaten and bloody. "I don't think they'll bother you, but let's be careful."

"Yes, I'd be grateful," she replied with the hint of a smile. "I live just next door."

A tiny bell tinkled as the young woman opened the door to the shop. Anne followed her in. A woman at a table looked up from the garment she was sewing. A smile flashed across her broad brown face, then yielded almost instantly to a frown of concern. "What's the matter, Sarah?"

"Nothing serious, Mother." The young woman turned to Anne. "My mother is called Hester, Hester Smith. But I don't know your name, sir."

Anne introduced herself as "Cartier. Monsieur Cartier," a visiting French nobleman's valet. She told Hester what had happened at the inn. The mother's lips parted, her brow furrowed in consternation. She stared at the wound on Sarah's neck. "I'll close the shop and put some ointment and a bandage on that cut. Then we'll have tea."

When Hester had disappeared into the back room, Sarah gazed inquisitively at Anne. "Even visiting valets aren't likely to stop for a pot of ale in The Little Drummer. And they wouldn't bother to save a black woman from a seaman's claws."

She's perceptive, Anne thought, scrutinizing her for a long moment. Her color was much lighter than her mother's; her eyes, a luminous golden brown; her hair, black and curly. She met Anne's gaze frankly. Sensing she could be trusted with the truth, Anne removed her cap, shook out her blond hair, and spoke in her natural voice. "I'm Miss Anne Cartier of Combe Park on a special mission in Bath. It involves you accidentally."

The young woman's eyes grew large, taking in Anne's altered appearance. "I'm delighted to meet you, Miss Cartier. Jeffery has spoken about how you found him in the attic. You were kind to him." Sarah began to clear a small table and beckoned Anne to a chair. "Your disguise is really very good. You must be an actress." She smiled half-apologetically.

"That I am, thank you, though not quite as clever as I had hoped." Anne added, "I followed you and Jeffery today."

Sarah gasped with surprise. "Why?"

"I'm concerned that Jeffery is getting into serious trouble."

"Yes, he's being followed by Mr. Critchley's spies. Jeffery shrugs, takes what precautions he can. I'm helping him. Bath is too small a city for him to escape notice, so eventually Critchley is sure to discover what he's trying to do."

"Why did you go to the Quaker Meeting House?" Anne asked, though she could guess the answer.

"Jeffery wants his freedom. Mr. Woodhouse is making arrangements. Sir Harry doesn't seem to know it yet. In any case, he won't do anything until after the boxing match tomorrow. And then...I think I shouldn't say more."

The mother returned from the back room, stopped in midstep to take in Anne's transformation, then smiled like a person who could not be easily shocked. After applying ointment and a bandage to her daughter's wound, she served tea.

Their conversation shifted to the family. Anne learned that Sarah Smith was twenty-one years old. Her father, a Bristol sea captain, had died a few years ago. Hester, a West Indian mulatto, had been his mistress. Shortly before his death, he had freed her and set her up in this shop. She would have a better life in Bath than in a seaport such as Bristol. He also had seen to his daughter's education. She could read and write and was attempting to teach Jeffery, thus far with modest success.

During the conversation, Anne struggled with a delicate question, not wishing to offend Sarah or seem to pry into her affairs. Finally she found an opportune moment. "I can't help wondering why you sat with the nymphs, giving the appearance that you were one of them."

"I don't resent the question," Sarah said with a patient smile. "The bartender and most of the patrons know who I am and why I'm there. I'm a seamstress like my mother. We make clothes for those women. Nothing I do or say suggests that I wish to sell my body."

"But your manner with the women is friendly...."

"The Pharisees condemned Our Lord Jesus for sitting at table with sinners and for allowing them to touch him. He did not judge them. I follow his example." She held Anne's eye in a steely grip, her voice husky with pent-up passion. "You sit at table with Sir Harry Rogers, a proud greedy man, who carries on a cruel trade in human flesh. I sit with three poor ignorant girls who have no choice but to sell themselves."

"I take your point," said Anne, feeling ashamed. As an actress, she had felt the harsh judgment of modern hypocrites.

A smile softened Sarah's expression, her voice cleared. "The three young women at The Little Drummer are kindly, generous girls, loyal and brave. You saw how they prevented the other sailor from attacking us. I enjoy their company. They see the funny side of life, as well as the misery."

While the young woman spoke, Anne began to feel a kinship with her despite their obvious differences of race and class. They were both independent spirits and lived without regret beyond society's respectable circles.

On the way back to Combe Park, once more in her own dress, Anne sorted out her impressions. Contrary to his master's will, Jeffery had gone to Sarah Smith to learn to read and to make contact with the Quakers. The footman knew he was being followed and would be reported. Sir Harry would surely be furious and resort to drastic measures. Yet, the footman took only simple precautions. He must believe he would be freed very soon.

Anne sensed the making of a tragedy. Jeffery seemed desperate for freedom, prepared to risk everything. She could not bring herself to imagine the consequences.

Chapter 16

Partners

Tuesday, April 3

It was now midmorning. Bath was fully awake; carts and carriages clogged its streets. Colonel Saint-Martin made his way through the traffic on foot to the York Inn. By this time, Georges was trailing after Fitzroy. Anne was somewhere in the city. She had been seen walking from Combe Park, dressed like a housemaid. Curious, he thought, she hadn't left a message. Investigating on her own, he supposed, a little disquieted.

At the entrance, the colonel was surprised by a sudden anxiety at the prospect of meeting Dick Burton. Would he see a conflict of interest between them over Captain Fitzroy? Last night in the Tea Room, the Bow Street officer had asked why Fitzroy had struck Roach. Saint-Martin had told him the rumors concerning Charlie's parentage and the alleged affair between Lady Margaret and Fitzroy. Burton had kept a straight face, had not commented.

That worried the colonel. When engaging Burton to search for Anne last April, he had gathered only a superficial impression of the man. His character and opinions had not been an issue then, but they were now. Burton was a patriotic English policeman and might object to any French attempt to kidnap the rogue Irishman. He might also want Fitzroy as a possible witness against Roach in an extortion trial.

Now was as good a time as any to find out. The colonel squared his shoulders and strode into the inn determined to turn Dick Burton into an ally. After all, they shared the goal of ending Roach's depredations in Bath and his threat to Anne. They would have to negotiate their differences.

At the front desk the colonel inquired after the officer and was directed to the breakfast room. A cool northerly light filtered through lace curtains into the oak-panelled interior. Only a low murmur of voices, an occasional clatter of tableware disturbed the hushed silence.

Saint-Martin paused in the entrance and surveyed the patrons. Few tables were occupied at this hour. The Pump Room was already open and had drawn many of the guests away to the water. The colonel spotted his man sitting by himself at a small table near a window, a newspaper to his left and a pot of coffee to his right.

The colonel took a few steps into the room, then paused for a closer look. Last night had not offered him a good opportunity to study Burton. They had met by candlelight in the hubbub of the Assembly Rooms and had also been distracted by the conflict between Roach and Fitzroy. Now, in the window's cruel daylight, the man looked unhealthy, his face creased and gray, the sabre scar a dull blue line. A cane lay on the floor under his chair.

At the colonel's approach, Burton stirred as if to rise. As he shifted his weight, a brief spasm of pain flashed across his face.

"Stay seated, please." Saint-Martin took the chair opposite the officer.

"Chronic arthritis. It's gotten much worse since we first met. Mornings are hell." Burton smiled wanly. "Couldn't sleep overnight coming from London. My coach hit every bump on the road. Didn't sleep well last night either."

The colonel gazed sympathetically at his ailing companion. "I hope you'll soon feel better. You've come to the right place. Perhaps a hot bath will help."

"Thank you, Colonel. Hot water does usually ease the pain. Didn't help much today. Just got back from King's Bath. I've tried the doctors too. Quacks, every one of them. They've no cure. By the looks of it, Jack Roach will be my last case." He gestured to the pot of coffee. "May I order one for you?"

Although he had breakfasted earlier, Saint-Martin agreed for fellowship's sake and out of self-interest. In view of Burton's infirmity, he might welcome assistance even from a pair of Frenchmen, though he could not be expected to admit it.

Another pot of coffee arrived. Saint-Martin leaned forward to pour, but Burton waved him back and took the pot. "You're my guest. I'm not helpless," he remarked with asperity. Though his hands trembled over the cup, he didn't spill a drop.

While the colonel stirred a lump of sugar into his cup, he reported on Lady Margaret's panicked return to her room in Combe Park. Someone had spied on her with a hidden optical device and had stolen something precious to her from a secret drawer.

"I see the Red Devil's hand in this," said Burton, a hint of admiration in his eyes. "Provoking Fitzroy was a clever ploy."

"A skillful villain, indeed," said Saint-Martin, his voice heavy with scorn. He surmised that Roach's criminal talents had won the officer's respect over the year he had been pursuing him. The colonel went on to describe how the theft had thrown Fitzroy into a fury and led him to beat Lady Margaret.

Leaning back in his chair, Burton listened attentively and asked a few brief questions. When Saint-Martin finished, the Bow Street officer sat up, took a drink from his cup. "Whatever was stolen concerned Fitzroy in some way and had been wrongly concealed from him. Love letters, I'd guess. Sounds like evidence Roach would want to sell to Harry Rogers."

"But if Critchley still has it," countered Saint-Martin, "he might try to bargain with Roach. Or, better yet, ignore Roach and sell directly to Rogers."

Burton shook his head. "And risk Roach's wrath? Not likely."

Saint-Martin raised a warning finger. "Consider Captain Fitzroy. To save what he has invested in Lady Margaret, he might lash out at Roach." He handed Burton a basket of bread and a pot of butter. "By the way, Roach must also be behind Critchley's spying on Jeffery. What should we make of that?"

The officer smiled his thanks and buttered a roll. "Roach can't expect to extort money from a black slave. Perhaps he could force him to spy on Lady Margaret. Or, he might try to influence the boxing match tomorrow and hedge his bet."

Saint-Martin idly stirred his coffee, drank slowly. His inner gaze focused on Jack Roach, trying vainly to grasp the man's mind. Exasperated, he looked up at his companion. "Roach may be juggling more balls than he can manage."

Burton rose stiffly from the table and reached for his cane. "Let's watch him."

The Pump Room was doing a lively business as Saint-Martin and Burton entered. They looked around for Roach, but he wasn't to be seen. This morning, the room seemed filled with bent middle-aged men shuffling painfully about, clutching glasses of hot spring water. Burton stared at them, then bent over, tapped his cane, and mimicked their grimaces. "I'll soon come to this," he snapped. In the next instant, he straightened up and turned to Saint-Martin. "Sorry for the self-pity."

The colonel smiled reassuringly. "Perhaps the water will help." With Burton hobbling behind, Saint-Martin pressed through the crowd. At the counter he bumped into Madame Gagnon. "Pardon," he said, startled.

"Good morning, Colonel Saint-Martin! What a pleasant surprise!" she exclaimed in French, then noticed the companion behind him. If she were concerned she had compromised herself, she didn't show it. She turned back to the counter, paid the attendant, and took her glass.

Saint-Martin had no choice but to introduce her to Burton, adding, "Madame Gagnon owns a fine millinery shop on Milsom Street." He dared not reveal her connection to Baron Breteuil, a secret best shielded from the sharp prying eyes of a Bow Street officer. The government might call upon him one day to investigate French espionage in Britain.

Saint-Martin placed an order at the counter and wondered how to disarm Burton's suspicion. The officer was surely asking himself how a French colonel, apparently on a secret mission to Bath, had come to know this woman. To say they had met accidentally in her shop, or at church, or any other simple lie would insult Burton's intelligence. Saint-Martin opted for a partial truth.

He handed the officer a filled glass. "Madame Gagnon and I have a mutual interest in restraining Jack Roach. He's as troublesome to some of her customers as he is to Miss Cartier."

Burton's eyebrow arched a bit. He raised his glass in a mocking toast to Roach. "Amazing! He touches so many lives!" He bowed to the milliner. "Would you allow me, Madame, to pay you a call and discuss his depredations in greater detail?"

She took his measure with a glance. "Of course," she replied, "I'm across the street from the Somerset and Avon Bank." With a wave and a wink, she disappeared.

Roach arrived a few minutes later, looking pleased with himself. He strutted through the room, greeting almost everyone on his way to the counter. A glass of hot spring water in his hand, he surveyed the crowd like a bird of prey.

Observing Roach from a few paces away, Burton leaned toward Saint-Martin and whispered, "You have to give the Red Devil credit. He enjoys his business."

"But he's so brazen about it."

"With the excisemen behind him, he thinks he can't be touched."

When Critchley arrived, Roach's face brightened. They exchanged a few words. Roach appeared momentarily startled, then frowned. He beckoned Critchley to follow him from the Pump Room.

Saint-Martin and Burton set off after them, the latter limping, grimacing with pain. Roach and Critchley crossed the church yard through a light mist, walked around the Abbey Church, and continued through Orange Grove to the wall near the river.

Despite the cool wet weather, small clusters of people were walking in the grove, offering cover to Saint-Martin and Burton. They drew close enough to see the two men, but could not hear what they said. In the shelter of a tree Saint-Martin raised his small jointed telescope to observe their facial expressions and gestures. Suddenly, Roach shoved a hand forward as if to demand something. Critchley jumped back a step, shaking his head violently. Roach took a step forward, raised his fist to within an inch of Critchley's face and screwed up his features into a fierce scowl.

"Mon Dieu!" Saint-Martin murmured. "They are close to blows." He lowered the telescope and handed it to Burton. "I think Roach desperately wants whatever Critchley has stolen from Lady Margaret. And Critchley refuses to give it up. If that's the case, why doesn't Critchley go directly to Sir Harry?"

Burton peered through the telescope for a few minutes, then said softly, "Because Roach has power over Critchley and is threatening him. They are probably arguing over a price. Critchley wants too much and doesn't trust Roach to pay."

Roach turned abruptly on his heels and stalked away toward the bridge to Spring Gardens. Critchley left in the direction of Combe Park.

Burton lowered the telescope and turned to Saint-Martin. "One of the balls Roach was juggling has just gotten out of control."

Early in the afternoon, Saint-Martin and Burton returned hungry to the York Inn. As they entered the public room, the aroma of beef stew and ale teased their nostrils. Patrons coming and going jostled with waiters serving the tables. Dishes clattered above the general din of voices.

The two men exchanged glances and engaged a small private room. At the recommendation of an honest-looking waiter, they ordered the stew and ale. After serving them, the waiter left a large pot of ale and a bottle of brandy on a sideboard. The door closed behind him.

Saint-Martin broached a matter that had intrigued him earlier. "Back in Orange Grove, you said Roach had a hold on Critchley. Would you mind telling me what you meant?"

Burton put down his fork, then swallowed a mouthful of ale. "From following Roach in London, I've learned he has employed Critchley as a spy before, especially in the homes and offices of wealthy merchants. I reasoned there had to be a dark spot in his past that Roach knew about. Eventually, I discovered that an employer had discharged Critchley under suspicion of having stolen a large quantity of silver plate. He escaped arrest and hanging because the Bow Street magistrate could not confirm the accusation or find the silver. I suspect he sold it to a fence whom Roach knew. He could have informed against Critchley and collected a reward, but chose instead to use him as a spy and earn more money through extortion. Roach can hand him over to the magistrate any time he wishes."

"Then Critchley's little more than a slave—one who surely hates his master."

"There's no love lost between them." Burton turned his attention back to his stew.

Conversation lagged until they finished their meal. Then, in search of common ground, Saint-Martin remarked, "You mentioned earlier having served with British forces at Minden." He cast a glance at the old soldier's scar. "My father was also there...on the French side. Lieutenant-General of Cavalry. He died of his wounds."

"I was lucky to have escaped with just this." Burton stroked the scar, then reached for the bottle of brandy and filled their glasses. "At the time, I hardly knew what happened. Thick smoke blanketed the battle field. French horsemen came upon us by surprise, sabers slashing, hooves pounding. In an instant, the battle ended for me. I awoke an hour later in a sea of blood and gore. French and British dead lay together all around me in a jumbled mass. I took no pleasure in our victory and vowed to serve God and country in another way."

The officer seemed to slip into reverie. His eyes gazed into a distant past. Saint-Martin leaned back in his chair and sipped quietly, recalling his father away at war and his mother in deep depression.

The silence of the room jarred Burton into the present. "Colonel, your father and I could have met at Minden." His voice was full of sadness. "The ways of Providence are puzzling! You would have been very young then."

"Ten."

"With no father. What became of you?"

"First, a cadet in the royal military academy, then a commission in the cavalry and service in America. After the war, a provost of the Royal Highway Patrol. Since the last time we met, I've broken up a ring of jewel thieves—with Miss Cartier and my adjutant, Georges, deserving most of the credit."

"You are too modest," Burton observed, toasting him with a glass of brandy. "A colonel and provost before the age of forty!"

Feeling self-conscious, Saint-Martin changed the subject. "And after Minden...how *did* you serve God and country?"

"I've hardly covered myself with glory," Burton replied. "Innkeeper for several years, then constable for as many more, and finally an officer of the Bow Street Court. I've sent scores of rogues to Newgate, where I hope to put Jack Roach."

Saint-Martin had noticed early on that Burton posed shrewd questions. His modest manner, his friendly face invited trust and must have enticed confessions from many a felon. When they first met more than a year ago, Saint-Martin had judged him to be a plodding, unimaginative sort. His speech indicated he was largely self-taught. Now, it was clear that he plodded according to well-considered plans and with sound insight into the criminal mind. Like an old experienced hunting dog, he would sooner or later run Roach to ground.

Leaving the York with his companion, Saint-Martin felt as if they had become partners. They shook hands. "Colonel," said the Bow Street man, "I believe I'll have a little chat with Madame Gagnon this afternoon. Might learn something new about the Red Devil." He winked to Saint-Martin as they parted.

Chapter 17

Confrontation

Tuesday, April 3

As twilight gathered over Combe Park, Colonel Saint-Martin sat at his table reflecting. It had been an eventful day: Critchley's theft of Lady Margaret's hidden secret, Anne's rescue of Sarah Smith at the Little Drummer, the new partnership with the Bow Street officer. And, there might be more. He glanced at his watch. He should have heard from his adjutant by this time. Could Fitzroy have become suspicious and tricked Georges or caused him harm? Saint-Martin shook off his anxiety. Georges might sometimes play the clown, but he was alert and cautious when in danger.

The colonel bent over the small account book he would present to Baron Breteuil at the end of this mission. The baron had set no limit on expenses, but would expect an accurate accounting. The colonel paused to study Georges' most recent report. He had paid out two hundred and fifty pounds in the past few days to various watchmen, inn keepers, chairbearers, cooks, maids, and other servants, and had promised at least as much to come. A useful network of informants did not come cheap. And there wasn't much time. With conflicts at Combe Park coming to a head, reliable information was essential. Baron Breteuil would agree.

Saint-Martin put the baron's account book aside and opened his own. How much could he afford to wager on Lord Jeff tomorrow? In the public rooms on the floor below, Sir Harry and dozens of sportsmen were engaged in a betting frenzy. The colonel had promised to join them.

Unlike most men of his class, Saint-Martin was not in the habit of betting. But he wanted to offer moral support to the black man, in whom he recognized a worthy spirit. Jeffery had the physical strength and courage of a warrior, combined with uncommon modesty and gentleness. A noble savage, as fashionable writers would say. And a skillful, well-trained boxer into the bargain. Saint-Martin quickly calculated his future expenses and reached a decision. One hundred pounds on Lord Jeff to win, risking the price of a fine horse.

There was a familiar knock at the door. Two short raps followed by two long ones. Saint-Martin put away the account books and opened for Georges. The stocky adjutant's face glowed with excitement. "Just got back. Guess what I learned in Bristol!" He went on to describe Fitzroy's visit to the port city and the American ship.

Saint-Martin listened with growing disbelief. "Do you really think Fitzroy intends to sail away and abandon Lady Margaret?" He motioned to the table and sat opposite his adjutant.

Georges thought for a moment before replying. "Fitzroy's a military man, trying to secure his rear. The ship to New York is his way out, if he needs it. He will probably try to resolve his conflict with Sir Harry before that American ship leaves Bristol. A duel perhaps, if the occasion arises. Or an assassination, carried out on his behalf by the two red-coated rogues who guard him. With Sir Harry out of the way, Fitzroy could marry the rich widow."

Saint-Martin furrowed his brow, still skeptical. "Sir Harry can deduce Fitzroy's motives as well as we. He'll anticipate the captain's moves and set a trap."

"They remind me," said Georges, "of two cats circling each other, looking for a chance to strike."

"Then we must come between them and prevent the fight if we are to steal Fitzroy away to France."

"We're likely to get scratched."

The colonel smiled. "No matter."

Georges tapped nervously on the table. "Where's Miss Cartier? I've asked Lord Jeff to keep an eye on her."

"In the ballroom," Saint-Martin replied, "singing for Sir Harry's guests. She followed Jeff this morning. Discovered he visits a young lady on Avon Street and is also making plans to flee Combe Park and become a free man."

"Good God! We're sitting on a volcano. If Jeff leaves, Sir Harry will erupt."

"And put our plans in jeopardy," added Saint-Martin. "I can hardly fault the slave for seeking his freedom, but I wish he'd do it after we've laid hold of Fitzroy." He walked over to the mirror, palmed his hair back. "I'll join the party downstairs and place a bet on Jeff."

The colonel made his way to the public rooms, amazed by the feverish atmosphere that reigned throughout the house: music and dancing in the ballroom, games of chance in the drawing room, food and drink in the dining room, betting everywhere. Distinguished visitors including the Duke of Portland were joining the crowd and placing bets. At the match tomorrow there would be more betting before and during the contest. Betting had become a consuming passion at Combe Park. Saint-Martin had seldom seen anything like it.

In the hallway, a servant told him that Sir Harry was in his study making final arrangements for tomorrow. Rogers and several other sportsmen had organized the match at a ruined abbey on the estate of Lord Bascombe, an earl who appreciated pugilistic prowess. The site was beyond the reach of magistrates who might otherwise condemn the match as a disorderly assembly. A crowd of thousands would come from Bath and London.

The door to Sir Harry's study swung open as Saint-Martin approached. Sir Harry strode out, leading a group of his sporting acquaintances, their faces flushed and jovial. "Colonel Saint-Martin! Come with us." They had apparently enjoyed a glass or two of Sir Harry's port wine. "We're on our way to the tennis hall to watch Lord Jeff spar with Sam the Bath butcher." Sir Harry took a boxer's stance—arms raised, fists clenched, and playfully traded punches with several like-minded sportsmen nearby. "These gentlemen want to see our bruisers before they settle on the size of their bets."

Jeffery was virtually unknown outside Somerset, while his opponent, Thomas Futrell, had fought in the presence of the Prince of Wales and was a celebrity throughout England. Most of this evening's visitors to Combe Park would bet heavily on him.

On the way to the tennis hall, Saint-Martin and Sir Harry ignored the drizzle and fell amiably in step. The Frenchman felt free to ask how he had come by his remarkable interest in boxing.

"It began dockside in Bristol," he replied, pleased to explain. "As a young man, I had to fight with brains and fists to earn respect from the brutes I worked with. I went on to rule the docks, then my ship, and finally my business. A year ago, on a trip to Jamaica, I discovered this slave, a young footman named Jeffery, fast as lightening, clever, strong as an ox. He was boxing for his master on a local market day."

Rogers' voice grew excited, his fists clenched, as if he were transported back to that match. "I learned that my own *African Rose* had brought him to Jamaica as a boy. I bought him on the spot. He was a natural fighter. Knocked out his opponent in ten minutes. I took him with me to Bristol, trained him, and put him in several easy local fights. Then I brought in the Jew, Dan Mendoza, the best boxer in London, who sparred with him, polished his style."

"Are you confident Jeff is ready to fight a national champion?" Saint-Martin asked.

"Confident?" Sir Harry chuckled. "Thus far, I've bet five thousand pounds on him at odds of two to one, and I expect to bet more. I grant you, Lord Jeff is smaller than Futrell but he's faster and in better condition. I sent Peter Hyde to London two weeks ago to watch Futrell in training. Peter says the man's slack and careless, hardly works up a sweat—claims he'll toy with Jeff for a while to please the crowd, then pound him to pieces."

Sir Harry patted Saint-Martin on the shoulder. "Colonel, mark my word. Tom Futrell is in for the surprise of his life. By tomorrow night, Lord Jeff is going to be the talk of Britain. Put your money on him."

As they entered the hall, Saint-Martin noticed that Captain Fitzroy and his two British army friends had already arrived and were watching the two fighters limber their muscles. Upon seeing Fitzroy, Sir Harry stiffened, snorted. With a brusk toss of his head, he led his companions to the opposite side of the sparring ring.

This was a light workout for Jeffery, who dodged the charges of his heavier partner and parried his powerful blows. An impartial observer might well have wondered whether the black man had the strength and the will to carry the fight to his opponent. Had Sir Harry designed this exercise to encourage the odds against his man? Paul asked himself.

After the two men had sparred for several minutes, Captain Fitzroy walked nonchalantly around the ring to Sir Harry. "I saw Tom Futrell fight in London. He'll beat your black man to bloody pulp."

"Do you think so, Captain?" remarked Sir Harry, loudly enough to be heard throughout the hall.

"Certainly," the Irishman replied. "Everyone knows that blacks are ignorant cowards. A manly bruiser like Futrell will bring craven fear to the eyes of your Lord Jeff." Heads turned toward the two men. The room grew quiet. The boxers lowered their mittened fists and returned to their corners.

"Then, Captain, you should be glad to back Futrell with the treasure you brought from France."

"Indeed, sir!" Fitzroy's words dripped venom. "I'll bet one thousand pounds your black beggar doesn't last a half-hour."

"Agreed, Captain," hissed Rogers through clenched teeth. On the spot, he wrote down the wager. Both men signed the chit, then stood for a moment glaring at each other. Saint-Martin could feel the hatred between them. Fitzroy beckoned his friends and they marched out.

"Good riddance," snarled Rogers as they left. He addressed the others, "Gentlemen, we shall return now to my study and place our bets." He nodded to Saint-Martin to join them and strode out of the room.

Anne sang the last words of her song, bowed to scattered applause, and stepped down from the chancel stage onto the ballroom floor. During the intermission, guests milled about in noisy conversation. Many were tipsy. She found herself alone in the crowd. Paul was with other gentlemen wagering in Sir Harry's study, and Georges was waiting on thirsty visitors in the dining room. Anne felt restless, tired, and hot.

If the weather had been fair, the windows would have been open. The crowd would have spilled out into the garden. Unfortunately, the weather was cold and wet, and the servants had closed the windows. The air had become unfit to breathe, the din intolerable. Though wearing only the light red gown Madame Gagnon had lent her, Anne escaped to the chilly, deserted portico off the entrance foyer. At the stone balustrade, she looked out over the mist covered city below her in the distance. A breeze stung her face with icy pellets.

She soon shivered from the cold and was about to go back inside when she sensed someone approach from behind. Before she could react, a hand clamped over her mouth, an arm gripped her across the chest, and a large heavy body pressed her up against the balustrade.

"I've been busy, but I haven't forgotten you."

Jack Roach, Anne realized with horror. She clawed at his arm, tearing his sleeve and scratching him. She tried to kick him, but her feet ripped her gown and became ensnared.

She felt his hot breath on her neck. "You fooled us on the Bristol Road," he whispered in her ear. "Met us like a goddam army. This time, you won't get away. Critchley's waiting down there to break your neck. Another accident, like Mary Campbell's." He lifted her up, as if to throw her over the balustrade to the flagstones some twenty feet below.

As he shifted his grip, she worked her mouth free and bit hard on his finger.

"Damn bitch!" His grip on her body loosened.

She jerked her head back violently. Bone struck soft flesh.

He uttered an obscene curse, tried to regain his grip.

She freed her feet and pushed away from the balustrade.

Suddenly, he released her. Anne spun around and saw Roach's face in the low, diffused light from the foyer. His eyes bulged. His mouth, twisted with pain, uttered soundless curses. Jeffery's powerful right hand was squeezing the nape of his neck in a vice-like grip. The footman duck-walked the bully across the portico and shoved him into the foyer.

By now, Anne was trembling from the cold and shock, one of Roach's buttons clutched in her hand. Jeffery pulled off his coat and threw it over her shoulders, then leaned toward her with a heart-warming smile, the first from him. "Sarah told me what you did for her at The Little Drummer. We're grateful." He paused, inspecting her carefully. "Are you hurt?"

"You arrived just in time," Anne spluttered, still trying to catch her breath. She struggled on in a worried voice, "He said Critchley's down below."

Jeffery leaped to the balustrade and looked over. "Nobody's there now." He returned to her. "I saw Mr. Critchley in the house just a few minutes ago. The Red Devil may have lied to frighten you."

"Yes, that must give him pleasure. But, one day, he will try again in earnest to kill me," said Anne in a voice so matter-of-fact that it startled her. Was she becoming fatalistic, losing control of her own destiny? "We should leave now, Jeffery. Please take care. It's true what they say about Roach. He always gets even—or tries to. You've just humiliated him."

He acknowledged her concern with a slight bow, then frowned. "I should report him to Sir Harry." His voice lacked conviction.

"Don't bother." Anne realized Sir Harry would regard the incident as a mere trifle since Roach hadn't hurt her. If accused, he would claim he had only been trying to steal a kiss. She would pass on to Paul and Georges his odd incriminating remark about Mary Campbell and Critchley. Another lie?

At the door to the hall, she returned Jeffery's coat and they stepped inside. Suddenly, persons nearby began staring at them. Some were snickering.

Georges came out of the crowd. "What happened?" he whispered. "First, Jack Roach stumbles through the door with blood pouring from his lips, his sleeve ripped. Then, you and..." He glanced at Jeffery, who was moving away, then at Anne. "Look at your dress! and your hair! You're a mess!"

Anne studied herself. The muslin was torn, smeared with blood, and a dirty gray where she had rubbed against the balustrade. "Roach tried to throw me off the portico. Jeffery saved me." Anne suddenly felt faint and leaned on Georges. "I'd better go to my room. Help me please."

Music from the party below drifted up to Anne's room. She was combing her hair in front of the mirror. After Georges left, she had changed to a soft rose woolen gown. Her cheeks were pale. The back of her head hurt where she had butted Roach. Her torn red gown lay strewn over a chair. Anger might come later. Now she felt cold, numb.

A soft knock on the door. She opened to Paul. He gazed at her, his brow lined with concern. "Are you well?"

"No serious damage. Just shock. Roach took me by surprise again."

"Georges told me everything. Who would have imagined Roach would dare to attack you on the portico while a party was going on in the next room! Fortunately, Jeffery was looking after you. We owe him a big favor." He took her hands, drew her near, and kissed her.

"Roach is toying with me, like a cat with a mouse," murmured Anne tremulously and held him close. "I don't feel safe anywhere."

"That's what he wants, but you made him pay for his pleasure. We shall find a way to stop him."

"What do you make of his remark about Mary Campbell?"

"Poor girl!" He stroked Anne's hair. "If she were pushed, Critchley might have done it—he no longer has an alibi. In this instance, Roach might have spoken the truth. Who can say?"

Anne drew back. "If so, then, did Critchley act alone? Roach would appear involved somehow. How else would he know what happened?"

"Perhaps he found out from someone he has engaged to spy on Critchley."

"William?"

"He's virtually Critchley's shadow.... But enough of that." Paul embraced her again. "Let's talk about us."

She pressed her head against his chest, heard his heart beat. Desire for him kindled in her body. His touch grew urgent.

Footsteps outside the door. Georges' familiar knock, then his voice. "Colonel, the Duke of Portland's expecting you in the dining room."

"In a minute," Paul shouted back, then muttered, "I'll strangle Georges one of these days." His face grew taut with unrequited desire. "It's no use, Anne. I must leave."

"Yet another time, another place?" She pouted for a moment, then smiled tenderly. "Just teasing, Paul. It can't be helped." She returned to the mirror and picked up her comb.

He stood behind her, strong hands stroking her shoulders. "Do you feel fit enough to return to the party and watch Captain Fitzroy and Lady Margaret?"

She lowered the comb, her jaw set firmly. "Yes, I'll go downstairs in a few minutes and find them."

"They're at the faro table in the drawing room." Paul gazed at her fondly in the mirror and caressed her cheek. "After I've finished with the duke, I must see what's become of Jack Roach." He leaned over, kissed her again, then left.

Anne stared at the mirror, her fingers feeling her cheek. Its color had returned. Paul had a healing touch. She listened to the sound of his steps fading away in the hall.

Anne found Lady Margaret still at the faro table, losing money but apparently enjoying herself. Fitzroy was not to be seen. He must have left Combe Park with his usual companions, Tarleton and Corbett. Anne was debating whether to stay in the drawing room, when a servant approached her with a message. Sir Harry wanted to see her in his study.

He was in fine fettle, sitting back in a large leather chair, a glass of port wine on the table by his side. His eyes were bright, his face florid. Clearly, he was exhilarated by the approaching contest. He rose to his feet as she entered, took her hand, and led her to the chair opposite his.

"A glass of port?" he asked with a smile.

Immediately on her guard, Anne wondered, what was he aiming at? But she replied politely, "No thank you."

"I've been thinking," he went on, settling back in his chair. He took a sip of his port. "I want Charlie to watch tomorrow's battle and learn about courage and manliness."

Anne's heart sank. The boy would learn nothing of the kind. More likely, he'd be amused by the raucous crowd and excited by the brutality of the combat. True courage and manliness would be learned elsewhere.

Rogers put his glass to the side and leaned forward, meeting Anne's eye. "And you, as his tutor, shall accompany him and help him understand the sport."

"Begging your pardon, sir, but...."

He cut her off with a wave of his hand. "You will claim that, as a woman, you can't be expected to stomach such a brutal sport. Rubbish! You may not grasp its finer points. Colonel Saint-Martin and other amateurs can help you there. But you *do* understand man to man combat. I've watched you. Lord Jeff's sparring with Sam fascinates you. Another woman would turn her face away. Your eyes follow every blow. You don't even flinch!"

Anne rose from her chair. Rogers' contempt for Charlie's feelings angered her. She was also disturbed by the insulting tenor of his remarks. "Our agreement," she said levelly, "allows *me* to decide how I shall tutor your son. I want him to remain at home tomorrow." She started toward the door.

In an instant, Rogers placed himself in her way. He seemed to have ignored what she had just said. Though he didn't raise his fists, yet he adopted in every other respect the posture of a bruiser—chest out, left foot forward, body tense. From his superior height he glared at Anne, a smirk on his face. "You are the ideal woman to train my son, to put steel in his backbone. You have experienced physical combat—and part of you must have enjoyed it. In Sadler's Wells, you beat Jack Roach to the floor with a chamber pot. Wonderful! I'm sorry I wasn't there to see it."

Dear Harriet! Anne thought. What have you not told your Harry Rogers!

"Just two days ago," he went on, "you wounded a pair of highwaymen on the Bristol road." He raised his fists, huge as hams, and inched closer to her. His eyes narrowed and darkened. "If I were to attack now, you would fight like a she-tiger with fang and claw."

The air in the room grew deathly still, as if he and she were awaiting a signal. Anne sensed Rogers was wound up tight, a steel spring at the point of snapping. A false move on her part and he might strike. Her heart pounding, she gathered her courage, gazed at him with a steady eye, and stood her ground.

After a few seconds, Rogers lowered his fists and stepped aside. "Charlie will attend the fight, with or without you."

Anne hesitated a moment. Rogers' eyes had grown cold and distant. The boy's fate was determined. Further protest was pointless. She squared her shoulders, raised her chin, and said firmly, "I'll go, for Charlie's sake."

Chapter 18

The Battle

Wednesday, April 4

Clouds scudded across an overcast sky as the coach left Combe Park, Peter Hyde driving and Georges at his side. Unpromising weather for the match, Anne thought. Rain seemed likely. She sighed at the prospect of a long, tedious journey, then an hour or more in a cold, soggy field, watching two big men batter one another, while thousands frantically placed bets on the outcome. But she had to go, never mind that she'd be the only woman in a crowd of raving madmen. Early this morning, Sir Harry had routed Charlie out of bed and ordered him to attend the fight. At risk of a beating, he had whimpered, pleaded to stay home but had yielded when told Anne would go with him.

The traffic out of Bath was a veritable exodus, as if every grown man were leaving the city. Coaches of all shapes and sizes rattled eastward on the road to Calne. Hoping to find a silver lining in the day's dark prospect, Anne stole a glance at Paul sitting opposite her. His eyes were bright with anticipation. The contest seemed to have captured his imagination.

She wasn't surprised. Curiosities of British life, like boxing, fascinated his inquiring spirit. This match took on special meaning for him because it involved Jeffery. Anne had noticed

Paul taking a more personal interest in the footman and his dangerous passion for freedom. Yesterday, he had inquired about her meeting with Sarah Smith and the Quaker and said something must be done.

The coach left Somerset behind and rolled on eastward into the Wiltshire countryside. A pale sun thrust thin rays through dark bundled clouds. Halfway to the site, the sky cleared enough for Anne to enjoy fresh green pastures, pink and white apple blossoms, and wild flowers blooming in the hedges along the road. Charlie slumped in his seat next to Anne, listless and morose, taking no notice of the beauties of spring.

Anne nudged him and asked, "What's the matter?"

"Mother wouldn't see me this morning. Said she was sick."

Sick indeed, Anne recalled. Lady Rogers had drunk far too much brandy last night and had to be carried to bed. To rally the boy, Anne reached into the bag at her feet and pulled out several *Punch and Judy* hand puppets. Charlie sat up, his interest piqued. Anne offered him a choice of the clown Scaramouche or Punch. To her surprise, the boy frowned, pointed to Punch, and said clearly, "Father." Then he picked for himself the clown's dog Toby. Anne and Paul chose the remaining characters.

A ragged version of the play ensued. The boy became curiously absorbed in the story and oblivious to the players. It hadn't gone far when Anne realized he was acting out his resentment toward his father. When Punch beat his wife Joan, the dog Toby snarled, then bit Punch viciously and with relish, and hid from sight under the boy's coat. An odd expression of satisfaction came over his face. Anne exchanged worried glances with Paul. Charlie clearly recognized the discord between his parents and took his mother's part. His resentment toward his father was deeper than Anne had suspected.

This concern retreated to the back of Anne's mind as the coach drew near to Lord Bascombe's estate. They met excited countrymen on foot pouring through gaps in the hedges and down narrow lanes, swelling the flood toward the site of the match. Bailiffs at the estate's main gate collected a shilling per head. A day's wages for many of the men, Anne calculated, but they smiled as they paid it, eager for the spectacle, eager to bet more.

At eleven-thirty, the coach reached the edge of a wide natural bowl now rapidly filling with men. Anne gazed down a grassy slope to the abbey ruins, a large picturesque enclosure on a low rise of land at the base of the bowl. The boxing ring, a raised platform covered by a canvas, stood in what was once the transept of an immense church. Its fragmented vine-covered walls rose chest high in some places. The walls of the apse, pierced by empty Gothic windows, stood one full story. The sanctuary, once the most sacred place in the church, now served as a gambling venue, a scene of false good cheer among gentlemen placing bets. Often for large sums, she guessed. Her only previous experience of bare-knuckle fighting was in a village market place where brawny countrymen battled one another for a few shillings.

For a moment Anne closed her eyes, blotting out the present travesty of the place and encouraging her imagination to transform the ruins into an outdoor garden theater and the gentlemen into a cast of players. What a perfect setting for *A Midsummer Night's Dream*! She recalled those golden summers at Chateau Beaumont with her as Puck and her stepfather Antoine as Bottom.

A bailiff's shout brought her back into the present. He directed the coachman to the place Sir Harry had reserved in what had once been the church's choir. Black-robed monks had sung their ancient chants there. Spectators now perched awkwardly on the great stone bases of long-gone pillars. Vendors sold food and drink, and burly footmen and grooms kept the peace.

The passengers climbed down from the coach to stretch and look about. "Paul!" Anne exclaimed, venturing forth a few steps, "I never dreamed this would be such an enormous project. And, it's *illegal!*" The magistrates of Bath and many other cities had declared such contests to be disorderly assemblies and forbade them. This assembly seemed orderly enough.

"Lord Bascombe's the law on his own estate and an avid sportsman," Paul explained. "I wonder about his financial interest in this match."

Peter Hyde leaned over from the coachman's seat. "Begging your pardon, sir, but I overheard Sir Harry this morning speaking to a sporting gentleman as they were about to leave Combe Park."

Paul glanced up and smiled. "Peter, my good man, we would be grateful for whatever you can tell us."

The man climbed nimbly down from his perch. Thick-set and middle-aged, he was still agile. His battered nose told Anne that he had been in the ring often in his younger days.

"Sir Harry don't mind me listening in. We often chat about famous pugilists I've known. And I've helped train Lord Jeff."

"So what have you learned about today's match?" asked Paul.

Hyde glanced left and right conspiratorially. "Lord Bascombe's the real winner! Five thousand men have come to watch the mayhem and give up two thousand five hundred pounds for the privilege—most of it from the Quality. His Lordship will observe the bloody proceedings from his grand coach." Hyde nodded to an open space near the ring. "It should arrive shortly and park there."

His voice took on an ironic tone. "At the end he will count out two thousand pounds for himself, then hand two hundred to the winner and fifty to the loser. What's left will go to expenses. His Lordship has also bet on Lord Jeff and hopes to put several thousand more into his pockets."

"There's much more money in this sport than I had ever imagined," Paul remarked with a hint of awe in his voice.

"Yes indeed, sir! Gentlemen are coming from as far away as London and beyond. The cream of the sporting set will be here, except for the Prince of Wales, who had another engagement." He pointed out a few coaches emblazoned with noble shields parked just beyond an outer ring surrounding the inner ring of combat.

Anne took her spyglass from her bag and surveyed the crowd. Within the outer ring, the timekeeper and the two umpires had gathered to confer. Vigilant guards, called whippers-out, kept the crowd from encroaching. Sir Harry, his face florid with excitement, was speaking with other backers and organizers near the ring. His archenemy, Captain Fitzroy, stood beyond the outer circle with Tarleton and Corbett, their gold epaulets shining in the sun. They had joined a group of fashionable young gentlemen drinking from silver flasks. Anne pointed them out to Paul.

He laughed. "If Jeff wins, Fitzroy will be a poor man." He explained that last night, goaded by Sir Harry, the captain had risked the money he had carried out of France and bet it on Tom Futrell.

Shifting the spyglass, Anne saw Jack Roach slouched against a ruined column, his red coat hanging over his arm. A pair of hard-faced ruffians accompanied him. A few steps away lurked Dick Burton, unobtrusive in a plain gray suit.

Roach glanced at his watch, then whispered in the ear of one of his companions. Seconds later, bailiffs parted the crowd. Jeffery and his handlers made their entrance, passing in front of Roach. Anne focused her spyglass on the black man. He turned his head sharply to the left. Roach must have called his name. Anne switched quickly to Roach, who faced her and spoke full-mouthed. "You shall pay, black bugger!"

Jeffery stopped, stared at him for a moment without replying, then looked straight ahead and went on his way toward the ring.

"*How* shall Jeffery pay?" Anne asked Paul, then explained to him what she had seen.

"Certainly sounds like retaliation for humiliating Roach on the portico. I guess Roach must have uncovered Jeff's secret dealings with the Abolitionists and threatens to expose him."

At that moment, Futrell and his handlers made their appearance. Paul asked the coachman for his opinion of Jeffery's opponent.

"He's a champion pugilist, comes from Birmingham," Hyde began, pleased to have been asked. He went on to describe Futrell. He had won over a dozen matches. His brute strength was legendary. "Look at the size of him," exclaimed the coachman, pointing to the bruiser, now stripped to the waist. He stood on the far side of the ring, barrel-chested, towering over the small circle of his handlers. Two of them were experienced pugilists, to judge from their battered looks. "Will Ward and Richard Humphries," said the coachman, who claimed to know them both.

Jeffery stood at the ringside closest to the coach in a similar circle of men. Hyde identified one of them as Dan Mendoza, a Jew and a very clever fighter, who had given Jeff some helpful lessons. Mendoza left the circle and tied a crimson scarf, Jeffery's colors, to the nearest corner post. On the opposite post hung Futrell's black scarf.

As noon approached, a fanfare of trumpets sounded. Jeffery and his opponent climbed into the ring. The murmur of the crowd grew to a roar. Charlie gaped at the boxers. When the umpires beckoned them to the center of the ring, Charlie turned anxiously to Anne and asked, "Will Jeff get hurt?"

"I hope not," she replied, concealing her fears from him. Boxers sometimes maimed or even killed one another in these contests. Taking the boy's hand, she led him back into the coach and settled down to watch the match from the windows. Paul and Georges stood outside. The coachman resumed his perch in the driver's seat.

Anne expected the brutality of the contest to offend her, but she must watch it to know how well Jeffery would do.

After the fight, she would report the results to Sarah Smith in case Jeffery could not visit her. The two fighters stood a yard apart, poised for battle. The crowd taunted them, goaded them to destroy each other. Her concern for Jeffery grew. A dread settled in the pit of her stomach.

~~~

At the umpires' signal, Jeff had stridden up to the scratch line and faced his opponent. The roar of the crowd seemed to fade away. For a few moments, Jeff stood alone with his thoughts. He trembled with wonder and amazement. How strange a path he had taken to this point in his life: from his family's home in Africa to a sugar plantation in Jamaica, then to a great house in Britain. Finally, today, he had come to this match, Lord Jeff, the center of a great spectacle. Thousands of men were staring at him, betting for or against him.

What an opportunity! If he could defeat Futrell, he would gain great honor in the eyes of the powerful men of this country. Even the Prince of Wales would hear of him. How could Sir Harry then keep him in slavery? By God, this was something worth fighting for, even to the death.

He and his opponent were fairly matched. Both men stood over six feet. Futrell was half a head taller, heavier, thicker in the body, but his weight was beginning to turn to fat. Jeff's body was lean, muscular; his arms longer.

His opponent stared at him, head tilted in a gesture of curiosity and contempt. Jeff felt tense but confident. He glanced at his handler. Mendoza smiled and shook his fist. An umpire shouted. The fight began.

In the early rounds, Jeff avoided close combat. He jabbed at his opponent's eyes, parried or dodged his blows, and evaded his attempts to grapple. The champion grew more and more aggressive. The crowd hooted and hissed at Jeff, clamoring for bone-shattering, flesh-ripping punches.

Jeff's confidence grew as he sensed Futrell had not trained well, expecting this to be an easy fight. Jeff's evasive tactics
~~~

exasperated and tired him. Finally, in a wild rush at his opponent, the champion lowered his guard. Jeff danced nimbly to the side, avoiding the man's grasp, then counterattacked with rapid left jabs that virtually closed Futrell's eyes.

In the meantime, the sky had darkened, thunder rumbled, and a thick cloud drifted in from the west. For a few minutes, it released a heavy shower of rain over the area. Out of the corner of his eye, Jeff could see umbrellas popping open among the spectators, but he refused to be distracted and launched a barrage of blows with both hands to Futrell's head and body.

The champion charged again, arms flailing wildly. Jeff attempted to dodge but slipped on the wet surface. Down he went, tripping his opponent, who fell heavily on Jeff's left arm. He wrenched free and scrambled to his feet, but his arm throbbed with pain.

Though the crowd howled in protest, the umpires stopped the fight. Futrell backed off to one side, scowling. Mendoza rushed out of Jeff's corner and examined his arm. Broken near the wrist. Mendoza looked up at Jeff and asked if he shouldn't quit. He risked ruining the arm for life. Jeff shook his head, having scarcely heard his handler's words. The fight was but half over. He *would* win, regardless of the cost.

During the match, Georges had slipped away from the coach and mingled in the crowd. When Jeff fell, a fever of activity had broken out. Betters frantically clustered and exchanged chits. Georges joined Dick Burton. A short distance away, Jack Roach was strutting about, proud as a rooster, hurling loud insults at Jeff.

"How's the Red Devil doing?" Georges asked.

"Forcing his luck," Burton replied. Before the fight had begun, Roach had placed a large bet on Futrell to win and had doubled it when Jeff fell.

"Sir Harry looks nervous," said Georges, glancing toward Rogers, who stood stock still, his eyes focused intently on his fighter. He had bet another five thousand pounds just before Jeff fell. When the umpires withdrew, directing the fight to begin again, Rogers visibly relaxed and smiled.

Georges winced. A slave's pain meant little to his master.

⁂

As the fight resumed, Jeff drew a deep breath, recalled his goal. Win and be free. He raised his left arm. It was now almost useless, but it had done its work. Futrell's eyes were swollen nearly shut.

The champion launched his attack like an enraged bull. Jeff continued his evasive tactics, dancing from side to side, bobbing and weaving. The crowd hooted in unison, "Fight like a man. Fight like a man." Their chant spurred him on. He would show them what it meant to "fight like a man." Smart, skillful, patient.

Futrell eventually tired, his assaults weakened, and for a moment he dropped his guard. Jeff feinted with his wounded hand, then caught Futrell with a powerful right hook just below the left ear. He fell senseless to the canvas. In the thirty seconds allowed by the timekeeper, he barely managed to struggle to his feet.

The mood of the fickle crowd now shifted in the black man's favor. They chanted in a crescendo of voices, "Lord Jeff! Lord Jeff!"

Jeff pressed home his advantage, striking repeatedly with his strong right hand while evading his opponent's wild blows and clumsy attempts to grapple. At the end of an hour, Futrell was staggering about the ring, blinded, his arms hanging helplessly at his side. The crowd cried for blood. "Finish him! Finish him!"

Jeff glanced toward Futrell's handlers. They exchanged a few hurried words, then drew their battered man into his corner. The crowd roared, "Lord Jeff! Champion!"

Moved by a powerful surge of pride, he strode to the center of the ring and lifted his right arm in a salute of victory.

After the match, when the crowd of spectators had thinned out, Anne and Charlie descended from the coach, emotionally drained. Their stiff limbs needed to stretch before the two-hour ride back to Bath. Like Anne herself, moved by affection for Jeffery, the boy had watched with greater interest than she had expected. It also dawned on her that the boy's initial recalcitrance to attending the match expressed a childish opposition to his father's will rather than a weakling's revulsion to the brutality of the sport. Paul joined them and they walked toward the ring, ignoring the gawking eyes of bystanders. Anne wanted to congratulate Jeffery when his handlers were done with him.

He stepped out of the ring into the outer circle, glistening with perspiration. Peter Hyde began sponging his body while Mendoza applied an ointment to the bruised, swollen knuckles of his hands and bandaged them. A doctor inspected his wrist and determined the fracture to be a simple hairline break that didn't need to be set. He applied a stiff bandage and fashioned a sling for the arm.

Realizing that the doctor's ministrations would take yet a little more time, Anne left Charlie in Paul's care and looked about for Jack Roach. A short distance away, Dick Burton stood by a ruined pillar. She went to him. Roach couldn't be far away.

"Over there," Burton said to her, leading her eye in the direction of the former sanctuary. In the shadow of the pillar, Anne raised the little spyglass. Roach was standing between his two ruffians on the edge of the crowd gathered around the treasurer of the fight committee. Arms akimbo, Roach looked down as if mulling over a decision. A menacing frown distorted his face.

Anne shifted her gaze to the crowd. At that moment, Sir Harry came into focus. He approached the treasurer to arrange payment on his bets. A broad smile on his face, he shared a flask of strong drink with other glad winners. Some of the losers nearby shrugged off their losses with the nonchalance of men who always expected to win next time. Others, among them Captain Fitzroy, looked darkly grim. Sir Harry turned to meet the captain's eye and smiled with cold, malicious satisfaction. The captain gave back a stare that could have killed, had it been a lethal weapon.

Meanwhile, Roach appeared to have made up his mind. Leaving his companions behind, he approached Sir Harry. They entered into an animated conversation, Roach with his back to Anne, Rogers facing her. Anne thought they were going to discuss a wager until Roach said something that directed Rogers' eyes toward Jeffery.

"What's he done?" asked Sir Harry, canting his head quizzically.

Roach drew closer to Rogers and spoke in his ear. Rogers listened intently, occasionally nodding. Finally, Roach stepped back.

Without any sign of gratitude, Rogers said merely, "I'll deal with him." Eyes narrowed, he stared at the black man. Her chest tight with foreboding, Anne hurried back to Paul and Charlie. Sir Harry composed himself and settled his affairs. His ruddy face glowed with his old enthusiasm. Approaching Paul, he shouted, "Lord Jeff's the best investment I've made in a long time!" He threw a cursory glance at Anne and Charlie. "The odds were against him, two to one. He's earned twenty thousand pounds for me today. That's twice what a whole ship's cargo of slaves will fetch in Jamaica after months at sea!" He pointed to Jeffery, who sat on a stool close by, still stripped to the waist, grimacing as the doctor applied an astringent ointment to an ugly cut on his left cheek. "Look at him—fifteen stone of pure black gold!"

His eyes fixed on Rogers, Jeffery repeated out loud the words "black gold" several times. Then he thanked the doctor and rose stiffly. His chin high, he walked up to Rogers. "Sir," said the slave in a strong, clear voice. "I wish to claim the winner's share of the door money. Two hundred pounds."

Jeffery's request momentarily stunned Sir Harry speechless. His brow furrowed with astonishment. Then, he bristled. "How dare you! Every penny a slave earns belongs to his master. I was prepared to give you a guinea to spend as you like. Now, you shall have nothing!" His face grew taut. "I know what you're up to. You are henceforth confined to Combe Park. Don't think for a moment I'll allow that wretched Quaker to steal you from me." He paused, his lips quivering with anger, then continued in a low menacing voice, "I'll soon decide what to do with you."

Chapter 19

Victory Party

Wednesday, April 4

A cold drizzle diffused light from the windows of Combe Park into a soft, luminous, enveloping cloud. The building glowed against the dark sky like a ghostly prince's palace. Jeffery stood outside the entrance, an exotic sentry, with a crimson cape over his livery and a powdered wig on his head. Sir Harry had ordered him back to his duties as footman. On probation until further notice. Forbidden to leave the estate. He must find a way to inform Sarah.

An oncoming coach interrupted his thoughts. He was soon busy. A caravan of coaches and cabriolets, some adorned with noble devices, pulled up to the entrance and discharged their distinguished occupants. They were greeted by music drifting out of the house. Sir Harry was celebrating Jeffery's victory and his own winnings.

For appearance's sake, Jeffery's left arm was without the sling, though still painful and useless. Nonetheless, he met the visitors with his usual courteous manner and inscrutable expression. He had learned to keep his feelings to himself. His soul at least remained free. But it was angry, churning within him like boiling water in a hot cauldron. Some of that anger had spilled over poor Futrell. A sad man tonight, eyes swollen shut, pride wounded. Beaten by a black slave! Jeffery felt a stir of pity for his adversary. The man had fought fair and lost.

Jeffery sighed, drew a deep breath of the cool, damp air. He preferred being outside this evening and Sir Harry Rogers inside. Had to keep a safe distance between them. Might break the man's neck if he met him alone. Rogers! A cruel and selfish man. Should have praised his fighter and freed him. Won the fight and a fortune for him. Did it with only one sound arm.

The arrival of coaches slowed to a trickle. Jeffery strayed from his post at the entrance and wandered past Sir Harry's study. Light seeped through the drapes. The footman stared at the window, hearkened to faint bursts of laughter. Sir Harry was in there with his friends, talking about the fight, about "black gold." Thinking, what should he do with his boxer? Worth twenty thousand pounds to him. Maybe more. But the boxer might run away. Then Sir Harry'd have nothing.

Jeffery turned and walked slowly back to the entrance, recalling the tall slender figure of Sarah Smith and her golden brown eyes. Now that he had come to know her and feel affection for her, he could not imagine leaving Bath without her. If Sir Harry were to decide to send him back to Jamaica, he would have to kill him first.

Hooves and wheels clattered on the paving stones, jarring Jeffery out of his thoughts. As he opened a coach door, he grimaced. His broken left arm had swollen to twice its normal size and was throbbing with pain. His bone-weary body ached at every joint. He felt nauseated. But he swore to himself to show no weakness. He must be worthy of his father and earn respect from men of honor. The visitors threw him sidelong glances, but paid him no compliments, then hastened on to congratulate Sir Harry and to enjoy his hospitality. Jeffery shrugged off the slights. Being ignored was better than being patronized.

From time to time, he glanced over his shoulder. He had to ward off fashionably dressed thieves and courtesans who might try to slip by him and ply their trade inside. Despite the chilly weather, they could walk up the road to Combe Park and enter the house behind his back while he tended to the coaches. Most noble households would have included Mr. Jack Roach among such pests, but Sir Harry had instructed Jeffery to send Mr. Roach to his study.

Late last night, after the guests had left Combe Park, Roach had come up to Jeffery at the entrance. "I had a score to settle with that Cartier woman out there on the portico," he had said. "It was none of your business." He had shaken his fist in Jeffery's face. "No proud black bastard can push me around and get away with it. I shall make you suffer. I know about Sarah Smith and the Quaker and about a big black slave trying to become free. When the time is right, Sir Harry Rogers will be told."

Jeffery had seized the man, spun him around, and kicked him out the door. He had felt the urge to kill him then and there, but thought better of it. Roach had cursed him, then vanished into the night, only to reappear at the fight today and make good on his threat to expose him.

Like a bad penny, Roach soon arrived alone in a cabriolet. Fighting back his anger, Jeffery approached to open the door.

"Back off, you black dodger!" exclaimed Roach. "You cost me a thousand quid today. Had you fought like a man, Futrell would've pounded you into mincemeat."

Jeffery stepped back, taking care not to show his pleasure at Roach's loss or his contempt for the man's logic. "Sir Harry has instructed me to direct you to his study."

Roach sneered. "Tell him, I'll come when I'm ready." He turned and glared at Jeffery, a malign grin on his face. "Oh, by the way, Sarah Smith's landlord owes me a favor. Tomorrow I'll tell him she's a trouble-maker helping a black man escape his master. We can't have that in Bath. To be sure, he'll say. By tomorrow night, your Sarah and her mother will be out on the street."

A surge of rage struck Jeffery. Raising his right arm and clenching his fist, he took a step toward his tormentor.

Roach reached swiftly into his coat and pulled out a pistol. "Another step and you're a dead man. I'd love to kill you."

Choking with anger, Jeffery lowered his arm.

For a few more seconds, Roach aimed the pistol at the footman, then put it back in his coat. He patted down his wig, tugged at his lapels, and sauntered into the house.

Dressed in crimson livery, Georges was busy serving in the dining room. Guests were coming and going, milling around the tables, chatting, drinking wine. Although he had hardly a minute to himself, he kept watch on Critchley, seated with William at a corner table. Both of them looked like proper gentlemen. The former had lightly powdered and dressed his hair. A deft application of rouge concealed his sallow complexion. His dark green suit, while out of fashion, was of high quality and fit him well. He carried himself with enough insouciance to fit into the present company of men of the world.

His young charge was similarly groomed and dressed in a light blue suit, handsome, save for a pouting mouth. He slouched sourly in his chair, apparently lacking money to wager in the gambling den. When the tutor spoke to him, he languidly studied the ceiling.

Then Jack Roach walked in and looked about, a scowl on his face. Thanks to the butt Anne had given him, his lips were still swollen. His finger was bandaged. Anne also deserved credit for that. And his jaw was taut. He had something urgent on his mind.

His eyes lit on Critchley and William. A waiter was taking their order. Roach stood just inside the door until the waiter returned to the bar, then moved quickly to the tutor's side.

A neighboring table signaled to Georges for service. He drew near enough to eavesdrop.

"I want it now," snarled Roach under his breath.

"We can't talk here," replied Critchley, glancing at William, who had pricked up his ears.

Georges, pretending to be busy, lingered as long as he dared.

"Meet me later," Roach said, then whispered something in the tutor's ear. William leaned forward, attempting to hear.

Critchley snapped at him. The young man slouched back, sullen, mumbling to himself.

"I'll be there, Jack," said Critchley with a sardonic twist of his lips, then added, "Remember, no tricks."

Roach glared at Critchley, abruptly turned on his heel, and left the room. The tutor's gaze followed him to the door. Then, with a shrug, he said something to William, who grimaced. At that moment, the waiter arrived with their drinks.

As Georges was mulling over this incident, Captain Fitzroy's valet walked by. He glanced furtively at Georges, then quickly averted his eyes. He, too, had been listening.

Anne and Harriet entertained in the ballroom most of the evening, country dancing with the guests, singing ballads and airs. The room grew warm, and they tired. During an intermission, they found an open window near the chancel. Harriet patted her brow with a kerchief, Anne pulled a fan from her sleeve. After a moment's rest, she considered speaking to her friend about the dangers of becoming involved with Sir Harry, but she couldn't get her attention.

The young woman's gaze lighted upon one handsome man after another. Finally, she tensed, her face brightened. "Captain Fitzroy is casting glances my way... Yes, here he comes. Good, we'll do the next country dance together." She tucked the kerchief away and gave the approaching captain a radiant smile. He responded with one of his own, extended his hand, and drew her toward the couples who were gathering on the dance floor.

With a sigh of resignation Anne moved off to the side of the room near the door. The musicians gathered, struck up a lively tune, and set the dancers in motion. The hall shook with the sound of voices and the pounding of feet. Anne was fanning herself when Georges slipped in next to her.

"Watch Critchley and Roach. They're bargaining," he whispered, leading her eye to the back of the ballroom. The two men were huddling under the mezzanine. "Try to read their lips with your spyglass. If you learn anything, you'll find me in the dining room."

Anne worked her way cautiously toward the men, hiding her face with the fan, until she came as near as she dared. In the shelter of a pillar that partially concealed her face, she raised her spyglass, shifted the lens to the diagonal position, and focused on them. She couldn't read Roach's lips; he was whispering into Critchley's ear. But she could see Critchley's face. His eyes were cast down, his brow creased with distrust. He merely nodded or shook his head in response. She had almost given up hope, when Critchley finally began speaking. At that moment, as luck would have it, a guest stepped into Anne's line of sight. Still, she caught two words: "tennis… thousand."

It was near ten o'clock when Anne joined Georges in the dining room. The guests' demands had abated, allowing him a few minutes with her. While pretending to order, she told him what she had learned spying in the ballroom. "The word 'tennis' has to mean a meeting will take place at the tennis hall."

Georges nodded. "And a 'thousand'? That must be pounds!" At a table nearby, a man and a woman glanced at him, then looked at each other with arched eyebrows. To disarm their curiosity, Georges added, "At the faro table." The neighbors shook their heads, their question apparently answered. Georges lowered his voice. "That's a small fortune. Must be Critchley's price for whatever he stole from Lady Margaret. With that much money he could retire and live comfortably for years."

"Can that be the sum Roach will demand from Sir Harry?" Anne asked.

"I doubt it," Georges replied. "Roach knows Sir Harry's willing to pay much more to be free to marry again." He paused for a moment, rubbing his chin. "Colonel Saint-Martin has to be told. Will you do it? I must go back to waiting on tables."

Anne agreed and was about to leave when she glanced over her shoulder. Fitzroy was at the door. He walked in with his usual nonchalance and called his valet aside. They exchanged a few quiet words. Fitzroy's expression grew tense, then anxious. Anne didn't need her spyglass to see the names being mentioned. Finally, the valet withdrew.

Fitzroy will go looking for Critchley and Roach, she said to herself, and find out what they're plotting. From the other side of the room, Georges signaled. She glanced toward the door again. The Red Devil himself had also arrived.

Roach and Fitzroy sat down at a table facing one another. They appeared to be bargaining, each man outwardly calm and collected, like bitter enemies discussing terms, having agreed to a truce.

Anne pretended to be drinking wine as she studied the two men over the rim of her glass. Since she could see them only in profile, she couldn't read their lips. At last, Roach rose from the table, turning his face so that Anne could finally study him. "Bring money," she thought he said.

When Roach left the room, Fitzroy soon followed. Anne lowered her glass, reflecting for a moment, while Georges hurried back to her. She reported what she had seen, then asked, "Is Roach giving Fitzroy an opportunity to bid for the stolen item?"

"That seems likely," Georges replied. "But he must find a great deal of money to replace what he lost at the fight. He'll get it from Lady Margaret. Her jewels perhaps. But he must act quickly. As we speak, Roach is probably bargaining with Sir Harry in his study."

Georges withdrew to his duties. Anne remained at the table for another minute, then set out to find Paul. In the entrance hall, she saw Jeffery at his post by the door. "Have you seen Colonel Saint-Martin?" she asked.

"No, Miss Cartier, I haven't."

She was about to leave him when she noticed he seemed troubled. "Are you well, Jeffery?"

"I'm ill," he replied. "In a few minutes, someone will come to take my place."

She hesitated. Should she ask if she could help in any way? No, she needed to find Paul quickly. Critchley's meeting with Roach in the tennis hall could take place at any minute.

He gazed at her, a cry for help in his eyes.

For another moment, she went on debating with herself what to do. Tongues would surely wag if they were seen together. Then, she made up her mind and signaled for him to follow her. She led him upstairs into the antechamber of her room, a quiet private place. She closed the door and stood facing the footman.

While the voices of guests below drifted faintly up to them, he told her that Roach was going to wreak his revenge on Sarah and her mother. "I must warn them and Mr. Woodbridge. Perhaps they can do something to change the landlord's mind or at least find another place to stay." He reached out his hands to her, pleading. "Could you deliver a warning to them? I can't do it myself, I can't leave Combe Park. The servants have been told to keep watch on me."

Anne felt her chest tighten, her heart pound. She had to help him. He was ashamed to admit he could not write. "I'll prepare the message and pay one of the grooms to deliver it. That's the most I can do tonight. Will that help?"

"Yes. They will begin to look out for themselves."

Jeffery seemed relieved and grateful, Anne thought. Perhaps Roach's malicious scheme could be thwarted.

A clock struck 10:30 when she showed him out. As he left, he said he would take some medicine and go to bed. She wished him good night and went into her room. As she sat at the table writing out his message, she had an unsettling feeling that he was withholding something from her. Before returning to the ballroom, she had to speak to Paul.

Jeffery took the servants' stairs down to his basement room, relieved that Miss Cartier would send his message to Sarah. He still seethed with anger, but there was nothing more he could do. Roach himself was beyond his reach.

In the basement hallway, he heard a burst of laughter from the kitchen. Peter Hyde was keeping the cook company. Jeffery managed to forget his pain and grievances for a moment. Their good natured banter always lightened his spirits. He joined them at a plain scoured wooden table.

"Mrs. Powell, would you kindly make a hot tisane for me?" He pointed to his arm in its sling. "It hurts."

"That's what you get for fighting," she replied, a teasing glint in her eye. "But I'll fix something anyway." She walked to a counter and started to prepare the concoction. Hyde nodded him to the seat across the table and they began to chat.

"How's the arm, Jeff?" the coachman asked solicitously.

"It's bad, especially at the end of the day."

Mrs. Powell came back with a glass in her hand. "This should make you feel better," she said. "Drink it up."

Jeffery did as he was told. In a few minutes the potion began to reduce his pain but made him a little drowsy. He understood she had added a drop of laudanum. In a short while, he was feeling well enough for a walk in the fresh air. "I'll just step outside for a few minutes and then go to my room." He rose from the table and wished them goodnight.

He left by the door adjacent to the kitchen. The night was misty and cool. At first, he intended only to walk back and forth in the dark a few times and then return inside. But he fell into reverie, yearning for Sarah. She would be anxiously waiting for word from him. Hopefully Miss Cartier's message would reach her soon. When the vision finally left him, he found himself in front of the tennis hall, chilled and damp.

He stepped inside to dry out, but didn't light a candle. It would attract attention. The steward might object to a footman wandering about outside in the mist, when he was supposed to be sick and in bed. A candle was anyway unnecessary. He easily found his way in the dark to the training room.

To warm up his body, he lifted weights with his good arm. After perhaps ten minutes, he was feeling much better. He had left the room and had come to the middle of the antechamber when he heard someone at the main entrance. He quickly slipped into the dressing room just as a large figure approached with a lantern. It was Jack Roach.

Jeffery's right arm yearned for a sixteen-pound iron shot. In his present frame of mind he would have hurled it at Roach's head. Instead, when the man turned his back, Jeffery stole out of the dressing room and through the tennis court. As he reached the back hall, he heard someone else at the front door.

"Jack! where are you?" cried a high nasal voice.

"Hurry up! You're late," Roach shouted back. "I'm in the training room."

Jeffery was tempted to find out what was going on. But that seemed dangerous. Roach was armed and would gladly shoot him. Still, who was his visitor? A certain person came to mind. And what were they going to talk about? Perhaps the fate of a troublesome black slave! Or, more likely, Lady Margaret's stolen package. Otherwise, why meet in such secrecy?

Frozen to the spot, he argued with himself. Should he creep up to the training room and listen? Or, should he leave? An insistent inner voice urged caution.

Peter Hyde saluted the cook and left her chuckling over his last anecdote. He had entertained her for almost an hour with his farfetched tales of youthful adventure. She had treated him to delicious tidbits meant for the guests upstairs.

He had hardly stepped into the hallway when the door to the outside opened and Jeff entered, his shoulders bent, his step heavy. The coachman shook a finger at him. "What have you been doing out there in the cold and damp? You're sick. Get to bed. I'll bring you a hot drink."

Jeff acknowledged the coachman with a grimace and went on to his room. Hyde returned to the kitchen wondering at the curious change in the footman. Then he recalled from his own experience how a feeling of depression set in some hours after a fight, even when he had won. "I know the remedy," he said to himself. He prepared a cold pack for the broken wrist and a steaming cup of hot buttered rum.

"Drink this, Jeff," Hyde commanded in his usual gruff way. "It'll cure whatever ails you."

The sick man gazed at Hyde with troubled eyes. "Thank you, Peter. You're a good friend."

In the entrance foyer, a clock struck eleven. Saint-Martin walked up to the drowsy footman who had taken Jeffery's post at the door. Anne had just told the colonel about the black man's predicament, and the secret bargaining she had observed during the party. Critchley, the tennis hall, and a thousand pounds were involved. What it all meant was still a mystery.

"Where is Mr. Roach?" Saint-Martin asked the footman. The Red Devil was surely somewhere in the picture.

"I don't know, sir. He came out of Sir Harry's study a few minutes ago and left the house. I heard him say he'd be back in half an hour. Sir Harry seemed angry. Cursed him roundly. Heard it even here."

Saint-Martin stepped outside. Mist was thickening on the path to the tennis hall. Judging from Anne's report, that's where Roach was likely to go. A gust of cold wet wind struck the colonel's face. He shivered. There wasn't time to go back to his room. The footman inside the door was trying vainly to suppress a great yawn. Saint-Martin pressed a shilling into the palm of his hand. "I need your cloak and lantern."

Open-mouthed, perplexed, the footman closed his hand on the coin, then threw the cloak over the colonel's shoulders and gave him the lantern.

Saint-Martin felt his way on the graveled path, aided by a small crack of light from the lantern. Roach was most likely already in the tennis hall, but it was best to be cautious. When the colonel reached the clearing in front of the building and fully shuttered the lantern, he was surprised to see a man—a bit too slender and timid to be Roach—hovering at the entrance, as if uncertain what to do next. Light shone faintly in the high windows of the training room. Roach must be there.

Saint-Martin stepped back into a grove of pine trees and pulled the hood of the cloak over his head. Who was the stranger at the door? Was he hesitating to enter? Or, had he already been inside? Finally, the person stole away into the darkness. Saint-Martin would wait to see if Roach or anyone else left the hall.

After what seemed like twenty minutes, he heard the sound of approaching feet on the gravel. Two hooded figures passed by the pine grove carrying lanterns. At the door to the tennis hall, they dropped the hoods. Saint-Martin recognized Captain Fitzroy and Lady Margaret. The Irishman opened the door, called Roach's name, listened for a few moments, then cautiously entered the hall followed by his companion. The colonel unshuttered his own lantern and checked the time. Thirty minutes before midnight.

Fifteen minutes later, Fitzroy hurriedly left the hall dragging Lady Margaret by the hand. In the faint light of his lantern, he seemed distraught and breathing heavily. She stumbled after him, clutching her throat. Something had gone wrong in there, Saint-Martin thought. No point in following them. They were going back to the house. Better to wait for Roach.

Saint-Martin scanned the windows of the hall. The light was out. Odd, he thought. Would Roach wait in the dark? Or, if he had left the building, why hadn't he used the front door?

At midnight, Saint-Martin again heard footsteps on the path. Sir Harry walked by with a small lantern and went into the tennis hall. After a few minutes he emerged, a puzzled expression on his face. What's going on? Saint-Martin wondered.

A short while later, with still no sign of Roach and no sound of anyone on the path, Saint-Martin crept up to the hall. Listened. No sound. He quietly opened the door. No light inside. He unshuttered his lantern and looked into the training room. No one there. He ventured on to the tennis court and called out. No answer, only his echo. He stood there motionless. The silence of the place was eerie.

Saint-Martin left the tennis hall, perplexed by what he had witnessed. At the entrance to the house, a preoccupied Sir Harry was bidding his last guests good-bye. The colonel hurried to the ballroom. Anne was on the stage, gathering her things and about to leave. Though weary from an hour of entertaining, she brightened when she saw him and listened eagerly to his account.

"So, Roach seems to have vanished into thin air. What can that mean?" she asked. "Lady Margaret has retired to her rooms, and Captain Fitzroy to his. Both seemed distressed. Had they met Roach or not?"

"It's difficult to tell," Paul replied. "Jack Roach follows his own whims. For whatever reason, he might have chosen to leave Combe Park unnoticed. Perhaps he sensed that someone was tracking him, that person hovering around the tennis hall door. I didn't notice any sign of foul play at the tennis hall. But something is amiss. We shall have to wait until the morning's light to find out."

"Paul, this may seem foolish, but Jeffery worries me. He was in an angry, desperate state of mind this evening. And now you tell me that Roach has disappeared. I shudder even to think of it, but there just might be a connection."

Paul nodded gravely. "I'll ask Georges to inquire among the servants in the basement about Jeffery's movements during the past few hours. Let's hope he stayed in bed."

Chapter 20

Foul Play?

Thursday, April 5

Shortly after dawn, Saint-Martin led Georges through a thin chilly mist to the tennis hall. It was still unlocked. Inside, a pale light sifted through the high windows, leaving much of the interior still in darkness. A hushed silence hung over the rooms. Saint-Martin was uneasy. Where had Jack Roach gone?

"The tennis hall must be searched thoroughly," he said to his adjutant. "We'll begin in the training room."

Georges lit a pair of lanterns and handed one to Saint-Martin, who stepped cautiously forward, scanning the room. Nothing seemed out of order.

Since the building had not been cleaned during the past two or three days, a very fine dust had settled. While Saint-Martin held the lanterns, Georges squatted down and studied the floor from different angles, looking for telltale signs of violence.

He rose to his feet, held a lantern high enough to cast a wide arc of light, then pointed to an area at the far side of the room near a bench. "Scuffling feet have scattered the dust there." He peered into the closet in the adjacent wall where he had eavesdropped on Sir Harry and Roach. "Before I left, I put things back where I had found them. Since then, someone has cleared space for a large object, then dragged it away." He stepped back for the colonel to look.

They followed a barely visible trail in the dust out of the training room, across the tennis court to the back exit. Small strands of fabric had caught on the door sills and on the rough boards of the narrow rear hallway. A black shoe lay near a wall. In the soft sodden turf outside the back exit were hoof marks and wheel tracks, as well as a jumble of fresh boot prints.

Saint-Martin bent down and ran his fingers over the indentations. "Miss Cartier and Charlie sculpt objects with plaster. I'll ask her to cast these boot prints before someone disturbs them."

Georges grimaced. "It's hardly worth her effort. I see three, maybe four different sets, all mixed up."

"Why so many, Georges? Was a gang involved?"

"Not likely, sir. No sign of struggle. I think one man surprised Roach, stored his body in the closet, then came back later with servants and carted it away."

"Roach? Are we sure?"

"He's the only missing person we know of. The bits of fabric and the shoe must be his."

"Burton's problem," said the colonel. "But I think we can help him." Unbidden, a sense of relief swept over him. Anne was safe now. In all likelihood, Roach would not be found alive. His vices had overtaken him. "We'll close this building. Sir Harry said last night he would be too busy to play tennis and Jeff wouldn't train with a broken wrist."

"I'll get the key from the steward," Georges said.

"When you've locked up, we'll arrange to meet Mr. Burton."

The two men retraced their steps, careful not to touch the suspicious marks in the dust. As they left the tennis hall, Saint-Martin had already lined up suspects in his mind.

After breakfast, Saint-Martin and Georges rode to the city with the steward on his way to the city market. In Stall Street they left the wagon and walked the few remaining steps to the Pump Room. Before departing from Combe Park, Saint-Martin had sent a message to Burton concerning Roach's apparent disappearance. Now, together, they would see if Roach paid his usual visit. An unlikely prospect.

As he approached the Pump Room, Saint-Martin wondered how much he should tell Burton about last night's suspicious activity at the tennis hall. Supposing Roach were found murdered, should he help Burton investigate Captain Fitzroy's possible complicity and risk putting him in an English jail or in a hangman's noose? That could jeopardize his mission to bring Fitzroy to France. In the end, Saint-Martin decided to take that chance and tell Burton what he'd seen. The Bow Street officer had a sharp mind. Attempting to deceive him would be foolish. Build trust instead.

Burton was waiting for them off to one side of the room, surveying the crowd with a critical eye and drinking a glass of warm, tawny water with obvious distaste. His cane hung on his arm. When he glimpsed the two Frenchmen, his face brightened. He listened attentively to Saint-Martin's account of the previous evening, clearly pleased by his willingness to share.

"Colonel, it sounds like murder, but we don't have a body. If Mr. Roach doesn't come here this morning, we'll try his home."

The two Frenchmen walked to the counter, each purchased a glass of water, then joined Burton where they could watch the entrances. While they sipped from their glasses, Georges recounted the exchange between Critchley and Roach in the dining room.

Burton frowned, shook his cane. "Critchley's playing a dangerous game, holding something back, trying to bargain."

A half-hour passed. No sign of Roach, though a pair of his ruffians looked into the room, furrowed their brows, and asked if anyone had seen him. Apparently, no one could say they had.

When an hour had passed without any sign of him, Saint-Martin and Dick Burton left to visit Roach's rooms and Georges set off to search at The Little Drummer and among the riffraff of Bath. On North Parade, Burton stopped before a rather ill-kept house in an otherwise elegant row. Trash had been allowed to accumulate in the window well, and dark green paint was flaking off the surrounding wrought iron fence. He knocked on the door until it opened a crack. A thin middle-aged woman peered out warily.

"Dick Burton, ma'am. Officer, Bow Street, London. Is Mr. Jack Roach at home?"

She hesitated, glancing from one gentleman to the other, then shook her head. "I don't think he came home last night." She must have noticed a look of surprise in Burton's face, for she added, "He's often called away suddenly on business."

"Would you allow us to examine his rooms?" asked Burton in a tone more like a demand than a request.

"Sir! This is a respectable house. Mr. Roach wouldn't want me to let strangers into his rooms. Indeed, he would be very cross with me." She began to wring her hands and back away, as if about to close the door.

"Would you rather that I trouble the mayor for a warrant to search?" Burton paused to allow the dire implications of his threat to sink into the woman's mind. "We won't disturb anything. Mr. Roach has gone missing. We're looking for clues to where he might be."

Saint-Martin understood the woman might have good reasons, apart from Roach, to avoid a legal search. Contraband brandy or lace or tea. Probably implicated in Roach's schemes.

The woman chewed on her lip for a moment, then let them in. Gathering her skirts, she led them up to the first floor and unlocked a door to a small entrance hall. A pair of riding boots stood beneath a greatcoat hanging from a hook on the wall; whips and spurs and other riding gear were piled on shelves.

"Is this his only riding outfit?" Saint-Martin asked the woman.

"It's the only one I've seen him in."

He turned to Burton. "Then he hasn't ridden from Bath."

"That puts a small piece of the puzzle in place, Colonel. I'll check the coaches and livery stables later."

The entrance hall opened to a sparsely furnished parlor. Ink pots, quills, sealing wax, a stamp, piles of paper cluttered a table by the window. Nothing of interest. A small cabinet stood against the wall. Inside were boxes of bills and receipts which Burton fingered through quickly. None of them seemed remarkable.

Saint-Martin inspected the bedroom off the parlor. "Roach didn't sleep here last night."

"So?" said the woman. "Mr. Roach often has work that keeps him out all night."

"Could you tell me where he was most likely to have *worked* last night?" Burton asked.

"Sir!" she spluttered. "I don't pry into the private affairs of my tenants."

Burton waited, staring at her with steely eyes. Finally, she gave him an address on Alfred Street.

As the two men left the house, Saint-Martin remarked, "We haven't seen any notes to or from the excise officers, lists of his extortion victims, evidence of smuggling or scandal that he could use against them."

"That's true," Burton agreed. "And Roach must have kept such papers hidden close by. He worked in his rooms. I'll take a closer look at another time."

Alfred Street was ten minutes away through the busy heart of the city. At midmorning, the fashionable brothel was being cleaned and aired. Its front door stood ajar, its windows wide open. A servant led the two gentlemen into a small, richly furnished front parlor and disappeared. Saint-Martin noted the gold drapes embroidered in purple, the fine brown mahogany table and chairs, the costly Turkish carpet on the floor. Judging from first impressions, he concluded the house catered to a discriminating clientele. It wasn't where he would have expected to find Jack Roach.

"Surprised?" Burton asked with a chuckle, after he too had surveyed the room. "Roach comes from a noble family—by the left hand, as they say. Son of a lady's maid and a baronet. Never been shy about it. Indulges in the fine things when he's in money. As a youth, he wenched, gambled, and drank his way through Eton and Oxford, bent on wasting a small fortune. But his father cut him off. He's lived by his wits ever since."

Footsteps sounded in the hall. A handsome, stylish woman in a rose dressing gown entered the room, attempting to conceal the puzzled look on her face. For a long moment she studied the men with cold gray eyes, then her face relaxed in a tentative smile. Her visitors didn't mean to cause her trouble, but they weren't patrons either.

Yes, she told them, Jack Roach was a frequent and welcome visitor. Made no secret of it. No, she hadn't seen him last night and had no idea where he might be.

For the rest of the morning, the men went separate ways: Burton to inquire at coach inns and stables; Saint-Martin to visit shops on Milsom Street upon which Roach preyed. After a fruitless search, Saint-Martin stopped to visit Madame Gagnon. Leaving her customers in the hands of an assistant, she led the colonel upstairs to her parlor. To his questions about Roach, she replied with a scowl; she hadn't seen him either and suspected foul play. At least a hundred men in Bath would have gladly killed him.

"But I have something for you," she said, reaching into the drawer of a nearby table. "A letter. It arrived an hour ago by overnight post from London. Read it while I prepare tea." She handed him the letter and left the room.

Saint-Martin scanned the cover, noted Comtesse Marie's elegant hand and seal. Mailed from Paris. He opened the letter, dated March 27. Folded inside was a note sealed by the baron. He set it aside and began to read his aunt's message, his lips moving silently.

> *Dear Paul, I am sorry to send you sad news. Sylvie looks pale and haggard. Stares into space, never speaks, pushes her food aside. It's been five days since she attempted to kill herself in the stable. We have moved her to Chateau Beaumont for the fresh air and the garden she loves. The servants and I keep a close watch over her. I am also concerned about her godfather, Baron Breteuil, who seethes with anger, doesn't sleep well, and snaps at people. He has sent along a note to you.*

He laid the letter in his lap and looked inward. His cousin Sylvie appeared with brutal clarity, standing in her shift, the rope around her neck. She seemed to gaze at him with eyes dull and despairing.

He felt a rush of pity for the young woman, followed by a visceral urge to beat her assailant into a mass of bloody flesh and broken bones. Fitzroy had callously destroyed her spirit. Yet, revenge seemed inadequate and self-serving, and would do Sylvie no good. Saint-Martin groaned softly, bowed his head, and prayed she would find her way back to a healthy mind.

By the time Madame Gagnon returned with the tea, he had composed himself. Without comment, he read the letter aloud to her. And then the baron's note:

> *Bring back Fitzroy, whatever the cost.*

She listened grim-faced on the edge of her seat, her back stiff. When he finished, she drew a deep breath and slowly exhaled. "What can I say? The villain shows no remorse for what he's done. He's put himself beyond the pale."

"And perhaps beyond our reach." Despair threatened to overwhelm his spirit. "I may disappoint the baron—and Sylvie. If Mr. Burton were to discover that Fitzroy has murdered Roach, he would lodge the rogue in an English jail. His trial might take place months from now during what the English call Quarter Sessions. Fitzroy would then plead self-defense and Lady Margaret would back him up. The court might acquit him and set him free or convict him of manslaughter and transport him to one of the colonies. In the meantime, my hands would be tied."

She stared at him, wordless, with a mixture of horror and disbelief.

He felt stricken, rose from his chair, picked up his hat. At the door, he turned to her. "Fitzroy might escape justice entirely—the baron's included."

In the early afternoon, Georges unlocked the tennis hall for Dick Burton and Colonel Saint-Martin and stood aside as they entered. Neither of them had found Roach in the genteel parts of Bath. Georges could not find him on Avon Street or at his other vulgar haunts. The rogue had clearly come to a bad end. But where was his body?

The light inside the hall had much improved. In the training room Burton was shown where a heavy body had been recently dragged. Leaning on his cane, he lowered himself painfully to the floor. With a magnifying glass he closely examined several brown spots. "Blood. Beyond a doubt!"

Georges shrugged respectfully. "But you'd expect to find some in a room where bruisers spar."

The colonel raised a finger. "I believe shedding blood is less likely in a tennis match." He pointed out a few brown spots along the body's trail across the court.

Burton took note of them, then examined the fibers Georges had discovered earlier on the rough floor boards of the rear hallway and on the sill of the back door. They were red, presumably from Roach's coat.

Saint-Martin picked up the black shoe from the floor. "A big man has lost it."

Burton examined the shoe and put it in the bag he carried. "There's little doubt the person who was dragged to the back exit was Roach, but we don't know for certain if he was dead at the time."

The three men stepped outside to inspect the fresh prints and tracks close to the door. Scattered bits of plaster indicated Anne had made molds of some of the clearer boot prints.

"The hoof prints are too small for a horse. Must be a donkey's," Georges remarked. "And the tracks come from a two-wheeled cart."

A few minutes later, they found a young beast in a nearby pasture, quite strong enough for the task they suspected she had performed. Her hooves matched the prints by the tennis hall. Her harness and cart were in an unlocked gardener's shed next to the pasture. The cart's wheels fitted the tracks.

"Servants rise early. They might have seen something," suggested Georges. "I'll find out." He left his companions in the tennis hall and hastened to the stables in Combe Park's west wing. The stablemaster was standing, arms crossed, overseeing the cleaning of a coach. Georges waited until the man appeared to be free, then asked him about the movements of the donkey and her cart. He shook his head, he had slept through the night. The two men working for him shrugged that they knew nothing.

As Georges turned to leave, he caught the eye of a young groom polishing a brass lantern at the rear of the coach. He was listening, knew something, Georges could tell, but was afraid to leave his work or had reason to be shy of the stablemaster.

Georges lingered in the stable, feeding oats to a horse, until the stablemaster left and the groom seemed free. Georges beckoned him. The young man came hesitantly. Georges promised to say nothing to the stablemaster and showed the young man a handful of pennies. He bit on his lower lip, his eyes on the money.

Then his tongue loosened. He had spent most of the previous night with one of the nymphs of Avon Street. Walking up the road to Combe Park before dawn, he heard someone coming toward him. He crouched in the brush off to one side. Two hooded men wrapped in long cloaks led a donkey and cart to within a few paces of his lair. It was too dark to see their faces or the large object they had in the cart. But he recognized Juliette.

"Juliette?" asked Georges.

"The donkey. I feed and brush her. Give her treats. As she passed, she sensed me. Balked and whinnied. I was afraid they'd find me."

"What did the men do?"

"One of them stopped the cart. The other drew a sword and stared in my direction. I was terrified. The man stepped toward me, his head cocked, listening. I held my breath. Then he said, it must have been a rat scurrying into the brush. He sheathed his sword and told the other man to move on. When they were gone, I hurried back to Combe Park."

"Can you identify the men?" Georges could easily guess who they were.

"Their voices sounded familiar. Irish, for sure."

By this time, Georges and the groom had fed and brushed the horse and cleaned his stall. "Before we leave the stable, tell me the rest."

Upon arriving back at Combe Park, the groom had checked the pasture and found Juliette missing, her cart gone from the shed. "It was none of my business," he told Georges. "I went to bed in my room above the stable. But I couldn't sleep. I wondered what the hooded men were carrying down to the river. Finally, I got up and hid near the shed. In a few minutes the cart drew near. A hooded man led the donkey up to the door and unshuttered a lamp to find the latch. I recognized his face."

"Who was it?"

"Captain Fitzroy's valet."

"And the cart?"

"It was empty."

Georges gave the young man his pennies and dashed back to the tennis hall. Dick Burton and Colonel Saint-Martin were in the training room. Breathless, he told them what he had learned from the young groom.

Burton frowned. "Fitzroy and his valet, beyond a doubt, leaving with Roach's body." He gazed at Saint-Martin. "I believe we have a murder to solve."

As he approached the house, Burton saw Sir Harry Rogers at the main entrance shaking the hand of a departing guest. A business partner, judging by the man's sober appearance and ample girth. Sir Harry smiled as he turned to go back inside, apparently pleased by a profitable deal. Then he noticed Burton approach. His smile faded at the sight of a stranger.

Burton tipped his hat, introduced himself, and began to explain his mission.

Sir Harry cut him off. "Come to my study. We'll talk there."

Entering the room, Burton smelled the fresh aroma of fine Virginia pipe tobacco. A bottle of port and two empty glasses stood on a small table by the window. A scent of dinner still lingered in the air. And perhaps the sound of music—the harpsichord was uncovered. Burton applauded inwardly. Sir Harry treated his partners well, one of the reasons he was so successful.

He nodded to a couple of chairs by the fireplace and they sat down. "You started to speak about Jack Roach, I believe." Sir Harry appeared annoyed.

Burton knew Rogers had engaged Roach to spy on his wife. Hardly an unusual practice in London or Bath. Could the two men have had a disagreement that became violent? Burton watched Rogers' face. "Sir, I believe that Roach has met with foul play at Combe Park."

Rogers drew back, mouth open, as if someone had suddenly struck him. "He was supposed to bring a report to my office last night on some work he was doing for me, but he never came. A footman said Roach had walked out toward the tennis hall. I looked there but couldn't find him." Sir Harry slumped down in his chair, confusion in his eyes, his hands nervously rubbing the arms of his chair.

Burton wondered about Rogers' obvious distress. A great deal had hung on Roach's report. It might have contained evidence for a divorce that Rogers desired passionately. If provoked by Roach, he could have reacted violently. But, until Roach's body was found, it was premature to probe him any further. Burton stirred as if preparing to leave. "I'll need to speak to servants and members of the family who might shed light on Roach's disappearance."

Distracted, Rogers didn't respond at first, then looked up and nodded. "Of course. The steward will show you around."

The parlor seemed like the best place for the informal interrogation Burton had in mind. He had sent a footman to summon Captain Fitzroy but had not indicated his purpose. That he was an officer of the Bow Street Court in London was usually enough to encourage a prompt response. Burton was standing by the fireplace, leaning on his cane, when the Irishman entered the room. He walked toward the officer with uneasy nonchalance. Curiosity and apprehension blended with his arrogance. Burton gestured to the chairs near the fire and they sat facing one another.

"Word may already have reached you, Captain, that Mr. Jack Roach has disappeared."

Fitzroy raised an eyebrow. "I hadn't heard. Should I care?"

"It happened under suspicious circumstances, such that I think he may have been murdered." Burton leaned forward, meeting Fitzroy's eye. "And, I think you *should* care. Mr. Roach entered the tennis hall approximately twenty minutes before you and Lady Margaret. You two may have been the last persons to have seen him alive last night."

"Wrong assumption," observed Fitzroy, unruffled. "It's true we went to the tennis hall. Mr. Roach had asked us to meet him there. I presumed Roach would beg for money, for he had lost heavily at yesterday's boxing match. But when we arrived, we found no one. We waited for perhaps a quarter of an hour, then returned to the house."

"Captain Fitzroy, is it likely Mr. Roach would have wanted to *borrow* money from you? He'd more likely have *demanded* it. He also knew you had lost as much as he had."

The Irishman appeared momentarily speechless.

"I believe you are more involved in Roach's disappearance than you have just led me to believe. I have taken the liberty of examining your boots."

Fitzroy appeared surprised, then outraged. "What insolence!"

"No insult intended, Captain. I shall do the same to several other men. It appears someone found Roach in the training room and moved him during the early morning hours. There are boot prints outside the back door of the tennis hall. They match yours."

Burton opened a package on a nearby table, revealing the plaster models Miss Cartier had made during the morning. Folding his arms across his chest, he leaned back, head to one side, watching Fitzroy.

Fitzroy glanced skeptically at the models. "They might fit many boots besides mine. I don't see any distinguishing marks or distinctive shapes."

"Furthermore," said Burton, pleased to have rattled the Irishman, "during the early hours of the morning, a witness observed you and your valet going down the road to the river with a heavily laden donkey cart." Burton realized he was stretching the facts slightly.

"*Observed* in the dark of night?" countered Fitzroy with contempt. "Absurd!"

"Your voice gave you away, Captain, when you thought a rat had startled the donkey. About an hour later, your valet was recognized as he returned the cart to its shed and the donkey to its pasture. Can you explain what you were doing? Or, must I draw the truth from your valet?"

The Irishman walked to the window, hands clasped behind his back and stood there silent for a minute. Finally, he turned around and glared at Burton. "It's true, my valet and I moved Roach's body in the donkey cart. You've already discovered that. But I didn't kill him. He was lying sprawled on the training room floor, already dead, when Lady Margaret and I arrived between eleven and twelve. I didn't want his body to be found on her estate. So I hid him in a closet, then later took him down to the Quay and dumped him into the river."

"It seems fair to say, Captain, you moved Roach's body because, if it were discovered at Combe Park, the public would leap to the conclusion you had killed him to save Lady Margaret's honor."

Fitzroy shrugged. "As good a reason as any I can think of."

Burton pressed on. "How would you describe your relationship with Roach? I recall you slapping his face at the Fancy Ball."

"It's common knowledge in Bath, Mr. Burton, that I despised the man, as did many others. The truth is, he threatened to expose a non-existent love affair between me and my cousin Lady Margaret. I would have gladly shot him in a duel, but he was much too cowardly to accept my challenge. I went to meet him last night because he claimed he would show me some new incriminating evidence he had gathered against Lady Margaret. The brazen cad!" Fitzroy drew himself up as if insulted.

"Even under such provocation, sir, I would not have stooped to murdering him in the dark of night."

Burton believed the Irishman might be telling the truth. But, he might also be an accomplished liar. His appeal to honor was suspect. It had not restrained him from beating women on at least two occasions. Burton leaned back in his chair. "No more questions for now, Captain, but I must ask you to remain in Bath until I have discovered all the particulars of Mr. Roach's death. You have made that task more difficult by throwing his body into the river."

Saint-Martin entered the parlor, Georges Charpentier in his wake. Dick Burton had called for them and was sitting at a table set for three. He rose to greet them cordially, then stretched, swung his cane back and forth. A footman brought them a tray of tea and biscuits, poured for them, and withdrew.

"Fitzroy has admitted to moving Roach's body," Burton began. "I would also have liked to question Mr. Critchley, but he was out of the house. Probably at Spring Gardens. And, Lady Margaret. But she was indisposed. I'll talk to her later."

He paused to spread butter on a biscuit and took a bite. Then he turned to Saint-Martin. "Fitzroy's the prime suspect, wouldn't you agree? He had opportunity and motives for killing Roach."

"A suspect, of course," replied Saint-Martin, apprehensive lest Burton reach a hasty conclusion. "But not the only one. The killer could have been lying in wait when Roach entered the tennis hall, killed him, then fled when Fitzroy arrived. Any number of persons could and would have done it."

"Do you have a particular person in mind?" asked Burton, his tone slightly waspish.

"It's really too early to name one among many. But, I could point out that even Sir Harry had opportunity and motive."

Burton looked doubtful.

"He could have slipped out of his study unobserved and surprised Roach in the tennis hall. Or, they might have agreed to meet there. Rogers badly wants to end his marriage with Lady Margaret. If Roach had offered the needed evidence but demanded too much, Sir Harry could have grown desperate enough to kill for it."

Burton shook his head. "I spoke to Rogers a half-hour ago. He appeared genuinely distressed, like a man who has lost a business partner on whom he was depending."

"Facial expressions are difficult to interpret," Saint-Martin countered. "Business men are often skilled liars." He added, "We should include on the list of suspects the many friends and relatives of the smugglers whom Roach betrayed to the excisemen, as well as the ladies and gentlemen of Bath whose scandals he exploited. With little effort and less compunction, any of them could have hired a couple of assassins to surprise Jack Roach last night when he entered the training room."

"Allow me to make a suggestion," Georges said respectfully. "I think Critchley should be considered. I saw him leave the dining room a little before eleven and he didn't return. He also had a strong motive—to free himself from Roach's grip. And, they were quarrelling about something Critchley had stolen from Lady Margaret, something that Roach desperately wanted. Critchley could have met Roach in the tennis hall, been cheated by him, and killed him."

Burton broke in, apparently suspecting the Frenchmen were attempting to divert responsibility away from Fitzroy. "That *something*, the object of their quarrel, could also serve as Fitzroy's motive for murder. It's likely he and Lady Margaret were having an affair. Fitzroy feared Roach had proof and intended to use it, so he killed him."

"Let's not rush to judgment," cautioned Saint-Martin. "Other suspects had equally strong interest in whatever was stolen from Lady Margaret."

"Thank you, gentlemen." Burton waved a hand to end the discussion and rose to leave. "I intend to question everyone who knew Jack Roach would be in the tennis hall between eleven and midnight and would have a reason to kill him. If you can think of one we've not yet identified, let me know. At the moment, Fitzroy is my chief suspect." At the door the Bow Street officer stopped and glanced back. "I need to know why Roach was blackmailing the captain and Lady Margaret."

Chapter 21

A Strange Letter

Thursday, April 5

From supper in the servants' hall, Georges walked with Peter Hyde to his room in the house's detached west wing where the stable was located. The coachman had invited the Frenchman to enjoy a pipeful of Virginia tobacco. Sir Harry had given it to him after Wednesday's fight for helping to train Lord Jeff. Though Georges didn't care to smoke, he feigned enthusiasm and brought along a flask of French brandy to share.

Hyde lodged comfortably in spacious quarters above the stable's harnass room, from which seeped up the distinctive odor of oiled leather. The furnishings were of good quality: simple, solid, and sensible, like the man himself. They also reflected his privileged status among the servants, one of the master's favorites. On the whitewashed walls hung mementoes of an adventurous life. A cavalryman's sabre and pistols, a boxer's blue scarf and sparring mittens held pride of place.

The coachman waved Georges to a worn but comfortable upholstered chair by the hearth, stirred the glowing embers to a bright fire, and lowered himself into a similar chair opposite. Georges brought out his flask, poured for Hyde and himself, then set the flask on a small table between them.

"To your health," they said, lifting their glasses together. The coachman drank a mouthful and smacked his lips with pleasure. Georges sipped uneasily from his glass, a twinge of guilt nagging his conscience. Drinking a brandy this fine, purchased with a baron's money, smacked of aristocratic self-indulgence. But it hadn't seemed right to drink it under the envious eyes of the other servants, and there wasn't enough for everyone.

The brandy was meant to dispose the coachman to talk freely. For some time Georges had wanted to meet privately with him, a knowledgeable, keen-sighted man, well-placed to observe the Combe Park household. He and Georges had become fast friends since that day on the Bristol road when together they had defended their coach and its passengers against a horde of bandits. Or, so it seemed to Hyde, who never tired of recounting the incident to anyone willing to listen.

After lighting their pipes, the two comrades exchanged small talk about the main house and its servants and reminisced about their military experiences. As young men they might have fought one another in the wars between their countries. But nostalgia banished any lingering trace of old hatreds or hardships.

At a lull in the conversation, Hyde peered over his shoulder conspiratorially, then caught Georges' eye. "So the captain dumped the Red Devil in the Avon, did he. Now that's a shame. The fish won't be fit to eat."

"Who told you that?" Georges asked irritably. "We are trying to keep it secret until tomorrow at least." He and Dick Burton hoped to search Roach's rooms early in the morning before news of his death led excisemen and other interested parties to interfere. Roach, if surprised by death, could have left behind a large collection of scandalous and otherwise incriminating material. Georges wanted to be the first to examine it.

Hyde made a soothing gesture. "The young groom, the one who saw the donkey cart on its way to the river. I overheard him telling his tale in the servants' hall. I said to him, now you've got it off your chest, I want you to stop. And I told the others to be quiet about it until the Bow Street man says it's all right."

The sound of footsteps outside the door interrupted Hyde's account. He opened for Jeffery, who stood there politely until invited to enter. "May I speak to you, Mr. Charpentier?" He glanced at Hyde and added with a courteous bow, "Privately."

"Of course," Georges replied. He turned to Hyde. "I want to talk to you later."

Hyde settled back with his pipe. "I'll keep the fire going and guard the brandy."

"Brave lad!" Georges handed the coachman a folded newspaper. "Here, read the latest *Bath Chronicle* while I'm gone. You may find a horse you'd like." Georges then followed Jeffery by a back way into the basement of the main house. He opened the door to a room little more than a closet with space for a bed, small table, and chair.

"What can I do for you, Jeff?" asked Georges with genuine concern. He sensed the footman came to him as a last resort.

The footman pulled a sealed letter from his coat. "This just arrived, addressed to Mr. William Rogers. Bad business, I think. Help me decide what to do with it." He explained that a well-dressed stranger, Mr. John Twycross, had come to the house earlier, demanding to see young Rogers. The visitor's grim demeanor had alarmed Jeffery, who left him standing outside while he consulted Lady Margaret. She knew the man and refused to let him in. One of William's bad companions, she had said.

"Twycross came back a few minutes ago, this time with a letter," said Jeffery. "I can't ask Lady Margaret—she's gone out for the evening. Would you read what's inside and help me decide what to do?" Jeffery smiled innocently. "I believe you know how to open it."

Georges nodded gravely. The letter might shed light on Roach's death, since William was one of his spies in the house.

"I may be able to help you." He took the letter and studied its wax seal. Prying it open shouldn't be difficult. While working for Lieutenant-General Sartine, he had opened diplomatic correspondence of the most eminent statesmen of Europe, and had come to enjoy their gossip.

"Wait here, Jeff," he said, tapping the letter. At first, he was inclined to open it in front of the footman but then changed his mind. Jeff should be able to say without lying that he had not seen the letter opened. "I'll bring this back to you in five minutes."

The footman bowed slightly, his expression blank except for a sly look in his eyes.

At a table in his own room, Georges held his knife's thin sharp blade in the flame of a candle. When it was hot, he deftly slipped it under the seal and lifted it from the paper. He unfolded the letter and began to read:

> *Mr. Rogers:*
> *It troubles us greatly to be obliged to send you this letter. We would have preferred to discuss our matters face to face, but you have studiously avoided us. Three months ago you asked us for a large sum of money in order, as you said, to enjoy the privileges of our establishment. You offered us a document, stating you were the nephew and ward of Sir Harry Rogers and requesting that you be extended the courtesies owed to a gentleman. Sir Harry's signature and seal authenticated the document. Privately, you claimed to be heir presumptive to Sir Harry's fortune, since Sir Harry, for reasons that are common knowledge, would soon set*

> *Master Charlie Rogers aside. On that basis, we the undersigned lent you two hundred pounds. You agreed to a repayment schedule of fifty pounds per month with interest of five per cent. Unfortunately, we have not received any of the scheduled payments. Furthermore, and more seriously, we now have reasons to believe the document is fraudulent and Sir Harry's signature is forged. You have until next Thursday to meet the payment schedule and to prove you are the heir you claim to be. Otherwise, we shall take the matter to Sir Harry and to the magistrates. This is the last warning. Indicate below that you have received this letter and return it to the bearer who will wait for it.*
> *Mr. John Twycross & Mr. Richard Wetenall*

Georges copied the letter's salient points and resealed it, then returned to Jeffery's room. The footman's guarded expression betrayed a hint of curiosity.

"As best I can determine, the letter doesn't directly concern Jack Roach. Bring it to William." Georges handed the letter to Jeffery, who glanced at it and smiled. The seal appeared unchanged.

"William is in serious trouble," Georges added, then explained the charges of deception against the young man.

"That doesn't surprise me," Jeffery remarked. "The servants talk much about his gambling."

"I noticed something else, Jeff, that you should know about." Georges engaged the footman's eye. "William would like to replace little Charlie as Sir Harry's heir. That could pose a threat to the boy. Do you understand what I mean?"

"Yes, sir, I do," he replied softly. "I shall be watchful." He flourished the letter. "I shall take it to William now."

A short while later, Jeffery returned with the letter.

Georges took it to his room again and opened it. William had written, "*I shall satisfy you by Thursday*," and signed his name. Georges resealed it and returned to Jeffery's room.

"How did he look when he read it?" Georges asked as he handed the letter over to Jeff.

"He pretended it wasn't important, but his hand shook as he handed it to me. I'll give it back to Mr. Twycross now."

Georges found Peter Hyde still in his chair by the fire, noticeably mellowed by the brandy. The *Bath Chronicle* lay spread open on his lap. The room stank of tobacco, affronting Georges' nostrils and watering his eyes. Like a stoic, he took his place opposite Hyde and poured himself a brandy.

"So, Georges, what has caused such concern to our champion, Lord Jeff, that he would search you out?"

The coachman was prying, Georges thought. But there was mutual benefit in sharing confidences, so he told him what he had learned.

Hyde frowned. "Sir Harry will be very angry about the forged signature. William's not his ward, and he's not willing to pay his gambling debts."

"How can the young man gamble away two hundred pounds so quickly?" Georges asked.

"Much of it went to Critchley. I'm sure he's behind the scheme. He has no credit, so he had to get money through William. They gamble together at Twycross's place. Critchley probably wrote the letter, signed Sir Harry's name, and used his seal. If anything went wrong, William would be blamed."

"Is there any truth at all in William's claim to be Sir Harry's heir-presumptive?"

The coachman grimaced. "For the time being, his heir is still little Charlie. And…" Hyde lowered his voice. "William doesn't stand a beggar's chance. I've overheard Sir Harry say he'd like to leave his fortune to a son of his own. Can't hardly blame him. Little Charlie's a fine boy, but he's not Sir Harry's." The coachman paused, cleared his throat. "Or, so they say."

Georges played innocent. "I guess that means Sir Harry wants to divorce Lady Margaret, disinherit Charlie, and marry again. Does he have a woman in mind?"

"Why Miss Ware of course! He can't take his eyes off her pretty face. Mind you, she's proper when I see them together. Friendly like, but not romantic. I'm not the one to ask how this will turn out. I know horses much better than women."

"Better than gamblers?" Georges asked, grinning. "Tell me about Mr. John Twycross and Mr. Richard Wetenall."

"Partners in a large fancy gambling house on Alfred Street near the Upper Assembly Rooms. There's much talk in the city about prominent hidden partners in the business. Some folks, including the mayor, call it a den of iniquity. Others praise its fine food and beautiful women, its high-stakes games of chance. Country gentlemen lose huge sums at its faro table. That's an open secret. The mayor of Bath is about to charge the two men in his court. He'll fine them one or two thousand pounds, only a small fraction of the profits they've made."

"Crooked characters!" Georges exclaimed. "Worthy successors to Jack Roach. Perhaps they will take over his extortion practice where he left off."

"And meet the same end," observed Peter, knocking the ash out of his pipe.

On the way back to his own room, Georges found Colonel Saint-Martin at his table, writing in his diary. He pulled up a chair and told him about Twycross' letter. "It gives William a motive for killing someone," Georges argued. "He desperately needs money. And he has the nasty character, as well as the physical strength to do it."

"But why would he want to kill Roach?" the colonel asked.

Georges rose and began to pace the room, hands clasped behind his back. "Let's suppose William thought Roach had the stolen package. He might conclude, if he got his hands on it, he could sell it to someone in the city or give it to Twycross in return for canceling his debt. So, he sneaked into the tennis hall between Critchley's and Fitzroy's visits, caught Roach unawares and killed him. Then, too late, William discovered Roach didn't have the package after all."

The colonel nodded. "A plausible scenario. William could be the person I saw at the entrance to the tennis hall before Fitzroy arrived. We can add the young man to our list of suspects."

"Critchley must have the package," Georges added. "If William had it, he would have no reason to avoid Twycross." He shook his head as he got up to leave. "There's still too many dark corners in this case. I'm hoping to throw some light on them tomorrow at Roach's house."

Chapter 22

Discoveries

Friday, April 6

On the broad sidewalk of North Parade, Georges Charpentier could see only servants and tradesmen moving about. The rich folk who would display themselves here later in the day were either at the public baths or still in bed.

The bells of the Abbey Church struck seven. A carriage approached. Georges checked his watch and murmured, "Right on time." He was waiting for Dick Burton.

Yesterday, when Burton had proposed to search Roach's rooms for hidden papers, Colonel Saint-Martin had offered his adjutant's services, claiming that Charpentier could ferret even the most reluctant rats from their holes. Burton had gladly accepted the offer and said he would arm himself with authority from the mayor of Bath. He would also engage men to search the river for Roach's body.

"Look's like they got here before us," the Frenchman remarked dryly as he walked up to Burton's carriage. "News of Roach's disappearance traveled fast."

Burton stepped out on to the pavement and glanced at a coach standing in the street, marked with fading royal insignia. "Excise officers?"

Georges shook his hand. "Three of them pulled up to the house just as I arrived a few minutes ago. Pounded on the door, like they meant to knock it down. Charged in, pushed the landlady aside."

Burton frowned. "They're a law unto themselves. We'll drive around the corner into Duke Street and wait until they leave. Won't be long. They can't find a thing without these." He waved a bundle of papers he had been carrying under his arm. "Architectural plans," he said with a sly grin. "John Wood drew them for the construction of the building in the 1740s."

As Burton had predicted, the excise officers came out of the house twenty minutes later, empty handed and irritated, and drove away in their coach.

Georges and his companion returned and knocked on the door. The landlady opened for them, pale, trembling. Burton flashed the warrant to search, but she hardly took note of it. She stood aside speechless as they climbed the stairs to Roach's apartment. The door was ajar. Inside was chaos. The officers had overturned furniture, spilled ink, scattered papers and quills about, ransacked the cabinet, slashed the straw mattress.

"They might think of the architectural plans later and find out I've got them." Burton laid the sheets on a table. "They could trace me here. Let's get our work done before they come back."

Georges studied Roach's rooms, then the rooms above and below and to each side, measuring the walls, floors and ceilings, all the while consulting the architect's plans. Finally, he pulled the bed out of its alcove and examined the wainscoting. It seemed to fit snugly to the wall. To the left of the alcove was a water closet; to the right, a storeroom. More measuring, then a low whistle. "There's a large empty space behind this section at the foot of the bed." He stepped back to study the alcove, muttering to himself, "Could Roach have found a way to use it?"

The excise men had torn down the curtains that closed off the alcove from the rest of the room. But the stout rod still remained in place. Georges reached up and tried to turn it. It seemed firmly fixed into a pair of cylinders pegged to the walls on the left and right. He examined the cylinders closely. A thin iron pin ran through each cylinder from top to bottom piercing the rod and holding it in place.

Georges removed the pins and began to turn the rod clockwise. Nothing happened. Then, counterclockwise. There was a faint sound of gears working, latches withdrawing. Georges stepped back as the wainscoting dropped to the alcove floor. In the opening stood two large boxes.

"Incredible!" exclaimed Burton, peering over Georges' shoulder. The Frenchman moved to the side to allow his companion to finger through the contents of the boxes. "Roach's treasure-trove of scandal and perfidy," he said, lifting one of the boxes out of the opening. "Take the other one, Georges. We'll haul them to the carriage."

"I'm sure Colonel Saint-Martin would be interested in what we've discovered," Georges remarked, convinced that Fitzroy would figure prominently in Roach's collection.

Burton hesitated hardly a second. "Of course. Tell your colonel to come to the York Inn. He and I must go through these things together." In ten minutes' time, they put the wainscoting and the pins back in place, moved the boxes into Burton's carriage, and drove away.

Saint-Martin hastened eagerly to Burton's room. Georges had told him of Roach's papers, then left to join in the search for his body. Burton received the colonel with a wide smile. "There may be some pearls here," he said, pointing to the two boxes on the table. "I thought it best we share them. By the way, thanks for Georges Charpentier. He's a gem."

They sat down immediately and emptied a box on the table. It contained personal things: financial records, bank notes worth several thousand pounds, journals, letters to friends, and a large collection of exquisite unsigned sketches of Bath scenes, portraits of men and women, as well as several erotic pieces signed J.Roach.

The colonel leafed through a journal. "This is a side of Roach I wouldn't have imagined. His handwriting is hasty, as one would expect, but vigorous and graceful. He had a gentleman's taste and a sharp eye for what's interesting."

"A pity he turned out so badly," conceded Burton, pushing the personal papers aside and emptying the other box. "But we must now consider his criminal side." The two men set to work sorting the contents into separate piles according to subject.

When they had surveyed whatever related to scandal in Bath, Burton laid a hand on the pile and looked up at Saint-Martin. "I believe I should return these to Roach's victims."

"It's the fair thing to do," the colonel agreed. Bath scandal concerned him only where it might implicate Madame Gagnon or compromise her usefulness. He was relieved to see that Roach had not mentioned her.

Detached yet curious, Saint-Martin looked on while Burton skimmed through Roach's correspondence with excise officers and other pieces related to smuggling. When he had finished, he handed Saint-Martin a packet. "Instructions from excise officers to Roach and his reports to them. Dirty business. He sent several smugglers to the gallows." A few minutes later, Burton gave the colonel a smaller packet. "Here are notes to and from smugglers." He added with a wry face, "To keep their trust, Roach sometimes warned them away from excisemen's traps."

The packets told Saint-Martin a fascinating story of Roach's treachery to both sides in the war between excisemen and smugglers. "A skillful juggler, I must say, though it's possible one or the other party did him in." He shuffled the packets back together into a pile and patted it down. "These are of no use to me. You might want to hold them, until we're sure who *did* kill Roach." The size and danger of the illicit trade, not only in tea but also in French brandy and lace, amazed Saint-Martin. Smugglers and excisemen clashed daily in bloody battles off the Channel coast of England.

Into a third pile had gone whatever appeared to concern Combe Park. Saint-Martin was fingering through a journal when the name "Campbell" leaped out at him. He read an entry dated March 16, the day she died.

> *Critchley, the cretin! Stole some spoons. The Campbell girl discovered him. He pushed her down a stairway and broke her neck. Or, so William claimed. Lucky no one else was there. I warned Critchley of dire consequences if he were ever again to do anything so stupid. He could have ruined my scheme at Combe Park.*

Saint-Martin stared at the page with cold fury. Roach hadn't cared that the girl was killed, only that Critchley had foolishly risked his position in Sir Harry's household. The colonel handed the journal to his companion without comment.

"What's this?" Burton exclaimed, staring at the page. His eyes widened as he read it, his lips shaped its words. He said softly, "So, Miss Campbell's death may not have been an accident. Why would William implicate Critchley in a capital crime?" He set the journal to one side. "I'll need it tomorrow when I interrogate them."

The two men resumed their search of Roach's papers until Burton sat up straight, holding a document. "This alone is worth a trip to Bath!" He showed it to the colonel. It was a signed receipt from the jeweler in London to whom Critchley had sold his stolen silver more than a year ago. According to an attached note to himself, Roach had threatened to denounce both Critchley and the jeweler, forcing the former to surrender to him the money from the sale and the latter to give him the silver. Roach had hidden it in his London apartment.

While Saint-Martin was still reading the note, Burton got up from his chair. With a grimace he stretched, then limped back and forth across the floor. "Damned leg. It's stiff. Need to move it." Stopping behind the younger man, Burton reached over his shoulder and pointed to the receipt. "That's Roach's lever on Critchley. I've suspected it all along! Now I've proof! The case is as good as closed and the silver recovered!"

"Congratulations!" said Saint-Martin, genuinely pleased for his companion. The silver was valued at six hundred pounds. Burton should receive a third as his commission, sufficient to live comfortably for a year or two. Fair enough. He had doggedly pursued the case long after others would have given up.

Saint-Martin returned the receipt and the note to Burton and reached once more into the Combe Park pile. Several reports to and from Roach piqued his interest. Critchley had discovered the steward pilfering from the pantry but had reported it to Roach rather than to Sir Harry. This confirmed the colonel's impression that, in contrast to Rogers' slaving business, his domestic staff was poorly supervised—for the most part, left to Lady Margaret. Roach could ply his trade easily among the servants.

Roach had instructed Critchley on the use of the optical device which Sir Harry had manufactured in order to spy on Lady Margaret. Critchley had described her bursting into the room the night of the Fancy Ball and running to the table to assure herself the secret drawer had not been disturbed. After bribing Lady Margaret's maid to gain entrance to the room, he had stolen the compromising item from the drawer. Roach had scrawled "Well done!" on Critchley's report and had added, "Will get it soon from C."

The name Harriet Ware, Anne's friend, came up unexpectedly. Critchley's report mentioned small presents Sir Harry bought for her and other signs of their affection. In a lurid passage Critchley described them making love in Rogers' study. Stunned, Saint-Martin asked himself, was Critchley describing what he had seen, or was he embellishing an incident in order to titillate Roach? In the margin Roach had placed a large question mark.

The Red Devil wasn't easily fooled, thought Saint-Martin. He reflected again on the lurid passage. Suppose Roach could expose an adultery between Rogers and Harriet? If it were flagrant, it could jeopardize his attempt to divorce Lady Margaret. He might pay handsomely to avoid exposure. Or...he might kill Roach to silence him.

Saint-Martin put it to Burton as a question.

"I doubt it," Burton replied. "Roach would feel he needed much more than Critchley's word to blackmail a man as powerful and dangerous as Rogers."

Burton sat down and browsed through the Combe Park pile again. Suddenly, he started, frowned. "Colonel, you should look at these." He pushed several pages across the table to Saint-Martin.

They began with Critchley's report on Jeffery's visits to Sarah Smith and to the Quaker David Woodhouse. Saint-Martin wasn't surprised. Anne had already informed him. But Critchley went on to claim that Anne had met Jeffery surreptitiously in Combe Park's attic for an orgy of passionate love-making. Critchley's obscene images tore through Saint-Martin's mind. He slapped the pages with the back of his hand. A tissue of lies! He stared numbly at the report for a long moment, then looked up. Burton was gazing at him.

"A curious monster, that Critchley! It's good he isn't here. You'd strangle him."

"Indeed!" growled Saint-Martin, and jammed the sheets into his valise.

As the colonel was about to walk out of the York Inn, Georges rushed up to him, breathless. At midmorning in the fish market, he had heard the news of a body, just discovered in the river. A fisherman had found it fully clothed a few hundred yards below the Bath Bridge and had carted it to the hospital on Upper Borough Wall. Georges had hastened to view the body and had identified it as Roach.

Saint-Martin left Georges at the door and immediately fetched Burton from his room. The three men hurried to the hospital. By the time they arrived, a doctor had already made a preliminary examination of the body. He showed them into the room where it lay stretched out on a table.

A day in the river had torn his red coat and tangled his hair. His face had a waxy sheen; the skin was soft, bloated, and yielding. Saint-Martin searched the face for its crafty malignant gaze, its haughty lift of eyebrows and sneering curl of lips. They had gone with Roach's evil spirit. Into Hell's fiery pit? The thought jolted the colonel. He couldn't remember ever having believed in Hell, with or without the fire. Yet, there it was, an idea lodged in the deep, dark recesses of his mind. Hell seemed a fitting place for Roach. Perhaps it *was* real.

Drawing the three men closer to the examination table, the doctor pointed to a wide shallow indentation at the right temple. "Caused by a powerful blow from a smooth round object," said the doctor. Death had been instantaneous. Roach's expression was blank, uncomprehending, as if he never knew what had hit him. He had certainly been dead before entering the river.

Georges pointed to the wound. "Since he was apparently taken by surprise, he must have been hit from behind by a right-handed assailant or by an object thrown from the side."

That didn't mean much, thought Saint-Martin. All the suspects he could imagine, including Jeffery, were right-handed.

"You've searched the body, I presume," said Burton, turning to the doctor.

"That we did. And found nothing of great value—only a few coins and small bills of exchange. He was carrying a little leather pouch containing a flint, black powder, and a half-dozen balls for a small caliber weapon."

"He was known to be armed," Saint-Martin interjected. "Last night at Combe Park, he had threatened Jeffery, the black footman, with a small pistol. We haven't found it in the tennis hall. Perhaps it fell from his body while he was tumbling about in the river."

"I don't think so," said the doctor. "A holster with a strap to hold the weapon is sewn into his vest at the small of his back. If the pistol had been in the holster, it would not have fallen out."

"Roach's killer must have taken it," said Saint-Martin. "And it's presumably still loaded. Roach didn't have an opportunity to fire it."

"Another indication that he was surprised," Burton added, then addressed the doctor. "You may remove the body. We're finished here. Would you write an official report for the record?"

It was ready in a few minutes. With the report in his hand, the Bow Street officer turned to Saint-Martin. "I'm off to the mayor. When he's read this, he'll surely agree I have a murder to investigate."

As Anne and Charlie entered the servants' hall, Mr. Cope the steward approached them, breathless with excitement. "Have you heard? In the market they say Jack Roach's body has been fished from the Avon. The whole town is buzzing."

To Anne this news came as no surprise. She already knew he had disappeared and was presumed to have been killed. Now she was curious how certain other persons would react. She and the boy waited just inside the door. They were supposed to meet Mr. Critchley and William at noon for a meal and French conversation.

A few minutes later, the two men walked into the hall, visibly agitated. The steward rushed up to them. "They've found Roach's body...."

Critchley cut him off brusquely. "In the river. Yes, I know."

The steward stared blankly at the tutor, then with a sniff recovered his dignity and left the room.

Anne stepped forward, clearing her throat. "Would you have any idea how he died?"

Critchley jumped a step, startled apparently by her sudden, unexpected question. "How in God's name would I know," he exclaimed testily. He glanced about the hall, then looked sharply at Anne. "Why isn't our food ready?"

"It will come in a few minutes, I suppose." She often had to rebuff his attempts to put her down as an inferior servant. She led the way to a table set near the windows looking out over the park. A soft northern light bathed a vase of daffodils that served as a center piece. The group of four took their places. A servant asked what they wished to drink and left the room.

Several months ago, Sir Harry had decided to provide training in French and good manners for William with a mind to eventually sending him abroad on a grand tour of Europe's art and antiquities. Mr. Critchley would presumably accompany him as tutor and guardian.

At Lady Margaret's insistence, little Charlie and his tutors, first Mary Campbell and then Anne, had been included in the program. Anne had told Charlie to pay close attention to Mr. Critchley's speech and his gestures, for he spoke more clearly and distinctly than anyone else in the house. But he wasn't to let the tutor catch him at it, she had added.

When Anne had met Critchley previously, she found him unpleasant company—too much given to cynical asides and a sardonic grin. At last Friday's meal, to her surprise, he had shown he knew how to behave at the table and had spoken excellent French. Despite her feelings about him, she had listened with interest. He appeared to know a great deal of history, literature, and art. His comments were often trenchant and witty.

At her prompting, he had spoken readily about himself. Years ago, he had accompanied young gentlemen to the continent. Fluent in Italian as well as French, he preferred Italy to any other country in the world.

"If fortune were ever to favor me with money and opportunity," he had said in full round tones, "I would live under Naples' sunny skies, gazing at its magnificent bay, studying its Greek and Roman antiquities. And, I would yield gladly to the charms of its dark-eyed, buxom young women."

Anne had detected in his voice a note of anticipation, as if Italy weren't entirely out of reach.

Critchley rapped on the table, interrupting Anne's recollections. "Mademoiselle Cartier!" He glared at her. "Let us begin." No doubt about it, she thought, Critchley's manner had changed today. She stared at him across the table. Anxiety creased his brow. He wrung his hands while he spoke. The discovery of Roach's body must have troubled him. A likely suspect, she concluded.

He appeared to sense what she was thinking. His head drew back as if he dared her to accuse him. Anne refused to blink. He turned to William for support. The young man frowned, apparently resenting the request. Did he bear Critchley a grudge? Anne wondered.

Conversation in French proved difficult and soon flagged. When it came to a halt, Critchley took a book from his bag and glanced at Anne. "Mr. Roach's atrocious death has dampened our spirits. While we wait to be served, I shall read in French some familiar passages from the *Fables* by Jean de La Fontaine."

Anne saw no reason to challenge his choice. A reading from the *Fables* would benefit Charlie more than the French conversation he could hardly understand. He already knew many of the stories in English translation and enjoyed reciting bits of them to his mother. At Anne's suggestion, Critchley chose "The Pumpkin and the Acorn," one of the few fables Charlie also knew in French.

With a flourish of throat clearing, Critchley opened the book and commenced. It was a simple tale. A rustic simpleton thought his Creator had made a foolish mistake, fitting the huge pumpkin to a low slender vine and the tiny acorn to a great tall oak tree. Then one day the man fell asleep under such an oak. An acorn dropped precisely on his nose, stinging him painfully and causing blood to flow. Good God, the man cried, what if this acorn had been a pumpkin! He left the oak tree and went his way, praising God who knew His business after all.

Anne sat quietly, intrigued by a change in Critchley's appearance. As he read, his voice grew lively and resonant, teasing nuances out of the rhymed verses. His face brightened and, for the moment, shed the bitterness that otherwise corroded his spirit.

Almost unawares, Anne was drawn into the tale. Its moral seemed to touch upon her own recent experiences. The ways of Providence *were* truly wondrous. Jack Roach was dead, killed most likely by someone he had wronged. A fitting end. This also closed a distressful chapter in her own life. Her spirit still bore the scars from his assault over a year ago. He had walked away from his crime with impunity and had continued to threaten her. But no more. She breathed a sigh of relief.

Distracted by her sigh, Critchley looked up from the book. She gave a little shrug of apology. He stared at her malevolently, head bent to one side, as if about to question her, then said nothing. She wondered what had come of Roach's plan to gather evidence against Lady Margaret? Had Critchley inherited it? Anne felt uneasy, but for Charlie's sake she tried not to show it.

The servant brought them a lamb stew, with ale for the two men, cider for Anne and Charlie. The meal was mercifully brief. William slouched in his chair and played with his food, paying little attention to Critchley's admonitions. Between the stew and the dessert, a honey cake, Critchley attempted to read again. William stared sullenly out the window, finger-tapping a rhythm on the table. Exasperated, perhaps intimidated by his pupil, the tutor had had enough. He slammed the book shut, declared the meal over without the dessert, and left the hall.

Anne and Charlie exchanged bewildered glances, then retreated to her room where they spoke about the fables for a few minutes. He had watched Critchley's lips like a hawk. Though he hadn't been able to decipher each and every word, he caught the gist of the stories and could retell them to Anne in his own original way.

Preoccupied by Critchley's strange behavior at the meal, she had to struggle to pay attention to Charlie. It dawned on her that, after all, Critchley had higher aspirations than to tutor spoiled, ungrateful William. He dreamed of a life of leisure in Italy! She sensed that his dry, sour appearance concealed roiling envy, resentment, anger, hunger for sensual pleasure. What desperate steps might he be willing to take in order to break loose from the bonds of his present dismal existence?

Anne sat alone in her room. Charlie had left with reading assignments for the afternoon. She felt pensive and restless. Critchley was still too much on her mind. What had happened in his youth to warp his character so badly? Learned, well-spoken, he obviously came from a cultivated family. She had heard his father had been vicar of a church near Oxford.

She walked to the open window and leaned out. The morning mist had lifted hours ago. A warm bright sun stood high in the sky. A perfect time to walk in the park and forget about Critchley. At least for the moment. Perhaps Paul…

A knock on the door startled her. She sighed. Charlie again with a question. Something that could probably wait. The boy was lonely, sought every opportunity to be with her. He needed deaf playmates his own age, but Lady Margaret was too distracted to make the arrangements. Anne squared her shoulders. She'd do what she could for him.

She pulled the door open and gave out a little cry of pleasure.

Paul stood there, unsmiling. "Roach's body's been found. In the river. Georges and I identified it at the hospital."

"Yes, I've heard." She drew him into the room while he spoke of the medical examination.

"Let's walk in the park," she said. "I need fresh air. You can tell me more about Roach."

In a few minutes she was ready. They left the house and walked down a steep winding path to a lovely ornamental covered bridge. Like an ancient temple, its roof was supported by rows of Ionic columns. A stream, swollen by the recent rain, cascaded beneath the bridge into a fishpond below, where a pair of swans glided gracefully.

Anne and Paul leaned side by side on the bridge's stone balustrade, studying their distorted reflection in the pond's agitated surface. He told her about Roach's papers. "Now we know how Mary Campbell died, or more precisely, how it appeared to Roach." He summed up for her what he had learned.

A feeling of sadness swept over her. "This strengthens my belief that it wasn't an accident." She lifted her face to the sky and cursed the heartless cruelty that cut the young woman's life short. Anne would write immediately to Mr. Braidwood. Mary's parents also needed to know, even though it would pain them.

Paul must have sensed her mood for he put a hand gently on her shoulder. When she had quieted herself, she asked what else he had learned. He then mentioned Critchley's fabrications about Harriet. Even though Anne discounted the lurid parts, Critchley's account distressed her. Harriet appeared caught in a compromising relationship with Sir Harry.

Paul and Anne walked back to the house at a leisurely pace. The early afternoon sun warmed their faces. Spring was bursting out around them. Thick clusters of daffodils dotted the open green upward slope. A soft fresh breeze carried the scents of spring blossoms from the adjacent woods.

As they neared the entrance to the building, he turned to her. "Tea in my rooms? I have something you probably should look at."

Her curiosity aroused, she agreed, then began to feel apprehensive. This was the first time he had asked her to visit him. She judged from the earnest tone of his voice that his purpose was not romantic. As they walked through the building and up the stairs, he had little to say. His face was taut, his smile strained.

His parlor was a bright, sunny room facing south. He called a servant who served tea at a table by the fireplace and then withdrew. Paul reached into his valise on a nearby chair and pulled out several sheets of paper. "From Roach's apartment," he said. "Critchley's crude fantasies about you and Jeffery. Burton agreed I should have them." He hesitated, uncertain. "I'm sorry, they may hurt. Do you want to read them?" He offered her the sheets.

Though her hand trembled, she took them and began reading. She soon gasped in disbelief, and finally thrust the sheets back to Paul. For a few moments at a loss for words, she wrestled with Critchley's malice. Then, with an exasperated sigh, she spluttered, "The man is contemptible!"

She breathed deeply, fighting back her anger. Finally, she calmed down enough to speak. "As I told you earlier, I had gone to the attic that morning to find toys for Charlie. In the room over the chancel I stumbled upon Jeffery asleep...."

Paul broke in, waving his hands. "You don't have to explain, Anne. Scandalous tales like Critchley's are best ignored, otherwise they may gain credence."

"But I must explain! You've raised the problem, Paul, and it won't go away—at least not from my mind." And, it will linger, perhaps fester in his, she thought. "You should hear me out."

He fell silent. A pained, stubborn look came over his face.

She went on to describe Jeffery in the attic learning to read, his panic when discovered, Critchley coming up the stairs looking for her and her quick reaction. "I honestly don't understand why he invented this horrid tale."

Paul looked at her as if he could guess the reason. She rose to her feet, shocked into a new awareness. He, like Critchley, had sensed a certain sympathetic understanding between her and the footman. Critchley had grossly distorted it into a sexual coupling.

That look in Paul's eye triggered Anne's memory of them riding back from Allen's quarry and meeting Jeffery. He had stared at her riding astride in boy's britches and Paul had reacted brusquely.

"Do you *think* I have given Critchley any reason to believe Jeffery and I are..."

"Please, Anne, we must put this matter to rest. You are guiltless. Critchley indulged in the fantasies of a sick imagination. He slandered your friend Miss Ware as well." Paul hesitated for a moment, chastened. "I suppose when I see another man showing interest in you, like Jeffery did, I feel the bite of jealousy. I love you beyond measure, but not as wisely as I ought. I'm sorry and ask to be forgiven."

She rose from the table and knelt at his side, caressing his cheek. "There's nothing to forgive, Paul. I love you dearly."

He lifted her to her feet. She put her arms around him and drew him to her. They kissed, holding each other closely. Then he stepped back and led her to the fireplace. "I brought Critchley's papers here so we could destroy them. No point allowing them to fall into the wrong hands and cause mischief." He stirred the glowing embers and threw the offensive sheets among them.

Anne stared into the fire. Within seconds Critchley's tale was reduced to wisps of ash.

Georges found himself waiting again for Dick Burton, this time in Combe Park's tennis hall. Colonel's orders. Georges had protested. "It's beginning to look like I'm working for Bow Street instead of the Royal Highway Patrol." The colonel had chuckled. "Burton's investigation is bound to touch Captain Fitzroy. We want to know what happens and, if possible, influence the outcome."

Steps sounded at the entrance. The door opened and Burton limped in, leaning on his cane. He needs me, Georges thought. The Bow Street officer was his age but looked ten years older.

He greeted Georges warmly. "I've come with full authority to investigate Roach's murder," he said. "Let's look for the weapon that killed him."

Georges led him into the training room. "The wound in Roach's temple suggests that the murderer could have struck him with one of those." He pointed to a dozen iron shots that lay lined up against a wall. Burton and Georges examined each of them but found no traces of blood or hair.

"The murderer could have improvised a weapon," Georges added, as he picked up a sixteen-pound ball, slipped it into a sack hanging nearby, and swung it at an imaginary victim. "Or, he could have held the shot in his hand and used his arm like a club, or even thrown it, then carried the shot away when he left." Georges rubbed the shot thoughtfully and returned it to its place in the line.

Burton drew the inference Georges expected. "In either case, he had not planned ahead, but had picked up a weapon on the spur of the moment. That theory would rule out hired assassins and Roach's enemies in the city and among smugglers. It would shrink the field of suspects to the Combe Park household and its guests."

Georges agreed, then suggested they look again at the boot prints outside the back door of the tennis hall. They already knew that the two sets grouped around the donkey cart's tracks belonged to Fitzroy and his valet. The other prints were less well defined and trailed off in different directions. To whom did they belong and at what time during the night were they made?

"We should check Sir Harry's boots," Burton said as they left the hall. "We know he had reason to meet Roach—as did Critchley."

Georges remained respectfully silent for a moment, then suggested, "Before troubling those two gentlemen, I think we should try something else first."

Inside the house to the left of the entrance, Georges opened a closet door and pointed to a row of boots of various sizes. "I'll wager we'll find a match here. Our suspect might have selected a pair of these for the short, wet walk to the tennis hall rather than go to his room for a pair, then march through the party wearing them."

A quick comparison with Anne's plaster molds proved Georges' guess to be correct. Holding a pair of the boots that did match, Georges remarked, "The footman on duty at the door the night of the party could not always see the closet. Critchley, Sir Harry, any of the guests could have slipped in here and taken these."

"That's true," Burton granted. "It's too soon to draw conclusions. I'll have to interrogate the lot of them."

Georges smiled inwardly. Fitzroy was still free for the taking.

Chapter 23

Quandary

Friday, April 6

Early in the afternoon, Harriet Ware came to Sir Harry's study. He had invited her to dine with him and one of his ship's captains scheduled to sail for Jamaica in a week. She had entertained for Harry on similar occasions and had grown comfortable with this setting. But recently she had begun to feel apprehensive. This had increased in the measure that he pressed his infatuation upon her.

Since speaking to Annie on Monday, she had hoped Harry would come to his senses. This week's boxing match had distracted him from his marital problems and put him in a very good mood. But was that likely to last? Pausing at the door, she bit her lips to bring out their color, then knocked lightly.

Sir Harry opened the door with a smile, took her hand, and drew her in. "Are you in good voice today, Harriet? My guest, Captain Fairbrother, loves Irish airs and he's not likely to hear any for a long while. I want you to sing for him."

"I'd be ever so happy to please the gentleman," she replied, thinking a seaman would be appreciative. Yesterday, she had sung Scottish airs at Harry's dinner for a proper businessman, who had hardly noticed her. In any case, Harry enjoyed her voice and paid well to hear it.

He took her cloak, offered her wine, and led her to a table by the window. While waiting for the captain, they chatted easily about music and the theater. Harry admired her gown, an elegant yellow wool, the bodice low-cut. Purchased with money from her first concert at Combe Park, she fondly recalled. She lightly fingered the lace trim, then looked up guardedly into his eyes.

His mood was tender but lusty. He plainly wanted to touch her and to have her. But she held back, warned by a small inner voice of caution that had thus far served her well.

Their conversation turned to the news that Jack Roach had been found dead. The Bow Street officer had informed Harry a few hours ago. Harriet sensed he didn't want to talk about it. But his feelings were so pent up, he couldn't hold back.

"Jack Roach was a scoundrel," he blurted out. "His death hurts no one—but me!" Harry's ruddy face grew nearly purple with anger. "Roach was investigating a most delicate matter."

Harriet listened quietly. She understood what Harry meant, although he had never openly spoken to her about it. He had hoped to receive the legal evidence he needed to end his marriage to Lady Margaret and marry again. After raising Harry's hopes, Roach had disappointed him. And had been arrogant and rude into the bargain.

Harry's frustration threatened to grow out of control. He rose and gripped the back of his chair. "Now Roach is dead and what had appeared to be within my grasp is lost." After a few moments of strained silence, he released the chair and began to pace back and forth, trying to calm himself. He glanced out the window, then turned to her. "Get ready, Harriet." His voice became almost normal. "Captain Fairbrother has arrived."

During the meal, Harry put on a good face for the captain, sharing sea stories from his youth on a slave ship. He had had several narrow escapes from ship wreck, mutiny, and insurrection. The captain had similar tales to tell. The adventure of a slaver's life seemed to blind these two men to its horror. Harriet lost her appetite, picked at her food, straining to appear interested.

Between courses, Harriet accompanied herself on the harpsichord in several of the captain's favorite airs. He settled back in his chair, a wistful expression on his weathered face. Probably dreaming of an Irish lass he had known. Seemed like a kindly man. Harry noticed his captain's pleasure and smiled at Harriet. Her spirits rose. Appreciation always made her feel better. After lunch, she left the two men to their pipes and port.

Half-way down the hallway on her way out, she recalled leaving a pair of gloves in the ballroom the night of the victory party. She turned around, walked past the study door and into the ballroom. After searching for a few minutes, she found her gloves set aside on a table. She breathed a sigh of relief, then retraced her steps. As she neared the study again, the door opened and the two men stepped out into the hall just a few paces away. They turned in the other direction and didn't notice her.

She was about to cough or say something, but she stopped herself—she didn't know why. The two men leaned together, their bodies tensed. Her heart beat wildly. She edged behind a column.

Sir Harry nodded toward Jeff standing unawares in the entrance hall and whispered to the captain, "That's the man."

The captain stared at the footman, a massive pillar of ebony, then glanced sharply at Rogers. "Good God! Not him!"

"Don't worry. He'll be drugged and bound."

"Aren't you sorry to lose a great boxer?"

"Sorry? Yes indeed. But if he stays here, I'll lose him anyway. At least this way, I'll get a good price for him. There are other big, fast black slaves where he came from. I'll train one of them."

The captain shrugged. "Next Friday, then. Three seamen will come with a wagon to carry him to Bristol and put him on board."

Rogers and the captain stepped back into the study, their voices a bare murmur. Harriet slipped away, shaking with disbelief.

Anne leaned back in her chair, staring at the ceiling. The scent of burnt paper lingered in the room, reminding her of Critchley's slanderous tale. Fortunately, it had brought her and Paul closer together. She warmed at the thought.

Her rest was interrupted by a knock on the door. She opened to find Harriet Ware, her face ashen. Anne put an arm around the young woman's shoulders and led her to a chair. "What's the matter, Harriet? Sit down and tell me about it." Anne poured her a small brandy.

As Harriet sipped from the glass and color returned to her cheeks, she related what she had heard at Sir Harry's door. "It's like a bad dream. I allow Harry to lose his temper. That's in his nature. And I can understand his hatred of Captain Fitzroy, who has betrayed him. But Jeff's done nothing to harm Harry. He even risked his life in Wednesday's match to win a fortune for him! It's wrong to drug him and ship him away."

Her composure broke down and she began to cry. "Harry's been so generous and kind—just wonderful to me. But now he acts like a stranger. I feel like walking away from him. Am I ungrateful?"

"Not at all!" Anne replied. "Your instinct is sound. Sir Harry is to blame." She was silent for a minute, reflecting on what could be done for the slave. A plan came to her mind, but sharing it with Harriet seemed too risky. She took her friend's hand. "For the time being, carry on with Sir Harry as if nothing has happened. I'll speak to Mr. Woodhouse."

Dark clouds scudded across the sky as Anne left the house. Georges was waiting for her at the door with a carriage.

"Going to Jeff's friend, the seamstress?" he asked.

"Yes. I just found out that Sir Harry plans to send him back to Jamaica soon. Sarah Smith needs to know." She explained how Harriet had brought the news to her.

"Heartless villain!" exclaimed Georges without regard for whoever might be listening. "But Burton might frustrate Sir Harry's plans. Jeff could find himself in a courtroom facing royal judges instead of cutting sugar cane. A few minutes ago, I found out that he's one of Burton's suspects in Roach's murder."

"Jeffery had good reasons to hate Roach, but so did many others. Please explain, Georges. I need to tell Sarah."

"Jeff stands out among them because of his ability to pitch."

"What?"

"Roach was killed by a single, powerful blow to the right temple by an assailant he didn't see—or sense. At first, we thought someone could creep up behind him and hit him with a heavy, round object. But that would be difficult to do. Roach was unusually alert. The man who killed him might not have come from behind. He could have stood off to one side in the dark, thirty paces away, and pitched a sixteen pound ball at Roach's temple. With deadly accuracy."

Georges paused, then measured his words. "Jeff's the only man at Combe Park, or in Bath, for that matter, who could do it. The servants say he often pitches at old pots and pans to amuse them."

Anne recalled him pitching at a wooden block on the bowling green. "True, he could have killed Roach, but I doubt that he did." She was less sure than she let on.

"In any case," Georges continued, "Burton can't show that Jeff was near the tennis hall at the time of the murder. The cook and the coachman swear he was in the basement of the house, ill and in bed. At about 10:30 she prepared a tisane to help him sleep and a cold pack to reduce the swelling of his wrist. No one admits to having seen him leave his room."

"That sounds like a good alibi for Jeffery," Anne observed.

"But Burton senses that the cook likes him and may be covering up for him. He's helpful to her. Peter Hyde is also protecting him. So, Burton still considers Jeff a suspect, though not the main one. This makes little difference to Jeff. He's already under virtual house arrest."

The horses shook their harness and snorted impatiently. "I'd better go," Anne said. She sniffed the air. It didn't smell like rain. "Let me out on Avon Street. I'll find my own way back."

Georges pulled down the step for her. "Do you have a plan for helping Jeff?"

She took his hand and climbed up into the carriage. "Yes, but I'm open to suggestions."

"You may need a miracle. Sir Harry has surely anticipated all the easy solutions."

When Anne entered the shop on Avon Street, Sarah Smith was alone. A look of surprise, then pleasure flashed across the young woman's face. She laid aside the gown she was working on and rose expectantly, lips slightly parted as if about to ask if she could be of service.

"I've come from Combe Park with news of Jeffery," said Anne quietly. "Could we go where we won't be disturbed?"

"This room will do. Mother has just left for the market." Sarah's brow began to furrow with anxiety. She locked the front door and sat facing Anne. "Is something the matter? I know Jeffery won his fight—the news is all over Bath. Was he badly hurt?"

Anne removed her bonnet and shook her hair. "His wrist is broken but seems to be mending well. He has a few bruises." She hesitated, gauging the concern in Sarah's face. "I'm sorry to tell you, Sir Harry has secretly arranged with a ship's captain to take Jeffery back to Jamaica next Friday. He doesn't know this yet. In the meantime he can't leave Combe Park. He's also suspected of killing Jack Roach."

"How awful!" Sarah clenched her hands before her mouth. "I was hoping to hear from him after the fight. Now I know why I didn't." Tears began to flow down her cheek.

Anne offered her a handkerchief. "I think we should visit the Quaker who has shown interest in Jeffery's situation."

"David Woodhouse. Yes, of course." Sarah dried the tears and returned the handkerchief. "Jeffery is gentle. He wouldn't kill anybody."

Anne gazed at Sarah, admiring her generous, trusting heart. But she couldn't banish the thought that even gentle men can be violent if sufficiently provoked.

Sarah bent over the table and began writing. "I'll leave a note for Mother."

Mr. Woodhouse was at work in the printing room of his shop in St. James's Parade. A young apprentice stood alongside him setting type. Sarah introduced Anne and asked if they could speak about a private matter. Woodhouse's eye searched Anne discreetly, as if he had heard of her but still wasn't sure he could trust her.

Anne understood his caution. The slave trade enjoyed strong support in Bath and Bristol. Their commerce and the employment of many of their citizens depended on it. Defenders of the trade felt encouraged to harass Abolitionists like Woodhouse. Or do worse.

After an uncomfortable moment, Woodhouse smiled tentatively. "Sorry, I have to be careful." He instructed the young man to watch the shop, then turned to the women. "Please follow me." He led them into a small room in the back of the building that served as an office. Anne searched for a place to sit. Stacks of paper covered every surface. The

Quaker grinned apologetically, cleared three plain wooden chairs, and asked what was on their mind.

Anne explained to him Sir Harry's plan to drug Jeffery and secretly ship him back to Jamaica. "He's holding him like a prisoner and might at any time put him in irons."

The Quaker sighed. "I confess this news comes as a surprise. I had thought Jeffery was safe for now, having proven to be so valuable as a boxer. But I see he has angered Sir Harry by claiming his share of the gate money. That was like asserting his right to freedom."

"What can be done for him?" Anne asked, casting a concerned glance toward Sarah Smith, who sat rigid on the edge of her seat. "I've heard of cases similar to his in which magistrates freed slaves."

"True," Woodhouse replied, "slavery is contrary to English Common Law, and courts have freed slaves in recent years. But, like many slavers, Sir Harry has found a way to evade the law. While still in Jamaica, he had Jeffery put his mark on a contract of indentured servitude for seven years, which is perfectly legal in England. If he were to flee from his master, as many slaves do, he would become a fugitive and subject to arrest and prosecution. I don't doubt for a minute that Sir Harry would pursue him vigorously."

"Perhaps he could flee to a foreign country, like France," Sarah offered quietly.

The printer shook his head. "France doesn't welcome fugitive slaves. Its slavers are rich and powerful and think as ours do about property rights."

"Has Jeffery no other choice?" asked Anne, feeling increasingly desperate.

"Yes, he does," Sarah interjected in a choking voice. She struggled to gain control of herself. "Jeffery told me, he would kill himself rather than submit to a slave's life on a plantation. He had signed the indenture to escape it." She covered her face with her hands. Anne moved to her side and put an arm around her.

Woodhouse sat silent for a while, then spoke carefully. "None of his choices are good, but life as a fugitive is better than going back to Jamaica or killing himself." He paused to allow Sarah to recover and for Anne to return to her seat. "Weeks ago, I began to study escape routes for him. They all lead to London. I have associates there who can hide him—big as he is. Sir Harry's wrath will slacken. He'll find something better to do with his money than chase after a poor black man. A powerful patron may appear. Then...well, we'll see."

Preparations for Jeffery's escape would require five days, the printer said. It should take place no later than Thursday morning before dawn, April 12, since on that day, probably in the evening, Sir Harry would try to subdue Jeffery.

Woodhouse glanced at Anne. "We'll need a reliable person at Combe Park to inform Jeffery of our plans and to remain in contact with him."

"I'll do what I can, but Mr. Critchley and his young spy, William, watch me closely. I'll ask my friend Georges Charpentier to help. He often works as a servant and has better access to Jeffery than I do."

Anne glanced sideways. Sarah Smith was sitting stiffly, biting on her lower lip. She seemed to be clinging to a slender, vanishing hope.

It was evening at Combe Park. Inside the dining room, the steward Mr. Cope looked hurriedly left and right. Everything seemed ready. Georges heard voices echoing in the hallway, then a stir outside the door. He brushed lint from his crimson livery and touched his powdered wig. The steward signaled to Jeffery. He opened the door and the guests streamed in. Their silver and gold embroidered garments glittered in the candle-light. Georges came to attention by a sideboard, ready to help serve the supper.

An hour ago, Anne had called him aside, told him about her meeting with Sarah and the Quaker. Georges was to pass the information on to Jeffery. And not a word of it to anyone else. If it were to get back to Sir Harry, things would go very badly for Jeffery. Anne had seemed so earnest and concerned. Georges had promised to do his best.

Resplendent in a dark green suit richly embroidered in gold, Sir Harry chatted loudly. But his affability seemed exaggerated, forced. As he approached the table, his face came into the light from several sconces on the wall. Thin lines of worry fanned out from the corners of his mouth. His hands trembled slightly. He operated a fleet of ships without sweat, Georges thought, but he couldn't manage his own household, much less his private life.

At the other end of the table, Lady Margaret nervously smoothed her russet silk gown embroidered in silver. She beckoned Captain Fitzroy to her side, her green eyes defiant. Scanning the guests, she cast a gracious smile to a French marquis, a wealthy tennis enthusiast. Since his English was hesitant, she had invited Anne and placed him next to her. He gazed with delight at Anne in a fetching lightly patterned yellow gown. From the opposite side of the table, Colonel Saint-Martin glared at him.

During the meal, Georges found it impossible to have a word with Jeff. Too many people in the room. Too much to do. Several wealthy men of affairs and their wives had joined Lady Margaret and Sir Harry at the table.

After the meal and the clean-up, when servants were supposed to have free time, Mr. Cope ordered Jeff to the stable to polish brass on Sir Harry's coach. It fell to one of the older grooms to watch him.

"My bad luck," the man muttered to Georges, "to watch a black man polish brass when I could be enjoying the company of a lively wench on Avon Street."

Georges saw an opportunity. "I have some work to do in the stable this evening. Saddles to clean." He cocked his head toward Jeff, who was standing close by, expressionless. "I could keep an eye on him for you."

With a sigh of relief, the groom glanced at the black man, then thanked Georges profusely and hurried away.

The Frenchman beckoned to Jeff and they set off for the stable. Georges closed the door behind them, got Jeff started on the brass lantern of the coach, then searched the stable to make sure they were alone. He lifted a saddle on to a bench near the coach and began to clean it, just in case someone walked in unexpectedly.

In a low voice Georges explained Sir Harry's plan to Jeff. Drugged and bound, he would be stowed on a ship sailing to Jamaica. But Mr. Woodhouse and his companions had begun to prepare for his escape before dawn next Thursday and to arrange a hiding place in London. Miss Cartier and Georges himself were to keep him informed.

Throughout this explanation, Jeff continued to rub methodically on the lantern. When Georges finished, the black man looked up. "And Sarah?" he asked, without breaking the rhythm of his work.

"She'll remain in Bath, at least for the time being."

Jeff was silent for a minute. "She must come with me."

"Why?"

"When I'm in hiding, the only way Sir Harry can hurt me is to hurt Sarah, and he'll find a way to do it."

Georges agreed inwardly, Jeff had a point. Sarah would need protection. It might be wise to move her also. And, Sarah's mother? Would she leave her shop? Would Sarah leave without her? Sir Harry had surely paid someone to spy on them. It would be difficult for the two women to leave unnoticed. Jeff's escape threatened to become complicated and unwieldy.

The two men worked silently at their tasks for several minutes. Over the past week, Georges had spoken to Jeff many times, served side by side with him, eaten with him in the servants' hall. Jeff also had seen him with Miss Cartier and realized that she and Georges were friends. A friend of a friend is a friend. Jeff had nowhere else to turn.

Finally, Jeff broke the silence. He laid down his polishing rag and began to confide in Georges about his love for Sarah. How hard it would be for him to live as a fugitive in London without her.

Georges countered gently with the question, what kind of life would she have there? Without work. Hiding from the police. A man shouldn't ask a woman to make such a sacrifice.

Jeff frowned, then shook his head. "No one is going to drug me. I'll go down battling."

"Let Sarah make her own choice," Georges said, leaving the bench, drawing closer to Jeff. "She's old enough and strong enough." He added, with more confidence than he felt, "Don't despair. I see prospects of hope. Hiding in London will only be temporary. When the Prince of Wales and other sportsmen realize Sir Harry is trying to send the country's best boxer to cut sugar cane in Jamaica, they'll scream. Sir Harry will be forced to call off his dogs."

A drowning man will reach for a straw. Jeff nodded tentatively, then picked up his rag and began polishing again. Georges went back to work on the saddle. Minutes passed. Finally, Jeff drew a deep breath, turned, and met Georges' eye. "Next Thursday. Before dawn."

Chapter 24

A Tissue of Lies

Saturday, April 7

In the second story classroom off the portico, Charlie laid down his quill and stretched. He had just finished his morning lesson in penmanship with Mr. Critchley, who sat facing him. The tutor was leaning forward, left elbow on his desk, chin in hand. Lines of worry creased his forehead. He was staring down at a sheet of paper on which he idly scribbled with a pencil.

Charlie lowered his eyes just as Critchley seemed to sense his pupil was no longer writing. The tutor looked up, his mouth fixed in a scowl. With an impatient sigh he beckoned Charlie to the desk, sent him back for his book, then pointed out the next lesson he expected the boy to prepare. Critchley didn't say a word, as if he thought the effort would be wasted. He turned his attention again to his scribbling.

Charlie picked up his pen without complaint, dipped in the inkwell, and began to write. He had reconciled himself weeks ago to Mr. Critchley's indifference. The tutor was supposed to teach him writing—*and* reading, arithmetic, Latin, French, and English, but he didn't try very hard. Charlie had trouble grasping the lessons until Miss Cartier began to help him on the side. Now he was doing much better. Even Mr.

Critchley had noticed—and complained she was meddling in his business.

Suddenly, the door to the hallway flew open. William rushed in shouting, his eyes wide with fright. Immediately alert, Charlie closely watched the young man's lips and guessed the Bow Street officer was here with questions. William frantically threw up his hands.

Critchley grimaced. With a jerk of his head he sent William to the far side of the room by the window. As he rose from his desk, he cast a glance at Charlie, who had bent over his book just in time. William stood glowering, his back to the wall. Critchley walked up to him and the two men began a conversation.

Miss Cartier had asked Charlie to keep watch on his tutor. He could help protect his mother. Unfortunately, Mr. Critchley now had his back to Charlie. Still, the boy could glean something from his gestures. And he could see William's face clearly.

The young man shook with anger, his eyes bulging, his lips quivering. "Where's…package?"

Critchley's back stiffened. He said something.

William looked doubtful. "Roach…no money…Pay later."

Critchley nodded.

William drew close to Critchley. "You…package or money."

The tutor shrugged his shoulders, lifted his hands, palms up.

William shouted, "You're lying!"

Critchley slapped the young man's face.

William stepped back, glaring at his tutor, then stalked across the classroom and out the door.

Charlie quickly lowered his eyes and resumed his lettering exercise.

Critchley swung around, his face pinched and wrathful. He strode past Charlie without giving him a glance and left the room. On the tutor's desk lay the paper with his scribbling. Charlie hesitated for only a moment, then snatched the paper and dashed out the door.

Anne was at her table, puzzling out a note from Georges. For safety's sake, he had written in cryptic French. Jeffery, she learned, would be ready Thursday at dawn. She was to tell the Quaker. A spasm of anxiety tightened her chest. The plan was set and would work, God willing.

A loud, sharp knock on her door made her jump. She dropped the note onto glowing embers in the hearth. When it had burned, she opened the door. Charlie rushed in, clutching his book, his face flushed with pride.

"What do you have to tell me?" she asked, pleased by his trust.

"I watched Mr. Critchley and William in the classroom. I think they talked about a package Mr. Critchley stole from my mother and tried to sell to Mr. Roach." The boy carefully enunciated each word. From his book he took out a paper with phrases he had jotted down and described the gestures he had observed. He also handed over the paper Critchley had scribbled on. As the boy told his story, he grew distressed. "Is my mother in trouble?" he asked.

"Perhaps," Anne replied gently. "But we'll do what we can to help her."

When Charlie had returned to his room, Anne took up his report and constructed a semblance of the dialogue between Critchley and William. It suggested to her that Critchley had secretly met Roach at the tennis hall Wednesday evening to negotiate a sale of the stolen item. William believed the sale had taken place and had protested he was wrongly denied a share of the money.

Critchley's hasty scribblings were more difficult to decipher. Thick strokes of his pencil had crossed out the initials JR referring to Roach. Beneath the initials HR, referring to Sir Harry, were numbers ranging from 1,000 to 20,000. He had crossed out all but the highest number. It seemed he was demanding a sum of money equivalent to what Sir Harry had won in Wednesday's boxing match. A small fortune.

Critchley had also written a list of cities, underlining London and Paris, circling Naples. Anne groaned. The man dreamed of escaping to a life of luxury in Italy. How pathetic! He was more likely to end his days hanged in front of Newgate Prison for the murder of Mary Campbell—and perhaps Jack Roach as well.

Anne recalled Mr. Burton was interrogating the household staff in the parlor downstairs. He wanted to talk to her. But she felt reluctant. For Charlie's sake. The stolen package surely contained matter damaging to his mother, perhaps a secret diary. Anne didn't want to expose her unless an innocent person would otherwise be harmed. Still, Burton already knew the stolen object was embarrassing. Lady Margaret was hopelessly involved in the case.

Anne leaned back in her chair and went on debating whether to step forward or not. Finally, she decided Charlie's report and the scribblings might implicate Critchley in Roach's death. That was evidence Burton needed to have. She gathered the papers and walked to the door.

William Rogers slouched at the table, his head tilted at a cocky angle, his arms folded on his chest. Only his furtive eyes betrayed his apprehension. Georges studied the young man. Like his uncle—tall, broad frame, square face, ruddy complexion. But the nephew's jaw hung slack; his lips were sensual and self-indulgent, his eyes sly and mean. He lacked entirely Sir Harry's rugged charm, his vigorous resourceful nature.

Across from the young man, Dick Burton settled into his chair, then asked Georges, whom he had engaged as a clerk, "Are you ready, Mr. Charpentier?"

Pen in hand, Georges nodded. He was prepared to observe as well as to take notes. He had also informed Burton of the letter William had received from Twycross. The young man was deep in debt and in danger of being exposed as a fraud. He could have killed Roach in a failed attempt to rob him of the stolen package.

The parlor was still, a quiet broken only by the occasional pop of glowing embers in the fireplace. Burton stared silently at the young man until he began to shift nervously in his seat. He had some explaining to do, Georges thought. On the table lay the young man's statement from the day before. He had offered an alibi for his tutor and claimed to know nothing relevant to Roach's death. Next to the statement lay little Charlie's report which Miss Cartier had just brought down to the parlor. She had cautioned Burton and Georges to avoid mentioning Charlie by name. Critchley and William might retaliate against him.

"I understand Mr. Critchley employed you to spy on Lady Margaret," Burton began quietly. With a start William sat up, surprised and annoyed, suspecting that someone had snitched on him. He appeared to quickly reckon who that person might be. Burton broke into his calculations. "I have that information from several sources—nearly everyone at Combe Park. No need to guess whom."

Burton leaned forward, thrust out his jaw. "Where was Mr. Critchley Wednesday night between eleven and eleven-thirty?"

The young man tried to evade Burton's gaze but failed. "We were in the dining room," he stammered. "About twenty minutes before eleven, Mr. Critchley said he was tired of the party. We went to his room and played cards."

Burton raised an eyebrow. "That's what you told me yesterday. But it isn't true, is it?"

William hesitated, apparently sensing Burton was about to catch him in a lie. His resentment against Critchley won out. "No, it's not. I followed him through the house to the basement. When he thought no one was watching, he sneaked out the side door and went to the tennis hall."

"Why did you spy on him?"

"I didn't trust him. He cheats everyone. Why wouldn't he cheat me?"

"Cheat you out of what?"

The young man was caught. Burton forced him to admit that Mr. Critchley had stolen Lady Roger's package and was supposed to sell it to Jack Roach Wednesday night. Critchley had agreed to share the money with William. The sale took place and Roach promised to pay for it later. Or so Critchley claimed.

"When did you see Mr. Critchley again?"

"Thursday at noon. He said we had to get our stories to match and not mention the package. He looked worried."

"You have just admitted your previous statement was a lie." Burton tapped the sheet in front of him. "How can I believe you now?"

"Yesterday," he hissed, "I covered up for him. But not any more. He didn't treat me right."

"How did you know that Mr. Critchley walked toward the tennis hall after he sneaked out of the house? You must have followed him. How far?"

William lowered his head for a second, sensing a trap. He looked up, his eyes uneasy. "To the tennis hall. Then I came back to the house and went to my room."

Burton gazed at him silently for a moment, then signaled Georges, who indicated he'd soon be ready. "Sign your statement, William," said Burton, "and you're free to go, but I may want to speak with you again."

As William was leaving the room, Burton called out to him. "By the way, William, I just read in Jack Roach's journal that Mr. Critchley killed Mary Campbell. Roach was very angry. Called Critchley a cretin." The young man stopped in mid-stride, nearly stumbled. "How do you suppose Roach found out? Critchley would have been afraid to tell him."

William slowly turned around, a desperate expression on his face. His mouth opened, but only a gagging sound came forth.

"You told Roach, didn't you."

Still no word from William, as if his mind were paralyzed by fear and confusion.

"But how did you know her death was murder rather than an accident?"

"I saw Mr. Critchley standing by her body. He told me..." William searched for words. "He had found her dead at the foot of the stairs. Didn't want anyone to think he had pushed her or was even in the house. They had quarreled. Told me to say nothing. But I hate him so I lied to Jack Roach to get him in trouble."

"Why didn't you tell the magistrate instead?"

"I was afraid. Roach said not to tell anyone else. He still needed Critchley."

Burton stared at the young man for a minute, then waved him out of the room. When the door closed, Burton turned to Georges. "The problem with liars is that you never know when they just *might* be telling the truth. I believe William saw more than he's willing to admit."

"He has cast doubt on the credibility of Roach's journal. Its reference to Critchley may be based on a lie by William."

Burton sighed with exasperation. "Let's return to Roach's murder. Shall we keep William on our list of suspects?"

"I think so," Georges replied. "He might have done it for the money. Caught Roach off guard and killed him." As Georges laid down his pen, he reflected darkly on William. A spiteful lad as well as a suspect of murder. The young man had serious reasons to hate Charlie and do him harm. Miss Cartier's concerns were well taken; she must be warned.

"Mr. Critchley's next," said Georges. "He's a major suspect now."

"Yes, indeed," replied Burton, "if we can believe William's latest story." He sighed with the weariness of a man who had spent too much of his life cutting through falsehood.

"Look at this." He handed Georges the statement Critchley had written yesterday. He claimed he had left the dining room before eleven and had gone to his room with William. He also insisted he had no reason to kill Roach. They had a congenial relationship.

"A web of lies!" Burton exclaimed. He rose from his chair and stood by the fireplace. A few seconds later, the hallway door opened and Critchley entered the parlor.

Georges took his clerk's post and studied the man walking toward him. Sir Harry hadn't hired him for his good looks or his sweet nature. In the subdued light of the room, the man's tall thin figure, sallow complexion, deep-set eyes, long arms, and long lank hair gave the impression of a living, breathing specter. Georges examined once more the statement in his hands. Beautifully rounded letters, polished phrases. The man *could* write.

"You wish to see me?" Critchley asked Burton, as he took a seat. His speech was precisely articulated; his voice, slightly nasal. He had a way of looking down his nose as if doing Burton a favor by speaking to him.

Burton remained standing, leaning forward on his cane. "Mr. Critchley," he began, "You need to explain certain factual errors in the statement you gave me yesterday." Georges handed it to the tutor.

He refused it with a wave of his hand. "I know what I wrote."

"Mr. William Rogers now denies seeing you in your room," Burton continued. "Instead, he claims you sneaked out of the house shortly before eleven and walked toward the tennis hall. That leads me to believe that you were with Mr. Roach at the time of his death."

Critchley remarked coolly, "William has chosen this way to show that he resents his tutor's efforts to make a gentleman of him."

"I'm inclined to think William may now be telling the truth. In your room I found a pair of boots that fit prints found behind the tennis hall."

Tricky, Georges thought. Boots in the downstairs closet also matched. The prints left in the wet sod simply weren't clear enough for a closer identification.

At the mention of his room having been searched, Critchley's eyes flashed with anger, but only for a second. Otherwise he appeared unperturbed, silent, as if disdaining to defend himself. A cold fish, mused Georges to himself. He paused with his pen, waiting for the man to speak.

Then he stirred. "Your case is flimsy, Mr. Burton. The prints prove nothing of the sort. I wear boots cast off by Sir Harry. Lord Jeff wears them also. Our feet, if nothing else, are similar. Why don't you arrest them? No one should believe the testimony of William, a disgruntled school boy. I had no reason to kill Jack Roach." Critchley crossed his legs at the ankles and leaned back in his chair, a smirk on his face.

Burton left the fireplace and paced back and forth in the parlor, limping a little.

Georges' pen scratched intermittently, while he mulled over Critchley's remarks. The similarity among the boots intrigued him.

When the pen quieted, Burton sat down facing the tutor and spoke in a low, deliberate voice. "Mr. Critchley, you had a powerful motive to kill Jack Roach. In his papers I've found the London fence's record of the stolen silver you sold him. For months, Roach has been holding that crime over your head. You were his slave." Burton paused to allow his words to sink in. "I believe you met Roach in the training room, quarreled with him about payment for a package you stole from Lady Margaret, and killed him. You fled in haste when Captain Fitzroy arrived unexpected."

Critchley sat bolt upright. His lips parted in disbelief. A look of terror spread over his face. "I didn't kill him. Fitzroy must have done it. I gave Roach the package and left him alive. You're trying to trick me about the silver. Roach wouldn't have kept..."

Burton cut him off. "Roach's papers also witness to your assault on Miss Mary Campbell." Burton reached over and pulled a bell rope. Alarmed, Critchley began to rise out of his chair, as if to flee. Georges moved quickly to his side and eased him down. A pair of bailiffs appeared at the door. "Gentlemen. You will escort Mr. Critchley to the city jail. Hold him there pending charges of theft being drawn up against him."

"Georges, would you ask Sir Harry to come here. He's waiting in his study. And tell a servant to bring us something to drink. My throat's dry." Burton shifted in his chair, seeking relief from his arthritic pain. His face also reflected an inner discomfort that Georges didn't expect to find in such an experienced officer.

Nerves? Georges asked himself, as he went on his errand. Why? Questioning Rogers should be merely routine. He might have seen or heard something helpful to the investigation. Still, Burton had reasons for concern. Sir Harry's relationship with Roach seemed murky, as did his intentions with regard to his wife, Lady Margaret. Rumor claimed that another woman had won his passionate heart. And his boots were at the scene! Was he wearing them? To put a man as powerful as Sir Harry under suspicion of murder might well make even a Bow Street officer dry in the mouth.

A short while later, carrying a tray of drinks, Georges returned with Sir Harry to the parlor. Burton greeted Rogers politely and they settled down in their chairs by the fire, Georges again off to one side, pen at the ready.

"A few routine questions, if I may, Sir Harry," Burton began with a deferential smile. "Please tell me where you were between eleven and twelve o'clock on the night Jack Roach was killed."

Rogers sipped from his glass, gazed at the ceiling, then explained he had met Roach in his study for about ten minutes.

Shortly before eleven, Roach left for the tennis hall to consult someone. The house was too noisy. He needed to talk without being disturbed and promised to return in a half hour.

"I waited, working at my desk. When Roach didn't keep his promise, I searched for him at the party until shortly before midnight, then at the tennis hall. In vain."

"Were you alone in the study while waiting for Roach?"

"Yes."

"There's a private exit from your study to the outside, I believe."

Rogers smiled easily and swirled the wine in his glass. "I could have slipped out to the tennis hall, possibly without having been seen."

Burton shifted in his chair and stretched his stiff leg. "Sir Harry, you may have been the last person—save the murderer—to see Mr. Roach alive. I hope you won't mind if I inquire into your relationship with him."

Rogers spread his hands, palms up, granting the dispensation. "I had engaged him to investigate certain matters of importance to me. To be sure, he had earned an unsavory reputation in the city, but he also had an uncanny ability to ferret out information."

"His unsavory reputation," Burton observed, "was earned in part by practicing extortion. Had you any reason to think he might turn his skill against you?"

Georges watched Rogers' face for signs of dissimulation. He desperately wanted to divorce Lady Margaret. But, adultery with another woman could ruin his chances. Roach might have tried to exploit Rogers' relationship with Miss Ware and triggered a violent reaction.

"Sorry," Rogers said slowly, eyes wary. "I don't follow the drift of your question."

Burton reached into the valise resting against the leg of his chair and pulled out a folder. "This contains a report Mr. Critchley sent to Jack Roach. I found it among his papers."

As he handed it over to Rogers, he added, "I regret having to distress you."

As Rogers read through the folder, his naturally florid face turned deep red, his lips worked with fury. "Critchley! That ungrateful, lying bastard!" Rogers threw the folder on the table, sputtering with exasperation. "There's not one scintilla of truth in what he says!"

Burton nodded sympathetically.

Rogers rushed on. "Miss Ware is a beautiful, charming young woman, a talented dancer with a lovely voice. I'm advancing her career. We're friends. Nothing more. She'd be most distressed to read this." He jabbed his finger at the offensive folder.

Burton leaned forward and retrieved it. "It occurred to me that Mr. Critchley might have imagined the lurid details." He held up the folder, regarded it with distaste. "The point is, how would it be read *outside* this room? In the city? In Bristol or London? What would it do to Miss Ware's peace of mind and to her career in the theater?"

"Are you suggesting that Jack Roach might have tried to extract money from me under the threat of publishing this report?"

"Hardly a farfetched idea, if I may say so, considering his character." Burton reached into his valise again and pulled out another folder. "Critchley's report on Lady Margaret," he said, handing it to Rogers. "Roach had engaged him to spy on her relationship with Captain Fitzroy. He even installed a hidden optical device to survey her rooms. Critchley then stole an item, perhaps a document, that was likely to seriously compromise her."

While Burton spoke, Rogers stiffened, his eyes darkened. "What are you getting at, sir?"

"Your marital affairs are none of my business, Sir Harry, except in so far as they give you a compelling motive for killing Jack Roach." He pointed to the folder in Rogers' hands. "A fair reading of those pages would lead one to believe that you wish to divorce Lady Margaret. Roach could force you to pay almost any price to discover grounds for your bill of divorce to proceed successfully through Parliament. He was bargaining with you on those terms the night of his death. You would be less than human if you hadn't wished to kill him."

"Your conjecture is barely plausible," said Rogers, thrusting the folder back to Burton. "I may have had the opportunity and the motive to kill him, but you are a long way from proving that I did." He rose from his chair, grim-faced. "If we are finished here, sir, I have business to take care of."

"One more matter, Sir Harry. I have arrested Mr. Critchley. He's charged with felony theft of silver in London and under suspicion of the murder of Mary Campbell. Should be in the city jail by now." Burton tucked the papers into his valise and told Georges to prepare a statement for Sir Harry to sign at his leisure.

Rogers appeared momentarily stunned, turned abruptly and strode to the door. As he went out into the hall, he looked back as if to say something, then shook his head and disappeared.

⁂

They were expecting Fitzroy in a few minutes. Still a serious suspect. While Burton limped to an open window for a breath of fresh air, Georges reviewed in his mind what the captain had already admitted. He had gone to the tennis hall at eleven-thirty Wednesday night, to meet a man he hated. He claimed to have found Roach dead on the floor of the training room, hid him in a closet until early morning, then carted his body off to the river. Georges's mind balked. Fitzroy could have found Roach alive and seized the opportunity to kill him.

Hearing steps in the hall, Burton returned to his chair. Georges assumed his post.

"Good afternoon, Mr. Burton." Captain Fitzroy extended his hand, and the Bow Street officer shook it. The Irishman's expression was amiable, as if he expected this meeting to be routine, having already explained his movements. They sat facing each other. Fitzroy casually crossed his legs. "I really have little more to say."

"Since we spoke on Thursday, Captain, new facts have come to light which I should discuss with you."

Fitzroy raised an eyebrow of mild curiosity. "Yes?"

"Mr. William Rogers claims Mr. Critchley went to the tennis hall, Wednesday evening, to sell a certain package to Mr. Roach. Critchley admits going there but claims he left Roach alive. He suggests that, when you arrived shortly afterwards, you killed Roach. It appears that someone is lying."

Fitzroy bristled. "It should be clear, sir, who is the liar."

Burton remained silent, inviting the captain to explain.

"Critchley's a sneak, a man without honor, who spied on a noble lady, broke into her room, and stole her secret papers to sell to Jack Roach. What man of good sense would believe the self-serving testimony of a Critchley!"

Burton pressed on. "Critchley also claims that he gave Jack Roach those secret papers." He paused, leaned forward. "Did you search Roach's body?"

"Yes." Fitzroy hesitated fractionally. "But I didn't find them."

"The truth will out," observed the officer in a flat, low voice. "As for Critchley, he's on his way to the city jail to face various charges unrelated to Roach's death."

Fitzroy started with surprise, then seemed to turn inward, as if studying the changing face of the battlefield and devising new strategies. His objective: that package!

"Oh," Burton went on, "I've also taken the liberty to contact the captain of the *Hampton* at the Bristol docks and cancel your passage to New York. I want you to remain in Bath for the time being."

A flash of alarm crossed Fitzroy's face.

At midafternoon, Anne and Paul rode back to Combe Park from the south after racing their horses in the countryside.

Anne's black mare chafed at the bit, yearning for the comfort of its stall. Paul's big chestnut hunter, a more docile beast, took the return in stride. They had lunched at a charming wayside inn, its walls ivy-covered, its roof thatched. The sun had broken through the clouds for much of their ride, and a soft spring breeze now caressed their faces. Anne felt happier than at any time since arriving in Bath.

Then the main house came into view, its great mass beginning to darken under a large gray cloud. Anne felt apprehensive, suddenly reminded of the conflicts raging within its walls.

Paul gazed at her with concern, sensing the change in her mood.

As they crossed the courtyard, Sir Harry galloped past them, his face flushed, a wild look in his eyes. "What's that all about?" asked Anne, startled.

"Georges must know." Paul pointed to his adjutant, just now leaving the stable. When he recognized them, he broke into a run.

"Critchley's in jail," exclaimed Georges, panting from the exertion. At the stable door, a groom appeared and took the reins of the horses. Anne and Paul followed Georges into the grooms' small social hall. It smelled of horse and leather but the tile floor was clean, the walls whitewashed. Georges stepped into an adjacent pantry, then returned with cider, bread, and cheese. He sat his companions at the room's plain wooden table. "You've not dined in a stable before, have you, sir?"

The colonel tasted the cider. It was cool and refreshing. "Until now, I wasn't aware of what I'd missed."

Georges waved his hands grandiloquently over the table. "Courtesy of Baron Breteuil. He has paid for dressing up this room and for the food. But among the grooms and stableboys, I give you the credit." He bowed to the colonel. "That's why you and Miss Cartier will always ride the best horses in the stable, and I'll be the first to know what's going on here."

At the table their conversation turned to Burton's strategy. Puzzled, Anne asked Georges, "Why has he imprisoned Critchley just now?"

"It's simple," Georges replied. "Burton wants to keep Critchley alive until the Roach case is finished. He may be needed as a witness. He surely knows more than he admits. And, Burton's a Bow Street officer after all. He'll earn a fat commission if Critchley is convicted of the theft of the silver and it's recovered from Roach's hiding place." Georges added darkly, "Judging from the look on Rogers' face, Critchley is much safer in jail than at Combe Park."

"What's become of the mysterious stolen package?" asked Paul.

His adjutant shrugged his shoulders. "Burton has searched Critchley's room thoroughly—even lifted floorboards and removed wooden panels from the walls. Found nothing. The package is hidden elsewhere—if it still exists."

Chapter 25

Lives in Crisis

Saturday/Sunday, April 7/8

Sir Harry urged his horse on with the whip, startling the foot traffic on the broad, well-beaten path that curved along the east bank of the river. This route took him past Spring Gardens into Bathwick and avoided the crowded streets of the city. He reined in his mount in front of the jail, a new three-story stone building in the Palladian style common to Bath. Warehouses separated it from the river. To the east lay the woods and meadows of Bathwick manor. To Sir Harry, the jail appeared conveniently isolated and remote.

At the entrance, Rogers met the jailer, a slightly-built older man. They knew each other from previous occasions when Sir Harry's ships' officers and men were imprisoned for drunken brawling and other misdemeanors. A shilling or two usually persuaded the jailer to make their confinement a little more comfortable.

"Sir Harry, are you here to visit your clerk?" asked the jailer with a deferential tilt of his head.

"Yes, my good man," replied Rogers, pressing a coin into his hand. He bowed and immediately showed Sir Harry into a small bare room with a table and two plain wooden chairs.

He had come to the jail with one overriding purpose: to gain possession of the mysterious package that Critchley had stolen from Lady Margaret. Since Roach's death, no one seemed to know where it was and what was inside. Love letters most likely, perhaps also a diary. Critchley might still have them. Never gave them to Roach. Hid them at Combe Park. But a thorough search of the house had failed to find them. Sir Harry's only recourse now was to bargain with Critchley. He would have preferred to cut the man's throat.

He had thought hard over what to offer someone who faced almost certain execution, especially if he were proven guilty of Roach's death. Money alone would do him no good. An alternative, the only one, loomed up in Sir Harry's mind like a monster. Should he risk virtually everything he had worked hard for in his life in order to be free of his wife and her lover who had cuckolded him? Free to marry the lovely, vivacious young Harriet?

A few minutes later, after what seemed an eternity, the jailer appeared with Critchley. Only a powerful effort of will restrained Sir Harry's impulse to throttle the prisoner. He had concealed his criminal past, had pilfered at Combe Park, had slandered Harriet and himself. And, he might have murdered Mary Campbell and Roach. For a brief moment, rage nearly blinded Sir Harry.

Critchley's wrists were manacled and his feet were in irons, but he was not humbled. Holding his tall thin body erect, he met Sir Harry's eye and did not flinch. He surely knew what his visitor wanted and was prepared to ask a very high price for it. The jailer withdrew, closing the door behind him. Critchley sat opposite Sir Harry at the table. They began to bargain.

Harriet Ware stared vacantly at a table setting arranged for two. The young maid waited patiently for approval, then coughed. Harriet put aside her anxieties for a moment, inspected the maid's work, and murmured well-done. The maid retreated to the kitchen to continue the preparations. Harriet lifted a spoon she had looked at only seconds earlier. Her hand trembled. Harry had sent word to expect him for tea at four o'clock. He would bring news she had to hear.

Harriet did not want to receive him. He had been to her apartment before with other guests but never alone. Most of all, she had not yet recovered from the shock she received yesterday. What kind of man would drug Jeff and send him back to Jamaica? Harry appeared to her now as a monster!

Simple prudence required her to keep a safe distance from him and in no way encourage his infatuation. But, the tone of his message implied he would come whatever excuse she might offer. She could not muster the courage to confront him head on. He might explode. And how would that end? A sense of foreboding paralyzed her. She stood at the table, absently fingering the tea service.

The front doorbell startled her. She called the maid to answer it. His steps echoed in the hallway. Her heart beat faster. She checked the tea water and placed the cake tray on the table. He knocked. She smoothed her rose silk gown, moistened her lips, and opened the door as if she were on stage. Her anxiety retreated behind a friendly mask.

He rushed in, a broad grin on his face. He kicked the door shut with his heel and swept her off her feet. Around the room they whirled in a wild country dance, threatening to upset the tea table. The maid fled back into the kitchen. Harriet gradually calmed him until he came to a panting halt and released her. His ruddy face was flushed with exertion, his eyes unnaturally bright.

"Harriet, I've finally found the evidence to end my unhappy marriage! It will soon be in my hands. Three or four days at the latest." He stopped for breath.

Overwhelmed by his enthusiasm, Harriet had said almost nothing. She welcomed this break and led him toward a basin on the sideboard. He smiled gratefully, then washed his hands, splashed water on his face, toweled himself, palmed his hair. Meanwhile, she lightly brushed his coat.

"I can't go into details, my dear, but this time I'm confident." He took her hands in a strong grip and gazed at her silently for a moment, as if she were a precious work of art. "You are so fresh, so lovely. And you sing with the voice of an angel. I know I've promised not even to speak of a commitment from you until I am free. Now, at least, I can see ahead to that time, and my heart is bursting with joy."

Harriet smiled automatically, but was still at a loss for words. How was Harry going to get the evidence he was talking about? She was afraid to ask. She had long suspected he had hired Jack Roach to find proof of his wife's infidelity. And Mr. Critchley had spied for Roach. That hadn't bothered her too much. Like Harry's trading in slaves, it was something that powerful men did. But only two days ago Jack Roach had been murdered, his body found in the river. And, less than an hour ago at the baker's shop, she had heard Mr. Critchley had been taken to prison.

Harriet pulled free from his grip and directed him toward the chairs at the tea table. "Make yourself comfortable," she told him. "I'll pour."

They had set to eating the cakes and had sipped some tea when Harry cocked his head, caught Harriet's eye. "Is something disturbing you, my dear?"

She put down her cup, gaining a moment for thought. His question was reasonable, but its tone was almost threatening. When Harry wanted someone to share his joy, he was not to be denied. She turned to him, but she couldn't bring herself to tell him the plain truth. "I heard at the baker's shop that Mr. Critchley had been arrested, then I thought of Jack Roach's murder. Terrible things like that aren't supposed to happen in Bath."

"Don't trouble yourself, Harriet," he said. "The Bow Street officer arrested Critchley for other crimes, not for killing Roach. Personally, I think Fitzroy did it." He leaned solicitously forward. "Forget about those men. Think of us."

Harriet put on her best smile and poured more tea. They chatted for a while as if nothing were amiss. Afterwards, they moved to the harpsichord in the corner. She accompanied herself in several popular airs until he rose to take his leave. He took her hand and kissed it. She gently withdrew it and, sensing his desire, took a step back.

"I'll see you in the Upper Assembly Rooms this evening," he said.

"Yes, thanks to Maestro Rauzzini, I'll sing in the chorus."

"And soon you'll sing solo!" he added emphatically.

When he left the room, Harriet leaned her back against the door, listening to the heavy tread of his boots in the hallway, down the stairs, out the front door. It slammed shut and the house was quiet. But his presence lingered on in her mind. He would get the document he wanted, cost what it might. Sooner or later he would be free. Then marriage? She shivered.

She scanned the parlor, lingering on the harpsichord. Had she been foolish accepting his patronage? She recalled when she had first met him. A year ago. He had said he intended to do something for her. Bring her forward. Since then, he had been true to his word. But, at a cost she was only now beginning to reckon—and was unwilling to pay.

The Upper Assembly Rooms on Alfred Street bustled with activity. The annual concert of sacred music on the eve of Easter was about to take place. A swelling flow of people poured into the ballroom. Their excited babble mixed with the tuning of violins and violas, and echoed throughout the building. From the Card Room the voices of the chorus in rehearsal penetrated the din.

One of six sopranos, Harriet stood poised, holding the score of Handel's *Messiah* in her hands, her eyes fixed on the lines, "*All we like sheep have gone astray. We have turned every one to his own way.*" A sharp clap of hands startled her. She looked up. Maestro Rauzzini stared at her, smiled when he had her attention. "We'll go through the first six bars again. All together now."

"All we like sheep,...all we like sheep, have gone astray." Some twenty voices raised Isaiah's plaintive words in perfectly measured allegro moderato. In full song, Harriet sensed the prophet speaking for her. She had to fight for control of her voice.

"Good. You've got it right," said Rauzzini, stepping back. "Get ready. In five minutes we shall enter the ballroom."

Harriet nervously smoothed the folds of her lemon yellow brocade, aware of sidelong glances from the tenors nearby. She still felt restless, anxious. She had hoped the excitement of the concert would distract her, but her mind drifted unbidden back to Harry.

Their meeting had added greatly to her sense that something was going wrong in their relationship. Harry's moods seemed to swing too swiftly. A dark, ruthless side of his nature was coming to the fore. Ending his marriage with Lady Margaret was becoming an obsession. And he simply assumed Harriet would marry him, even though he had never proposed to her and she had never indicated she was interested.

Her career in the theater now began to weigh upon her conscience. Had greed and vanity subtly undermined her common sense? Her parents had cautioned her about seeking profit and applause. It was one thing to sing for God's glory in the church choir, quite another to dance for a shilling or two at Sadler's Wells. They had sighed when she left home to work in Bath and would surely have warned her against accepting Sir Harry's patronage. Had she gone astray on a dangerous path?

Peering into the ballroom, Harriet could see Sir Harry in the middle of the fifth row of the audience. Had she been honest with him? Encouraged his interest in her? On the way to the stage, she looked rigidly straight ahead. On stage she kept her eyes on Maestro Rauzzini.

Nonetheless, she was keenly aware of Harry staring at her, straining to pick out her voice from all the others in the chorus. When it came time for the song from Isaiah, Harriet could simply not help herself. She looked at Harry and her voice went out to him. "*All we like sheep have gone astray. We have turned every one to his own way.*" Tears welled up in her eyes. She now feared the man and must avoid him or court disaster.

Georges was outside the Assembly Rooms during the concert, gathering rumors and gossip from the chairbearers while he waited for Anne and Colonel Saint-Martin. When the audience began to leave the building, he stationed himself in the vestibule. After several minutes, Miss Ware and Sir Harry walked through the corridor towards him. She appeared tired and very tense. He was in good spirits, though he seemed concerned about her. They were on their way to the vestibule to wait for Sir Harry's carriage.

In the press of the crowd they didn't notice Lady Margaret and Captain Fitzroy enter the vestibule at the same time. At the last moment, Georges saw what was about to happen but could do nothing to prevent it. The jostling crowd shoved Lady Margaret into Miss Ware so forcefully that, had Sir Harry not caught her, she would have fallen to the tiled floor.

Several bystanders realized an accident had taken place and stopped to stare. An eerie silence fell over the room. Lady Margaret turned and saw Miss Ware in Sir Harry's arms. She gasped. Anger flashed across her face.

Sir Harry, who hadn't seen the crowd pushing Lady Margaret, assumed she had deliberately shoved Miss Ware. He bristled, then snarled, "Mad Irish bitch."

Captain Fitzroy started, as if struck. He stepped toward Sir Harry. "Sir, you have insulted my cousin."

Sir Harry took a step toward the captain. Miss Ware, who had regained her balance, tried to restrain him. He shook her off. "Sir, she's my wife and I can call her anything I like."

Fitzroy's hand gripped the hilt of his sword. "I demand satisfaction." The spectators of the scene edged back.

Georges realized he was perhaps the only one who clearly understood what had happened. He forced his way through the crowd and came between the two men. "There's been a most unfortunate misunderstanding," he said calmly, glancing at one and then at the other. Supposedly a servant, Georges spoke with surprising authority. The men gaped at him.

"I witnessed the incident," he continued. "Allow me to explain." He drew the two men aside and in a few words told them what had happened. "This calls for apologies, not a duel," he concluded. After some hesitation and fuming, and with glances to the distinguished crowd around them, they agreed. Apologies were rendered through clenched teeth, and the two couples went their separate ways.

Georges breathed a deep sigh of relief. A duel, however it ended, would almost certainly frustrate Baron Breteuil's plans for Captain Fitzroy.

A joyful peal of bells rang through Bath and announced Easter Sunday. From the rear of the Abbey Church, Anne and Paul scanned a congregation of the curious and the devout, mingling easily on this bright feast day. Light poured through the colored glass of the west front and the south clerestory and flooded the sacred space with a golden glow.

"Look for a dark red bonnet," Anne told Paul, as she began to edge into the crowd. "It's what she usually wears here." They detected several such bonnets, but Anne narrowed the search down to one young woman in a matching red dress. Harriet stood alone in the south aisle, half-hidden by a thick pillar. Anne and Paul chose places at a short distance behind her.

During the service, Anne found herself paying more attention to her friend than to the reading from Holy Scripture, the chanting of psalms, and the sermon. Harriet gave no indication of her state of mind until the service ended. While the congregation filed out of the church, she remained in her place. After a few minutes, she stiffened, then suddenly sank down on a nearby bench, face buried in her hands, shoulders heaving.

Anne glanced at Paul. He nodded toward Harriet. She went to her friend's side and put an arm around her shoulders, but said nothing until the sobbing ceased and Harriet sat up.

"Shall we walk in Orange Grove?" Anne asked.

Harriet agreed quietly.

Paul withdrew, saying he would visit Mr. Burton at the York Inn. The two women left the church and walked toward the grove. The sun had reached its zenith in a clear blue sky. The temperature was mild. Hyacinths, daffodils and other spring flowers bloomed in profusion. Everyone who could walk, it seemed, had come out to enjoy the day, crowding Orange Grove and presumably all the other gardens and parks of the city.

"We could have gone to my apartment," said Harriet. "But I'm afraid Harry might come at any time."

"I know where we can be undisturbed." Anne led Harriet into John Street to the rear entrance of Madame Gagnon's shop. She glanced left and right to ensure they had not been followed, then unlocked the door.

Harriet appeared surprised.

"The milliner is an acquaintance. We had a mutual interest in Jack Roach," Anne offered. "She lent me a key to her shop." In the back room, Anne brewed tea while Harriet filled a tray with shortbread she found in a cupboard. When they had sipped some tea, Anne asked her friend why Sir Harry felt free to call on her without notice.

"During the last few days he has sensed that I'm pulling away from him. That aggravates him and makes him push me all the harder."

"Push you?" asked Anne. "How?"

Harriet hesitated, began biting on her lip. Her voice dropped to barely a whisper. "Lately, he seizes every opportunity to touch me—decently, mind you. Though he never asks, I know he wants me in his bed. I've been holding him off. Last night at the concert, I reached the end of my rope. The way he stared at me on stage! As if I belonged to him, like Jeff! After the concert, in the vestibule..." She stammered for a moment with embarrassment. "But Georges must have told you what happened."

"Some of it," Anne admitted. "But I'd like to hear it from you."

"I was shocked. Harry was eager to duel Captain Fitzroy right there in front of everybody." She lowered her eyes, as if ashamed.

"Please go on," Anne said gently.

Harriet looked up hesitantly. "Afterwards, when he had driven me home, he wanted to come to my apartment. I could see in his face what he wanted—he was panting! I said, no, I was too tired and upset. I couldn't bring myself to say outright, no, meaning never. He became jealous and suspicious. He claimed I wasn't paying him the attention I should after all he had done for me. 'Have you been seeing another man?' he asked. 'You had better not.' Then he shook his walking stick at me and left."

She stared at Anne in despair, trembling, unable to speak.

"Take your time, Harriet," said Anne, holding her hands. "You'll be all right."

After a few minutes, still trembling, Harriet continued, "I'm afraid of Harry. I don't know what to do. I can't go on like this."

Anne stroked her friend's hands. "There's hope. You have time to make plans. Even if Sir Harry gets the document he needs, he must still go through Parliament before he'll be free to marry again. That could take several months. In the meantime, keep him at a safe distance. Remind him that you come from a religious family. When the season ends in a few weeks, return with me to London. With your beauty, talent, and experience, you will easily find work to do."

Harriet stood up to leave, a wan smile on her face. "You're a dear friend, Annie. I'll follow your advice." The two women fell into an embrace, then Harriet stepped back, holding Anne's arms in a firm grip. She was silent for a moment, staring at Anne. Finally she spoke in a low, level voice. "If Harry were ever to learn that I'd actually leave him, I believe he would kill me."

I fear that he would, Anne said to herself. Or, hire someone else to do it.

Chapter 26

Approaching Storm

Sunday, April 8

After leaving Anne and Harriet at the Abbey Church a little past noon, Saint-Martin stopped in the church yard and shielded his eyes from the sun. A riot of sounds, colors, and gestures assaulted his senses. A brass band clashed and clanged its way through the yard. A troop of Italian acrobats in gaudy checkered tights cartwheeled, built human pyramids, and juggled before a rapt audience of children. Vendors hawked their wares. Several young dandies preened themselves, ogling pretty young women in muslin dresses, their faces guarded from the sun's rays by wide-brimmed, brightly beribboned hats.

Soon the square, energetic figure of the colonel's adjutant snaked through the crowd. The colonel hailed him. "Learn anything this morning, Georges?"

"A few interesting bits." The adjutant patted his stomach. "I've followed Captain Fitzroy around Bath for hours. Now I'm hungry. Could we talk over lunch?"

Saint-Martin agreed, leaving the choice of an eating place to Georges. He led the way to the Shakespeare, a coach inn at the city market. "Good seafood, decent wine," he said as they took seats in a quiet corner of the large public room. "And we can speak safely."

A sturdy, pink-cheeked barmaid came to their table, smiled coyly at Georges, and took their order. She returned in a few minutes with a steaming platter of mussels, country bread and cheese, and a carafe of dry white wine from the Loire valley. As she moved on to another table out of earshot, Georges leaned forward, glancing over his shoulder. "That's Flora. I've paid her to eavesdrop on Fitzroy. He usually meets his two British officer friends here for drink, cards, jokes about women."

Georges forked a mussel, dipped it in the juice, then in butter, and slurped it with obvious relish. After half a glass of wine, he resumed his story. "This morning was different. Just coffee and serious talk. They were cautious when Flora came around. Still, she heard Fitzroy tell the officers that Burton had canceled his passage to New York and had him under constant watch."

Saint-Martin grew impatient. "We know that much already!"

"There's more," Georges continued apologetically. "Flora said the three men lowered their voices. Laying plans. She could pick up only scattered words until at the end Fitzroy spoke loudly enough for her to hear: 'Tuesday morning, then!'"

"Not much to go on," remarked Saint-Martin, pushing his plate to one side. He was less fond of steamed mussels than his adjutant. "Sounds like desperation, either flight or fight." He leaned back, chin in hand. "Flight's no longer a good option for Fitzroy. He's not one to live like a hunted animal. He needs to strut about in public like a peacock. Besides, he and Lady Margaret seem bound together, even though he abuses her. Miss Cartier and I watched them during the concert last night. Not exactly love-birds. But they touched, smiled and nodded to one another, even swayed together with the music. And you saw him defend her afterwards."

"And don't forget her money!" added Georges, breaking off a piece of bread. He dipped it in the mussel juice and stuffed it into his mouth.

The colonel gently swirled the wine in his glass, smiling indulgently at his adjutant's table manners. "Georges, if you were Fitzroy, what would you do at this point?"

The adjutant saluted Saint-Martin with his glass and emptied it. "I'd go for her money. After all, I'm a gambler. Lady Margaret and Charlie will inherit Rogers' fortune. I'd make sure her marriage lasted until she became a widow. Then I'd become her legal guardian or husband."

Saint-Martin leaned forward, arms resting on the table, hands clasped. "Hasten Sir Harry's death, would you?"

"I couldn't do it myself. I'm closely watched and my motive would be obvious. But, my friends could arrange it for a share in the inheritance. Wouldn't be difficult. Sir Harry often rides to Bristol without a guard. He left a note in the stable for a cabriolet on Tuesday. He'll drive it himself."

"They would attack him, Tuesday morning!" exclaimed the colonel in a hushed voice. "Suppose they are successful, how would Fitzroy deal with Critchley and the stolen package?"

Georges replied for Fitzroy. "With Sir Harry dead and me in control of his business and Lady Margaret's wealth, the stolen item would matter less. The marriage would be over and who would care much about the love letters, if that's what's in the package. I'd let Critchley hang."

"And the British officers would do Fitzroy's bidding?" Saint-Martin was unconvinced.

"Their brutality in the American War is notorious—a pair of thugs in red coats. They've not improved their character since then. They'll do whatever Fitzroy wants if he pays them enough." Georges tore off another piece of bread, cut a piece of cheese, poured more wine for Saint-Martin and himself.

The colonel stared into his glass, twirling the stem. Finally, he glanced at Georges. "I think we must protect Sir Harry, our best hope for capturing Fitzroy and shipping him back to France. If the rogue acquires Harry's widow and her wealth, he'll become nearly untouchable." He saluted Georges with his glass, who responded in like manner, and they finished their drinks. "Keep a closer watch on those two redcoats," Saint-Martin said. "We won't tell Harry yet. The danger to him is still guesswork."

Georges frowned. "Are we going to let him get hold of the stolen package, divorce Lady Margaret, and take Charlie away from her? Miss Cartier believes he needs his mother, weak though she is. Sir Harry hates the boy and will abuse him, perhaps disinherit him if he gets a son of his own."

The colonel rose from his chair, leaned over the table, and stared at Georges. "Remember why we're here. To capture Fitzroy. That's how we judge everything else. I don't see how we can recover the package or stop Sir Harry from ending his marriage." He uttered his words through thin, tight lips. "Don't forget Sylvie de Chanteclerc."

From a clerk at the York Inn, Saint-Martin learned that Mr. Burton had left after breakfast. He was expected back soon. The colonel glanced at his watch. Almost three o'clock. He decided to wait. He found a chair in the parlor to the left of the main entrance. Burton would have to pass by him to get to his room.

In the meantime, Saint-Martin observed his fellow human beings, a useful exercise for a policeman. Perhaps because of the fine weather, he felt kindly disposed toward them today. A stout, ruddy-faced, well-dressed Englishman and his wife peered into the parlor, exchanged smiles with him, then walked on into the public room. Their good-natured candor was what he'd come to expect from people of their class. Even from Dick Burton, though he had a police officer's wary curiosity. Saint-Martin recalled in contrast the sly, sardonic expressions so common among the French.

The next person to glance into the parlor was Burton himself, who also smiled when he noticed the French colonel. The two men shook hands and went upstairs. By the time they reached Burton's door, he was breathing heavily and limping. "It's been a long day," he said, mustering a cheerful expression. "I'm looking forward to giving this leg a rest."

At ease in a comfortable chair, Burton explained he had spent the day with several of Roach's victims, returning scandalous documents that had been used for blackmail. "People of quality, they were, and most grateful." Irony crept into his voice.

Saint-Martin suspected that Burton, like other Bow Street officers, must have received financial rewards for his kindness for he had to pay a clerk, probably several informants, and his own travel expenses.

After learning that Sir Harry had visited Critchley in jail, Burton had interrogated the prisoner again. "He wasn't forthcoming. Repeated his claim that he had left Roach alive and insisted it was Fitzroy who killed him."

Saint-Martin looked askance. "It's not likely Sir Harry went to the jail to offer solace."

Burton smiled. "According to Critchley, Sir Harry promised him a character reference if he were put on trial for Roach's death and would try to persuade his former employer to drop his accusations about the stolen silver."

"Would that save Critchley from hanging?"

"No. His former employer is unforgiving." Burton fell silent, lines of sadness at his mouth, as if he had seen too much human misery during his many years on Bow Street.

"Did you learn any more about the stolen package?" the colonel asked.

"Critchley still claims he doesn't know where it is. Nor does William Rogers. Critchley has surely hidden it—and is using it to bargain with Sir Harry."

"That's likely," Saint-Martin agreed. "Are you going to charge Critchley for the murder of Roach?"

"Yes, I shall."

"Why Critchley rather than Fitzroy or one of the other suspects?"

"A fair question," replied Burton easily. "The black footman's alibi is supported by the cook and the coachman. I couldn't shake their story. In my view, Sir Harry and his nephew William lacked sufficient motive. Fitzroy remained a serious suspect until I questioned Lady Margaret. I was persuaded that her testimony corroborated his." Burton hesitated briefly before going on, as if less sure of himself. "I'm also inclined to believe Fitzroy wouldn't have killed Roach in her presence."

Hmm, thought Saint-Martin, recalling Sylvie's battered face. Fitzroy's respect for women was erratic at best.

Sensing the colonel's skepticism, Burton quickly added, "I don't mean that honor would have restrained Fitzroy. He simply wouldn't have wanted Lady Margaret to witness him killing Roach. If she were interrogated, he couldn't depend on her testimony and he couldn't afford to get rid of her."

"Sounds reasonable," granted Saint-Martin, concealing his true feeling. In fact, Burton's reasoning failed to convince him. Critchley was a convenient scapegoat, already charged and virtually convicted of a capital theft. Roach's true killer was still unknown. Fortunately, Fitzroy remained available for abduction and the rigors of French justice. Could that possibly be Burton's intent?

"A magistrate will charge Critchley on Wednesday morning," Burton went on to say. "He'll be held for trial in Taunton castle, several months hence, during the royal judges' next quarter sessions. On Thursday, I'll return to London and search Roach's apartment for the stolen silver."

"Have you finished investigating the tennis hall?" Saint-Martin asked. "Sir Harry and I would like to play a game soon."

"I envy your good health," Burton replied. "No need to keep the tennis hall closed. Georges has sketched the scene for me." He suddenly caught Saint-Martin's eye. "Will *you* accomplish what you've set out to do here?"

The colonel wasn't sure how he should answer the question. Its ironic tone, the skeptical curl of Burton's lips meant he knew why Saint-Martin was in Bath. Nonetheless, it seemed wise to maintain the fiction of a vacation trip. "Yes, I believe I may. God willing." Depending also, he thought, on how helpful Sir Harry proved to be.

The clock in the servants' hall struck four o'clock. Jeffery sat down at the table with Mr. Cope the steward, the housekeeper, Peter the coachman, and a maid. To his surprise, William Rogers joined them a few minutes late. Their Easter meal of roasted lamb, potatoes, and green peas lay steaming before them. They had this time for themselves. Upstairs, the dining room table had been set. In the kitchen, the cook and her helpers were preparing the evening meal for the family. The night footman had already eaten and was minding the main entrance.

Jeffery had come to the servants' table with a mixture of apprehension and satisfaction. He was supposed to eat at a small table apart from the others. Yesterday afternoon, without warning, Sir Harry had barred him from wearing Combe Park livery or serving the family and had consigned him to menial tasks in the basement or the stable. When Lady Margaret heard of it later, she had objected, but Sir Harry ignored her.

This evening, he was not at home and would not return until late. Lady Margaret ordered Jeffery back into livery and assigned him to serve the family meal. He believed she had done this to spite Sir Harry, but he also suspected other motives. There was a certain gleam in her eye whenever she looked at him.

The weakness of his arm wouldn't matter upstairs. A maid would help him. She was seated now at his left, solicitous of his injury, holding the platter while he served himself with his right hand. The servants were usually sympathetic, obeying Sir Harry's orders as leniently as possible. But they had to be mindful of his spies.

From across the table, William glared at Jeffery, then turned abruptly to the steward. "What's this black slave doing here? My uncle ordered him to sit by himself." William pointed to the small table in the corner.

Mr. Cope stammered helplessly, "We thought...."

Peter Hyde broke in, "Since Lady Margaret put Lord Jeff back into livery and ordered him to serve upstairs tonight, we thought he should eat with us. We've important matters to discuss." He glanced around the table at his companions and snickered. "Like his great fight last Wednesday."

Jeffery felt pleased but suppressed a smile. The coachman was his best friend among the servants. A bluff man, he could risk speaking up because Sir Harry was fond of him.

The coachman reared back in his chair and looked down his battered nose at William. "And to what do we owe the honor of *your* presence among us? Master Charlie's going to eat upstairs." The steward stirred uneasily, pursed his lips, and shot the coachman a warning. The others looked down at their food.

William started, as if slapped in the face, then glared at Hyde. But the coachman held a level gaze, the hint of a smirk on his lips.

Red-faced with wrath, William sputtered nonsense, as if he had lost control of his tongue. Finally, he burst out, "The little devil hates me, poisons his mother against me." William's eyes narrowed to mere slits, his jaw tightened. "But I'll get even with him someday. Soon."

The force of William's malevolence was shocking, almost tangible. For a moment, the table grew deathly still. The smirk left the coachman's lips. The steward grew pale. Jeffery felt a tightening in his chest. A moment later, conversation resumed as if nothing had happened. William ate silently, sulking.

Anne guided Charlie into the dining room, her hand on his shoulder. She looked at the table with surprise. It was set for only four persons. Charlie smiled up at her, then pointed across the room. Jeffery, a massive ebony figure, crimson-clad, was standing rigid by a sideboard, his left arm in a sling. Anne was delighted to see him. She had heard he was banned.

Lady Margaret took her seat at the lower end of the table; the place at the other end was empty. "My husband asks to be excused," she remarked to Paul, who had accompanied her. She added with a quick sardonic smile, "Business in the city, he said. Odd, don't you think, on Easter evening. But there you are."

She invited Paul to the place on her left usually occupied by Captain Fitzroy. "My cousin, the captain, isn't the kind of man who offers excuses. He declared he would sup—and I expect he will also gamble—with his friends this evening." She inclined her head slightly toward Paul, her hand lightly touching his. "The two men on whom I must rely have both deserted me. Fortunately, there's at least one gentleman in the house to escort me to the table."

"My pleasure," he said politely, as he took his place.

Anne sat to his left, across the table from Charlie so he could more easily try to read her lips. The boy sought his mother's attention, timidly waving his hand. She ignored him, engaging Anne in a conversation about last night's concert. "Did you notice Miss Ware?" she asked coyly. "She usually sings like a princess, fearless, at ease in her part. But on this occasion, she appeared nervous, as if overwhelmed by old Isaiah's lamentation. And...by my Harry's hungry stare."

"I'm afraid I failed to notice what you observed," Anne replied, grateful that she could not have watched Sir Harry from where she sat. "Harriet is a religious person. The prophet's sentiments may well have touched her deeply."

While Anne turned the conversation to other matters, she kept an eye on Jeffery serving the meal. His expression was enigmatic. Only his tired eyes betrayed the stress he was under. As he offered the meat platter to Lady Margaret, he seemed to stiffen slightly. A flicker of self-awareness broke through his mask. She was staring boldly at him. Anne had earlier noticed Lady Margaret's interest in the black footman. Beneath her cool indifference stirred strong, unsatisfied human passions. Jeffery's virile body—exotic, yet elegant in crimson and silver livery—his swift, graceful, cat-like movements, seemed to catch her fancy. Her conscience, however, seemed unaffected. The indignity and injustice of his bondage, even the injury to his arm didn't appear to concern her in the least. Like Sir Harry, she regarded Jeffery as property, a fascinating pet.

At a break in the conversation, Paul turned to Charlie and, speaking clearly, asked him, "Have you learned to bowl?"

"Yes," the boy replied, his soft blue eyes brightening. He explained with nearly perfect diction how Lord Jeff had taught him the game.

Anne covertly signed to Charlie, "Well done!" She and Paul had rehearsed this little conversation with the boy during the hour before supper.

Lady Margaret's cool demeanor vanished. She stared at her son, startled, as if seeing him for the first time. She reached for his hand and patted it. "I'm proud of you, Charlie," she said, her voice breaking a little.

"Thank you, Mother," he replied and squeezed her hand.

For a moment, she regarded her son, taking in his long, wavy black hair, his fair skin, his fine, regular features. Then she turned to Anne. "I *have* noticed what you've done for Charlie in the twelve days you've been here. Before you came, I thought I might lose him, so far had he withdrawn into himself. Now he's happy." She gazed at her son, a hint of concern appearing in her face. "I've watched him practice reading my maid's lips. How hard it is!" She smiled at Anne. "You've made his task much lighter and I'm grateful."

Anne thanked Lady Margaret for the compliment, then seized the opportunity she had been looking for. "Charlie would be greatly encouraged," she said respectfully, "if you could train the household how to speak more clearly to him.

Include him in company. Encourage him to speak. Listen to him patiently."

For a few seconds it appeared that Lady Margaret might have resented Anne's unsolicited advice. A frown crossed her brow. Then, she sighed. "Perhaps I should do as you suggest. Later. When my mind is free."

The meal passed pleasantly with Charlie taking part. Lady Margaret engaged in the conversation, but from time to time appeared preoccupied. When the meal ended, Paul and Charlie went off for a walk in the mild evening air. Lady Margaret drew Anne aside and asked in a low, strained voice, "Miss Cartier, would you come to my room, please?"

While Lady Margaret rang for a maid and changed into a dressing gown, Anne surveyed the room, noting the peephole in the ceiling, the table with the secret drawer. Could Critchley have slipped the package back into the drawer? Who would ever think of searching for it there? Anne's fantasy was interrupted by the maid coming with a decanter of brandy and two glasses. Lady Margaret gestured that they should sit at the table.

The offer surprised Anne. The noblewoman had previously kept a strict class barrier between them. Anne looked into her eyes. The hauteur was gone, replaced by hints of trouble and uncertainty.

Lady Margaret dismissed the maid and poured a full glass for herself, then asked Anne, who indicated a half glass would suffice. The two women raised their glasses, toasted each other, and tasted the brandy. It was excellent.

Settling in her chair, Lady Margaret briefly assessed her guest. "You're a stranger at Combe Park, but I've learned to trust you. And I've got to talk to someone. My cousin will not listen to me. My husband surrounds me with spies, like his despicable nephew William. And my little Charlie's deaf..."

She broke off, as if she were sorry she had slighted her son, then she went on, "and he's only eleven."

Anne studied Lady Margaret over the rim of her glass. Thin lines of worry creased her forehead, and her deep green eyes had lost their lustre. Her hands trembled. Anne felt sorry for her and remarked she'd be happy to listen.

"You and I have Jack Roach in common. Over a year ago in Islington, he nearly killed you. Last week, he tried again on our portico, and you gave him a bloody lip." She ventured a wry smile, then drank deeply of the brandy. "He has also been a nightmare to me, probing into my life without mercy. And I've not been able to get back at him. Someone has even robbed me of the pleasure of killing him. Now his evil lives on in Critchley. With his help my husband intends to rid himself of me and Charlie. My cousin defends us with such passion that I foresee a bloody end to it all. Soon!" She took another long sip of brandy and sighed. "There's nothing I can do to stop it, but I warn you to stay clear of us. Or you, too, will suffer."

Chapter 27

Nightmare

Sunday, April 8

After the diners had left, Jeffery arranged the chairs and doused the candles while the maid cleared linen from the table. He was about to close the door when he saw Colonel Saint-Martin in the hallway sending Charlie to his room to change his shoes. They were going for a walk in the park. The boy dashed up the stairs two at a time.

Out of the corner of his eye, Jeffery noticed William Rogers loitering in the hallway. His sullen gaze followed the deaf boy like a cat watching a mouse at play. With alarm, Jeffery recalled the ugly scene in the servants' hall and William's ill will toward Charlie.

His concern mounting, Jeffery slipped back into the darkened dining room and hid where he had a view of the stairway. It was early in the evening. The light from the window above the stairwell was failing. In the hallway below, a pair of sconces cast a dim, fitful glow. William had disappeared into a dark narrow passage to the left of the stairway.

A few minutes later, Jeffery heard Charlie run down the stairs from the chamber story to the halfway landing. Jeffery leaped into the hallway just as William popped up from the passage and held a stick over one of the upper steps.

"William!" Jeffery shouted. The villain pulled back the stick a second before Charlie reached the step. The footman's sudden apparition startled the deaf boy and he stopped, mouth gaping, one foot raised. Meanwhile, William slipped away through a service door at the end of the passage. Jeffery beckoned the boy, who was growing anxious, to continue down the rest of the way. He reassured him with a hug, then escorted him into the entrance hall where Colonel Saint-Martin was waiting.

"Sir, watch out for William," whispered Jeffery to the colonel, whose brow had begun to crease with concern. "He's seeking to hurt Charlie."

William peered through a clump of newly leafing bushes at the Frenchman and the boy passing by. The sun had almost set. Trees soon blocked his view. He ground his teeth in frustration. Finally he caught sight of them walking a path that snaked through the woods. William followed at a safe distance.

In a few minutes they came out in the open, the Frenchman leading the boy down the hill to the covered stone bridge over the stream that flowed into the pond below. They threw bread to a white swan swimming near them. Then they started back up the hill. As they drew near, the boy looked up into the man's face, trying to read from his lips.

"The little snitcher!" muttered William under his breath, taking cover again in the twilight shadows of the pine grove. Charlie could read lips better than he or Critchley had thought. Yesterday morning in the classroom, the boy had spied on them and had divined what they had been quarreling about. He had told Miss Cartier and she had spoken to the Bow Street man. Now, Critchley was in prison.

"And I'm cheated out of my share of the money. I'm a pauper without prospects," he muttered. "If I could only find the package Sir Harry wants. Where did Critchley hide it?"

The colonel and the boy walked through the pine grove to the bowling green, passing close by William. He hunkered down behind the bushes and listened. Charlie tried to say, "bowling." It came out, "poling." The colonel rolled a ball, then formed the word again, this time more clearly. Charlie repeated it a couple of times and came close to getting it right. The colonel patted him on the shoulder and let him win a game. In the failing light, they walked back to the house, the boy looking up to the colonel and smiling.

"Mother's pet! He'll get his father's money," William murmured through clenched teeth. "You just wait, Charlie, I'll wipe that smile off your face."

When evening chores were done, the steward locked Jeffery in his basement room for the night. The slave resented this injustice, but it could be worse. Though a prisoner, he had certain resources. Through a barred window to the air well a few feet to the right of the main entrance, Jeffery could hear people coming and going above. He could also observe much of the basement hallway through an air vent above his door. He could even escape, if need be, for Georges had secretly given him a key. A useful precaution in view of Sir Harry's plans for him.

As he rested on his bed, he reflected on the dangerous trick William had tried to play on Charlie. A fall down the stairway could have seriously injured the boy, even killed him. Like Mary Campbell. Jeffery felt certain William would try again at the next opportunity. That would be after midnight when the house had quieted down. The night footman was supposed to patrol the house until dawn, but he often shirked his duty. A busy spy like William must be aware of the footman's practice and the chance for serious mischief.

As Jeffery had anticipated, the footman left his post at midnight and returned to the basement. Peering through the air vent, Jeffery saw the man walk in the direction of the pantry, then come back with bread and cheese. After visiting the beer cellar, he went to his own room on the other side of the stairway. Within a few minutes one of the maids joined him. Jeffery strained to listen. Apart from the faint sound of lovers' laughter, the basement grew still.

At midnight, when the footman had left, William stole down the dark, silent hall of the chamber story, a bundle in one hand, a lamp in the other. Combe Park slept. No one in sight. He quietly let himself into the antechamber shared by Miss Cartier and Charlie. Still no sound. He opened the bundle and quickly donned the costume, then inspected himself in the full-length mirror on the wall between the rooms. Perfect!

A hideous mask, black hat and gown, and long, claw-like gloves had turned him into a witch. The boy was going to get a fright he'd never forget. William glanced at Miss Cartier's door. Another night, he thought, he'd figure out a trick for her too. Clever woman. She had blocked the peepholes. For a brief moment he recalled his pleasure watching Miss Campbell. Bold bitch!

But tonight was the boy's turn. William shuttered his lamp, opened the door, and glided silently to the boy's bed. He felt gingerly for the alarm rope, and tied it up as high as he could reach. Then he leaned over the sleeping boy and unshuttered the light in his face. Charlie woke up dazed. William cackled madly, though he knew the boy couldn't hear. With one hand he turned the lamp toward his ghastly mask. With the other he clawed at the boy's face.

For a moment or two the boy stared blankly, then grimaced and uttered a choked, barely audible cry. William had expected him to leap out of bed and start running. He'd chase him around the room like a scared cat. Instead, the boy stiffened, gagged, and gasped. He couldn't seem to draw air.

William drew back in panic and ran out of the room. The boy was going to die. They would blame him. In the antechamber he tore off the mask, shuttered his lamp, then rushed out the door and down the hall to his room. Still in black hat and gown, he sat on his bed trembling, panting, soaked with sweat. "God damn," he muttered again and again. "Stupid little brat."

Jeffery peered through the air vent. Nothing stirred. He lit a lamp and shuttered it, removed his shoes, and slipped his key into the lock. The door squeaked open. He crept up the creaking stairs, listening for sounds of alarm. The laughter from the night footman's room continued unabated. Jeffery breathed more easily and climbed the steps faster. At the first floor, he glanced up and down the hallway. It was dark and deserted. He felt his way up to the chamber story.

At the top of the stairs, he heard a door opening. He stood still, then peeked into the dimly lighted hallway. A figure ran toward him, a witch's hat on its head, a long gown flowing behind. As the figure swished by, it came into the flickering circle of light from a sconce on the wall. It was William! Terror etched his face.

When the sound of the young man's footsteps had disappeared, Jeffery stepped out into the hall, debating which room to check. The door to the antechamber between Charlie's and Miss Cartier's rooms stood ajar.

Best to look in on Charlie first. As the footman drew near to the bed and unshuttered his lamp, he sensed immediately something was wrong. The boy lay rigid, stared with a haunted look. His breathing came in short labored gasps. Jeffery hurried through the antechamber, knocked on Miss Cartier's door, called to her, then rushed back to the boy.

Awakened by the pounding, still drowsy, Anne heard Jeffery's muted shout, "Charlie's sick!" Alarmed, she threw a robe over her night gown and dashed to the boy's room. Jeffery was seated on the bed, cradling Charlie in his arms, rocking back and forth, side to side, cooing softly over Charlie's whimpering form.

"Young Rogers dressed like a witch and scared the boy," Jeffery remarked, glancing up at Anne. "Charlie was near choking to death when I got here."

Stunned speechless for a moment, Anne struggled to gather her wits. "How is he now?" She knelt on the floor near the bed.

"He's still in shock but not, I think, in any real danger." Jeffery gazed down on the boy tenderly. Anne felt a catch in her throat. How extraordinary! This giant, bare-knuckle fighter was rocking and cooing again. The troubled lines on the boy's forehead seemed to relax. His breathing returned to near normal.

Jeffery must have sensed the wonder forming in Anne's mind. He looked levelly at her. "Charlie's a good boy. Has a hard life in this family. I feel sorry for him."

Anne met his eye, detected the irony in his remark. The slave's compassion embarrassed her. She averted her gaze, glanced at the boy. "Charlie's still in a stupor. We must not leave him alone, especially in this room. He should be with me for the rest of the night."

Jeffery carried Charlie into Anne's room. She pointed to her sofa. "Lay him there. I have extra blankets for him."

As he laid the boy down, Jeffery grimaced. For the first time, Anne noticed the footman's sling hung loose from his neck. "Your arm..." she exclaimed.

He shrugged and put the arm back in the sling.

"You're remarkable, Jeffery. You knew exactly what to do. Charlie could have died."

"I learned from my mother in Jamaica. She comforted children whom the overseer had frightened." He was about to say more but stopped, then looked at her in a new way as if assessing her as a woman.

She grew self-conscious, suddenly aware her robe had come loose. She drew it around her and tightened the cord. He gazed at her silently for a few seconds, then bowed and opened the door. "Charlie will be better in the morning," he said, adding, "but he'll need a few days to recover. He might have nightmares."

"I'll watch him closely."

"Latch the door behind me." He smiled, then vanished.

Chapter 28

Spring Ball

Monday, April 9

Saint-Martin gripped his racquet and squinted through sweat at his opponent. On the other side of the net, Sir Harry positioned his feet, preparing to serve. Rogers had more than tennis on his mind. He had summoned the colonel out of a sound sleep, and they had begun to play without breakfast. The early morning sun had barely lighted the court enough for them to see the ball. For an hour, the tennis hall had echoed with the sharp snap of the racquets, the thudding of the small leather ball, the stomping of feet, the grunts of the players.

Sir Harry hammered the ball as if it were his worst enemy. But he remained in full control of his game, playing skillfully off the shed roofs and laying down difficult chases. His returns rarely went into the net. Saint-Martin had to muster all his reserves of stamina and coordination to keep the score even at five games each in the set they had agreed to play.

As they began the sixth game, Sir Harry's serve weakened, his pace slowed down. He gasped for air. Saint-Martin made him earn his points, but let him win the next two games and the set. Winning, Saint-Martin realized, was Sir Harry's single-minded goal in life to which he devoted his extraordinary strength and intelligence. He looked pleased with himself as he walked up to the net to shake Saint-Martin's hand. They walked off the court together, commenting on the games.

In the dressing room they continued their chat about tennis. After a few minutes, Sir Harry fell silent, looked out into the antechamber to ensure they were alone, then closed the door securely. Saint-Martin waited with mounting curiosity.

"Colonel, I've a proposition to put to you. Been thinking about it for several days." His voice had the edge of cold steel. He pointed to a couple of benches and the two men sat down facing each other. "Let me say, first, I've investigated you, and I know precisely why you're here. We have a common point of view where Captain Fitzroy is concerned—the vile brute who beat and raped Sylvie de Chanteclerc, who tried to kill you on the road from Bristol."

His eyes black with anger, Rogers leaned toward Saint-Martin. "The captain has cuckolded me, foisted his bastard son on me, made me the butt of jokes in Bath. He thinks because the government protects him, he can do as he likes." Rogers' voice thickened and rasped. Saint-Martin strained to hear him. "I assure you, Colonel, the Irish rogue has met his match. Saturday of this week, my ship, *The African Rose*—you saw it in Bristol—will set sail for Africa. It will stop in Bordeaux to take on a shipment of cognac brandy in exchange for bales of fine English woolens and…Captain Fitzroy. He will leave behind a note, saying he had freely decided to return to France to clear his name and vindicate his honor."

Saint-Martin raised an eyebrow. He hadn't expected Sir Henry to be so forthright. "An unusual trade! What would I be expected to do?"

"My men will secure the person of said captain on Saturday and stow him bound and gagged on the ship. I would like you to sail with *The African Rose* as my guest in comfortable quarters and remove Fitzroy from the ship at Bordeaux. I'm sure you have the proper papers to bring him into France. I'm confident that, once Baron Breteuil gets his hands on him, he will receive the punishment he deserves but would escape in England. The voyage should take no more than a week."

"And Fitzroy's friends?"

"I shall arrange for the arrest of his two red-coated bodyguards on charges of swindling." He smiled malevolently. "Roach brought the evidence to me last week."

"It's as reasonable and generous a plan as I could imagine," remarked Saint-Martin, admitting to himself that something could go wrong. Fitzroy was elusive and armed. No one should imagine that apprehending him and returning him to France would be free of risks. But Sir Harry had both the means and the will to carry out his plan.

For a few moments, Saint-Martin stroked his chin, balancing risk and opportunity. Then he met Sir Harry's eye. "On Saturday, then. I'll be ready." The two men rose from their benches and shook hands.

At the door Sir Harry glanced back at Saint-Martin. "I needn't remind a provost of the Royal Highway Patrol that secrecy in this matter is of the utmost importance. Fitzroy must have no warning. I also trust that the Bow Street officer will leave before we set our plan in motion. In any case, he must not know about it or he might interfere." With a wave, Rogers let himself out. The firm beat of his boots faded, the outer door closed.

In the silent building, the colonel remained seated on the bench for a short while, trying to sort out the impressions he had just gained. Behind Sir Harry's charm and geniality was a powerful, ruthless will. He had conceived a daring plan which most men would shrink from, a plan Dick Burton would oppose. Saint-Martin felt torn between the loyalty he owed to the Bow Street officer and the mission he had received from Baron Breteuil. He recalled the battered face of Sylvie de Chanteclerc, and he knew what he must do.

Dressed in a pink satin robe, Lady Margaret was drinking her morning coffee. An uneaten roll lay on a plate in front of her. She waved the maid out of the room and invited Anne to take a seat at the table facing her. "Coffee?" she asked.

Anne hesitated momentarily, studying the noblewoman. No sign of duplicity. None of the usual cool detachment. Instead, there was warmth and tenderness. Lady Margaret was feeling for her son, Anne realized, and was rewarding her for the happiness she had given him. "Yes, that would be lovely."

"Where's Charlie?" Lady Margaret glanced toward the door as if expecting the boy to enter at any moment.

"I left him sleeping. He had a difficult night."

The mother's eyebrow shot up. "Oh, what happened?"

Anne explained how William Rogers had terrified the boy and the shock had nearly killed him. She stopped short of mentioning Jeffery, since he was supposed to have been locked in his room.

While Anne spoke, Lady Margaret clenched her hands on the arms of her chair. Her face flushed with growing anger. "William! That wretched bastard!" she exclaimed. "I'd send him packing this very minute, but Harry insists he stay with us. Uses him as a spy. No point telling Harry what happened. He'd only say, boys will be boys and Charlie's a timid little coward."

She reflected for a long moment, her face clouding with confusion. "You were asleep. Who saw William and saved Charlie?"

"The black footman, Jeffery," Anne replied calmly, though her heart was pounding. "He suspected William would attempt to injure Charlie during the night."

"But the slave was locked in his room!"

Anne shrugged, then lied. "The steward apparently neglected his duty. The footman found the door unlocked."

"No matter," said Lady Margaret emphatically. "I don't care if he tore the door off its hinges, or broke through a wall! From now on, he will sit in Charlie's hallway during the night until dawn. He's the only footman I can trust. Sir Harry be damned!"

Charlie woke as Anne entered her room. He sat up on the sofa, his eyes still full of sleep. Then the memory of the night's horror returned and threatened to overwhelm him.

"William tried to kill me," he cried, so agitated that Anne could hardly understand him. His breathing grew short. He began to wheeze.

She sat by his side and put an arm over his shoulder. "He probably only meant to play a mean trick on you. Don't worry, we won't let him do it again." She stroked him gently until he relaxed and his breathing returned to normal. She puzzled in her own mind about William's intentions. He must have known that Charlie suffered from asthma. Frightening him badly could trigger a fatal attack. Is that what William wanted to do last night? He could have killed Charlie without leaving a mark.

Anne kept this troubling conjecture to herself. She rose, drew the boy to his feet. "I've just spoken to your mother, Charlie, and explained what happened last night. You don't have to worry anymore. Lord Jeff will watch over you."

The boy mustered a wavering smile.

"You may go to your room now and dress. I'll order breakfast for you."

When he had eaten, and was nearly his old self again, Anne assigned some lessons to occupy his mind. She had temporarily taken over Critchley's tutorial duties, though the boy knew better than she how to conjugate Latin verbs and the like. After a few minutes, she left him busy at his desk and returned to her own room.

She opened her closet, hoping to find a suitable gown for tonight's Spring Ball at the Upper Assembly Rooms. Harriet would sing during intermissions and had asked her and Paul to come for moral support. The thought that Sir Harry would also be there had unsettled her. Anne could think of much she'd rather do than see and be seen in a noisy, crowded ballroom. She had even less desire to play whist for pennies and share gossip in the Card Room.

She sighed softly. Her wardrobe from London offered little to choose from. A white silk gown trimmed with gold thread would have to do. She walked to the window and looked out. It was midmorning. Paul must have been delayed. At that moment, she heard a knock on the door. She opened for him, beckoned him in, and sensed immediately that something weighed on his mind.

"Sorry I'm late." He closed the door behind him. "I've just been speaking with Georges. An hour ago, Sir Harry told me he'll put Fitzroy in my hands." He went on to explain Rogers' plan to abduct the Irishman to *The African Rose* and send him off to Bordeaux. "I'm to sail with him on Saturday and bring him to Paris. Baron Breteuil himself couldn't have designed a plan more to his liking."

Paul's news shocked Anne, triggering a riot of conflicting feelings. Her hands leaped to her face. She struggled to compose herself.

Paul stared at her. "What's wrong, dear?"

She hesitated before answering. "I realize you must leave on the ship with Fitzroy. That's why you came to Bath. But, I'm concerned for Charlie. He's in danger here." She told him how William had attacked the boy and Jeffery had saved him. "You've become his friend. Your leaving will discourage him."

Paul sighed softly, but he remained silent.

She put her hands on his shoulders, looked into his eyes. "Perhaps, deep down, my anxiety has more to do with our parting than with Charlie, with wondering if I shall ever see you again."

Paul held her in his arms, gazed at her tenderly. "Who could have imagined just a few weeks ago that we would be together in Combe Park? We should have confidence in our future."

Her lips met his, then she broke away, fondly tousling his hair. She drew him to a bench by the window. "What's to become of the boy?" she asked. "Sir Harry told Harriet he'd have Lady Margaret out of the house by Wednesday. He's shipping Jeffery to Jamaica and Fitzroy to Bordeaux by the end of the week. You, Georges, and Mr. Burton will also be gone by then. Charlie and I will be left here alone with Sir Harry." She shuddered violently. "I'm convinced he's half-mad! And dangerous!" She stared out the window, hugging herself.

Paul stood beside her, his hand on her shoulder. "Sir Harry would send the boy back to Braidwood in Hackney, and you with him. I should think that would please Charlie."

"That's what a reasonable man would do," she agreed. "But toward Charlie, I fear Sir Harry might not act reasonably. He's convinced the boy is Fitzroy's son. And, if Jeffery tries to escape sometime this week, Sir Harry might react violently. At the least, he would suspect me of aiding Jeffery and send me away. Then Charlie would be alone with him. The thought of it is almost more than I can bear."

"Unfortunately, the law gives a father exclusive rights over his son," Paul replied gravely. "Sir Harry may do as he wishes, short of killing the boy, and we may not interfere." He turned silent for a moment, as if hunting for a straw of hope to give her, then added, "As a last resort, you might bring the matter to the mayor or another magistrate."

She drew a deep breath and sighed. "There's no point imagining the worst. You're probably right. Either this week or the next, Charlie will return to Hackney, hopefully a happy boy. Who knows what will happen to the others." She walked to the closet and opened it. "This much is certain. We are going to the Spring Ball tonight." She held up the white gown against her body. "Help me decide. Will this do?"

He gazed fondly at her and smiled. "It's lovely. I look forward to this evening with you."

At the entrance to the Upper Assembly Rooms, sedan chairs and carriages disgorged their passengers. With Anne on his arm, Paul gaped in amazement at the social stew milling around them. In the ballroom the mixing of classes was even more glaring. Mr. Tyson, the master of ceremonies, had assigned seats according to rank and honor. The first places went to a sprinkling of aristocrats; the next best to people of quality: professional men, prominent military officers, wealthy gentry. The rest of the seats were left to plain-looking men and women decked out in fine clothes.

In a low voice, Paul asked Anne, "Have these people—tailors, grocers, and the like—come into more money than they know how to spend? In Paris, on such a formal occasion as the Spring Ball, the lower classes would be strictly excluded."

Anne replied, "Society in Bath is like a masked ball. People high and low escape from convention without harm to their reputations. Unless you are a prince, or a bishop, or a general, social distinctions mean little. Money and appearance are what counts."

"Let's see what they make of us." Paul presented himself to Mr. Tyson in the formal velvet suit of a French nobleman: a knee-length, cutaway medium brown coat embroidered with metallic yarns, a light brown waist coat, and dark brown breeches. Taking note of his aristocratic bearing as well as his title, the M.C. directed Paul and Anne to sit between an earl and a bishop.

Tyson then admired Anne's gown. On a mischievous impulse, Anne acknowledged his compliment with a strong French accent and a slightly supercilious air. This earned her the M.C.'s deep bow. Would they honor the assembly with a minuet a little later in the evening? he asked. Paul and Anne glanced at one another, considered the offer, then agreed with a mixture of nonchalance and grace.

While waiting for their dance, they scanned the crowd. Sir Harry was talking business somewhere and wouldn't attend the ball until the intermission, when Harriet would sing. Lady Margaret and Captain Fitzroy sat among the people of quality. He appeared relaxed, throwing her a brilliant smile from time to time. She also performed as if on stage, nodding graciously to him and to her neighbors. A green velvet gown showed off her creamy skin and a tiara of diamonds glittered in her auburn hair.

In due course, the M.C. beckoned Paul and Anne onto the dance floor and introduced them as Comte and Comtesse de Saint-Martin, distinguished French visitors to Bath. "I think the title suits you, Anne," whispered Paul, pretending to be unaware of his remark's implication.

"Mr. Tyson has exceeded his authority. I'm not a comtesse yet." She gave Paul a teasing smile. "But I shall enjoy playing the role."

As they began to dance, the crowd craned their necks for a view of Anne in her white silk dress. Its delicate gold embroidery took on a rich amber tone in the light of five great chandeliers blazing with burning candles. A buzz of voices rose, threatening to drown out the orchestra. Within minutes the crowd reached agreement: the elegant woman in white was a maid of honor to Queen Marie Antoinette and her gown followed the French queen's latest fashion. Captain Fitzroy and Lady Margaret might have protested, but they had already left.

Anne and Paul executed the dance with a graceful passion, their mistaken celebrity adding to the pleasure. Anne delighted in the skill of her partner and the working of an inner harmony between them. Holding hands at the end, they bowed to the crowd, then left the floor to hearty applause.

As the evening wore on, the crowd grew more boisterous. The level of noise became deafening, the air hot and stuffy.

After a round of country dances, Anne suggested to Paul that they quit the ballroom and find a more comfortable corner of the building. They made their way into the Tea Room to a table with a view of the patrons.

Sir Harry had arrived in the meantime and sat on the opposite side of the room with Harriet Ware. She flashed a look of desperation to Anne, then retreated behind the mask of rapt attention she affected for Rogers. He seemed restless, at times staring at Harriet as if to devour her, at times detached from her, absorbed in his own dark thoughts.

While preoccupied with Harriet and Sir Harry, Paul and Anne had not noticed a short, thick-set bewigged waiter in a blue and buff silk suit. Carrying a tray under his arm, he approached their table from the side.

"May I serve you?" asked the stranger with a high-pitched, accented voice.

Anne started with surprise, then recognized him. She threw back her head and was about to burst out laughing, when he brought a finger to his mouth and hushed her.

"Georges!" Paul whispered. "What are you doing here?"

"Keeping close watch on those two redcoats." He gestured toward a half-hidden table where Fitzroy's officer friends sat, brandy glasses in their hands, their attention fixed on Sir Harry. "Remember, Fitzroy told them, 'Tuesday, then.' We assumed he meant they should attack Sir Harry on his way to Bristol sometime during the day. Well, Tuesday begins in less than five minutes."

Paul stiffened, then glanced toward Tarleton and Corbett.

Georges leaned forward. "I've overheard Sir Harry and Miss Ware. At midnight, he's going to walk her to her apartment, like he usually does when the weather is good. On his way back to the Assembly Rooms, he'll be alone in a dark street for several minutes. Those two scoundrels know his route and intend to intercept him. I've made sure they won't."

"How?" whispered Paul and Anne together.

Georges took a small bottle from his pocket. "Laudanum. In their brandy." He pointed toward the officers. "Watch."

One of the men was slowly bending over; the other, sliding back in his chair. Within a few minutes they had both passed out. Georges beamed with satisfaction.

At that moment, midnight struck and Sir Harry and Harriet left the Tea Room. Paul turned to Anne. "I haven't seen Fitzroy and Lady Margaret for at least an hour."

"They left with some friends to go to a private party," interjected Georges. "They'll probably spend the night there. She was already tipsy when I last saw her."

"There seems to be no reason to stay here any longer," Paul remarked to Anne. "Shall we return to Combe Park? I think the danger's past."

"I'm not so sure." Anne shivered. Lady Margaret's dire warning echoed in her mind.

From a shadowed corner of the entrance, Captain Fitzroy observed Colonel Saint-Martin and Miss Cartier leave in a carriage. The Irishman hastened into the building.

The Spring Ball was still in progress and its guests were too tired or drunk or dazed by the noise to notice him hurry toward the Tea Room. His heart pounded; his mouth felt dry. What had gone wrong? An acquaintance, who had arrived late at the private party, had remarked offhandedly that Tarleton and Corbett had disgraced themselves. Notorious for their tolerance of brandy, they were seen drunk at the Assembly Rooms before the Spring Ball was half over.

The Tea Room was thronged with people coming and going, jostling one another. All the tables seemed full. Quickly scanning the room, Fitzroy saw his friends. His heart sank. Even as he watched, they were lifted limp from their chairs and hauled away.

"I must look to the matter myself," he growled as he left the building.

Chapter 29

Final Reckoning

Tuesday, April 10

Following his routine at the city prison, the night guard glanced into the small cell. Its sole occupant, a tall thin lank-haired man, lay sound asleep on his pallet. They said he was a scholar who had studied too closely his employer's silver; many of the finest pieces had stuck to his fingers. He was also suspected of killing Jack Roach, but it seemed a shame to hang a man for that.

The guard returned to his post by the entrance and settled into his chair. He yawned, then dozed off in the quiet of the early morning hours. A knock on the front door woke him. Eyes half-closed, he shuffled to the door and opened its small barred window. A watchman stood outside with a lantern in one hand and a cowed, ill-dressed man gripped in the other.

"A pickpocket!" announced the watchman. "He's yours for the night."

The guard rubbed the sleep from his eyes, complained that one's personal property was no longer safe in Bath, and unlocked the door. The watchman shoved his prisoner forward. The guard turned his back to them as he closed the door and began to lock it. Suddenly, he sensed a movement behind him. A hard object struck his head. A spray of light enveloped him, then darkness.

ꕥꕥꕥ

Since he came to this prison on Saturday, Critchley had avoided sleep as much as he could. The nightmares were torture. He had seen himself again and again on the scaffold in front of Newgate, hands tied behind his back, the crowd taunting him while a minister prayed. A leering hangman fitted a hood over his head, then slipped a noose around his neck. Sweat poured from his body. The stool beneath his feet was kicked away and he hung by his neck, fully conscious but slowly choking to death. The crowd roared and roared and roared. Then he woke up shaking violently.

Late this evening, when the night guard came by, Critchley had feigned sleep. Now, as the appointed hour drew near, he sat on his pallet wide-awake, trembling with anxiety. Suddenly, keys rattled in the lock; the door swung open. A man dressed as a watchman entered and tossed a small bundle to him.

"A change of clothes. Your disguise. Hurry."

On the way out, Critchley saw a second, ill-dressed man, tying a gag on the night guard, who was now strapped to his chair. The two strangers walked Critchley a short distance through a dark wood to a clearing where four horses waited. On one of them sat a large man, his features concealed by the hood of his cloak.

The night watchman helped Critchley mount, then walked back to his companion.

"Follow me," ordered the large man, the hood muffling his voice.

Critchley's throat tightened. He barely stammered, "Yes." Too frightened to speak, he rode silently behind the large man until they reached the broad footpath along the river. The rushing water drowned out all other sounds. The large man had not said another word nor showed his face, yet Critchley knew beyond a doubt, it was Sir Harry. Who else rode like he owned the place he was riding through!

Last Saturday, Sir Harry had said, "Be ready shortly after midnight on Tuesday morning. The stolen package in exchange for your freedom. A new life in America with enough money to live comfortably."

Critchley would have preferred Italy, but America was better than hanging! The plan was daring, but Sir Harry had the resources to carry it out. So, Critchley asked himself, why did his heart pound, his hands tremble? What had he to worry about?

South of Spring Gardens, Critchley and his hooded companion left the river path and turned onto the road up to Combe Park. The sounds of the river grew fainter, then disappeared. In the growing quiet of the early morning, Critchley thought he heard someone behind them. He had sensitive ears, tuned to the slightest whisper or the fall of a leaf. But now, he thought, his ears were playing tricks on him. He was tired from lack of sleep and overwrought by his misfortune. He stared at the large dark hooded man ahead of him. Unbidden, a memory surfaced from his youth. A picture on the vicarage wall. A large dark hooded figure, the Angel Death, led a sinner to Hell.

Georges dodged to the side of the Pulteney bridge over the Avon as two mounted men from Bathwick rode into the lamplight. An odd pair, he thought, as he studied them. One was dressed like a night watchman. Georges frowned. He had made the acquaintance of virtually all the watchmen of Bath. This man was a stranger. The other was unshaven and wore a long ragged derelict's coat. But beneath the coat Georges saw sturdy riding boots. Both men sat astride their mounts with assurance, as if they were at home in the saddle.

A pair of highwaymen, Georges guessed, as he followed them out of the corner of his eye. He hastened his steps. He couldn't give himself a good reason for going to the city jail, only a suspicion. Sir Harry had not returned to the Spring Ball. According to a chairbearer whom Georges had hired to follow Sir Harry, he had escorted Miss Ware home, then walked to a stable and emerged on a horse. He rode as far as this bridge before the spy lost sight of him.

Why would Sir Harry go to the other side of the Avon into Bathwick so early in the morning by himself? Spring Gardens were closed. The only other place anyone might visit was the city jail. Sir Harry did have a reason to go there. Critchley! But, at one o'clock in the morning?

The jail was dark as Georges approached. He knocked. No response. The night guard had probably fallen asleep. Georges knocked again, loudly. Still no response. He began hammering on the door. To no avail. He stepped back and examined the door. Thick solid oak. Its little window was shut. He ran back to the New Road, stopped a coach and sent it off with urgent messages to Dick Burton and the warden, who had keys to the jail.

Waiting restlessly by the roadside, Georges recalled the two suspicious horsemen he had just met on the bridge. Brigands hired by Fitzroy? Had they enticed Sir Harry into Bathwick fields and killed him, then somehow entered the prison and killed Critchley? A farfetched idea, Georges admitted, but it removed the two obstacles standing between Fitzroy and Lady Margaret's inheritance. Or, what was more likely, the men were in Sir Harry's pay and met him at the jail. Why? Georges racked his brains, but the only answer he could think of seemed incredible.

Jeffery sat obediently at his post in the hallway of the chamber story. It was early in the morning at Combe Park, the quiet hours, before birds would begin to sing. The deaf boy was safe in his room, sleeping peacefully. His tormenter, William Rogers, was away for the night, visiting the nymphs of Avon Street. The night footman who was supposed to mind the main entrance had also gone to the city. The other servants were sound asleep in their basement and garret rooms. The master and mistress, and Captain Fitzroy were at the Spring Ball and wouldn't come home until dawn—if then. The French colonel and Miss Cartier had returned early and retired to their rooms. Everyone was accounted for.

Unnerved by the stillness, Jeffery fell into troubled thoughts. He hadn't heard from Sarah Smith or Mr. Woodhouse. Had they met obstacles arranging his escape? Sir Harry might have changed his mind, moved up the date for the abduction, intending to take him by surprise. Jeffery argued with himself, what to do. Did he dare to sneak into the city to Sarah's shop? That seemed foolish. He decided to ask Miss Cartier later in the day if she had any news.

In the meantime, he needed fresh air and exercise. Cooped up inside for days, he felt sluggish, missed his training and sparring. Charlie was safe, the house secure. Having eased his conscience, Jeffery walked downstairs, through the darkened entrance foyer, and out the front door. The moon cast a hazy, spectral light over the courtyard. He had reached the far side when he heard the sound of horses approaching, their hooves crunching in the gravel. His heart began to pound. Fearing discovery, he crouched down in the shadow of a retaining wall and waited.

Two men rode by slowly, silently. That's odd, Jeffery thought. Why didn't they go to the stables or stop at the entrance to the house? Instead, they kept riding toward the pine grove and the tennis hall. He sprang from his lair and dashed back to the house.

At the pine grove, Sir Harry pushed back his hood and beckoned Critchley forward to take the lead. He veered off the gravel road onto a path, Sir Harry following close behind. Moonlight shafted in thin rays through the trees, lighting their way. In front of the tennis hall, they dismounted and tied up the horses.

"It's in here, is it?"

Critchley nodded and led him into the hall. He lit a lantern. It shook in his hand.

"Where have you hidden it?" Sir Harry threw aside his cape.

Critchley hesitated. The moment had come when he must give away his secret, the only power he had. But, he had come too far to turn back. His knees nearly buckled beneath him. He summoned what little courage he had left and pointed to the training room.

Sir Harry shoved him into the room. "Show me," he growled.

∞∞∞

Saint-Martin stared open-mouthed at the black footman standing before him. "Two tall men just rode across the courtyard? Are you *sure* one of them was Sir Harry?" He could scarcely believe what he had heard. He had just been roused from sleep and was rapidly dressing.

"I didn't recognize his horse," Jeffery replied patiently, "but I would know *him* anywhere. He sits so firmly in the saddle, holds the reins like a king."

"And the other man?" Saint-Martin pulled on his boots.

"Thin, long hair. Awkward on the horse." Jeffery hesitated, as if unsure. "Mr. Critchley, I think."

"Critchley! Good God! What's happened?" Saint-Martin took his pistol from a drawer, laid it on the table, stared at it. He shook his head and put the weapon back in the drawer. Better to rely on one's wits. More to himself than to Jeffery, he said, "Sir Harry has freed Critchley from jail. They're riding toward the pine grove and...perhaps the tennis hall. For a good reason, most likely the missing package."

As he rushed out of the room, he told Jeffery to alert Miss Cartier. "Tell her to warn Georges Charpentier and Mr. Burton. There's an emergency at Combe Park."

In the pale moonlight he made his way quickly over a familiar path. In the pine grove, he heard a horse trotting toward him. He ducked behind a bush. The rider dismounted and tied his horse to a tree not more than ten paces away, and stalked toward the tennis hall. At the edge of the grove, he halted for a moment, his hand gripping the hilt of his sword, then stepped out into the clearing. Watchful, as if reconnoitering an enemy camp, he crossed the clearing and stopped in front of the tennis hall. A light shone in the high windows of the training room.

The moon showered its thin pale rays on the man, as he cocked his head, listening at the door. Saint-Martin gasped. Captain Fitzroy! He cautiously slipped inside, leaving the door ajar.

Meanwhile, Critchley had led Sir Harry into the training room to the cabinet where tennis racquets were hung. Sweating profusely, he stumbled to a halt and stared blindly ahead. His arms refused to move.

"Give it to me!"

Critchley dared not look back over his shoulder. The anger in his companion's face would have turned him to stone. Finally, he grit his teeth, bent down, and reached into the narrow space beneath the cabinet. Just as he grasped the thin flat package, he heard faint sounds outside the room. He rose with a start and hearkened. A sword unsheathed. A floorboard creaked.

Rogers leaped to the door and crouched to one side. In the next moment, Captain Fitzroy burst into the room, sword drawn. Rogers jumped out of the shadows and plunged a long sailor's knife into the Irishman's side. Fitzroy's sword clattered on the floor. He uttered a short cry, stumbled forward. His body twisted, dropped to the floor, and came to rest on his back. For a few moments, he jerked and twitched, then lay still, three paces from Critchley's feet.

Rogers stood over his fallen enemy, gazing down at him without pity. Life appeared to linger in his face. "Do you hear me, Captain?" Rogers bent forward and stared into Fitzroy's eyes. They flickered. Rogers shook his head. "I had not planned to kill you, Captain, to stick you like a pig. A worse fate awaited you in a French prison. You've cheated me again. But now I'm glad to be rid of you and soon to be rid of my whoring wife and your bastard son." Rogers looked sharply at the man's face, then straightened up and said without feeling, "He's dead."

Fascinated by the ghastly scene before him, Critchley clutched the package with trembling hands. Rogers stepped over Fitzroy's body and picked up his sword from the floor. Flourished it. "Now, Mr. Critchley, we shall have our reckoning."

Chapter 30

Justice and Honor

Tuesday/Wednesday, April 10/11

For a minute, Saint-Martin stared across the clearing to the tennis hall, then hurried to the entrance. He leaned inside, and listened. The sound of voices drifted faintly from the training room. He slipped into the building, then suddenly stopped. With a slight rasp, a sword had left its scabbard. A few seconds later, quick footsteps, then a sharp cry of pain, and the thud of a body hitting the floor.

He crept stealthily through the antechamber to the open door of the training room and peered in. Rogers stood with his back to the door and a sword in his hand. In the next instant, he hissed "Treacherous ingrate!" and thrust the sword into Critchley's body. "You *would* insult the woman I love."

"What have you done?" exclaimed Saint-Martin aghast and stepped into the room. Before him, Fitzroy lay sprawled on his back on the floor, the handle of a knife protruding from his side. At the far end of the room, Critchley staggered, then fell back against the racquet cabinet and slid to the floor.

Rogers spun around, sword in hand. His eyes wild, his jaw taut, he strode toward Saint-Martin. "Unfortunately, Colonel, you have seen too much." He held the bloody weapon at his throat. "I intend to blame the captain for Critchley's death and for yours. This is his sword after all."

Saint-Martin stood his ground. "Have you found what you were looking for?" He spoke as evenly as he could. Rogers appeared deranged.

He lowered the sword a fraction, reached into his pocket, and pulled out a slim, square package. Holding it aloft, he shook it like a trophy. "Here's the proof I need to put before Parliament. I'll soon be rid of the Irish bitch and her son." His face hardened. He raised the sword again. "Time to say your prayers, Frenchman."

Suddenly, a loud explosion shook the room. Rogers lurched forward. The sword dropped from his hand, striking Saint-Martin's left arm and tearing his coat sleeve. An echo rang in his ears. The acrid stench of gun powder stung his nostrils.

For a moment he was too stunned to realize what had happened. Then his vision cleared and he saw Rogers crumpled at his feet and Critchley sitting slumped against the cabinet, a pistol in his right hand. Saint-Martin picked up a lantern, held it over Rogers, felt his pulse. None.

He approached Critchley warily, even though his pistol had fired its shot. The wounded man's eyes followed him, his lips moved. Barely a whisper. Saint-Martin strained to hear.

"I'm dying, Colonel. Better than hanging." His eyes were unnaturally bright and watering. He gasped for breath.

"Did you kill Roach?" Saint-Martin still had in the back of his mind the nagging fear that Jeff had done it.

Critchley nodded. "Gave him the package…asked for money. He laughed. Called me a fool…his slave. He opened the package, wasn't looking. I hit him." His eyes drifted to the rack of iron balls nearby.

"And Mary Campbell?"

"No," he murmured. "Dead when I came home. Ask…" Blood dribbled from his mouth. His eyes glazed over.

Saint-Martin leaned closer and asked softly, "Yes? Yes?"

For a second, the man's face seemed suffused with an inner light. "*Italia! Come bella...Ital...*" His head slumped to one side.

"Beautiful Italy, indeed!" Saint-Martin felt a tinge of pity for the dying man, despite the evil he had done. He turned to Fitzroy and found no pulse. The face still wore a look of surprise, the eyes staring into the void, the mouth slightly open. Saint-Martin knelt down on one knee and gazed at the dead man. A vile brute, Sir Harry had said. True enough. Fitzroy had scarred Silvie de Chanteclerc for the rest of her life.

The colonel sighed. He would return to Paris empty handed, having spent a great deal of Baron Breteuil's money and much valuable time. He couldn't even claim credit for Fitzroy's death. Sir Harry had killed him for his own reasons, depriving the baron of the satisfaction of vengeance. Fitzroy would not slowly rot away in prison. He died, as he would have wished, in combat—quickly, deftly, believing his honor still intact.

Footsteps and hushed agitated voices sounded in the entrance hall. Still on his knee, Saint-Martin looked up apprehensively, then relaxed as he recognized Anne, pale and drawn, carrying a lantern. Behind her loomed Jeffery, a long iron bar in his good right hand.

"We heard the shot," she exclaimed, slowly scanning the carnage. "Horrible! Are they all dead?"

"Yes," Paul replied, pointing to Fitzroy and Sir Harry. "And Critchley's dying. He confessed to Roach's death but not to Mary Campbell's."

Paul rose to his feet and picked up the package that had fallen from Sir Harry's hand. "You must help me decide what to do with this. I'll keep it safe for now." He slipped the package into his pocket. To Jeffery he remarked, "Forget you've ever seen it." The footman nodded gravely.

Anne glanced at Paul's left arm. "You're wounded!" she cried. Blood was soaking through his sleeve.

"Sir Harry nicked me as he fell. It's not serious."

With a boxer's familiarity, Jeffery pulled medicine and bandages out of a cabinet and dressed Paul's wound. Anne assisted, since Jeffery's broken arm was still causing him pain.

"Police work is dangerous," the footman said, as he put away the medicine. He glanced over his shoulder at Paul. "You should box instead." Jeffery's brow wrinkled with apparent concern. "Yes, sir, we both must be careful. If we hurt our right arm as well, who will cut our meat into dainty morsels?" His gaze shifted mischievously toward Anne.

For a moment the black man's impertinent wit nonplussed Paul. He shook his head as if to clear away his confusion, then noticed the flicker of a smile on Jeffery's lips, a tentative twinkle in his eyes.

Paul turned to Anne. A smile had spread across her face. "You were wise to bet on him. Sly fellow, just like Georges."

"Jack Roach's pistol," said Colonel Saint-Martin, handing the small, deadly weapon to Dick Burton. The colonel had just finished reporting what he had witnessed in the training room. "He always carried it on his person, but mistakenly thought he wouldn't need it when dealing with Critchley. The man's spirit *seemed* broken."

Burton studied the pistol in the light of a lantern. Dawn's rays were only just beginning to break through the high windows of the tennis hall. "We searched everywhere for this thing. Where did he keep it?" He dropped the pistol in his bag.

Saint-Martin bent down and slipped his hand into the space under the racquet cabinet. "Critchley must have hidden the pistol there after we had searched the training room. He could reach it from where he fell."

Burton had arrived at the tennis hall with several watchmen to inspect the scene and remove the bodies. While they worked at their task, he told Saint-Martin that Georges had captured the two highwaymen a mile outside Bath on the Bristol road. They might have escaped, had they not stopped for an early morning drink at The Little Drummer. Under questioning, they claimed they didn't know who hired them. They never saw his face, only his money.

When Burton finished and was about to leave, he turned to Saint-Martin. "Sir Harry took too great a risk in freeing Critchley. Still, if you hadn't interrupted him, he might have succeeded." His gaze fell. He tapped the floor with his cane, as if pursuing a thought. Abruptly, he looked up. "The package, Colonel, the one stolen from Lady Margaret. Have you found it?"

Saint-Martin had foreseen the question as soon as he studied the package's contents. He also understood Burton's viewpoint in asking. He had shared Roach's papers. Fairness seemed to require Saint-Martin to share the stolen package. It might also earn Burton a financial reward from Lady Margaret. "Yes, I have," Saint-Martin replied, adding, "Critchley gave it to Sir Harry. He dropped it when he was shot. I picked it up."

"May I see it?" Burton's voice was low and insistent, his eyebrows lifted. The question was a challenge.

"I am not at liberty to show it to you, for it touches a woman's honor. And, since the thief, Critchley, and his accomplice, Jack Roach, are dead, the object they stole should simply be returned to Lady Margaret."

Burton frowned. "I had hoped you would trust me to respect her honor. I'm not prying into common Bath scandal. That package contains the key to understanding four violent deaths."

"I mean no insult to you, and I understand your desire to resolve this case fully in your own mind. But I simply cannot run the risk of the package's contents becoming more widely known."

Burton's expression grew irritated. He leaned heavily upon his cane.

Weighing his options, thought Saint-Martin. He could arrest him but with no likelihood of getting the package. Or, he could accept the fact that it didn't matter. The case was closed, all the villains dead. Finally, Burton straightened up, started toward the door. He turned, met Saint-Martin's eye. "I trust you will appear at the coroner's inquest."

"Of course."

"Then we shall resolve our differences there. Otherwise, I believe my work is nearly finished." With a straight face, he added, "And yours, too."

"Not quite," Saint-Martin rejoined, the fate of Lord Jeff on his mind.

Early afternoon on the next day, a maid showed Anne and Paul into Lady Margaret's room. Dressed in a black silk gown, she sat staring out a window, a closed book on her lap. Her thick auburn hair had been brushed into lustrous waves, but her face was haggard. Paul wasn't surprised. At dawn on Tuesday, she had been roused out of a drunken stupor at a friend's house and brought back to Combe Park to identify her dead husband and her cousin. She had fainted away and been put to bed.

Anne and Paul had gone to Bristol and persuaded Betty to nurse Lady Margaret. Leaving her cottage in a neighbor's care, Betty had returned with them to Combe Park late in the afternoon.

Betty now sat nearby, knitting. She rose as Anne and Paul approached. "I'll go to my own room. Tell me when you leave."

Lady Margaret gave them a sidelong glance, sighed, then gestured for them to be seated. Unsmiling, she asked why they had come. "You needn't express regrets. All three men are better off dead. Even Fitz, and a part of me loved him." Her eyes were heavy lidded from fatigue but clear. No sign of tears.

Anne turned to Paul, who began, "Lady Margaret, we have come here to speak on behalf of Jeffery, your footman."

She frowned. "I understand Sir Harry was displeased with his impertinence. Planned to sell him, I suspect. What concern is it of yours?"

Anne spoke up. "I am in his debt." She went on to describe Jeffery saving her from Jack Roach on the portico. "And, I may add, little Charlie owes him much."

"He only did his duty," Lady Margaret said irritably. "If that's all you wanted to talk about, you may leave. I can't be bothered about a black footman." With a haughty stare she challenged them to contradict her.

Paul and Anne glanced at one another with a shared understanding. Mr. Woodhouse's plans to free Jeffery were going forward on the assumption that Lady Margaret could not be trusted to do the right thing. When she began to settle her affairs, she might decide to sell Jeffery. Woodhouse and his companions would have to act within a couple of days. There was no time for delay.

Paul leaned forward, his voice took on a stern tone. "Lady Margaret, we do have something more to talk about: your certificate of marriage to Maurice Fitzroy from February 11, 1776, signed by Rev. John Blair, vicar of St. Bride's church in London, witnessed by a sexton and by your nurse, Betty. And, recently stolen by Mr. Critchley."

Her hands flew to her mouth. She gasped, "Do you have it?"

"Yes, I do." He drew the package from his pocket and smiled gently, inviting her confidence.

She fell into an uneasy silence, drawing up buried memories. "I was just nineteen and recently widowed. My father arranged my engagement to Harry Rogers, who would pay his debts and settle a large income on me. I protested in vain that I didn't love him."

She stared out the window, as if uncertain whether to continue, then went on in a low voice. "While Harry was on a visit to Jamaica, I fell in love with my cousin Fitzroy and we married secretly in London. Shortly after the wedding, my father called me home to Ireland. Fitzroy fled to France to escape his creditors. No one knew of the wedding, except Betty, the feeble-minded sexton, and the old vicar who died soon after. I couldn't tell Harry. When I married him, I was already pregnant with Charlie though I didn't know it until a month later."

"Why did you keep the certificate?" Anne asked softly.

At first, Lady Margaret appeared not to hear the question. She gazed quietly at the distant hillside. "Yes," she murmured finally, as if talking to herself, "Why *did* I keep it?" She smiled. "Fitz was a fine lad then, handsome, full of mischief and laughter. Our wedding night was the happiest moment of my life." She turned and pointed to the certificate. "Through the years, this reminded me that I wasn't really married to a Bristol slave trader, but to Fitz. We were joined together forever."

Paul tapped the package. "This certificate also is evidence that your marriage contract with Sir Harry is null and void. By the terms of Sir Harry's will, Charlie—illegitimate in the eyes of the law—is no longer his heir. Another male relative should inherit Sir Harry's wealth." Paul patted the certificate. "If William knew of this, he would surely challenge Charlie's claim."

Her expression grew hard. "I see what you're going to do with that certificate." She stuck out her hand. "Give it to me. It's mine."

"It's material evidence of a crime. I should bring it to a magistrate." He handed it to Anne, who put it in her bag.

Lady Margaret glared at him. "Extortionist! You're as bad as Roach, trying to force me to free your black friend." Her lips curled with disdain. "I thought you were a man of honor."

"Justice before honor, Lady Margaret. Sir Harry tricked Jeffery into signing an indenture of servitude before coming to England, since slavery is illegal here." He held her eye. "As Charlie's guardian, you must legally revoke that indenture and free Jeffery. And, give him the two hundred pounds, the gate money from the boxing match, which Sir Harry wrongfully denied him. If you meet these two conditions, I swear on my honor, I'll burn the marriage certificate now."

She crossed her arms, threw a contemptuous glance at him, then stared at Anne. "What do *you* say? Would you beggar my son Charlie with this certificate? Expose him to ridicule?"

"I love Charlie, but his fate is in your hands, not mine."

Lady Margaret looked silently out the window, chin high, nostrils flared, fingers tapping angrily on the arms of her chair. Finally, she turned to Paul. "Have you something for me to sign?"

He produced a legal agreement declaring Jeffery to be free from the indenture and entitled to the sum of two hundred pounds. She read it, then went to her desk. "Burn the certificate," she said, her pen poised over the agreement.

Paul sensed guile in her voice. "Sign first."

"Goddam Frenchman!" She hurled the pen against the wall, tore the agreement to pieces, beat on the desk with both fists. She turned on Paul and shouted "Goddam whoreson!"

Anne started with alarm and began to rise from her chair.

Paul waved her down. "Wait," he mouthed.

The litany of abuse gradually subsided. Lady Margaret sat still, staring down at the desk. She picked up another pen.

Paul walked over to her and placed a second copy of the agreement in front of her. She signed it without hesitation. Paul and Anne witnessed her signature, then Paul folded the agreement and put it in his pocket. He turned to Anne. She drew the package from her bag and gave it to him. He opened it and showed the certificate to Lady Margaret.

She glanced at it and grimaced. "Destroy it!"

He stirred the glowing embers in the hearth to a flame, then laid the certificate in the fire. In seconds it was reduced to ashes.

Lady Margaret rose erect from her chair and tossed her head scornfully. "Now I'm safely mistress of this house." Her voice was low, her words measured. Fixing Anne and Paul in her gaze, she went on, "You will get out of Combe Park immediately and take Monsieur Charpentier and your black friend Jeffery with you. The steward will give him the gate money as he leaves. And you, Miss Cartier, will receive your stipend." She pulled a bell rope.

Betty was outside the door as they left, having listened to what had gone on inside. As Anne and Paul passed her, she whispered, "You've done the right thing. I'll try to bring her around to a better frame of mind."

"And take good care of Charlie," said Anne, pressing the woman's hand.

Chapter 31

Aftermath

Friday/Saturday, April 13/14

On a late Friday morning, three days after the deaths at Combe Park, an inquest was held at the White Hart Inn in Widcombe across the Avon south of Bath. Anne sat in the front row with Paul and Jeffery in the banqueting hall, a large simple room in the floor above the street. At the table before her sat a Mr. Bennett of Widcombe House acting as coroner. A justice of the peace whose estate lay near Combe Park, he knew Sir Harry and the circumstances there. A jury of thirteen local men sat to the left of the coroner, their faces alive with curiosity and expectation.

Anne had awaited this moment with apprehension. Little Charlie's future seemed to hang in the balance. Should the inquest reveal his mother's bigamy, the boy might face life as a pauper and not return to Braidwood's school.

A commotion erupted at the door. People standing there struggled to make way for someone to enter. Erect, veiled, and dressed in black, Lady Margaret glided into the room. Betty and Charlie accompanied her. All eyes followed the trio to reserved seats in the front row. A loud buzz rose from the crowd, then subsided at the coroner's command.

From her place, Anne had a clear view of Charlie slouched in his chair, staring glumly at his feet. He apparently had little idea of what was going on, and no one had explained it to him. Before Anne left Combe Park, she told him what had happened to Critchley, Fitzroy, and Sir Harry. He had seemed withdrawn, more confused than grieving. Had he begun to wonder who was his father?

At least he was no longer in danger. Lady Margaret had ordered William out of Combe Park as soon as she was its unchallenged mistress. He had vanished almost immediately, fearing Mr. Twycross and life in a debtor's prison. Peter Hyde claimed the young man had indentured himself to a ship's captain for passage to America.

The coroner rapped on the table and announced the first item of business: an inquiry into the deaths of Sir Harry Rogers, Captain Maurice Fitzroy and Mr. Edward Critchley.

"Will Colonel Paul de Saint-Martin come forward."

Paul rose, faced the jury, and told them simply who had killed whom, without mentioning Lady Margaret's stolen package or alluding to the motives of the three men. The coroner asked him to describe the scene in the training room: was the light of the lantern sufficient for his observations? Where exactly was he standing? Where were the victims? Saint-Martin responded directly to the questions in clear correct English, prompting murmurs of approval from the crowd.

After Anne and Jeffery had supported the colonel's testimony, the coroner summoned Mr. Burton, who came forward with the aid of a cane. The crowd buzzed again at a high pitch of expectation, hungry for scandal. The jurors sat up alert. The coroner brought quiet to the room, then asked the Bow Street officer to explain what had happened.

Anne's chest tightened with anxiety. Burton could accuse Paul of concealing the stolen package, evidence of a scandal relevant to the case. The coroner might then call for further investigation and uncover Lady Margaret's bigamy. Burton could also bring up Harriet Ware's liaison with Sir Harry in order to account for his disturbed frame of mind. Her reputation could be stained.

The Bow Street officer stared at Saint-Martin and Anne with cool regard, his face ashen, his sabre scar livid. He acknowledged Lady Margaret with a slight bow, then approached the jury and met their gaze one by one. They watched him eagerly, some with mouths agape.

Leaning on his cane, Burton began to speak. The enmity between Sir Harry Rogers and Captain Fitzroy was common knowledge, he said, having to do with a private dispute. To a man, the jurors turned their eyes toward Lady Margaret and Charlie. Burton gathered their attention once more. Privy to certain delicate information, he continued, Critchley had apparently been caught between the two men and triggered their final bloody confrontation.

To the evident chagrin of the curious and the scandal mongers, Burton went no further into the tangled issues of the case or its salacious details. He ended his testimony with a few perfunctory remarks and turned to the magistrate, indicating he would receive questions.

The coroner requested some minor clarification and then inquired into the death of Jack Roach. A preliminary coroner's inquiry had led to a verdict of homicide, perpetrator unknown. Could Mr. Burton shed more light on that case?

Burton obliged with a brief response. Roach's killer was most likely Mr. Critchley, who had confessed while dying. He had acted alone in the course of a dispute over money. The coroner sought confirmation from Colonel Saint-Martin, then declared himself satisfied. He instructed the jury and sent them out. They came back promptly with a verdict of three homicides, whose perpetrators had killed one another.

The crowd stirred in their seats, grumbling, their desire for scandal frustrated.

Anne leaned back, breathing easier. Persons of authority and influence in Bath had chosen not to rake up the Rogers' household muck for public view.

Lady Margaret had risen from her seat, head high, when the coroner rapped for order. "Mr. Burton has just cast doubt upon the verdict of the original inquest into the death of Mary Campbell," the coroner announced. He nodded to the Bow Street officer, who had joined him at the table. The crowd hushed. Lady Margaret sat down uncertainly. Anne and Paul stared blankly at each other.

"Now, Mr. Burton, explain what you mean?" The coroner's was waspish.

"Your Honor, I have only this minute received evidence strongly suggesting the death of Mary Campbell was a homicide, not an accident." Burton sent a bailiff out. In a few moments he returned with a box. The crowd gawked as Burton reached into the box and retrieved something so thin Anne could barely see it.

"I submit to the court this piece of wire from an old harpsichord in the attic at Combe Park. Mr. William Rogers stretched it across the top step of the servants' stairway by means of these hooks." Burton placed the items before the coroner. "In the dim light of a candle, the wire was virtually invisible. For several nights Mr. Rogers studied Miss Campbell's movements through hidden peepholes and learned when she went to the kitchen for Charlie Rogers' medicine. I believe that in the early morning hours of March 16, William Rogers hid in the darkened stairway to the garret floor above. As Miss Campbell approached, he raised the wire and caught her foot, causing her to fall."

"His motive?" the coroner asked.

"She had accused him of excessive gambling, harassment of the young maids, cruel teasing of little Charlie and other misbehavior. According to the servants, William claimed that was none of her business and he would make her pay."

"Why has it taken until now to bring the matter before this court?"

The investigation had been difficult, Burton explained. Several days ago, he had studied the stairs, found holes for the hooks, and guessed a wire had been used. Yesterday, he found a harpsichord with a wire missing. A painstaking search of William's room discovered the wire, as well as the hooks. Under a microscope, a medical doctor identified bits of blood on the wire where it had cut the young woman's ankle, a cut indicated in the original medical report.

"Do you believe the fall killed Miss Campbell? Or, if it merely injured her, could someone else have killed her while she lay unconscious?"

"She died of a broken neck. I have three suspects but cannot say which one of them caused it. Captain Fitzroy and Mr. Critchley are dead. William Rogers has vanished."

The coroner remarked that a later court might determine who killed her and sent the jury out to deliberate. It brought back a verdict of homicide, overturning the earlier verdict of accidental death. The coroner thanked the jurors and quickly closed the inquest.

The crowd dispersed in a noisy rush to the doors. Anne stood waiting with Paul.

"Miss Cartier. May I have a word with you?"

Anne nearly jumped. In the confusion she hadn't noticed Burton. Suddenly, he was at her side.

"I shall leave Bath this afternoon. Becoming acquainted with you has been a bright spot in my visit. I heartily wish we might meet again."

Anne replied in kind, then shook his hand. "Do you think William killed her?"

"Yes, though I'm not sure he fully intended to. Does that make sense?"

She nodded.

He stepped back and bowed to her, then turned to Paul. "Colonel, I leave Bath, grateful for our cooperation. You and your adjutant have helped make these, my last cases, successful. The good citizens of Bath have also made them financially rewarding. About the mysterious stolen package, I feel the lady in question does not deserve consideration but her son may. I presented my opinion in that light." He offered his hand. Paul shook it. As Burton walked off, he remarked over his shoulder, "Henceforth, I'll hold the French police in high regard."

Anne shut the lid of her trunk, then surveyed the room for articles of clothing she might have missed. Satisfied she was ready, she fastened the lock. Since her summary expulsion from Combe Park, she had stayed at the York Inn, together with Paul and Georges. Their business finished, they were preparing to leave for London today. Anne felt happy to put Bath behind her. A beautiful city, but tarnished in her mind by the evil she had encountered.

She put the key to the trunk in her pocket and began to pace the floor. Though she had packed, a sense of unfinished business nagged her. She was leaving Charlie without a tutor. Mr. Braidwood would be disappointed. She felt sad, but nothing could be done.

Paul had arranged for breakfast in one of the York Inn's small private dining rooms. Anne went there early to talk privately with Jeffery. Dressed in the hotel's red livery trimmed with black, he was setting out plates, holding them with his right hand and wiping them with his left. She noticed he favored his left arm. It was only ten days since he broke it, and it had not yet healed.

But he had to work nonetheless. Yesterday, at Mr. Woodhouse's request and on Paul's recommendation, the manager had grudgingly hired Jeffery as a footman. He had warned that the inn could not make allowances for his injured arm.

The manager had also voiced concern that some patrons might hold the inn in less regard for having a black man in its livery.

Woodhouse had countered that most patrons would be pleased. A large handsome man like Jeffery was agreeably exotic and fashionable. Many of the "quality" included liveried black servants in their household staffs. The Quaker had proposed trying Jeffery for thirty days and the manager had agreed.

Anne took a step into the dining room. Jeffery became aware of someone watching him and turned around. When he recognized her, he smiled and bowed smartly, then flourished an arm over the table setting. He had laid places, he said, not only for her, Colonel Saint-Martin, and Georges Charpentier, but also for Mr. Woodhouse, Sarah Smith, and her mother. "And I shall serve them," he exclaimed, "as a free man!" He smiled tentatively. "I can hardly believe what's happened to me."

"Where are you living?"

He pointed upward. "In the attic. For now."

"And your plans for the future?"

"Sarah and I would like to get married, but we'll wait for a while. Lay aside a little money. Sarah and her mother will still have the shop. Roach died before he could bring about their eviction. I'll learn to read and write better and look for a permanent position, perhaps in the house of one of the wealthy sporting gentlemen. Give him boxing lessons. Spar with him." He gently patted his weakened left arm. "No more battles for me."

Paul was the next to arrive, dressed for travel in a brown suit, his hair tied back with a brown ribbon. He embraced Anne, then smiled a greeting to the footman.

Jeffery left the table and approached them. "I've waited until now to thank both of you for helping me gain my freedom. I know Lady Margaret didn't want to give it to me. And I'm also grateful for the gate money!"

"It's yours. You earned it," Paul said. "And you shall have another two hundred pounds that I won betting on you."

Partial compensation, Anne thought, for the years of slavery Jeffery had endured.

After breakfast, Anne went to her room to oversee the removal of her trunk. It had just left when a maid delivered a message.

> *Please come to the parlor. I need to speak to you. Betty*

Anne sat down to think. Why would Betty come here unless something had happened to Charlie? Anne felt a tremor of apprehension. She rose, squared her shoulders, and went downstairs.

Betty was standing in the middle of the small entrance parlor with Charlie close by her side. They smiled hesitantly when they saw Anne enter. She gestured toward the chairs. They sat down facing her.

"What can I do for you, Betty?" Anne asked gently.

"I'm embarrassed, Miss Cartier, to come here unannounced." She put an arm on Charlie's shoulder. "The boy's mother sent me. She knows you're leaving Bath, now that the coroner has finished the inquest. She wants you to take Charlie back to Braidwood's institute in Hackney. His things are in the coach outside."

Anne gazed at Charlie's expectant face. "Of course. I'm delighted to do it. We have room. Colonel Saint-Martin has hired a coach for the journey." Anne wasn't sure the boy fully comprehended what she had said, so she repeated it to him. He broke into a big smile and threw his arms around her.

She hugged and kissed him. Holding his hand, she turned to Betty. "How is Lady Margaret?"

"Presently at sea, in a manner of speaking, though I think she's getting better. Leaves her rooms, walks in the garden. She loves Charlie and would like to keep him at home. But on her terms. She's not ready to accept him just as he is, deaf and all. And he's unhappy because he can't please her. Two days of them just staring at each other brought her to her wit's end. That's why we're here."

"Leave Charlie with me. Go back to his mother. With time and your help, she may see what she needs to do with her life."

"I hope so." Eyes brimming with tears, the old nurse embraced the boy. "God be with you, Charlie."

"Thank you, Betty," he said carefully, and walked with her to the door.

It was noon and the sun had broken through the clouds when the coach finally set out for London. Anne, Paul, and Charlie sat inside. Georges rode outside as guard, a musket resting by his knee. Harriet Ware had come to wave good-bye. She and Anne spoke for a few minutes while the coach was being loaded. Sir Harry's death had given Harriet pain, but also a sense of relief. She had decided to stay in Bath at least through the present season.

As the coach rolled through the lush green countryside of Wiltshire, Paul drew a letter from his pocket and handed it to Anne. "Madame Gagnon forwarded it to me this morning. From Comtesse Marie in Paris."

Settling back with the letter, Anne learned that Sylvie de Chanteclerc was still under the comtesse's care at Chateau Beaumont. Anne paused at the final paragraph:

> *Yesterday, though, I noticed improvement. Michou has joined those who take turns attending Sylvie every hour of the day. When I entered the room, she was looking over Michou's shoulder while she sketched birds feeding outside the window. Today, I saw Sylvie with crayon and pad, sitting next to Michou who was*

> *teaching her how to draw the birds. She was smiling! My heart leaped for joy.*

Anne looked up from the letter. "There's a glimmer of hope for Sylvie." She leaned toward Paul. "Don't chide yourself that you couldn't bring Captain Fitzroy back. That lay beyond your control. You've done what duty required of you in Bath." She nodded toward Charlie, who had fallen asleep, the book in his lap, his head resting on Paul's shoulder. "And you've gone beyond the call of duty for him and for Jeffery."

"The baron will be disappointed but I can cope with that."

Something else was bothering him, she sensed.

He began anxiously searching her face. "When will you return to Paris? I'll keep this coach for the trip from London to Dover. Will you ride with me?" He paused, opened his mouth as if to say more, then looked away.

Anne grew concerned. "I beg your pardon, Paul. May I ask what's on your mind?"

He flushed with embarrassment. "Anne Cartier's on my mind. I can think of little else. It's almost a year since we met at Wimbledon in the Quaker's parlor. The sight of you brought back memories of our summers together at Chateau Beaumont before I went off to the American war. In hindsight, I believe I may have lost my heart to you already then." He leaned forward and took her hand. "Will you marry me, Anne?"

Anne's throat tightened. She spoke in a whisper. "We need to come to an understanding."

In response to a nudge, Paul glanced down at Charlie awake now, who pointed to a picture in his book. Paul examined the picture with a show of interest that satisfied Charlie, then turned to Anne. At first his voice quavered, then grew strong. "I want you to be my companion, friend, lover. I want us to walk through life together, arm in arm."

Old anxieties rushed to her mind. "How much does it matter to you what others, particularly your relatives, will think of you marrying a commoner, an actress, a Protestant?"

"Some of them despaired of me long ago." He smiled wryly. "This will confirm their worst fears. I've taken leave of my senses, they will say. I've dishonored the family's name and foolishly imperiled my career." His chin rose a little higher. The smile vanished. "But enlightened men and women will judge me, and you, on our merits. And that's what matters."

Anne fell tensely silent. Her love for Paul clamored for their union, but she was less sure than he that his family's predictable opposition to their union could be so easily disregarded. And, her spirit still bristled at the unjust laws and conventions of marriage. *Now* was a crucial moment, full of danger and risk. But, after knowing Paul for a year, often in circumstances that severely tested his character, she believed she could trust him to be fair and true, as well as loving.

She gazed at him tenderly. "I shall marry you, Paul, first at my church in Hampstead and then at yours in Paris."

"Agreed, with all my heart." His face brightened. A great weight seemed to lift from his chest.

For a moment she entertained an afterthought. "I wonder if Baron Breteuil would allow you and Georges to stay for a few days at my grandfather's home in Hampstead. He would enjoy talking about guns and horses—and getting to know you better. I need time to gather my things. And, we must speak to the vicar at Saint John's."

"The baron would gladly agree to the delay, I shall assume, and Georges and I would be delighted." Suddenly, Charlie stirred, shifted his position. Paul put an arm around his thin shoulders and gazed out the window at men and horses turning the fertile soil, rich with the promise of spring. A look of contentment came over his face.

Anne sat back, adjusting easily to the rocking motion of the coach, and to the prospects of a new life in Paris.

Author's Note

Bath in 1786 was a city of some 30,000 inhabitants. Since Roman times it had been a health resort, noted for its mineral hot springs. In the eighteenth century it developed into Britain's premier spa, offering in addition to its water a full program of amusements: gambling, music, theater, sport. Affluent visitors came from all over Europe. The 1780s were a period of robust growth. Edith Sitwell offers an elegant introduction to the eighteenth-century city in her *Bath*, London: National Trust, 1987. For a more scholarly treatment, read Peter Borsay, *The Image of Georgian Bath, 1700-2000: Towns, Heritage, and History*, New York: Oxford University Press, 2000. Walter W. Ison's *The Georgian Buildings of Bath from 1700 to 1830*, London: Faber & Faber, 1990, is a rich source of architectural plans, illustrations, and maps.

Combe Park in *Black Gold* is a thinly fictional representation of Prior Park, one of Bath's greatest landmarks. Robert Allen [1693-1764], a wealthy, self-made business man and organizer of Britain's postal system, conceived a house in the Palladian style and placed it adjacent to his quarries of Bath stone. It was completed by the middle of the eighteenth century.

In the nineteenth century the wings of the house were much enlarged and the central building received the addition of an italianate stairway to the portico on the north front. Sir Harry's tennis hall in *Black Gold* is on the site of a gymnasium, added to Prior Park in the 1830s.

The combe [rhymes with room] at Prior Park is a steep narrow valley extending from the ridge, a short distance above the country house, down to the Avon. In this valley Allen laid out an English landscape garden, then one of the finest in the country. It commands a splendid view of the city to the north.

Prior Park during Allen's lifetime was the center of a lively social and cultural life. Among his many guests were the poet Alexander Pope and the novelist Henry Fielding. Following Allen's death, his property passed to his niece, Gertrude, who sold the furnishings and leased out the buildings. In 1785 she moved back and was living there at the time of *Black Gold.*

Subsequently, Prior Park has had a checkered history, including two disastrous fires, the significant alteration of its interior spaces, and the neglect of the park. Since the 1830s its buildings have housed a Roman Catholic school, presently Prior Park College, which has beautifully restored the main building. Allen's quarry lies buried beneath the cricket field. The National Trust owns the park and has undertaken to bring it back to its former glory.

In the eighteenth century, despite sporadic condemnation by magistrates, bare-knuckle boxing became a popular sport and adopted the rules and other conventions that are found in the "battle" between Lord Jeff and Tom Futrell.

In the 1780s the sport also became fashionable and its champions, such as Dan Mendoza, were celebrities. Futrell *did* fight in the presence of the Prince of Wales and many other dignitaries. Victor in twenty matches, he was beaten by John Jackson, who resembles the fictional Lord Jeff in his quality of decent, modest gentleman, as well as in his physical strength and skillful style of fighting. The chief difference between them lay in their skin color and social condition.

Lord Jeff also bears a physical resemblance to Tom Molineaux, a freed American slave and a giant of heroic strength, who fought for the British championship in 1810. For a popular account of the sport, see Bohun Lynch, *The Prize Ring*, London: Country Life, 1925.

At the time of *Black Gold* there were 35,000 blacks living in London and several thousand more in Liverpool, Bristol, and Bath. Many were slaves, or fugitive slaves, or freed from slavery. Most worked as grooms or domestic servants, sometimes for distinguished personalities, such as Dr. Samuel Johnson. Despite the Common Law's principle that a slave becomes free the moment he lands in Britain, the courts continued to treat slaves as property and affirm the right of owners to recover fugitives.

For an overview of the transatlantic slave trade, read Hugh Thomas, *The Story of the Atlantic Slave Trade, 1440-1870.* New York: Simon & Schuster, 1997. Slavery in Britain is discussed by Gretchen Gerzina, *Black London: Life Before Emancipation*, New Brunswick, NJ: Rutgers University Press, 1995, and by James Walvin, *Black Ivory: A History of British Slavery*, London: HarperCollins, 1992.

Gainsborough's painting of Elizabeth Linley and her brother Tom (1768) is one of the treasures of the Clark Art Institute in Williamstown, Massachusetts. In 1784 the painter sold it to John Sackville, the Third Duke of Dorset. Poetic license has placed it in Harriet's apartment. In 1787 it was most likely in the ducal residence at Knole Park, Sevenoaks, Kent, unless its owner brought it with him to Paris, where he was British ambassador to the French court.

Gambling was a scourge of eighteenth-century society. Mr. John Twycross and Richard Wetenall did in fact operate a gambling house on Alfred Street near the Upper Assembly Rooms.

On April 11, 1787, the magistrates closed down the house and brought the two men to trial. They were convicted with great fanfare and initially fined 1800 pounds. Powerful hands worked on their behalf behind the scenes, and the fines were reduced to 550 pounds. Whether they resumed their profession is not known, but gambling continued unabated in Bath.

To receive a free catalog of other Poisoned Pen Press titles, please contact us in one of the following ways:

Phone: 1-800-421-3976
Facsimile: 1-480-949-1707
Email: info@poisonedpenpress.com
Website: www.poisonedpenpress.com

Poisoned Pen Press
6962 E. First Ave. Ste 103
Scottsdale, AZ 85251